THE JORDAN INTERCEPT

J. ALEXANDER McKENZIE

Bethany Fellowship INC.
MINNEAPOLIS, MINNESOTA 55438

The words, "I am come as the warm spring rain, and that which was dead lives, and that which lives . . .. loves," used in whole or in part by the author herein, are taken from the publication *A Song for the Night*, copyrighted 1980 by Russell Patch, and are used by permission of the copyright owner.

The Jordan Intercept
J. Alexander McKenzie

Library of Congress Catalog Card Number 80-68581

ISBN 0-87123-269-3

Published by Bethany Fellowship, Inc.
6820 Auto Club Road, Minneapolis, Minnesota 55438

Printed in the United States of America

For Gary and Carol Johnson,
fellow laborers

The Canaan Trilogy

Prologue

Tuesday, October 3, Corpus Christi, Texas.

It had been dark about an hour when the black limousine pulled in to park at the rear of the deserted motel. Coming out of the rear of the air-conditioned car, Joshua Bain was at once conscious of the night's heat and humidity. The odor in the still air was damp, smelling organic and decaying, and he caught his breath once through his mouth. He looked up to help orient himself, but the Gulf Coast of South Texas was under a dark cloud cover, a foreboding slate blanket, so that no stars were visible.

"Follow me and stay close." His escort's voice, soft spoken and made even more congenial by his heavy Creole accent, belied the peremptory command.

Joshua fell in stride behind him, noticing that the other man was light on his feet, moving with an athlete's control and rhythm. He picked up the sound of a nearby surf, and he remembered from the flight chart in the DeHavilland Otter that they must be somewhere along the Gulf side of Padre Island. They quickly crossed the rear of the motel grounds, reaching the beach and a narrow wooden pier. As they started down the short gangplank to a waiting launch, his escort turned to face him.

"Are you armed?" he asked Joshua politely.

"Your friend asked me that at the airport," Joshua reminded him, but he held up his arms anyway.

The frisk was perfunctory, and once again the Viper was missed. The small automatic, strapped high on the inside of Joshua's right thigh, normally escaped detection during a routine search.

A few minutes later they were on the open water, and Joshua was careful to note their heading was south by southeast. "How long?" he asked the other man at the controls.

"About fifteen minutes."

Joshua had already checked the speedometer. Thirty-five knots and steady. Roughly twelve more miles. Which meant the rendezvous was probably going to take place in international waters.

He moved his right leg, feeling the assurance of the Viper. The weapon was only a precaution, since at this point he had no reason to fear for his safety. Otherwise he knew little else about what he might now be heading for. There was still over four thousand dollars in his billfold, the balance of the five thousand included in the mysterious package delivered to him by a Palm Desert messenger service yesterday morning. There also had been a note in the package instructing him to fly the ranch's private plane, a DeHavilland Otter, to the Corpus Christi International Airport, where he was to be met by an escort. With the note had been a small item of great personal interest to Joshua Bain, one which had prompted him to accept the invitation which he might have otherwise ignored.

The unsigned note had not given the purpose for the trip.

He tried to relax into his seat, turning his mind to certain known quantities. As usual at this time of the year, the foremost matter was Rancho Canaan, which at the start of its third season seemed about ready to produce a profit. Such was the prediction of his partner, Alan Hunt, who was holding down the fort during his brief absence. Joshua realized he was smiling to himself, thinking that Alan and his recent bride, Anne, had not had much of a honeymoon after all.

The timing of the trip was thus awkward.

The swell action on the sea around them was sluggish, and he again glanced apprehensively up at the low and threatening overcast, remembering the Corpus Christi forecast. "There's a front moving in, you know," he said to the man next to him.

"Yes, sir; but we still have at least two hours."

The man's confident manner did little to pacify Joshua's rising concern. Assuming twenty minutes back on the water, plus another twenty in the limousine, add these to his refueling and clearance time at the airport, and he knew he could not afford more than thirty minutes at their destination.

"We're almost there," the man was telling him.

The launch was throttled back in a few minutes, and Joshua could make out the shadowed profile of a ship. Apparently dead in the water, the huge yacht was at least a hundred feet long, sleek and powerful looking even in the bad light. Joshua noted curiously that the ship was totally dark. His stomach began to churn as he realized this had to be it. Idling in from the aft quarter, Joshua was able to make out the name, *Swanya II*, on the fantail.

At the top of the boarding ramp, he stepped warily into the shadows of the main deck, his subconscious recording a slight hum. Air conditioning?

"Mister Bain?"

Joshua turned toward the speaker. For some reason he was surprised to be facing a woman. "Yes," he said after a passing moment. It was too dark to tell much about her, except that she was tall, only two or three inches shorter than he was.

"Welcome aboard," she told him. "My name is Karen Laswell."

"So what now?" he asked, impatient with the social amenities.

"The note please."

Anticipating the request, Joshua reached into his inside jacket pocket. The brief note he had received yesterday included the proviso that he was to use it for identification. He handed a folded-up piece of paper to her. She briefly examined it with a small penlight.

"This is a photocopy, sir," she said. There was now a trace of annoyance in her carefully controlled voice. "The instructions were specific, that you produce the original."

Joshua shrugged indifferently. "I normally tend to obey orders," he said in the same manner, "when I agree to do so." He looked aside then, out to the open sea. "Don't misinterpret my presence here as an indication of my acceptance of any such prior agreement."

She hesitated only briefly before telling him to follow her.

They moved out forward to turn into a hatch which Joshua guessed would lead them to the main cabin area. Near the center of the ship, his escort stepped aside to allow Joshua to enter an open doorway. As Joshua stepped through, an overhead buzzer sounded. He felt the woman's hand on his right shoulder, restraining him before he could take another step.

"You're not supposed to be armed, sir," she said, polite yet insistent.

Joshua glanced around the spacious room, apparently the main cabin or salon. Indirect lighting, with a ton of money in just the furnishings. He turned to face his escort, realizing that the Viper must have tripped a surveillance alarm. "You've got two choices," he said, also politely but firmly. "We can either get on with it as things are, or, I'll find my own way back to the launch."

For a moment there was silence. Karen Laswell stood before him—not all that beautiful, but yet with the demeanor and appearance of a classic model. Despite her height, she was slenderly proportioned in a decidedly feminine way, perfectly groomed even in her dark deck jeans and matching turtleneck sweater. Her hair, richly dark, was pulled away from her face into a hardly discernible knot, so that against the darkness of the hallway her high forehead and face seemed even more creamily translucent. She wore no makeup that he could see, and she obviously disliked the sun. He guessed she was in her late thirties.

"Please wait here," she said finally, averting her dark brown eyes. She then moved down the hallway, as if this time she was unwilling to take the initiative.

Joshua moved slowly into the salon, deliberately walking toward the mahogany bar on his left. The room was air conditioned, and the chill felt good on his face. He ran his right hand across his chest under his jacket, feeling his shirt limp and damp. He thought that he could use a shower and change of clothes. Then crossing behind the bar to open the refrigerator, he decided he could use a good meal most of all.

"Help yourself, Joshua."

The rumbling bass voice came at him from his back, and there was in Joshua's mind the kind of instant recognition that caused him to freeze in his tracks. He closed his eyes once, and then opened them before straightening up to face Colonel Calvin Price.

Small wonder the ship was running without lights.

The Colonel's presence also explained why they had to be beyond the twelve-mile limit, since there were those in the U.S. Government who would probably be willing to double the national debt just to lay their hands on this one man, whose former exploits at home and those more recently overseas had him at the top of everyone's most-wanted list. As usual, the Colonel stood easy, confident and assured, as if being one of the ten richest men on the face of the earth afforded him the right to be solidly in control.

Joshua simply stared at him, saying nothing.

"If you're hungry," Price said congenially, "I'll call up something from the galley." He pulled the door closed behind him. Calvin Price was about Joshua's height but more slender. No one knew his age exactly, but Joshua supposed the older man was in his middle seventies. His silvery white hair was more thin on the top now but long as usual down the sides and back, still not combed and at the nape of his neck looking like the belly hair on a wet collie. His face, too, was a bit thinner, and he was heavily tanned. It seemed to Joshua that Calvin Price looked even healthier than the last time they had seen each other.

Joshua turned up his watch, "I'll take a steak and eggs," he said wearily, "if you can have it here in five minutes."

The Colonel turned to a wall intercom and issued the order for the food.

Watching, Joshua leaned forward on the bar counter, again wondering what it could be that had brought him two thousand miles and could be worth five thousand dollars for just expenses. It didn't really matter now, anyway, and he reached into his back pocket for his billfold.

Price sat down on one of the leather-covered bar stools, as he studied Joshua for a moment, the hint of a smile on his weathered and heavily lined face. "Why the rush?" he finally asked. Calvin Price did not speak in the normal fashion of one accustomed to being equal, offering options, being considerate, or expecting argument or debate. His voice rumbled out of his mouth with an authority, deep and demanding, formidable. His style was that of a freight train, slow moving but powerful.

Joshua Bain, however, was not about to be intimidated. "There's a storm brewing," he answered calmly. "And I'm on a tight schedule." He extracted the balance of the five thousand from his billfold. Carefully folding the bills, he stood them on edge in front of Price. "Here's what's left of the cash."

Price picked up the money, turned it once in his hand before dropping it indifferently into a nearby ashtray. "You look well, Joshua," he said, "and I understand you've turned the Canaan ranch around."

Joshua consented to endure the small talk, figuring he owed Price something for his steak and eggs. "We're making it all right," he confirmed.

"What's your partner's name, the young Indian?"

Joshua stared at him for a moment before answering, "You remember his name. Or at least you should. He was the one who talked me into giving you your passport . . ."

The older man nodded once, looking down at the counter. "You mean your heart wasn't in it?"

Joshua shook his head. "If it had been entirely up to me,

I'd have socked you away so deep in a Federal pen that it would cost a hundred dollars and take a month just to get you a postcard."

"Ah, Joshua!" Price exclaimed, and he turned on the stool to face the open cabin. "That's what I always admired about you; you never did pussyfoot around much."

"So why don't you get to it now?"

The Colonel turned back to face him again. His eyes were narrowed down now, putting Joshua on guard. "Be patient, my friend," said Price. "You've come a long way—"

"Let's keep the record entirely straight," Joshua interjected. "Had I known you were here, I'd never have made the trip. And what surprises me is that you should have known that. Be that as it may, the only reason I'm here is because of the item you included with your note," and he reached into the left front pocket of his slacks to pull out a small tissue-wrapped packet. He removed the paper, placing its contents, a small silver cylinder, on the counter top.

Price picked up the object, turning it slowly in his hand. "What is it?" he asked Joshua.

"You don't know? I thought you sent it."

"I provided the money and the note," said Price, "but this was supplied by an associate, a person who said it would guarantee your presence here."

"Who's your associate?"

"Confidential for the moment."

"Now who's pussyfooting?"

Price ignored the question. "Looks like it's been burned," he said, looking more closely at the cylinder. "This writing— it's Hebrew, isn't it?"

"Yes," Joshua confirmed. "It's a mezuzah. It was worn by a friend of mine."

"Then your friend must've taken a beating," mused Price. "This thing is hardly recognizable."

"He's dead," Joshua told him, and there was a break in his voice. The history of the mezuzah was an intensely private matter to him, and he reached out to retrieve the battered cylinder. He carefully folded it up in the tissue paper.

"I'm sorry," said Price sincerely.

"No matter," said Joshua, and he had to clear his throat, fighting against the lump forming there. He pushed away from the counter. "I'm ready to leave," he said flatly.

Price held up his left hand in a placating gesture. "You've

got food coming, and you've got the time to at least hear me out."

Joshua shook his head, but he did not move.

"The reason you're here," Price started, "is because the Canaan team is desperately needed to act as an intermediary, a go-between, in a transaction of great importance, one which also involves a considerable sum of money. For example, your fee for services rendered will be one hundred thousand dollars."

"And you're one of the parties?"

Price nodded slowly.

"Then forget it," said Joshua.

Colonel Price drew a deep breath, obviously struggling to control himself. "Come on, Joshua," he offered. "You don't hide yourself very well. So maybe you're doing fine at the ranch, and I can understand your loyalty to Alan Hunt. But, deep down, I'd bet half your fee that both you and Alan are not altogether happy catering to the golf and tennis bums—"

"Beats going to jail," Joshua noted, "and I see you do remember Alan's name."

Price broke into a smile, showing his perfect teeth. "Your part in the operation is virtually clean, and I can guarantee your immunity. It's your dependability and honesty that we're buying."

"That still doesn't make it legal."

Price reached up to pull on his right ear, a gesture which Joshua knew indicated the older man was problem-solving. "You sound like Alan Hunt has done a real number on you," Price suggested wryly.

Joshua felt his jawline hardening. "You'd best watch your mouth," he said evenly.

Calvin Price was glaring at him then.

The knock on the door broke the tension.

Price turned toward the door. "Come in!" he said harshly.

The uniformed servant entered the cabin with a tray of food, placing it nervously on the counter before Joshua. Price dismissed him with a flick of his hand.

"You go ahead and eat," Price said, "and I'll be back in a few minutes."

Joshua lifted the corner of the silk napkin covering the tray. The spencer steak looked like it was rare, the three eggs done over easy. There were biscuits and butter, and a side dish of diced fresh fruit. A pot of hot coffee was also included.

Joshua swallowed hard. Why not? he thought, and he pulled the napkin away.

Calvin Price went directly to his own sleeping quarters, a smaller cabin located down the connecting hallway. The man on his bunk came to his feet when he entered the cabin. Karen Laswell was standing near the small bar, opposite the bunk. Price moved directly across the room to turn off the intercom switch.

"You heard it all," he said resignedly.

"Yes," the man said. He was shorter than Price, his upper torso disproportionately long and muscular. His thick, muscular neck supported a head which had been shaved bald. When he turned to look at Price his upper body rotated with his head, pulled around by the neck brace cupped under his chin. The man moved and looked like a wrestler. "He doesn't care much for you," Michael Brav suggested quietly. His voice was low and thoughtful, accented just enough to suggest he might also speak another language.

"He hates my guts," Price snapped. "And I warned you how he would feel." He sat down heavily on his bunk.

"You're positive you can trust him?"

"Absolutely," said Price. "*If* he commits, and especially if they commit as a team. If Bain starts to waver, Alan Hunt backs him up. Together, they're so clean they squeak."

"What about the girl?"

Price gestured toward Karen Laswell.

"Our dossier indicates she is a new addition," Karen reported. "She and Alan Hunt were recently married."

"She's just baggage," Price suggested tartly, and he looked at Brav. "Why, are you now having second thoughts?"

"No," responded Brav quickly. "Of the three principals we suggested, we also feel that the Canaan team is the strongest. We in fact still feel indebted to them for their help in the Rahab operation."

Price was pulling on his left ear. "The obstinate fool," he said after a moment.

"He angers you," Brav suggested, "because he is unaffected by your wealth, and, perhaps, by your power—which further recommends him."

Calvin Price was shaking his head negatively. "If you think Bain is a problem, wait until you meet his partner."

"Let's for the moment concentrate on Bain."

"I'm wide open for ideas."

Karen Laswell had stepped next to the bunk to put her hand on Price's shoulder. "Regardless of what you decide to do," she said softly, "just be sure you let him finish eating first. Isn't there some ancient tale about selling one's birthright for a mess of pottage?"

Michael Brav watched the trace of a smile cross the Colonel's face. "I know it's normal to try to shade the odds," Price said to her gently, "but Joshua Bain is the most unpredictable man I've ever known." He shook his head then. "If he were an ant on an anvil right now, the best odds I could give you would be fifty-fifty, assuming you had a sledge hammer in each hand."

"He's got you psyched out," she suggested.

The Colonel laughed ironically. "You were with him less than two minutes, and he put you on the spot twice."

"One half of one percent has done it for us before," she reminded him.

Michael Brav took a step toward the door. "It seems you've done your best with the cash incentive," he proposed, "so let me try the real reason instead."

"Good luck," said Calvin Price. Watching the other man push out through the door, the Colonel then remembered that his parting comment favored and reflected the personal conviction of one Alan Hunt, who had once suggested to him in the most profound way that luck was not luck at all but was indeed the will of God.

Cutting into the last of his steak, Joshua was thinking that Alan Hunt would be disappointed to learn that Calvin Price had probably not changed during the past two years. His partner always held out the most optimistic hope that people could change, no matter what their condition. Perhaps Price was the exception that proved the rule. The influence of Alan Hunt now brought to Joshua's mind the further truth that men ought not to judge one another. The salon door opened, and the stranger entering the cabin brought his mind back to the present.

"My name is Michael Brav," the man said cordially.

Joshua put his fork down as the man strode across the distance between them. "Joshua, Bain," he said indifferently, figuring now that Calvin Price, the known gambler, was turning his hole card in the person of the man called Michael Brav.

After shaking his hand with a firm grip, Brav slid onto the stool at the far end of the bar. Joshua caught himself staring at the neck brace.

"Coffee?" he asked.

"No, but you go ahead and finish."

Joshua picked up his fork to probe at the remnants of his eggs. "I presume you're a friend of Colonel Price?"

"No, not really. I'm here to pick up the mezuzah."

Joshua was suddenly no longer interested in his food. He placed his fork carefully on the edge of his plate. "So you're the one who gave it to Price."

"Yes."

"Why do you want it now?"

"To return it to the mother of Benjamin Caplan."

Joshua stared at him frankly and suspiciously.

"That's where it belongs," Brav added. "She agreed to let me borrow it."

"Why?"

Brav crooked his mouth in an indifferent grimace, a casual and off-hand gesture. "Because she thought it might help persuade you to help us."

Joshua let the comment settle in his mind before responding, "And that's the real reason why you're here." He was now studying the man from a new viewpoint, one which began to make sense. What had thrown him off was the man's appearance, his blue eyes, his stature, demeanor. "You don't look Jewish, you know," he finally offered.

Brav smiled broadly, as he reached up to scratch the neckline at the back of the brace. "I'm beginning to appreciate," he admitted then, "why Colonel Price endorsed you for the job."

Joshua was at once wary of the flattery. He glanced at his watch. "If you've got a point to make, you've got about five minutes left."

"That's plenty of time," said Brav. He had clasped his heavy hands before him on the counter, and he now looked down at them before going on, "A warning first, so that there will be no misunderstanding. Don't be misled by the calm and serenity of this meeting. What we may become involved in will be both tricky and dangerous. If you become a part of it, you must constantly be on the alert. Trust no one. Your best protection will be to follow your instincts and forget the book."

Aware that Brav was trying to pique his interest, Joshua simply frowned at the tactic. "You sound like you know that

Ben Caplan was killed because he went by the book."

Brav lifted his eyebrows in an appreciative gesture. "You know, his mother spoke affectionately about you."

Joshua was thinking that the world was not so large a place after all, and he figured by now that he knew why he had been brought to this remote place. The feeling was in his bones. And he suddenly resented the man before him, and he wanted to turn away, to escape before it went too far. "I've got to be going," he stated tartly.

"I've got over three minutes left," Brav reminded him.

Joshua pulled the small packet out of his pocket, pushed it down the bar top. "You said this is what you really wanted. I'm banking on you to return it to Ben's mother."

Brav picked up the small packet. He nodded slowly then, almost understandingly as he proposed, "You can't keep on running away from yourself, Joshua. That's a luxury only the most selfish and intolerant enjoy."

Joshua stared hard at him, thinking that the man had done his homework, or, that he was a gifted mind reader. "Now you're getting personal," he said icily.

"I haven't even started. According to Caplan's mother, her son would've jumped at this kind of opportunity."

Joshua felt his hands starting to clench up.

"If Ben Caplan were alive today," Brav went on unmercifully, "we wouldn't even give you a second thought."

Joshua turned the corner of the bar. "If you mention his name one more time," he said thickly, "I'll be tempted to forget that you're a cripple."

Michael Brav slipped off the bar stool in one easy, fluid motion, facing Joshua in a slight crouch.

The two men stood opposite each other, their respective anger and emotion showing in their faces. Joshua could hear his own breath moving like a wind in and out of his nostrils.

Brav began to relax first, pulling his shoulders back slightly, a sign to Joshua that the moment was perfect, that the man who had suddenly become his opponent was either a very good gambler or a rank fool.

"It's strange, isn't it," Brav then proposed quietly, "that we Jews always seem to wind up fighting before we can settle anything."

Joshua questioned who between the two of them was really the fool. "You're down to about thirty seconds," he reminded the other man.

"If you haven't guessed it already," said Brav, "then you should know that I represent the State of Israel. And we expect to be the top bidder in negotiations with Colonel Price for certain material that we desperately need."

"Illegal arms?"

"Not exactly. The point is that we want the material, and we're prepared to pay the asking price. I might add that there are others who are known to be after it also, and they too must be counted on to go to any limit to get their hands on it."

A natural enough consequence for the competition, Joshua thought to himself. Price and his organization operated in a world apart, in an environment without law or moral conscience, where one survived strictly by his wits. Whatever the material might be, it was literally up for grabs until it was safely in the hands of the Jews on Israeli soil. Joshua sensed that Brav had somehow finally managed to arouse his interest.

"You should also know," Brav added quietly, "that the containers holding the material at one time bore the ID label of a company called Armatrex."

Joshua closed his eyes instantly. *Armatrex!* The name aroused a host of images, and he blinked once before taking a deep, liberating breath. Colonel Calvin Price had just turned his hole card, the ace of spades!

Taking note of the following silence, Joshua decided that he had to break it off, to turn the moment around. He needed time to think. He then noticed that Brav still hadn't said anything more and didn't appear ready to now. Joshua cleared his throat before observing, "It is the trick of a hard-close salesman to make his final pitch, then to shut up. Because, between him and the customer, the next one to speak is usually the loser."

Michael Brav was smiling thinly.

Part One

THE INTERCEPT

And the Lord said unto me, A conspiracy is found among the men of Judah, and among the inhabitants of Jerusalem.
They are turned back to the iniquities of their forefathers, which refused to hear my words; and they went after other gods to serve them: the house of Israel and the house of Judah have broken my covenant which I made with their fathers.

—Jeremiah, chapter 11

Chapter one

Wednesday, October 4, outside of Palm Desert, California.

The action on the one-meter diving board was still too stiff, and Alan Hunt made a final adjustment on the pedestal tension rod before turning back toward the main building. As he cleared the deep end of the fifty-foot pool, he noted that the rising water still had about a foot to go before the pool would be filled. Like practically everything else on the ranch, the pool had been recently serviced and declared ready for the upcoming season.

He paused next to a redwood table near the shallow end to inspect the next item on his three-page check list, the recently installed therapy spa. Smiling, he ticked the item off, remembering that he and Anne had already checked out the unit the night before. Sighing contentedly, he placed the clipboard on the table. It was getting dark now, and he had done enough in the past fourteen hours to make it a day.

Barefoot and dressed only in a pair of worn Levi cutoffs, he settled into a nearby chaise lounge to stare out across the ranch they called Canaan. The long dusk was a favorite time of the day for Alan Hunt during most of the year, because with the sun behind the mountains to the west, the air temperature at their high-desert location dropped toward a comfortable level. It was also quiet now, except for the murmur of the well water moving through the pool fill line, and Alan figured that right now should be a time of assessment, of counting his many blessings. There was the fact of Rancho Canaan, which he still couldn't fully comprehend. He was in the best health of his life. And his recent marriage to Anne was in itself a miracle of immeasurable proportion. And Joshua, too, who had become a kind of friend closer than a brother—

"You seem preoccupied."

Alan turned his head to smile at Anne standing next to the table, a tray in her hand. She was also barefoot, dressed in a pair of weathered jeans with a loose cotton top. Her long black hair was pulled behind her head, tied back to keep it out of her way, and she was smiling as she placed the tray on the table.

Watching her, Alan felt a kind of warmth engulf him, along with a sinking feeling of helplessness, a special sort of yielding sensation, which was still strange to him. He reached out for her, and she moved to sit down beside him.

"Joshua is up," she told him quietly.

He took her hand. "He's probably hungry as a bear."

"You're right," she said as she pushed herself up with her free hand. "So I pulled three steaks out of the freezer."

"And you want me to barbecue them."

She was smiling again, and he noticed the thin black line around the pupils of her dark brown eyes. He reluctantly let her hand go. "You've got a deal. But I'll do a couple laps in the pool first."

She frowned. "You must be kidding. That well water has to be freezing."

"I know," he admitted freely, and as he stood up he cupped her chin with his left hand, kissing her gently.

The first floor of the main ranch house was largely occupied by the dining room, whose cathedral ceiling reached to the second-story roof. To the right of the dining room and behind the front office were two long rectangular rooms, one behind the other. The first was a recreation room, the other a library. The second floor, balcony fronted around the dining room, was given to the private quarters for the ranch management personnel.

Joshua Bain moved listlessly down the balcony stairway. He stopped on the tiled landing, debating which way to turn. Business first, he thought, as he turned toward the office, aware that he was in fact stalling. Soon now he was going to have to face Alan and make the decision to either go or not to go. In the office he first went through the mail, finding nothing of importance. His call slips were also routine, except for one from Rabbi Feldman, upon which Anne had added the remark to "See Alan re this." Joshua folded the slip once before putting it in the pocket of his pullover. The silence in the building irritated him, and on his way out he stopped by the registration desk to turn on the stereo system.

He assumed his timing was right as he came onto the patio near the shallow end of the pool. The food was on the table, and Alan gestured for him to sit down.

"Welcome home," said Anne warmly as she handed him a linen napkin.

Joshua was smiling as he sat down.

Alan said grace, and they all chorused a final "Amen."

Picking up his knife and fork, Joshua noticed that Alan's open Bible was next to his plate. There was still light enough to read, with at least an hour of daylight left. The passage of time itself had become a burden, and Joshua cut into his steak, feeling awkward in the brief silence. "What are you reading?" he finally asked Alan.

"Ecclesiastes."

Seems appropriate, Joshua thought to himself. A time to keep silence, a time to speak. "For any particular reason?" he heard himself inquire.

Anne answered him, "He's feeling a little guilty."

"About what?"

"Not guilty, really," Alan put in. "Maybe a little uneasy, though, because things are going so well for us all. I've been especially blessed this year," and he looked at Anne, his meaning clear on his face.

"Indeed you have," Joshua agreed, and he too looked knowingly at Anne.

"The author of Ecclesiastes was kind of in the same boat," Alan explained, "so I was checking out his response."

"So," said Joshua, "why don't you just eat, drink, and be merry. Or, like the man says, enjoy it while you can."

Alan was looking at him sideways. "You've been reading too, haven't you?"

"You're the one who practically ordered me to do it, remember."

"Yeah," said Alan after a moment. "Which reminds me, Rabbi Feldman called again this morning."

Joshua sensed he ought to say something, but he didn't.

"This time," Alan was saying, "he rather pointedly suggested that you should call him."

Joshua acknowledged the message with a tip of his head, thinking that he would have to call the Rabbi tomorrow. He had been absent without explanation from the last two sessions at Palm Desert synagogue. Not wanting to discuss the matter with Alan now, he turned the conversation to the issue of immediate concern. "We have something to settle tonight, a very serious item which could affect our work schedule."

"Your trip?" Alan asked.

"That's right."

Anne started to get up.

"Please stay," said Joshua.

Anne sat down, moving closer to Alan.

"First," Joshua began, "what would you say our schedule status would be as of tomorrow morning?"

Alan gestured toward the clipboard at the far end of the table. "We're in good shape," he proposed. "Maybe as much as a week ahead of schedule. Yesterday, after you left, I had Tony pick up an extra hand in Indio. We've only got holes eight and nine left to finish landscaping."

A good sign, Joshua was thinking. They'd spent the entire summer putting in the nine-hole practice course, hoping to have it ready for the season.

Alan went on for the next several minutes, detailing their progress on the all-important check list. He finished his report with a performa estimate of their bank balance as of the middle of the month—roughly fourteen thousand dollars. "We are thus solvent," he added confidently.

Listening, Joshua had helped Anne clear the table. "We'll have to program in the hundred-hour check on the Otter," Joshua reminded him thoughtfully.

"We can trim eight grand off the first quarter," Alan suggested, "if we replace the maitre d' with a receptionist," and he put his arm around Anne. "She wants to give it a try."

Joshua studied her for a moment, briefly recalling her background, which certainly qualified her to deal with even the most obnoxious of customers.

Anne was not at all embarrassed as she reminded him, "You said yourself that we are all working partners."

"Then it's done," agreed Joshua.

"So what's the serious item?" Alan asked bluntly.

Joshua contemplated where to begin. All three of them were already familiar with the background details, so he started by saying, "I have reliable information that the Armatrex plutonium has surfaced."

Alan Hunt made an appreciative sound in his throat, while Anne simply lifted her eyebrows.

Joshua then reported the details of his trip, ending up, at Alan's request, with a second account of what would be expected of them. "Our function will be that of a responsible intermediary. We will, in effect, represent both sides during the final negotiations and transfer of both the material and the payment. We will oversee inspections and meetings, the locations of which we will select at our discretion. We are, you might say, in charge until it's finished."

"And we're responsible," Alan reminded him.

"But there's no liability, as such."

"What if it falls apart at some critical point?"

"That's a risk the principals enjoy, for the most part. Remember, too, they each have veto power over any plans."

"So how do we get paid the hundred grand?" Alan asked.

"They offered fifty now, plus the balance when it's over."

Alan laughed disdainfully.

"I know," Joshua said. "I reminded Mike Brav that we'd been that route before and that the terms were not acceptable."

"What do you think?" Anne asked him.

"They'll be calling in the next day or two for our answer. If we decide to go, why don't we ask for seventy-five now, in cash, with the balance payable at some midway point."

"Better yet," Alan said, "go with the fifty now, but put the balance in escrow, payable to us at the end of the time period—say, in two weeks."

Beautiful, Joshua thought. The escrow move guaranteed them a lock on the final payment. He noticed then that Alan was staring out over his shoulder. Turning to follow Alan's line of sight, he picked up the sound of an approaching airplane. An experienced pilot, Joshua began tracking the aircraft at once. Despite the poor light in the lee of the mountain range, he could see enough of the small ship's trim to identify it. "A twin-engine Piper," he said under his breath. The aircraft was low, no more than a thousand feet above the ground, and on a heading taking it right down the center axis of the ranch.

"Maybe an early check-in," Alan quipped.

The aircraft winged over into a slow turn to the east.

"He's heading for Bermuda Dunes," Joshua suggested, and he turned back to the table, dismissing the incident since small planes were occasionally over the area. The ranch's private landing strip was a well-known landmark, and it was likely the plane's pilot was getting his bearings in the diminishing light. "So what do you think," he said, "do we go or forget it?"

Alan was studying his coffee cup. "If it weren't for Calvin Price, I'd say let's do it right now. The money will help us, without any doubt. Which, in a way, troubles me more than anything."

"Why?" questioned Joshua. "They made the offer. I didn't hassle them over the amount." He held up his hands. "We work and we get paid for it."

"You don't think it's too much?"

Joshua mulled over the question. "Hadn't really thought about it," he admitted. "On a deal like this, it's hard to assess what is really a fair price. We're not buying a used car, you know. We don't have a blue book for a guide."

"It may be," Anne suggested, "that you both have underestimated the risk factor, which they are more aware of."

"Perhaps," Joshua conceded. "We might have to deal with an upset competitor. However, by careful enough planning, especially on timing and location, we ought to be able to frustrate any effort to intercept."

"All right," said Alan, "so that leaves us with Calvin Price."

Joshua tried to put together a reply, offering finally, "There are millions of dollars involved, as well as material precious enough to some to almost be above value. Both Calvin Price and the Israelis desperately want to trade what they've each got for what the other has. It seems clean to me from both sides."

"Okay," said Alan. "I'd still like to take the rest of the night to kick it around, to pray about it. How about tomorrow morning for an answer?"

"Take your time," said Joshua, and he stood up to look down at Alan Hunt and his wife. "How did it really get started?" he wondered aloud. "I mean, like I've tried to figure it out, from the beginning, but I can't seem to get a handle—"

Alan held up his left hand to stop him. "Isn't that interesting, my dear friend. Yesterday makes little sense to us, even though we've lived it, documented it, can even recount and recall every move; even so, the best we can do is to propose that most of it was a mystery, inexplicable. Yet, here we sit, in somber committee, trying to plan out tomorrow. The real absurdity of our position is that on the day after, we shall again look back, on tomorrow, with the same perplexity."

Joshua could only shake his head. "So you make worse what is already a problem."

"Not really," Alan insisted gently, "because we've omitted the third corner of the triangle of time. We hit upon yesterday and tomorrow, and we are rightfully baffled."

"You mean today."

"Right on, brother. And, remember, today is 'sufficient unto itself.' "

The operations log of the Bermuda Dunes Airport tower

reported that the twin-engined Piper had landed at 2030 hours. The commercial aircraft was a special charter out of the Long Beach Airport, whose brief employment instructions to that point only directed the pilot to report into room 23 at a local Palm Desert motel not later than 9:00 p.m. After picking up a prearranged rental car at the airport, the pilot drove directly to the designated motel, arriving a few minutes before nine o'clock. His contact in room 23 turned out to be a young dark-complected man of slight build who spoke English with an accent and who curtly introduced himself as "Hafiz Barca."

"Cliff Pearson," the pilot said, extending his right hand. Barca ignored the gesture, turning instead to the nearby dresser to pick up a small briefcase. A tough professional accustomed to rude customers, Pearson turned without further comment to sit down next to the table near the front of the small room.

Barca opened the briefcase, putting it on the table across from Pearson.

"As of now," Barca told him, "you are on standby." He handed Pearson a motel key. "This is for room 21, where you will stay until you receive word from me. If you leave for any reason, you must check out with me."

Pearson took the key. "Can you tell me when?"

"No, not now. The best I can say is within a week, probably."

Pearson sighed heavily, shaking his head. "I only brought one day's extra clothes."

Barca had removed an envelope from the briefcase, from which he extracted several one-hundred-dollar bills. "Here is an advance on your perdiem. Buy what you need and keep a record," and he laid five of the bills on the table. "Remember, from this point on, you are not to discuss your reason for being here with anyone, including your employer."

"That's no problem, since I don't know myself."

Barca removed a large piece of paper from the briefcase, which Pearson could see enough of to guess it was a hand-drawn map of some kind.

"You flew over the ranch coming in?" Barca asked him as he spread the paper on the table.

"Yes. It was dusk, but I located the strip. I can use Hiway 74 as a reference. I could probably find it in the dark."

"What is your recommendation for the best time, if we have an option?"

"Early morning, the earlier the better. The winds are down then."

"How about shortly after dawn?"

Pearson nodded approvingly. "So long as we have enough light to land."

Barca pushed the map next to his elbow. "How is this for scale?"

Pearson studied the paper briefly. "From what I can remember, I'd say you're close. But then it was nearly dark."

"Then we'll fly over it again tomorrow, just after dawn, so we both can get a good look." Barca then returned the rough map to the briefcase. "After we get back in the morning, prepare the aircraft for its maximum range."

"How many passengers?"

"Two, with minimum baggage."

"Flight plan?"

"Do not file one, which, I understand, is permissible procedure."

"That's true, but for our own safety, I should know our final destination. There is the weather, charts—"

"*Se hable Espanol?*"

"I know enough," Pearson responded to the obvious hint, and he smiled for the first time. He came to his feet, assuming that the meeting was near its end. "It's possible the owners already advised you," he said carefully, "that anytime we book a foreign charter that we want it understood we will not be a party to any illegal activity. It is, simply enough, a matter of strict company policy."

"I understand, and the owners did make the point."

"For my part," Pearson went on soberly, "I would like it further understood that my contract does not include, shall we say, any hazardous duty."

"Try to relax," Barca said reassuringly, "and do not be overly concerned or intrigued because of the secret nature of our plans. Per our agreement, you have been hired to fly your airplane to any legal and otherwise acceptable destination whenever I say. Nothing more, nothing less," and he hesitated briefly before adding sarcastically, "I presume we've hired a pilot, not a lawyer."

Cliff Pearson chuckled appreciatively. The thin skin of one Hafiz Barca suggested that he, too, might be a little on edge.

After they had finished in the kitchen, Joshua excused himself to try out the new spa. Left alone in the house, Alan and Anne moved together into the library. He took his own separate chair, settling down to stare thoughtfully across the large, furnished room. Anne toured down the nearer wall, reaching up absently to rearrange out-of-place books on the darkly stained oak shelves. "Why is it," she finally asked quietly, "that you are so undecided?"

"You mean Joshua has already decided to go."

"Of course he has, which seems obvious."

"You're very perceptive; I don't recall him saying he'd made up his mind."

"I may not know why, but he wants to go. He also wanted to talk to you about it."

"I know, but it wouldn't do any good. You see, we've gone over it all before. Joshua's cross is his sense of responsibility. He's a moral accountant with a ledger full of IOUs, which, in actuality, are probably all bad debts and should be written off."

"I haven't noticed," Anne observed quietly.

"He keeps the ledger locked up. For example, the ashes of Jerrie McKennan are still in the hills, and every time Joshua rides up to the higher ground, he communes with her spirit, or, so he believes."

"Is that so unusual, considering he loved her very much?"

"While it's true he loved her, it is also true that he feels responsible for her death. And, that's the key with Joshua Bain. His inordinate sense of responsibility. It's the same with the Armatrex plutonium. He was hired to find it, and he feels he actually had it in his grasp, and he let it slip away."

Listening, Anne had retraced her steps to sit down on the couch opposite from him. "I suppose you're right. The worst mood I've ever seen him in was a couple months ago when Ben Caplan's name came up."

Yes indeed, Alan thought to himself. Of all the acts of Providence that Joshua had been exposed to during the past several years, the tragic matter of Ben Caplan had to be the most significant.

"He's changed," she insisted gently.

"Not really. While Ben's death has Joshua obliged, its further service has been to awaken in him an awareness of his Jewishness. That's why he's been going to the synagogue. He's on an identity search. And, that's why he must volunteer for this mission." Alan let his head tip forward, opening his eyes to stare at her. "Which is why I didn't give him an answer earlier.'"

"You mean because you'll be helping Israel?"

"That's right."

"How about that," Anne offered after a moment. "I thought about it while we were in the kitchen. As you must know, there is a part of me that wants me to say no, telling me that I must not be a part of it. However, I have just as strong a feeling that you, like Joshua, must also go," and she waved her hand once, as if to emphasize her dilemma. "It seems like it is all kind of inevitable. So, in other words, I don't feel I should say no or try to stop you; yet, I'm not about to say yes either . . ."

"Thanks a lot."

"You are out of character now," Anne reminded him. "You used to drive me up the walls with your sense of confidence, your trust."

"So you're saying it's already under control."

"That's for you to decide, since you're the one who needs to know whether to turn to the right or to the left."

Praise the Lord, Alan Hunt was saying to himself, and he pushed up out of the chair, reaching forward to take her in his arms.

By 11:00 p.m., within its time zone, the yacht *Swanya II* had cleared the Yucatan channel and was on an easterly course toward the island Republic of Haiti. Michael Brav entered the main salon exactly on the turn of the hour. Karen Laswell was behind the bar, the only one present, and Brav pulled up to look questioningly around the room.

"He'll be here in a minute," Karen told him, referring to Calvin Price.

Brav sighed irritably before sitting down on the nearest bar stool. Without asking him, she poured him a drink, a straight double Scotch, which he accepted without comment. He downed the liquor in one tip of the glass. As she refilled his glass, he noticed the expression of disapproval on her face. "If you're keeping score," he said caustically, "this is my first one since before dinner." He reached out then to take the bottle from her hand.

"There are other ways," she suggested quietly, "to dull the pain."

Michael Brav reached up to touch his neck brace, and he

felt his anger starting to ebb. "I'm sorry," he said then. "But three days on this ship is just about all I can take."

"We'll be in Port-au-Prince tomorrow morning."

"That doesn't help my nerves right now."

He saw Karen look over his shoulder, and he turned at the waist to see that Calvin Price had entered the salon. The Colonel had a leather valise in his right hand, and, apparently had some reason to be smiling.

"We have a go?" Brav said expectantly.

Not answering, Calvin Price walked casually across the heavy carpet to the salon's centerpiece, an enormous mahogany dining table, where he pulled aside the captain's chair, deliberately taking his time before he finally sat down, putting the valise on the floor beside him.

Watching him, Michael Brav was convinced the man was a sadist, showing by his manner and expression that he was savoring the moment. And he played the same game at five-card stud, especially if he had a winning hand, making his opponents sweat while he toyed with his chips. Brav realized he was holding his breath.

"Would you bring me coffee?" Price said to Karen.

Brav let his breath go, picking up his glass. The alcohol in the first drink had reached his brain, and he started to relax, knowing, too, that perhaps while Price was presently playing out a winning hand, the game was not over yet. Downing his second drink, he noticed that his hand was still shaking.

Karen placed the silver coffee service next to Price's left elbow, and he gestured for her to sit down before he finally addressed Brav, "Won't you please join us?"

Brav took his time pouring himself another drink, while he contemplated telling Price what he could do with his fancy yacht, his bid, the whole scenario. Instead, he slipped off the stool, making his way slowly across the room to sit down on Price's right.

"You can use the ship's radio," Price told him, "to report to your superior's that Israel has been awarded the bid."

The news was expected, yet Brav still felt a distinct surge of relief, which passed quickly as he realized that they had only cleared the first hurdle.

"You have nothing to say?" Price asked him.

"Tell Aviv will be pleased."

"They should be, since your bid wasn't the highest."

As Price leaned over to open the valise, Brav looked

searchingly at Karen Laswell, whose raised eyebrows suggested that she too was as much in the dark as he was. Price put a small black briefcase on the table, followed by several typed sheets of paper, one of which he handed to Brav.

"This is a package manifest of the material," Price told him. "Includes number of containers, weights, sizes, and so on, which will enable you to provide adequate transport. Notice that each container is numbered. On the reverse, you will find a detailed list of warnings and precautions you must observe in handling this material. Per your suggestion, we will retain the code name of Jordan for the material."

"We can use this as a check list," Brav commented as he briefly scanned the document, "when we make the exchange."

"Exactly," Price confirmed. "I don't need to warn you that all these documents are highly classified," and he handed Brav a second sheet. "Here is a list of three locations, arranged in order by the priority we prefer. It is imperative that both I and my people avoid U.S. waters, or any area serviced by Interpol."

"What about inspection?"

Price handed him a third sheet. "Here are the terms and conditions of both inspection and payment procedure. Inspection is clean. You can provide up to two inspectors, with whatever equipment you select, so long as they can hand carry it. Since you insist on inspecting the entire lot, security for us both becomes a problem."

"I don't understand, exactly."

Calvin Price looked down to the drink in Brav's hand, briefly showing the disapproving expression of a teetotaler, one not unfamiliar to Michael Brav. "You know, Mister Brav," Calvin Price suggested, "it is best we all keep a clear head, especially in our business—"

"My mind is perfectly clear," Brav snapped defensively. "So shall we get on with it," and he deliberately tipped the glass to his mouth, finishing it in one gulp. "Like what is the security problem?"

"All right," said Price resignedly. "For us, inspection of the entire lot means, simply enough, that we have to divulge its location. For you, assuming inspection is a day or two before delivery, there is the chance of a switch. The history of the Armatrex material itself is a classic example."

"We've already considered the problem," Michael assured him, "with a clear head, I might add. And, one inspector is enough, whom you can blindfold during the final critical leg of the itinerary. Our inspector can seal the containers, with seals we will provide. At the time of delivery, we can then make a final check.''

Calvin Price was shaking his head. ''You obviously are not experienced in this sort of transaction, and, your superiors are naive in assuming you can trust me. For example, no matter how complex or clever your seals, we could probably duplicate them in two hours.'' He simply held up his hands. ''Raising oranges is your business, duplicating seals is ours.''

''So we run the inspection immediately before the transfer.''

''Then I'm too vulnerable.''

''What's your alternative?''

''The Canaan team is the obvious answer, for both the material inspection and the payment transfer. Your inspector, who need not be blindfolded, will be accompanied by Karen, as my representative, and by one of the Canaan team, who will look out after both our interests. Once the inspection is complete, all three will simply remain with the material until it is delivered. They will not only provide added security but will also function as kind of hostages.''

Brav was careful to avoid looking at Karen Laswell. ''I'll discuss it with Tel Aviv. I expect the hostage angle will appeal to them.''

''Then to payment,'' said Price.

Brav looked down to the third sheet briefly, before observing, ''So you insist on the securities as payment.''

''Absolutely,'' said Price flatly. ''And, the Bonn notes in such a block size are only available through the Andreason group in New York. Plus, they can be relied upon not to publicize the transaction.''

Of course, Brav thought to himself, the New York source was obviously under the control, somehow, of one Calvin Price. Anyone else would be delighted to receive bullion, or some form of stable currency. ''We may be naive,'' he said, ''but you treat us like fools.'' He pushed his empty glass across the table toward Karen, who looked questioningly at her employer.

Price simply waved his left hand, a gesture of indifference, and she got up to move toward the bar. ''Let's keep our mood at a negotiable level,'' the Colonel suggested wryly.

''So the broker's fee,'' Brav pointed out, ''will run to as

much as two hundred thousand. A nice bonus, shall we say, for someone."

"I've often been accused of making a profit."

"Not at our expense, this time."

"All right," said Price, more amiably now. "So I'll pick up the entire tab for the Canaan team, plus their expenses."

Brav briefly considered the proposal before replying, "That still leaves you with a lift of nearly a hundred and fifty thousand, since you're absorbing only fifty thousand from the original agreement on the Canaan group cost."

"I told you that your bid wasn't the highest. Believe me, I'm losing more on the difference there alone."

"We only have your word on that."

Price's expression hardened perceptively.

Karen Laswell had returned to the table, putting Brav's drink down before him. "Why don't you forward the proposal to Tel Aviv," she said to Brav as she sat down in her chair.

"We're getting short on time already," Price said tartly. "And if the Jews have to make another committee decision, God only knows when they'll come up with an answer."

Michael Brav tried to deal with his own rising anger, occupying himself by watching the liquid in his glass shift in response to the easy roll of the ship. He bit down on his teeth, knowing he had to let the other man speak first.

"All right," said Price abruptly. "I'll absorb the first fifty thousand on the broker's fee."

"It would also help," Brav suggested softly, "if you could use your influence to get the fee reduced. One percentage point would help."

Calvin Price was obviously more relaxed as he nodded approvingly. "I will do my best." He gestured toward the papers before Brav. "Are we otherwise in agreement?"

"Yes."

Price handed him the small metal briefcase. "You will deliver the securities in this case. Be careful with it, for we will not accept payment in anything else."

Brav took the case, finding it heavy for its size.

"It's waterproof," Price explained. "It's made of stainless steel and the lock is not to be turned until we inspect the contents at the time of delivery. Only Karen will have the key. And, when the time comes, it can easily be inspected to confirm it is not bugged."

Putting the metal case beside him on the floor, Brav was

thinking that Calvin Price was totally paranoid.

"I am one who survives," Price was telling him, as if he might have read his mind. "Which is why I'm careful, very careful. Which is also why, at this point, that I must lodge a possible protest."

Michael Brav was again on his guard.

"The reason I was late for our meeting," Price explained, "is because I was going over a cable from my security chief concerning the background details on the woman recently married to Alan Hunt, who I'm not so sure now is merely baggage," and he looked to Karen for help. "What was her name before—"

"Anne Delemar," Brav interjected.

"That was an alias she used," Karen reminded them. "She was involved as a double agent in the Rahab operation."

"And before that?" Price asked.

"Our best information—" Karen started to report.

"The actual record is incomplete," Brav again interrupted. "She was planted, very cleverly I might add, by the Arabs to help them in the Rahab operation," and he paused for a moment. "The price she paid in order to initially deceive us was severe. She was only able to assume the identity of a young Jewish girl by allowing her face to be badly mangled. It took a team of our doctors six weeks to put her back together."

"I mean before that," Price insisted.

"We can only guess," Brav surmised truthfully.

"She was a terrorist," said Price.

"Our information," said Karen, "is that she was an active member of the Popular Front for the Liberation of Palestine. The PFLP is the most militant of the Arab commando movements."

"Does your information," Brav asked, "include her real name?"

"No," Karen admitted.

"Then your information is no better than ours, which, by the way, suggests you got it from our files." He shook his head appreciatively. "The truth of the matter is that we have no proof, no real evidence where she came from."

"I deal in probabilities," Price said evenly. "The odds are overwhelming that she is a former terrorist."

"*Former* is the key word," Brav went on. "Besides, between the two of us, it is we who should be concerned about Anne Delemar's background."

"She is privy to the bed of Alan Hunt," Price reminded him.

"She is also under his influence," Brav pointed out. "If your information is up-to-date, then you know she has accepted his religion. She became a Christian shortly before they were married."

"You omit the fact," Price said, "that influence can work in the other direction."

"Regardless," Brav went on, "we could not accept her if she were to be directly involved in the operation. However, Joshua Bain told me before he left that Anne Hunt would be completely out of it, since she would be needed to run their ranch while he and Alan were away."

"Okay," said Price, "but I want it on the record."

"I'll make a note of it," Brav promised.

"Aside from your approval of the payment," Price then proposed, "the only item left is the Canaan team." He turned up his watch. "You can use the ship's radio, if you like, to contact Joshua Bain."

The liquid drug in his system had diminished the pain at the base of his skull enough to allow Michael Brav to shift his weight to a more comfortable position in the chair. "I'll call him from Port-au-Prince, or, maybe Miami," he said slowly, trying to control the developing thickness in his voice. He was getting drunk, he knew, and his bodily responses were slowing down, a familiar enough consequence, but he imagined that he was still alert, that his mind had been conditioned to its daily dose of ingested alcohol.

"Then the meeting is adjourned," Price said.

Chapter two

Thursday, October 5, 2:30 p.m., EDT. The Justice Department, Washington, D.C.

The meeting was held in the office of special investigator Jonathan Malek, who was assigned to the special projects department of staff operations. Having just returned from a late lunch, Malek's first order of business was to meet with Patrick Shell, a staff member of the Central Intelligence Agency, whose current assignment involved analyses of friendly intelligence communications worldwide from all sources, including the NSA network. After brief opening amenities, Shell removed a folder from his attache case, putting it on Malek's desk.

Shell: Here is a compilation of three intercepts bagged from Israeli transmissions during the past ten days. As you can see, a common denominator is the code word Primo. Our computer gives us two answers on Primo. One, that it probably stands for one Calvin Price, based on known prior associations in Israeli traffic, and, secondly, that your office is the number-one agency most likely to be interested.

Malek: The subject involves Interpol primarily, and they've asked for our help.

Shell: If you say so. However, your entry indicator is class red.

Malek: So why did it take three inputs to get your tail in gear? You've already waited too long as it is to be of much help.

Shell: We adhere to the principle that three's a crowd. With our budget we usually can't afford to move until something becomes a mob.

Malek: There isn't much in these transmissions we don't already know. If Primo is your code word, then you can punch it in that it definitely stands for Calvin Price. And, you might as well know that more than Interpol is involved, since we're on the verge of coming to you for help anyway. The fact is, about a week ago, Fleming at State was contacted by a member of the Israeli ambassador's office with the message that Israel had a chance to secure the contraband material they identified as the Armatrex plutonium. And, provided we give them help, to return it to us.

Shell: Miracles will never cease.

Malek: Not really. A Ha Mossad man was originally involved in the diversion, and Israel still feels responsible.

Shell: Not to mention the Rahab fiasco, which I'm sure none of us will forget too quickly, especially Tel Aviv.

Malek: They haven't. We found out a few days ago that they've had a team chasing the plutonium for the past year.

Shell: So what kind of help do they want?

Malek: Logistics mainly. Transport for their teams and for the material itself, which is where you might have to be involved.

Shell: Who's picking up the tab? If Price is selling, it's going to cost plenty.

Malek: The Israeli government should foot the bill for the plutonium, or, at least we can now presume they will. There is mention here in the third and last message that Primo insists on option two for payment.

Shell: You sound like the gig has been approved.

Malek: It has, from the top. But don't feel offended, because until now it's really been a routine operation, one involving us, State, and DOD. We simply had to rule out the CIA in the beginning because of the oversight snoopers. In fact, your being here now authorizes me to confiscate this material, and, to advise you officially that you are to discuss it with no one, except for your immediate superior, under the authority of inter-departmental memo eighty-five, dated September twenty-eight. We'll pass the final plan through your people just before it goes into effect.

Shell: I understand. However, since we've gone blue-line, then you're safe to verify what I now suspect.

Malek: Perhaps.

Shell: It's not really the plutonium you're after, is it?

Malek: The lid just closed, Mister Shell.

3:30 p.m., Atlantic Time. The Boca Chica Hotel, San Juan, Puerto Rico.

A young black woman stepped off the elevator on the third floor. Satisfied that she was alone in the hallway, she stopped in front of room number 336 where she took a moment to compose herself. According to the hotel register, the occupant of the room was an Ibrahim Accad, systems engineer, and carrier of an Algerian passport. Her PFLP contact had told her his real name which he was to use to identify himself, but she figured his mission would have to remain a secret. Tapping lightly on the door, she conceded she was honored enough just to be permitted to participate.

The man who opened the door correctly identified himself as "Kasim."

She moved into the room after introducing herself as "Sylvia," her assigned code name. The appearance of Kasim surprised her, for this was the man whose exploits had made him into a legend among his followers. He was slightly built and short in stature, weighing perhaps no more than she did. He needed a shave, but even the heavy shadow of his day-old beard did little to hide his receding chin. Behind his dark glasses, Kasim did not in any way look grim or menacing. However, as she followed him across the room to a waiting table, she noticed a small caliber automatic in his belt at the small of his back. They both sat down opposite each other across the table. There was an open magazine in front of him, and as he closed it she saw that it had been covering a .38 caliber revolver.

Sylvia: Is the boat satisfactory?

Kasim: My men are checking it over now. I'll meet you here again tomorrow morning at eight hundred hours. If there are any changes needed, I'll give you the list then. I'll check it over myself tonight.

Sylvia: I understand there will be time for any modifications.

Kasim: We are in fact very short on time. Both I and my men are in the open now, and I want to get underway by this time tomorrow. Normally, twenty-four hours is my maximum allowable time to be in one place.

Sylvia: You should try to relax, enjoy yourself.

Kasim: You've obviously not been in this business very

long, and I guarantee you that you will not last with that kind of thinking. I spend much of my time trying to figure out ways to get my enemies to relax so that I can kill them.

Sylvia: I'm sorry—

Kasim: That's even a worse weakness.

Sylvia: Perhaps I should leave now.

Kasim: Without my permission, you wouldn't make it halfway to the door. Besides, you are not much of a professional if you so easily allow your feelings to get hurt. But, you can go after you make one or two mental notes. First, the air tanks you provided are inadequate. We need two per man with a spare for each. Also, we need provisions for ten days. The arms and explosives appear to be adequate. Otherwise, the only item left is the aircraft.

Sylvia: The charter has been arranged.

Kasim: Type of aircraft?

Sylvia: A DC-3. It's the smallest we could get to carry the weight you specified.

Kasim: It's acceptable, so long as it can operate out of the three strips we listed.

Sylvia: Anything else, sir?

Kasim: You are dismissed.

4:00 p.m., EDT. The Guantanamo Naval Base, Cuba, Base Communications Office.

The duty Comm' Officer, LTJG Bud Matthews, checked the wall clock before turning to his private phone directory. Locating the inter-base extension for SubOps, he dialed the number, impatiently drumming the fingers of his right hand on the closed folder in front of him. An enlisted man finally came on the line.

Matthews: Pass this to the operations officer at once. We've received a priority-one flash from SubCom and it's just cleared crypto. It's an immediate forward, so I'm alerting the old man because it's so late. It should clear typing within twenty minutes, which means you can pick it up by sixteen thirty hours. And, be sure your courier has top-secret clearance.

Hanging up, he opened the folder to proof the decoded tape before passing it to a typist. The DTG for the message was zulu time:

021458 X PASS TO SKIPPER USS BUSHNELL W./SAME PRIORITY CMA CODE CMA AND CLASS X IMPLEMENT PHASE ONE ONLY CMA REPEAT CMA ONLY OPN JORDAN EFF UPON RCPT X MODIFY STANDBY POS TO 18.13N BY 75.60W X GUARD CHANNEL SIXTY-TWO X CONTACT ID IS JORDAN X COMMENCE PHASE TWO AT UR DISCRETION X IF LOCATION OPTIONS ONE OR TWO CMA SUGGEST YOU MAINTAIN STANDBY POS AT PERISCOPE DEPTH X SUBMIT IMMED STATUS RPT AT START OF PHASE TWO X ALL OTHER PROV REMAIN THE SAME X

4:30 p.m., EDT. The stock broker firm of Andreason & Company, Ltd., New York City, New York.
One of the firm's account executives responsible for overseas accounts, a Ms. Jeannette Bourges, entered the office of the branch manager, Malcom Chandler, with a TWX message in her hand. Chandler was frowning as he took the TWX, because at this late hour he would rather take up more business the next morning. As he quickly scanned the message his expression changed to one of concern and interest. The TWX was in fact a purchase order from one of the firm's clients, a multinational organization known in financial circles by its abbreviated title, MERTEX.

Chandler: You were right in insisting on showing this to me now.

Bourges: I still can't believe it. Three and a half million—

Chandler: It's legit, and don't be surprised at the numbers. Wait until you get your first order from one of the Saudi groups.

Bourges: Which reminds me, you know that the main interests, if not all, behind the MERTEX group are Jewish.

Chandler: Does that mean we should turn the order down?

Bourges: Of course not, sir. I didn't mean—

Chandler: I hope I know what you meant. However, your future with this company revolves around your ability to keep your mouth shut, especially on a transaction of this size and sensitivity. Have I made myself clear?

Bourges: Absolutely, sir.

Chandler: Then you may go. I'll handle this myself.

The instant the door closed, Malcolm Chandler turned to the small computer console on the table to his right. He carefully punched into the keyboard the identification code for the securities listed on the TWX. The readout on the CRT informed him that the Bonn block was in storage at the company's Zurich office. The location of the securities was of secondary interest to him. Using a memo pad, he carefully listed the serial numbers of the block. He was careful to double check the numbers before shutting down the computer. Turning back to his desk, he called his secretary, instructing her to connect him with an overseas operator, with the specific orders that the connection was to be made on his private line.

5:45 p.m., Central Atlantic Time. On the open sea two-hundred and fifty miles south south-west of the Azore Islands.
The Portuguese trawler *Arosa* was on a steady course bearing west south-west. The *Arosa's* last port of call had been Ponta Delgada, the Azores, where she had provisioned for the Atlantic crossing and where she had taken on her only passengers, a team of six Israeli nationals. The senior member of the Israeli commando group was Major David Sheldon, an experienced field commander known for both his coolness and bravery under fire. His assistant was Lieutenant Hank Koman, a younger man of considerable less patience who was already restless with the confines of the small ship. Alone in the cramped galley, the two men had been huddled together while they decoded their last wireless transmission. When they finished with the brief message, Major Sheldon unfolded a small map, smoothed it out on the table.

Sheldon: So our rendezvous with the *Bushnell* has been changed. The coordinates indicate a point between Jamaica and Haiti.

Koman: The question is when.

Sheldon: You are always in a rush.

Koman: This time with good reason, sir. The food on this wreck is like everything else; it stinks. The American submarines are known for the excellence and variety of their meals.

Sheldon: Soon enough you won't have much time to think about your stomach, other than how to keep it intact. I've worked out our assignments, and we'll start the familiarization schedule at dawn tomorrow. Timing and risk are exceptional for the bravo team, so I'll assume that command.

Koman: I was hoping I might get bravo.

Sheldon: The alpha assignment requires the endurance and strength; you are by far the stronger. Besides, alpha team will spend most of its time on the *Bushnell*, which should suit you, since it will provide you with the opportunity to more thoroughly appraise the ship's cuisine.

Koman: The fringe benefit is small, considering the cost of this operation.

Sheldon: Your curiosity is exceeded only by your appetite for good food, and, from recent reports, an occasional loose woman.

Koman: Pressure from the work.

Sheldon: Which reminds me, we are far enough out now to give you the name of the alpha team contact. Do you remember Michael Brav? I believe you worked with him on Cyprus a couple years back.

Koman: The wrestler type with the neck brace?

Sheldon: That's him. Once on the *Bushnell*, you'll follow his orders to the letter.

Koman: I remember that he likes his booze.

Sheldon: Drunk or sober, he's the best negotiator in Ha Mossad. He's a tough pragmatist, pure and simple, and the best way for you to deal with him is to do exactly what he says and keep your mouth shut. In fact, you will consider such a procedure a matter of personal orders from me.

Koman: I guarantee you that Brav will find me a total bore.

Sheldon: I expect irritation will be a better word. Off the record, Michael Brav is a bitter and cynical product of too many years in what at best is a hellish business. To him, much of what is happening in our country today is foolishness, the new ways.

Koman: You sound like you know him.

Sheldon: By reputation mostly. After we were briefed last week, we went out for a drink, and he had a few too many. We talked for hours. So, just be careful around him. He tends to hold the young responsible for much of what he believes is wrong now.

Koman: So maybe it's time for the old man to retire.

Sheldon: He'll retire when he dies. Which, according to some, may never happen.

Koman: He will die, sooner or later. It even happens to the very young.

Sheldon: Do you know what they call Brav, his code name? Or, how he got the neck brace?

Koman: No.

Sheldon: They call him the cat. And, for good reason. In May of '48, Brav was still in his teens and was operating as a runner for Haganah. He was caught outside the Jewish quarter of the Old City by tribesmen fighting with the legion forces. His captors shot him repeatedly, at least sixteen or seventeen times. He wouldn't die, so they decided to hang him. The only thing handy was a piece of barbed wire.

Koman: Oh, my God—

Sheldon: Yeah. They hoisted him up by the neck three times before they finally gave up, reportedly, in disgust . . .

Koman: . . . It's both a hard thing to say and hear, but I

appreciate your telling me. It will help me, and I suppose it helps explain his heavy drinking.

Sheldon: Don't feel sorry for Michael Brav. He's more than evened the score. You see, learn the lesson that he did. His captors were orthodox Moslems, who, perhaps rightfully so, believe that if a man stubbornly resists dying, that it is Allah's will that he live. To them, such a man is even to be esteemed.

Koman: So he's got them psyched out.

Sheldon: It's something to think about.

Chapter three

Friday, October 6. A secluded villa on the western coast of the West Indies Republic of Haiti.

The Caribbean headquarters for Calvin Price was serviced by both a private harbor and landing strip, and the isolated estate was entirely self-sufficient. While no passable roads reached the estate, the international jet airport at Port-au-Prince was only twenty minutes away via helicopter. It was turning dusk when Calvin Price came out of the main house onto the pool veranda. The more lush undergrowth, common to the coast even in the time of drought, harbored a variety of night-flying insects, the first of which had by now begun to fill the more open air around the estate. Calvin Price waved his right hand irritably in front of his face while straining to look across the roof. The distant dry and eroded hills stood starkly hued in orange and red under the setting sun, as if they might be on fire, making it difficult to pick out the landing lights on the approaching helicopter. He saw the dust rising then from the vicinity of the pad, and he turned back to the house, hurrying now in the failing light. He very carefully avoided the grounds at night.

At the doorway leading to the den, he pulled up, turning to partially face the veranda. The bats were coming in now, flitting and jerking ecstatically as they gorged on the insects. He thought he heard one of them then, a tiny shriek, reminding him of the complaint of a terrified mouse. Shivering once, he fumbled in his pocket for the key to the door. "Nick," he said softly yet urgently.

The dark form of Nicholas Villon, his personal valet and bodyguard, appeared at his left elbow, materializing from someplace.

"Yes, sir," Nick said quietly, the Creole influence subtle and somehow or other belonging.

"Tell Miss Karen that I want to see her in the den."

The tall mulatto turned away without a word, padding silently off in the direction of the side gate, where he again disappeared in the developing darkness. Using his pass key, Calvin Price quickly unlocked the heavy outside door to the den. Inside, he let his hand linger on the door handle after he tested it several times to make sure it was latched. It was time to leave again, he told himself as he started determinedly across the room. The estate sanctuary was one of expediency for Colonel Calvin Price, who otherwise preferred a more civilized and palatable location. Here, however, he had absolute security and privacy, warranted not only by his own personal army but also by the local officials, whose cost of both cooperation and indifference was reasonable. But two or three days was all he could take of this island within an island surrounded by an organic jungle thick with voodoo rites and chants. He pushed through the door to the room which served as the estate's security office.

His security chief, Maurice Garand, was seated at the table supporting a massive radio transmitter. Several clocks were wall-mounted above the radio, each reporting a time zone which could be of interest to Calvin Price in his business enterprises.

"Karen will be here in a minute," Price reported as he moved to Garand's elbow.

Maurice Garand, in his usual taciturn way, didn't answer, choosing instead to finish an entry in the radio's log. The office, like the man who ran it, was in perfect order, well organized and functionally arranged. The long wall opposite the radio was covered with a fiber display board, on which Garand had assembled the graphic details relating to the Jordan operation. A former intelligence officer with the French Navy, Maurice Garand was a meticulous planner, and Calvin Price permitted his security chief to act as he wished, generally, because the man was a machine, one totally dependable, whose loyalty was without question, and one who had always produced with a remarkable record of efficiency.

It was also Maurice Garand's edge that he trusted no one, not even himself, and it was on this premise that all his plans were formulated.

Thus aware, Calvin Price was not surprised at Garand's response when it finally came.

"It was a mistake," Garand offered slowly as he stood up, "to have sent her to escort Brav to the airport." His only handicap was his eyesight, which was so poor as to require special trifocal glasses, and, since he was virtually blind without them, he protected the lenses by using an athlete's type of frame employing an elastic band around his head. Self-conscious of his appearance, he constantly wore a light woolen pullover type cap to hide the elastic band, causing Karen Laswell to once observe that Maurice Garand had the continual look of a downhill skier about to clear the starting chute.

Calvin Price filed away Garand's comment, which he knew constituted a mistrust of not only Karen Laswell but of his own personal judgment as well. "Brav is a fox," he suggested pointedly.

"It is debatable," Garand countered quickly, "who is more the fox and who is more the vixen."

Price heard himself chuckle, a gesture of admiration for the man's quickness of mind. "It was you," he finally said, "who suggested we use her. And, as I recall, you were certain Brav was the better of the two, which, supposedly, was to work to our advantage," and he paused for a moment. "Are you telling me now that you made a miscalculation?"

"No, not at all." Garand had a pencil in his right hand, and he pointed it directly at his employer as he went on, "On a scale of one to a hundred, I would rank Michael Brav as a ninety-five. Your protégée is probably a sixty, at best."

"What's your point?" Price snapped impatiently.

"That you don't miscalculate in allowing her to negotiate by herself."

"You prepared the script."

Garand simply held up both his hands. "And we only have her word that she followed it."

Calvin Price fought down his impulse to tell Garand that he was in fact nit-picking a situation which simply had to be, until he began to realize that the man was really going beyond filing a protest, that he was in fact probing. He was shaking his head as he turned to face the wallboard, sensing that it was necessary to change the subject. "So you think the Canaan team will select the Jamaica site," he said idly, reaching up to pull on his right ear.

"Absolutely," Garand replied, "assuming, of course, that your estimate of Joshua Bain is accurate."

"That's why I'm raising the point. While Bain is not especially cerebral, he's got a gut that's second to none," and he turned to stare coldly at his security chief. "You could get rich betting on Bain's hunches."

"That's what we intend to do," Garand assured him, and a rare smile crossed his face. "The man's skepticism is what will finally confirm the Jamaica site." He got up then to turn the corner of his desk, pulling up before the wallboard. "Bain's primary problem will be security during and after the transfer. Especially after, since they are responsible until Brav's team and our people get back to their respective base points." He reached up to tap the aerial photo showing a narrow lagoon extending in from a larger body of water. "So his first choice will have to be here."

"How can you be so sure?"

"Bain's transport," Garand answered quickly, and he moved back to his desk. "You might logically expect him to use a powerboat. But, Bain is a pilot, remember, and he happens to be experienced in amphibs . . ." And he sat down heavily to stare impassively across the room.

Calvin Price studied the photo for several seconds before observing, "So what do we do with that contingency?"

"We let Bain run with it, after what may be classed as an appropriately mild objection."

"You mean we actually want him to use a seaplane?"

"Because he will then be less of an obstacle to our intercept team . . ."

Calvin Price checked his watch, realizing that he did not fully understand the implication. "All right," he said impatiently as he turned toward the door to the den. "You can give me the details later."

"By the way," Garand said, "the call that was on the radio just before you came in was from our contact in San Juan."

Price pulled up in the open doorway.

"It seems our Arab friend is right on schedule," Garand went on, almost casually. "The local underground is going for the program full bore. They've even arranged for a DC-3 to be on standby starting this weekend."

So the plot was thickening, Price thought, and he nodded his head in obvious approval. "So you arranged for him to know about the probability of the Jamaica site."

"Early yesterday morning."

"Which means there is an airstrip near Morant Point?"

Maurice Garand allowed another smile to cross his face.

Calvin Price stared appraisingly at his security chief, taking note of the confidence in the man's face. "This is the last warning I'm going to give you about underestimating Joshua Bain. A nearby landing strip will spook him. Or, at the last minute, he may decide to use it himself. And, wouldn't that be dandy, having him and our people show up at the same landing strip."

Maurice Garand came up out of his chair. "The strip is twelve miles up the coast from the lagoon and another three miles inland," he explained. "The odds are that Bain won't even pick up on it. And, if he does, he'll have to reject it because of the distance factor. On the other hand, the strip is ideal for us. All we have to do is shuttle the aircraft in from Montego Bay after the transfer has taken place, by which time Bain will be long gone in the opposite direction."

There was a knock on the den's outer door.

Calvin Price pulled the door to the security office closed behind him, satisfied that he had adequately warned Maurice Garand. He moved thoughtfully to the near corner of his desk, where he reached down to depress the button releasing the outer door, allowing Karen Laswell to step into the room. As she took a chair opposite the desk, Calvin Price noticed that she appeared flushed, perhaps from the exertion of the long walk from the helicopter pad. She was smiling as she faced him now, and he was reminded of another woman and another time.

"What are you beaming about, my dear?" he asked idly.

"I'm just happy, I guess."

"The day went well, I presume."

"Like clockwork."

"So Michael Brav is on his way."

"I put him on the plane myself." She turned up her watch. "By now, he should be almost to Miami, the only stop between here and Los Angeles. He is scheduled to meet Joshua Bain and Alan Hunt tomorrow morning."

Listening, Price had been studying her critically. She was

not entirely like Britt Halley, after all, he thought then, because she so easily showed her emotions. "Is our friend Brav fully under control?" he asked then. "I suppose I should ask you how you feel about the arrangement?"

She pursed her lips before replying, "Very confident. Brav is so gullible; it's almost unreal how he went along with the program."

"That should be a warning to you."

"Not in this instance," she insisted. "He's got me pegged as an opportunist."

"Don't sell Brav short," he cautioned her.

"He's in over his head, and I mean it. He's totally hooked on the sauce, and it shows in his judgment."

He looked aside at the remark, not wanting her to see his eyes. And it occurred to him for the first time in his life that he would have made a lousy gunfighter. He was severely disappointed because she had so badly miscalculated in her appraisal of the hardened professional, Michael Brav. "Regardless," he said after a moment, "the Jews are looking to clean up on this operation, and we must not let it appear that we're going to disappoint them."

"That end of it should go smoothly, assuming, of course, that we make the Hong Kong connection in time."

"He'll be here by Sunday night."

"That will give us only a few hours—"

"Can't help it," he interjected. "Chandler called in the serial numbers only about an hour ago. Plus, Zurich still hasn't given us the exact paper type. However, don't worry, because it'll be taken care of by Sunday night at the latest. By then, we'll still have twenty-four hours left, plus, the added advantage of knowing Bain's selection of the transfer site." He paused thoughtfully. "We can go over the inspection routine with Maurice after dinner. Which reminds me, did Brav mention the inspector?"

"Yes, sir. He agreed to just one, and I got the impression that was acceptable to them from the start."

Standing up, Price filed the input away. "You've done well today, and I'm immensely pleased. Just be sure you give all the details to Maurice."

She also came to her feet, and she was smiling as she told him, "I'm grateful for the chance to assume the responsibility."

"It's my pleasure," he assured her. "Now, you must be

tired, so why don't you go ahead and do whatever it is that will help you unwind before dinner. I have a few personal calls to make now, anyway."

In her own room, Karen Laswell closed the door carefully behind her, standing with her back against the door while she tried to sort out the day's events, and, especially, an appraisal of her performance just concluded in the den. Moving across the room, she assumed she had pulled it off. She hesitated before her dressing table, still preoccupied while she studied herself in the mirror. There was a twitch in the reflected image of her right hand, and she reached down to the table to steady herself.

While she had managed to perform acceptably to the present time, she wondered if she could stay with it to the end . . .

The trust of Calvin Price seemed genuine.

Maurice Garand still needed convincing.

Michael Brav was the real question mark. For example, could he really be depended upon to betray his country? The question moved in her mind as she pushed away from the table. She knew she was absolutely alone in trying to determine the answer. For Calvin Price and Maurice Garand, the question and its answer had been reduced to a matter of probabilities, all of which could be dealt with in any number of acceptable ways. Garand had a contingency for every conceivable option, including the deceptions of Michael Brav.

Karen Laswell was aware that she had no such latitude.

It had to come down just the one way, exactly.

Or, it would all have been for nothing.

And her sense of confidence started to build again, because she finally felt she had the inside track she had spent two years developing.

If she couldn't make it work now, then she never could.

During the lengthening days of the fall months, the premature dusk came more slowly to the western rim of the Coachella Valley. The slowly developing shadows had tricked Joshua Bain into thinking it was earlier than he had supposed, and, as he hurried toward the rear door of the main ranch house, he checked his watch to see that they had less than an hour before dinner. Anne Hunt met him just inside the door to the kitchen.

"It's long distance and person-to-person," she told him, gesturing toward the nearby wall phone.

Joshua lifted the extension receiver and identified himself.

"This is Michael Brav," said the voice on the other end.

The call was expected, yet Joshua felt his stomach turn over.

"We have full approval on this end," Brav was saying conversationally, and then there was silence.

Joshua cleared his throat before offering, "It is affirmative on this end, if that's what you want to know."

"I'm in Miami now," Brav told him, "attending to the necessary details here. I'm on a National flight to LAX in a few hours which will put me there before noon tomorrow. We should meet then if possible."

"We'll have to arrange something close by the airport," said Joshua. "Can you be reached later on?"

"Forget it," Brav said flatly. "When you work it out, leave a message with the National information desk."

Before Joshua could confirm his agreement the line went dead. As he returned the receiver to its cradle, he turned to see that Anne was studying him curiously.

"It's set," he told her blankly.

"When do you leave?"

"I don't know yet. However, we have to take the Otter to LAX for its overhaul, so we can meet with Brav and get the details then." He reached up with his right hand to pull thoughtfully on his lower lip. "Which means we should know by noon tomorrow."

"So it could start at any time."

"Brav sounded anxious," he observed under his breath, "which suggests an early start." He checked his watch again. "I'll go tell Alan now. And, we might be a little late getting in for dinner." He stopped in the doorway and looked back over his shoulder to see that she was still standing there, a somber expression on her face. He suspected this might be the last time they could be alone before he had to leave.

"Alan told me," he began slowly, "that you wouldn't object to his going."

She looked down to the floor, not saying anything.

"I'm certain I'm being unfair," said Joshua, "perhaps even selfish. Because I suspect there are similar things pulling you which are pushing me." He held up his hands in a helpless kind of gesture.

"You don't have to apologize or be concerned," she told him. "I can only pray that you both come out of it safely. For my part, you already know that I spent most of my life trying to fulfill the kind of obligation you're talking about. And, as you also know, I found it to be a futile exercise." She gestured once, reaching out with her right hand. "Here, at least, with Alan, and you, the ranch, all of this makes sense to me, has so much meaning . . . "

"So you think I'm a fool."

She laughed, reaching up to cover her mouth self-consciously. "You know better than that, Joshua. You're entitled to the benefit of the doubt; maybe you can make it work where I couldn't."

"I see," Joshua noted.

"Let's just say," she went on candidly, "that while you go with my consent, you don't necessarily have my blessing."

"That's fair enough."

"Just bring Alan back home," she told him evenly.

Joshua pushed out through the door, satisfied that he had at least made his peace with Anne Hunt. With that loose end resolved, he realized there was still yet another item of some importance which needed attending to before he left.

Alan Hunt was locking the door to the tool crib when Joshua pulled in to park the pickup on the hangar apron. Joshua gestured for him to get in. As he pulled the door closed, Alan noticed that Joshua looked serious, even a little grim.

"Brav called," Joshua told him as he pulled the transmission into gear. "And we've got a go." He turned the truck away from the hangar, moving across the tarmac toward the back road leading up to the higher ground along the back of the ranch. "We'll meet with Brav tomorrow morning," Joshua went on, "when we take the Otter to LAX. Brav will give us the details then."

Alan simply nodded that he understood. "So, like where are we going now?"

The truck was on the narrow dirt road now, and their angle of ascent became steeper, causing Joshua to slow to a crawl. "You might say," he finally answered, "that it's time for some high-ground talk."

So that was it, Alan thought. They were going to the promontory, the one place which was something special to Joshua Bain. The memories were over two years gone now, yet they crossed Alan's mind as fresh as if they might have happened just yesterday. The promontory was a kind of sanctuary for

Joshua Bain, who from time to time would still make the climb. Joshua had agonized on the cliff, had even wept there, and it was his own private place.

The truck climbed steadily for several more minutes until they finally ran out of road. With the truck stopped, they both got out. It was cooler at the higher elevation, but the landscape was still harsh and foreboding. The terrain was rough, boulder-covered and cleft, and as Joshua led the way on up to the higher ground, Alan found himself laboring to keep up. It took only a few minutes for him to tire enough to ask for a break.

"You're getting out of shape," Joshua suggested as he stood straddle-legged, his arms crossed over his chest.

"You're probably right," Alan admitted breathlessly, and he sat down gratefully on the nearest rock. Trying to catch his breath, he looked to his left to notice a thin stand of the delicate smoke tree, one of the most unique of all the desert flora. He reached out with his left hand, pointing toward the steeply draining washbed. "The smoke trees look down this year," he said haltingly.

"The rains were light in the foothills last winter."

Alan felt his breathing returning to normal. "They'll make it. I guess all it takes is one or two to survive the season."

"You mean the lesson of the seed?"

Alan was chuckling to himself as he pushed himself to his feet, thinking that Joshua's memory and perception were especially keen. "So let's get moving," he suggested, "or else we're going to miss out on dinner."

A few minutes later, they reached the top of the cliff. The view across the Coachella Valley was breathtaking. While they were in the shadows, the rest of the valley was still under the light of the declining sun, briefly tinted a pastel orange under the more distinct purple of the hovering easterly horizon.

"I had forgotten," Alan said under his breath, "how beautiful it is up here."

"It's something else," said Joshua as he sat down against a granite outcropping. "It's not only the way it looks," he went on reflectively, "but it's the wind mostly, the way it moves back and forth. Together, somehow or another, it all works to clear the mind."

"I can imagine it does," Alan commented. "It's absolutely basic, in a way, and takes one back to the start of it all, or, at least it does for me, anyway."

"You mean creation?"

"It's right out of the first chapter of Genesis. The firmament, the light, even the herb yielding seed . . . "

"And God saw that it was good."

"Yes, He did," Alan consented, and he was pleased to hear Joshua quoting scripture. "He obviously got a kick out of putting all this together."

"There's even a little bit of Eden here," Joshua mused.

Alan finally broke the following silence, "So what's on your mind, Joshua?"

Joshua shifted his weight, sighing once as he seemed to settle himself down. "I'm sorry for the small talk," he said evenly, "but I'm not too sure where to start."

"Take your time," Alan told him cordially, and he moved back away from the forward edge of the cliff to lean against the same outcropping. "Is it about Jordan?" he asked idly, thinking he might get Joshua started.

"No, it isn't. I'm reasonably confident of the operation, but we'll go over it more closely after we meet with Brav. What I want to talk to you about involves me personally. The Jordan thing is involved only to the extent that it seems to be pushing me to get some things settled."

"Any one thing in particular?"

"Very definitely, and I can open it up by telling you that I had a talk with Rabbi Feldman on the phone this afternoon."

The remark caught Alan totally unprepared.

"And I agreed to meet with him again tomorrow night," Joshua was saying.

Now speechless, Alan tried to assess the implications, and he looked down to see that Joshua was staring hard at him.

"I need your help, my friend," said Joshua simply. "And I'd like for you to be frank and, especially, to stop trying to be nice to me."

Alan looked away.

"You know," Joshua went on with a carefully controlled insistence in his voice, "you're not really doing me a favor by holding back, because you're afraid you'll hurt my feelings, or whatever."

Alan had pushed away from the outcropping to start pacing slowly to and fro across the flattened area of the promontory, trying desperately to prepare his response. But he couldn't seem to get beyond his nervous excitement that here at last was the opportunity, the one chance that he had been praying for.

"You're really something else," he heard Joshua saying. "Like I've learned more about the Lord from listening to you talk to other people, like Anne for example, than I've ever learned from you directly. I mean, like I thought we were close friends—"

"I tried at first," Alan interjected.

"That was a long time ago."

Alan pulled up to look down at his feet, and he realized that there was considerable truth in what Joshua was saying. The complaint was valid, and he wasn't sure why, but he knew he had to say something now. "When I have the chance to witness to someone," he began slowly, "it's a special kind of joy for me. I feel great afterwards, for example. The sharing experience seems to do me as much good as the person I'm talking to. You could say that I get on a special kind of high when I'm talking about the Lord . . . " and he paused before adding, "but with you, Joshua . . . " and his voice trailed off.

"Why, my friend?"

"As time went by, I began to think it was because we were so close, and maybe I was taking advantage of our friendship. You know, like forcing myself on you," and again he hesitated.

"You're having trouble," Joshua suggested quietly, "in telling me because I'm a Jew."

Alan turned to look out across the Coachella Valley. He sensed that he had finally come to a critical juncture in his life. During the past few years he had thought about what special role, if any, that he might have to play in what remained of his life. After meeting and getting to know Anne, he had assumed that to be a good husband, perhaps even a father, in time, was an apparent and worthwhile mission. In his early enthusiasm, right after his conversion, he had even considered going into the ministry, but he had given that up because it just didn't seem to be in his nature. Now, as he prayed inside for help in what to say, he realized that he had made a wise decision because theology was obviously not his special gift. As he turned back to look at Joshua, his next following thought formed in his mouth, "You know that I'm not equipped to debate with Rabbi Feldman."

Joshua was smiling thinly, as if Alan had just confirmed his last suggestion.

Alan Hunt shook his head helplessly.

"What's the matter," said Joshua tartly, "aren't you able to say it?"

"All right," Alan snapped. "So it's because you're a Jew!"

Joshua smiled broadly. "So it wasn't so hard, was it?"

Alan sighed heavily, before going on, "It's much more difficult than you can imagine. I've read the material you've brought home from the meetings at the synagogue. I mean, like I'm supposed to be a soul-snatcher. Like I'm trying to destroy your heritage." He paused, at once sorry for his outburst, yet still unable to quit. "And, of course, there is the final clincher, the remark of last resort, which I'm at a complete loss to deal with . . . " and he paused once again, for he was finally ashamed.

"You mean the Holocaust."

Alan was nodding slowly. "It is all so confusing sometimes. If *you're* mixed up, how do you think *I* feel? Like I know your very own family had to suffer at the hands of those . . . those maniacs."

"Hey, man," Joshua interceded, "like I'm the one who's supposed to be looking for help," and he hesitated briefly before going on, "The matter of the death camps has to be dealt with, and by us all. However, you should give me enough credit to keep separate the matter of responsibility." He reached out with his right hand, waving it once to encompass the terrain falling away below them. "The memory of Jerrie is still here, wouldn't you say?"

Alan nodded slowly, and he waited, not understanding.

"And the lesson of her death," Joshua went on, "was one you taught me. And it was admittedly a bitter lesson. But, in time, I had to face it. And a great part of what I had to learn was that God, or your own Jesus Christ, was in no way responsible. Human beings laid the plans for their own selfish reasons and motivations." His voice began to trail off as he went on, "Perhaps my mistake was in presuming that God should have intervened."

"There were those who should have intervened," Alan suggested soberly, "on behalf of the Jews during the war."

"Ah, yes," said Joshua firmly. "But you miss my point. We're here at *my* request because I'm trying to find *my* way, my own personal thing. I'm not trying, at the moment, to solve the world's problems or to exact some higher justice."

"You mean like your own spiritual condition."

Joshua smiled once again. "That sounds kind of heavy, but it'll do." He then waved his right hand for emphasis. "Don't be misled into thinking that even for a second I've forgotten my family. But, how can I ever hope to understand Auschwitz if I don't first understand myself? First things first, like Genesis comes before Exodus. And, don't be discouraged by the material I've brought home from the synagogue. In all fairness, they're entitled to their opinion."

Alan felt a little encouraged by Joshua's apparent tolerance.

"At any rate," Joshua was saying, "both you and Feldman have been able to show me at least that it's best to start at the root of something. In fact, it looks to me that part of your problem, your awkwardness and uncertainty, in talking to me or any Jew is because you're bogged down with the upper end, the whole picture, so to speak. In a way, you're just as guilty, if that's the right word, because you're just as sensitive to their comments and criticism as they are to yours. For my part, at the present moment, anyway, I have come to the conclusion that there has to be a basic truth involved, and it's from that view that I'd like to proceed. After, of course, we both dump our respective guilt trips."

Alan considered Joshua's last statement before offering, "You realize this is the first time you've ever come right out and asked for this kind of help."

"I should think you'd be pleased."

Alan studied him carefully. "Is there something about Jordan that you haven't told me? I mean, I get the feeling that you're forcing yourself."

"Not at all," Joshua assured him impatiently. "Much of this has been on my mind for a long time, and I've been putting it off, I guess. You could say that Rabbi Feldman has been pushing me lately."

So it was the basics they were after, Alan was thinking, but he didn't have the slightest idea where to start. "We both know, Joshua," he finally offered, "that we cannot be argued into accepting the Lord."

"But you still tried."

Alan was also smiling as he shook his head. "I guess I have leaned on you once or twice."

"Seems to me I recall something about those who plant and those who water, or words to that effect."

Alan closed his eyes, offering another brief prayer for help. Joshua had been like a closed and locked door for the years they had known each other. Now, the lock had been turned by someone or some thing. At least, he thought, the door could now be opened. "It is likely you are closer to the truth than you realize. I know you've been studying, especially the Scriptures. And, therein is the certain key to the truth you seek. Be wary of anyone who advises you otherwise, for the Word of God is final in the investigation you've decided to undertake. You don't have to yield to my arguments, or the Rabbi's either," and he opened his eyes to look at his friend. "It is not simply a theological overstatement that God's Word is a two-edged sword."

"That's probably why I'm here now," Joshua admitted. "However, if the truths are indeed there, which I'm willing to accept, then why the conflict, why the almost implacable disagreement, between, say, you and Rabbi Feldman?"

Alan sighed heavily, aware of the apparent dilemma. "Your suggestion to stick to the basics is sound," he proposed, "and I expect you're also correct in taking it in stages," and he paused briefly before going on, "And, above all, to keep it simple."

"Right," Joshua agreed.

"Simply enough, then, you are the descendant of Abraham, one of God's chosen people. That is a truth which should be most obvious to you, without further elaboration. And, the books of the Old Testament, the sacred and inspired Word of God, is the history of your people. Which is another simple truth I'm sure you can accept. So, what essentially do those books teach? Without question, the theme is one of triumph and failure, of man's shortcomings and his glory, of God's incredible love for His people, of His mercy. And, of course, of His justice. He gave you the law, not as a stern taskmaster, but as a loving and concerned Father. His covenant was both gracious and fair, immeasurably so. Yet you couldn't cut it, so you fell, again and again, because you were human just like the rest of us, so that your history has been one of exile and exodus, of dispersal and wandering, and all because of the law and how you responded to it. And, if you wish to still accept it today, then you will be obliged to put yourself under the same yoke of legal bondage." He stopped then, turning to look out across the valley, on to the opposite quarter now turning black under a purple halo of the sky above.

"Is that it?" asked Joshua after several seconds. "You just want me to go over the Old Testament?"

Alan turned back to look at him. "And pay attention to the prophets, especially to review the hundreds of predictions concerning the coming of the Messiah. Otherwise, that's about the size of it. I suppose the covenant made with Abraham is critical, because sooner or later you will have to ask yourself why a loving God could make a deal with His children that He knew they wouldn't keep. You see, that means He is either capricious and cruel, or that He does things for reasons which are for our own good. So, I can only suggest you read it over again, carefully, to find the truth you seek."

"Are you sure that's as far as you want to go?"

"That's as far as Rabbi Feldman will go. Or, perhaps, I should suggest that's as far as he *can* go."

Chapter four

Saturday, October 7. A motel on Century Boulevard, Los Angeles.

As the yellow cab pulled into the driveway, Michael Brav noted with satisfaction that even with the stop at the liquor store it had taken them less than twenty minutes to make it from L.A. International Airport. It was only ten-thirty, which gave him a full hour and a half before his noon flight. Following his instructions, the driver parked next to the motel office. Brav got out without delay, taking his briefcase.

"Wait for me here," he told the driver, and he handed him an airline ticket folder. "I'll be out within ten minutes. While you're waiting, take this to the clerk and confirm my reservation. The baggage tags are from the flight I just came in on, so make sure my luggage gets switched."

Joshua Bain had been watching from the vantage point of their ground-floor room. He let the curtain go as Brav started limping hurriedly across the parking lot. "He'll be here in a second," he repeated to Alan Hunt, who was sitting at the room's only table.

"He didn't waste any time," Alan suggested.

"He's probably in a hurry."

The knock on the door was perfunctory, and Joshua pulled it open quickly.

Michael Brav paused only briefly, surveying the room once

before stepping inside. "Gentlemen," he said cordially.

Alan Hunt stood up as Joshua introduced him. Michael Brav showed the signs of a man who had been on the road for a long time, and a moment passed before Alan realized he was staring. Brav's cotton jumper was wrinkled and soiled. His heavy beard was at least a day or two old, and he brought into the room the sour smell of one needing a bath. Alan's first coherent thought about the man was that his age was difficult to assess under the camouflage of his shaved head, the neck brace, the large dark glasses with their reflecting mirror surfaces. Brav sat down, without invitation, in the chair opposite them. He exhaled noisily as he removed his dark glasses, looking across the table to appraise Alan, his smoke gray eyes showed a placid recognition. "Welcome aboard," he said simply, a kind of official and necessary statement, as he looked down to open his briefcase.

Alan returned wordlessly to his chair.

"I need a glass first," said Brav as he pulled a pint bottle of Scotch out of his case.

Joshua turned to the nearby dresser to pick up a drinking glass from a tray. As he handed Brav the glass, he declined the offer of a drink. Alan Hunt also shook his head, watching with amazement as Brav downed most of the six-ounce glass in one hungry gulp.

"It's been a long week," Brav proposed hoarsely. He wiped his mouth, refilled the glass. "Most people deal with jet lag by going to bed. I deal with it by getting on another airplane."

Looking at the nearly empty pint bottle, Alan thought irrelevantly that Brav might need some help in getting on the next airplane.

"It's going to be a long day for all of us," Joshua said pointedly.

"I apologize for complaining," said Brav, obviously in response to the impatient edge in Joshua's voice. "Your being here is most convenient for me."

"It's not that much out of our way," Joshua assured him.

"So let's get to it," said Brav, and he removed a heavy manila envelope from his briefcase. "I'm heading back to Florida in little over an hour."

"We can give you a lift to the airport," said Joshua.

"I've got a cab waiting." He handed the envelope to Joshua, who took it before sitting down on the nearby bed.

"Your preliminary instructions are all there," Brav went

on quickly, "and don't bother opening it now. Briefly, in sequence, we'll meet next on the morning of the eighth."

"That's tomorrow," said Joshua thoughtfully. "Where?"

"The King's Inn, next to Miami International Airport."

"Both of us?" Alan asked.

"Yes. Your reservations have already been made, and you'll rendezvous with our inspector there. You will by then have selected the transfer site. One of you will accompany our inspector to Price's villa on Haiti by late tomorrow night. The inspection party will stay with the material until it is transferred, which eliminates any chance for compromise."

"You figure Jordan is at the villa?" Joshua asked him.

"It's either in or near the villa, according to Karen Laswell."

"Alan will supervise the inspection."

"A wise assignment," said Brav, "which will free you up to pre-site the selected transfer point tomorrow afternoon."

"Why can't I do that on Monday morning?" asked Joshua.

"No way," countered Brav. "The transfer must take place on Monday night, the day after tomorrow."

Alan was not surprised at Joshua's quick reaction.

"Not enough time," Joshua was saying. "You're only giving us roughly twenty-four hours to gear up. We're supposed to have an advantage, remember, but you're putting us all on par, including you and Price."

"We've anticipated that," Brav reported, "so our inspector will arrive at the King's Inn rendezvous early tonight. She will be in bungalow seven."

"She?" repeated Joshua.

"Yeah," said Brav. "Sharon Iser is your Miami contact as of this evening. You must understand that a quickly executed program from this point on will give us badly needed extra security. So you will pass to Sharon whatever you need, either information or logistics, which will give you plenty of time. Price is aware of the situation. You can arrange what you wish with Sharon, so long as you guard the actual transfer point. Don't forget, you're responsible for both the payment funds and Jordan back to each base point. Your job isn't finished at the transfer site."

Alan was frowning. "I don't understand."

"Base point for each side," Joshua explained to him, "is that position where each party considers themselves secure, on their own ground, so to speak."

"That's correct," Brav said. "Base point for Price is Port-au-Prince. Thus, you are responsible to escort his representative, who will be Karen Laswell, with the payment funds received from us, back to Port-au-Prince. Once you deliver her, with the money, to Port-au-Prince, that part of your job is finished."

"And your base point?" Alan asked.

"We will probably be mobile," Brav told him. "It will depend upon your selection of the transfer point. Since all of your site options are either next to or near the open sea, we tentatively have arranged a suitable vessel as our operating base."

Alan nodded that he now understood. "Once the exchange is made, we are still responsible to escort both parties back to a designated so-called safe point."

"And for good reason," Brav suggested. "You two are literally in charge here, and both sides will feel a natural vulnerability once we start operating under your orders."

"It's a reasonable procedure," said Joshua. "But I'm still curious about Price and his private villa on Haiti. We both figure all this should be more logically taking place closer to home for you, say in the Mediterranean area. Also, I've done some checking around, and it seems most of the private traders in the ordinance world conduct their business in that area also. Monte Carlo seems to be the main base."

"That's true," said Brav. "But you're thinking about the *licensed* private arms dealers. Price actually got his feet wet in Monte Carlo, but he only lasted there about six months. In fact, that's where he picked up Karen Laswell, whom he pirated away from one of his competitors. And, while we don't know all the details, we do know that Price is a wanted man on the continent. The Straits of Gibraltar is a closed door to him and his organization. Besides, the bulk of his action in this half of the world is with the Central and South American republics anyway."

"You say in this half of the world," noted Alan.

"He's also very active in Asia," Brav explained. "He has a similar villa, or area headquarters, near Hong Kong, but we're not sure where."

"So he's totally illegal," Joshua remarked.

"Absolutely," said Brav. "However, we might say that in this regard he performs a worthwhile service, since he is one of a select few who could put this package together."

"I find it difficult to be impressed," Joshua observed wryly.

"You better be," Brav warned him. "If anything goes wrong, you can't pick up a telephone and call the police," and he hesitated for a moment. "Don't tell me you've underestimated—"

"You should know better," Joshua cut in sharply. "We're looking for inputs. Why, for example, has Price selected Port-au-Prince for his base point instead of his villa?"

"Who knows?" said Brav. "I assume he's trying to be helpful. After all, you yourself made the point that you didn't want to be around him—"

"Now who's underestimating?" Joshua snapped.

"It's your problem," Brav retorted sharply.

Tension filled the room instantly, and Alan Hunt cleared his throat. "What is the absolute time deadline," he offered on what he hoped was a less volatile subject, "that both you and Price must know the transfer point?"

Joshua looked aside, shaking his head.

"I would say noon tomorrow," Brav answered after a moment. "We both have to arrange final transport. There are many people involved. Communications."

"That's also reasonable," Joshua offered, his voice back to normal. "My only concern is that I figured we'd be working with you in the interim."

"Out of the question," said Brav, and he pulled a small camera out of his case. "After this morning, it will be next to impossible to contact me directly." He tinkered with the camera briefly before aiming it at Alan Hunt, who flinched as the flash unit popped in his face. "Passport pictures," explained Brav. He shot several more frames, turning to repeat the process at Joshua. "Your papers will be delivered to you tomorrow morning in Miami, so you will be covered no matter where you go." He returned the camera to the case and snapped it closed. Almost as an afterthought, he picked up the pint bottle, draining it.

"This Sharon Iser," said Joshua. "I presume she is more than just a qualified physicist."

Michael Brav was smiling as he returned the dark glasses to his nose. "She can take care of herself if that's what you mean." He came to his feet then. "She is also married, a fact which normally wouldn't be worth mentioning."

Alan was content to wait.

"So why mention it?" said the more impatient Joshua.

"Because she's married to a Christian."

Alan realized his own eyebrows had lifted.

Joshua was shaking his head again, the hint of a smile around the corners of his mouth. "A Gentile in the organization, even by marriage—"

"You're not paying attention, my usually alert friend," Brav chided him. "Unless you can produce a more kosher name than Iser."

"A converted Jew," Alan proposed under his breath.

"Score one for the younger man," said Brav, and he extended his right hand to Alan Hunt. "Good luck to you both," he added.

Shaking his hand, Alan observed, "I should think *Shalom* would be more appropriate."

Michael Brav turned to the door, opening it with his free hand. "I gave up on that kind of wistful idealism twenty years ago."

"In exchange for another," Joshua suggested good-naturedly.

Under the jamb of the open doorway, Brav looked back at Joshua over his shoulder.

"My partner here," Joshua went on, "believes that luck is the will of God, so that you have in effect just offered up a prayer for our good fortune."

Alan Hunt was wishing he could see through the mirrors of Brav's glasses.

"An interesting thought," Brav admitted after a passing moment, and he abruptly turned on his heel.

After closing the door, Joshua began to walk the floor, and Alan Hunt remained silent, allowing his friend to collect his thoughts. For Alan, the operation seemed routine. He was thinking he should call Anne when he noticed that Joshua had stopped before the front window to look through the split in the drapes.

"He's gone," Joshua reported quietly. He turned then, pulled his billfold out of his hip pocket. He fingered a bill out of the billfold before moving to the door. "I'll be right back," he said, and he left the room.

Alan decided to wait until Joshua returned before calling the ranch. The Sharon Iser development turned in his mind. He viewed it as a definite good sign, a positive note in an otherwise mass of unknowns. He filed the matter away, drawn to the more immediate list of chores they all would have to turn to at Rancho Canaan. Tonight would be their cut-off time, unless Joshua altered the plan. He started to build a mental checklist of things left to do, but the image of Anne intruded into his mind repeatedly, until he realized that today marked the first time they had been separated since their marriage.

Joshua entered the room to sit down at the table. "Our friend Brav has a noon flight all right," he said slowly. "According to the desk clerk, however, the cabbie confirmed a United flight direct to and terminating at Washington, D.C."

"So he lied to us," Alan offered.

"That fact doesn't really bother me, which is hardly even a sin to a man in his profession. It's *why* that has me curious."

"It's simple," Alan suggested. "He didn't want us to know where he was going. After all, it's really none of our business anyway."

"Anything he does which involves us is our business."

"So maybe Washington is other business. Brav is obviously a heavy operator in Israeli overseas affairs. He's probably got a dozen different things going right now."

"Maybe," Joshua seemed to admit.

"So you think about it while I call Anne."

Joshua leaned forward to pick up the heavy envelope left by Brav. "I'll go you one better," he said as he opened the clasp. "I'll go over this material on the bathroom counter while you call Anne." He dumped the contents of the envelope on the table. Another smaller letter-size envelope was on top, and he opened it to thumb through its contents. "There's fifty thousand here in cashier's checks," he said tonelessly.

So we're now committed, Alan thought to himself, but he couldn't help but notice the lack of enthusiasm in his friend's voice. Joshua got up slowly, gathering the material together. Watching him move toward the bathroom, Alan figured that to this point the morning had come down to a draw, one good sign, one bad sign. So be it, he thought, reaching for the phone to call his wife.

Standing before the counter in the bathroom, Joshua came out of his thoughts as Alan pushed into the room behind him. He turned up his watch to see that Alan had been on the phone for nearly thirty minutes. "How's the lonely bride doing?" he asked congenially.

"You hit it right on the head, and, I have to admit the feeling is mutual. However, she's keeping busy. We picked up three more bookings."

So business was booming, Joshua thought, almost disinterestedly, as he leaned forward again at the hips. He had arranged the Jordan material into four piles. The first, as he explained to Alan, included briefing details, which he suggested they go over more closely later in the day. The other three were the specs on the site options, which he had been studying in detail. An aerial photo was on top of each stack, and he picked up the first one, showing it to Alan. "I'm against this one because it's totally landlocked. It's a private landing strip of some kind, postage-stamp size." He turned the photo over. "It's located fifty miles northwest of Santo Domingo."

"Dominican Republic," Alan mused thoughtfully.

"Yeah, right in Price's backyard. Regardless, there's dense undergrowth right down to the strip. It's too tight." He dropped the photo back on its pile, picking up the second. "This is on the north coast of Haiti, which puts it on Price's back porch. A small cove with a fairly open beach," and he handed Alan the photo. "I like the idea of the water. However, note the choppy surf. That part of Haiti is probably on the windward passage."

"Water too rough?"

"I'd say so. And, if the weather is sour, we'd all have a bad time. According to the specs, the Jordan containers weigh ninety pounds each. There's ten of them. Can you imagine what it would be like trying to handle that cargo in rough weather?" He picked up the third photo. "As far as I'm concerned, this is it."

Alan took the photo, flipped it over. "Jamaica," he said simply, and he turned it over to study the aerial print, which showed a section of apparently isolated coastline. A red line had been drawn around a channel-like lagoon near the center of the photo.

"That channel is perfect," Joshua proposed confidently. "It's about a hundred yards across at the mouth, with practically no wave action, which indicates deep water at that point."

"Looks like about a half-mile long," Alan guessed.

"Plus or minus fifty yards," Joshua said, and he picked up another photo. "Here's a close-up of the area at the top of the channel. Note the small wooden pier, and, especially, the nearby vertical clearance."

Alan took the photo, studied it briefly before looking at Joshua questioningly. "There appears to be plenty of vertical clearance. That looks like Marsted matting next to the pier, between it and the building."

"I have my reasons for wanting this site," Joshua went on soberly. "To begin with, the one weak link in the whole program is the movement of Jordan from Price's villa."

"But that's his responsibility," Alan pointed out. "Brav has to get the money to the exchange site, on his own, and Price has to transport Jordan. We don't take over until the exchange at the rendezvous."

"That's correct. And, I'm confident that Brav will take the necessary security precautions to guarantee delivery of the money. However, in the case of Jordan, there is a more complex security problem. You will supervise the inspection, which means that both you and Sharon Iser will stay with Jordan until it is delivered to the exchange point, which from now on we will denote as Jamaica. Now, according to the briefing instructions, Price will move Jordan via a small ship of his own arrangement to Jamaica. Since Jordan is on Haiti now, then that movement will involve about twelve hours on the open sea. Even if he has a half-dozen armed guards, that ship will still be an open invitation."

"So it's a calculated risk."

Joshua shook his head emphatically. "You and the inspector's lives will be at stake. Plus, the Armatrex inventory is involved, and you know how I feel about that."

Oh, yes, Alan thought to himself, for he was aware that if it had not been for the Armatrex connection, they probably wouldn't be there now.

"The temptation is too great," Joshua was saying, "for an outsider wanting that plutonium. Besides, such exposure for you goes beyond my understanding of our original agreement."

"But it has to be moved, Joshua. Price has to deliver. And, the only other alternative is by air."

"Naturally."

"But how? That photo covers what, a two- or three-mile square, and there's no landing strip close by." He picked up the smaller of the two prints, looking at it carefully before going on, "There isn't enough open ground to accommodate a chopper big enough to carry that kind of load."

"We'll use a seaplane," said Joshua. "Which is the main reason for selecting this particular site. Both the pier and the channel combine to make a perfect anchorage. Plus, we can get in and out fast."

Alan pondered the suggestion for a moment. "I understand

the seaplane, but not the *we*."

"I'll arrange with Iser tomorrow morning to talk to Price. Unless I miss my guess, the old man will be delighted to turn that part over to us. The seaplane angle is ideal for both of us. His security for the trip is dramatically improved, since the exposure time is dropped from twelve hours to one."

"So, let Price use a seaplane."

"That's the first option I considered. However, it would be better to spring this at the last possible minute tomorrow. By then, Price won't have the time to arrange for the plane and a qualified, reliable pilot. Besides, and this is what finally convinced me, we've got to get in and out of there too. With Brav's team, Price's people, plus our end, that rendezvous is going to need a traffic cop. By doing it my way, we reduce the vehicle and personnel congestion by a third. It's just so much cleaner."

"It's not only cleaner," Alan observed, "it also extends our control."

"It's the only way to go. I had planned to use an aircraft for our end anyway. We can charter one out of Miami on a contract and have it delivered to Port-au-Prince by tomorrow noon. The delivery pilot can lay over there until we return the aircraft on Monday night."

"So you'll fly it?"

"I'm qualified, with over ninety hours in amphibs. And, we don't want an uptight pilot on our hands in case of trouble. I can use it tomorrow afternoon to pre-site the Jamaica site. Sometime on Monday afternoon, Price delivers Jordan, along with you and Iser, to the seaplane anchorage at Port-au-Prince. We'll also load Karen Laswell, who will pick up the payment. We then take off for the Jamaica site. We make the exchange there. You and Iser go on with Jordan to Brav's base point. I fly back to Port-au-Prince with Karen and the money." He held up his hands in a definitive gesture. "Presto, end of operation."

Alan nodded his approval of the rough plan. "How do I get back?"

"According to the briefing instructions, if we select either the Haiti or Jamaica site, Brav is going to hire a smaller boat to move Jordan to his base ship. Since we've selected Jamaica, he'll probably rent the boat in Kingston. Either you return the boat yourself or hitch a ride with whoever does. From Kingston, you catch a flight back home. Which reminds me, I'm going to specify that Brav's base ship be no more than five miles from the exchange point. I can then easily reconnoiter the area from the air prior to the exchange, giving you, in effect, what I consider necessary air cover."

"The only hitch I can see," Alan said after a moment's thought, "is the short time you've got to rent the aircraft. If we wait for Sharon Iser, it'll be too late tonight for her to make the contact. Don't forget, tomorrow's Sunday."

It occurred to Joshua Bain that another part of Alan's value had just surfaced again, his tendency to pick up on the small details. "You're absolutely right," he conceded, and he checked his watch to see that it was ten minutes past twelve. Michael Brav had been airborne now for ten minutes. He turned thoughtfully out of the bathroom, heading for the night stand and the telephone.

"It's too late to catch Brav," Alan said as he followed behind. "So we'll have to take care of it ourselves."

Joshua picked up the phone, asked the switchboard for the Western Union operator. Waiting, he glanced over his shoulder to tell Alan, "We might have to, but we'll try something else first." Straightening up, he was thinking that maybe now was as good as any time to run a check on how efficient their organization really might be.

After he had hung up the phone in his Palm Desert motel room, Hafiz Barca sat still on the edge of his bed. The message from Maurice Garand had been terse and to the point: he was to transfer his cargo on Monday, at any time he wished, but not later than noon. He reached out to lift the phone receiver before dialing room 21.

Cliff Pearson came on the line after one ring.

Barca told him to come to his room.

He then moved to the small table at the front of the room, where he began to ready the material he would need to review for his end of the operation. Only a few seconds passed before there was a light knock on the door. The quickness of the response suggested that the hired pilot was likely getting even more impatient. Barca opened the door and stepped outside.

"We depart on Monday," Barca told him after checking to make sure they were alone on the walkway.

Pearson appeared to look pleased as he nodded that he understood.

"You will land at the ranch strip at exactly five-thirty," Barca went on.

"Five-thirty on Monday morning," Pearson repeated to

himself, before adding, "Isn't it about time you told me our destination?"

"I'll have a map for you when we take off. All you need to know for now is that we'll be landing in the vicinity of Tampico, so you can provision the plane accordingly."

Barca noticed that Pearson was making no move to turn away, so he reached into his shirt pocket to extract two one-hundred dollar bills. Handing them wordlessly to the pilot, he watched with a sense of resignation as the man turned to move toward his room. As he turned back into his own room he was thinking that they were all mercenaries of one kind or another. But, then, the pilot was perhaps entitled to the small remittance, since the odds were high that he wouldn't live out the week.

The terminal foot traffic at Dulles Airport was lighter than Michael Brav expected, and he was relaxed as he moved contentedly along the connecting satellite to collect his baggage. It was still early, and he had over three hours before his meeting with his Justice Department contact. He needed a drink badly and was looking for a cocktail lounge when he heard his name coming over the intercom, which requested that he pick up the nearest white courtesy phone.

It took only a second for the impact of the page to register.

Tensed and on guard, he turned hurriedly into the first men's restroom, where he washed his face in cold water. He had drunk heavily on the plane, enough to put a normal man flat on his back, and he was trying desperately now to clear his mind. He doused his face again and again, breathing deeply in an effort to ventilate his system to hurry up the sobering process. He stood up ostensibly to look at himself in the mirror, glancing instead from side to side suspiciously.

The several other men present seemed to be normally going about their business.

He debated whether to even answer the courtesy call.

Jonathan Malek was the only person who had knowledge of his arrival in Washington, and he was enough of a professional to know better than to put an agent's name on the air in a public place.

Michael Brav glanced down to the wash basin to see that both his hands were shaking. He had been in the field for a generation, and all his experience, along with his instincts, warned him now that if he picked up the white phone he might be marking himself for an assailant.

He doused his face again, bending forward awkwardly at the hips. As he came erect again, he realized that anyone after him could easily enough recognize him. His own name was listed on the flight manifest. Also, to the present point, there was no danger factor anticipated in the Jordan operation. Continuing to breathe deeply, he left the restroom, forcing himself to act normally. He was more alert now, feeling secure on his feet, and he elected to try the United information desk first. The timing of the courtesy call suggested that whoever had arranged it was aware of his arrival flight.

He began to hope that he was over-reacting.

His logic turned out correct, for after he had casually mentioned his name to the girl behind the United counter, she immediately handed him a telegram envelope.

"It's collect, sir," the girl told him politely.

Brav hesitated, turning the frail envelope in his hand.

"We can put it on your air card," the girl suggested.

Brav grunted, reaching for his billfold.

As the girl filled out the charge slip, Brav opened the telegram, which was addressed directly to him. The text was also written in the clear:

UMPIRE URGENTLY REQUIRES RENTAL OF AMPHIB OR SEAPLANE TYPE AIRCRAFT FOR DELIVERY TO PORT-AU-PRINCE BY NOON TOMORROW. PREFER GRUMMAN TWO-ENGINE MODEL OUTFITTED WITH FREIGHT COMPARTMENT PLUS LONG-RANGE ACCESSORIES. IMPERATIVE THIS ITEM BE DELIVERED TO AVOID DELAY IN SCHEDULE. END OF MESSAGE EXCEPT FOR POST SCRIPT SUGGESTING YOU VISIT WASHINGTON MONUMENT AND WHILE THERE ASK ABOUT THE CHERRY TREE.

The wire was signed by Joshua Bain.

Michael Brav heard himself swearing under his breath.

"Anything wrong, sir?" the girl was asking him concernedly.

"No, nothing."

She put the charge slip on the counter before him, and he reached out to sign it after deciding he really had no other choice. "Perhaps you can help me," he said. "Do you know what a cherry tree has to do with the Washington Monument?"

She was smiling as she pulled the charge slip copies apart. "You are obviously not an American."

"That's correct, young lady, but what does that have to do with it?"

"Forgive me," she told him. "But it has to do with George Washington when he was a boy. The story goes that he cut down a cherry tree, and when his father questioned him about it, he admitted that he had done it with the explanation that he could not tell a lie."

"I see," said Brav as he took his copy.

"Parents use the story," the girl went on, "to encourage their children to tell the truth."

"I said I understand," said Brav gruffly, and he turned to stalk away in the direction of the baggage-claim area.

Chapter five

Monday, October 9, 4:45 p.m., EDT. Between Haiti and Jamaica.

Alan Hunt's calculations suggested their Jamaica ETA was about five minutes away. They'd been airborne for nearly an hour since Port-au-Prince, and he noticed that the steady roar of the seaplane's two engines had declined to a less irritable level, indicating an internal adjustment on his part, since their airspeed was still exactly the same. He gestured out with his left arm, pointing at his watch. "How much time?" he asked Joshua, who was seated next to him in the pilot's seat. The westerly sun was low on the horizon, and for some reason its intensity had been abruptly diminished.

"Only a couple more minutes," Joshua told him calmly. He had on his usual flying headgear, a grimy old baseball cap. His issue dark glasses were a relic from his flying days in the service. He had already removed the headset connected to the plane's radio, after confirming the Kingston VOR. They were on standard radio silence now, relying upon limited-range and portable transceivers to communicate with each other for the duration of the operation.

Alan glanced nervously at the fuel indicator. "What's our gas situation?"

"We've got enough," Joshua reassured him. "But we're going to have to pass on that part of our tour for Montego Bay and Port Royal."

Alan looked aside to see Joshua was grinning under his glasses. "Okay, wise guy, so what happened to the sun?"

"Cloud cover for the island."

So they were getting close, Alan thought, and he felt the anticipation turning in his stomach. He leaned to his right, straining against his shoulder harness, to look down and out the dirt-streaked, plexiglass cockpit window. The water rushed away below them, still less than two hundred feet away, and he took another deep, concerned breath. The low-level approach was necessary to avoid the Kingston radar, but it made him uneasy, and he felt better at once as he saw the land mass then coming up directly ahead. He realized that Joshua was saying something, and he turned to see him returning his intercom mike to its wall latch.

"What was that?" Alan asked him.

"Just told the ladies to buckle up. You better check your gear too, because we're going to have a bumpy landing."

Alan obediently checked his harness straps. Unlike Joshua, who had on a shoulder holster with a .38 revolver, Alan was unarmed because he felt no need for a personal firearm. There was a lightweight machine gun on the floor beside his seat, and he now secured the weapon under the small canvas bag holding Joshua's extra ammo and equipment. The sophisticated weapons, including a silencer for Joshua's handgun, had been supplied by an insistent Maurice Garand. Alan still felt awkward around so many guns, and he reached down to touch the right forward pocket on his dungarees. The compact New Testament was snug against his thigh, itself more a comfort than all their guns put together.

"Get the radio," Joshua told him.

Alan unzipped his bag, pulled out one of the transceivers, holding it at ready in his lap. He had no reason to be concerned about their two passengers, since Karen Laswell and Sharon Iser were quite competent to take care of themselves. Lulled by the steady drone of the plane's engines, Alan was hoping that the rest of the operation would move along as smoothly as it had gone so far. The Sunday morning rendezvous in Miami had been uneventful, even prosaic. Sharon Iser, the Israeli inspector, had turned out to be an efficient and no-nonsense element, and Alan had liked her at once. He had actually enjoyed the inspection phase, the time spent at Price's villa, where he had the feeling he was a tourist, for what little official duty he had to perform. He came out of his thoughts with a start as the plane's left wing dropped without warning.

"There she is," Joshua was telling him, and he took his right hand off the control yoke to point down across his chest.

Alan squinted through the window to spot the trawler. As the plane began a slow turn, he could also make out a second smaller boat next to the larger ship.

"Get Brav on the radio," said Joshua.

Alan lifted the radio to his mouth, punched the transmit button. "This is umpire calling trawler *Arosa*. Come in please." He released the button, waiting for several seconds before repeating the message.

He was about to try the third time when the answer came, "This is trawler *Arosa*; we hear you loud and clear."

"That cabin cruiser should already be on its way," Joshua said irritably. "Ask them what's the problem?"

"What is your status?" Alan said into the radio. "We have a five o'clock deadline at transfer site. Repeat, what is your status?" He was watching the ship now as Joshua held on a tight circling pattern.

"This is Brav," the answer came then. "We have a minor problem with the boat engine. Repeat, a minor problem. We will be underway in a few minutes. Suggest you land and wait at transfer site. Over."

Alan looked questioningly at Joshua, who responded by taking a deep breath and shaking his head. "It'll be dark in less than an hour," he finally said.

Alan's first impulse was to suggest they land and make the exchange at the trawler itself, but he then realized that the sea was far too rough; they'd never get the cargo transferred.

"Ask him for a change until tomorrow morning," Joshua snapped.

Alan quickly made the request.

"Negative," Brav answered at once, and there was obvious irritation in his voice as he went on, "An overnight delay is out of the question, and, I repeat, out of the question. All arrangements have been made for now. And, there is a weather front moving in to hit here by morning. You must land and wait for us. Over."

Alan again looked questioningly at Joshua. "Can you take this thing off in the dark?"

"That's not the problem. I wanted to give you cover during the return trip to the trawler."

Alan ran the situation across his mind. "Can't you still do it? I mean, couldn't I radio you when we get there?"

Joshua appeared to consider the suggestion before he replied, "That will probably work all right. Plus, we've got a couple thousand watts of landing lights," and he nodded his head emphatically. "Tell him we're going in."

Alan relayed the message. Several more minutes went by as Joshua made two short passes along the coast adjacent to the channel. Using binoculars, Alan inspected the darkening shoreline carefully, unable to spot anything out of the ordinary. Wanting to conserve fuel, Joshua elected to land downwind as they finished the second pass. Alan said two prayers when he flew, once on take off and again on landing. Per Joshua's suggestion, he usually sought the greater blessing on take off; however, on this occasion, he added a little extra as Joshua put the seaplane down. The first bump was alarmingly harsh, and he braced, closing his eyes, thinking that the wings were in danger of coming off. Then it was over before he knew it, and he looked out the window to see the beachline less than a hundred yards away.

"Praise the Lord," he exclaimed, and he let his breath go at the same time.

"Amen," Joshua added.

The temperature rise in the cockpit had become apparent by the time they started up the narrow channel. Joshua was totally occupied by the controls, working the engine throttles to obtain the subtle adjustments in power needed to coax the heavy plane over the water. Alan sat transfixed, staring at the dense undergrowth, a shadowy exotic wall passing by no more than a few feet from the wing's tip. The noise from the engines had alarmed hundreds of birds which were now swarming in the premature dusk brought on by the heavy cloud cover.

"Go now," Joshua told him.

The main cabin compartment was rigged for cargo and was fairly open with its light load. The Jordan containers, reminding Alan of a rack of squat milk cans, were grouped forward, lashed down with canvas straps on a custom recessed pallet. The two passengers were aft, one on either side, still strapped in their drop-down canvas seats. After stepping over the turnbuckles securing the pallet, Alan gestured for them to come to their feet. Karen stood up almost immediately, obviously prepared. Like her companion, Sharon Iser, she was dressed in a dark blue jump suit. Both women were also armed, with pistols holstered and attached to more military looking web belts. Alan moved to help Sharon Iser, who waved him aside as she, too, stood up. Sharon Iser was short, no more than five feet tall, with what Alan would estimate medium weight. Her hair was cut close, showing her ears, over a face which Alan had already reported as pretty. Now, she was a little flushed, and her olive complexion and dark eyes reminded him of Anne.

"Welcome to Jamaica," said Alan, trying his best to sound cordial. "The first you'll notice is the lush tropical jungle—"

"Forget the guided tour," said Karen, and she busily went about straightening her jumper, arranging herself in what Alan considered a definite feminine gesture. Moving to the nearby cargo hatch, he noticed that Sharon was ignoring the condition of her clothes, preferring instead to open her duffel bag, extracting her automatic weapon. He levered the hatch open. The warm damp air hit him like a wet towel.

A few minutes later he was on the narrow dock securing the second of two lines used to keep the seaplane next to the pier. Joshua shut down the engines, and with the prop wash gone the air was immediately filled with insects. Alan ducked quickly back through the hatch, pulling it closed behind him. Karen handed him a small bottle of repellent, looking at him with an expression suggesting he should know better.

"What's next?" Sharon asked.

Joshua had entered the compartment. "We wait," he said evenly. "I just talked to Brav again, and they are getting underway."

Karen turned up her watch. "What's going on? It's already five minutes past."

"Engine trouble on the launch," Alan told her.

"It's going to be dark soon," Sharon said thoughtfully. "Shouldn't we post a watch?"

Joshua tossed his machine gun to Alan. "I flew over the area yesterday, and there's only a rough trail leading in here. Otherwise, it's wall-to-wall jungle for miles."

"I'd much rather be outside," said Sharon quietly.

"Come on," said Alan. "We'll scout the area together," and he turned to lever the hatch open.

Sharon Iser hesitated, turning to Joshua, as she was about

to step through the hatch. "My orders are to not let it out of my sight," she said, glancing to the Jordan containers.

"How do you manage," said Joshua easily, "to take it with you to the bathroom?"

Standing next to her elbow, Alan saw a smile cross her face, the first in the brief time they had been together.

"I'll watch it for you," Joshua said.

It had started to mist, and it was suddenly cooler as they started along the old decaying dock toward the nearby line of trees. The moisture in the air had also thinned down the insects to a tolerable level. Shielding his eyes with his left hand, Alan surveyed the edge of the heavy jungle, sensing that there was really nothing he could see. He looked aside then to see that Sharon had her weapon at the ready. "We might as well relax," he suggested. "If there's anyone out there, we'd never spot them, anyway."

"You're probably right," she said, and she followed his example in letting her weapon slip into the crook of her left arm. Alan noticed that she did not, however, put the weapon on safety.

They were near the tree line now, and Alan pulled up. He could barely make out the remains of the abandoned roadway, which now was nothing more than a narrow pathway leading off into the trees. The mist was now coming in from a northerly quarter on the waves of the wind, bringing with it the sound of the trees and plants moving under the wet mantle of the heavy mist. She turned with him to look back at the seaplane, sitting now like some waiting animal, an invader made to look more menacing by the darkness and the intervening mist. "We are just about on the last leg," Alan said quietly.

"The sooner the better."

He laughed, more to himself, and his thoughts ran briefly back to Rancho Canaan and the clear image of Anne. "You better believe it," he added.

"So you want to get home also," she observed. "You mentioned that you're married," she went on as they started back toward the plane. "What is she like, your wife?"

"She is a lot like you," he said impulsively, and he didn't know what to say further on the subject, so he went on hastily, "And what about your husband; what kind of man is he?"

She was silent for a few steps before she answered, "Daniel Iser, in his own special way, is really a giant of a man. And, I love him very much."

"Do you love him because he's a giant, or, despite that fact?"

"So you already know he's a Christian."

Yes, Alan admitted to himself, and he wondered if he had said the proper thing. "I didn't mean anything—" he started to explain.

"That's all right," she assured him quickly. "I'm used to the inquiry, and it doesn't bother me anymore."

"You sound as if you're resigned to it."

"He has his right to his belief."

"You mean that Israel practices freedom of religion?"

They had pulled up next to the closed hatch, and she turned to face him. "Freedom of religion in my country, especially when it comes to what Dan believes in, is a lot like racial integration in your country. The matter is officially on the books, but then there is the popular acceptance. If you know what I mean."

"I think I understand," said Alan after a thoughtful moment.

At the same moment, the Israeli transfer boat turned into the mouth of the lagoon. The craft was a thirty-foot cabin cruiser chartered out of Kingston, selected because it could handle both the Jordan cargo and the escort team. Hank Koman, alpha team leader, was at the controls of the slowly moving boat. Directly behind him, Michael Brav stood braced against the port side of the small sheltered bridge. Two other heavily armed men, the rest of alpha team, were on the fantail, one on either side, keeping watch. There was a fifth man below in the cramped sleeping quarters, the courier from Tel Aviv with a black metal briefcase manacled to his left wrist.

The wipers on the windshield kept ahead of the mist, which started to slacken off as the boat moved into the more sheltered waters of the channel. Michael Brav relaxed against the nearby bulkhead, fishing in his jacket for his one remaining pint of Scotch. Taking a deep drink, he didn't bother offering the bottle to Koman, who had already declined the same offer on several occasions, not really bothering to hide his contempt for his superior's heavy drinking. Slipping the bottle back into his jacket, Brav considered for a moment that he might just order Hank Koman to indulge himself.

"How far is it?" Hank Koman asked him.

"Should be around the next bend."

Koman throttled down another notch, and Michael Brav realized that in a few minutes the responsibility for the exchange securities would be out of his hands. He had felt secure with the plan up until now, but he was beginning to have second thoughts. His own usual sense of invincibility was beginning to slip. It was probably because of his conscience, he supposed. Plus, he had not really cared before, either, which always gave him an edge. It was different now, for the first time, because there was a heavy stake involved for him personally.

So it mattered whether he could pull it off.

It was time, he told himself determinedly, to tighten up the program. Reaching into his jacket again, he began to review his options.

The transfer craft was docked next to the seaplane without incident. With Sharon Iser assisting, the plutonium containers were thoroughly inspected by the Israeli courier while they were still secured in the cargo compartment of the seaplane. Satisfied, the courier unlocked the briefcase from his wrist, handing the heavy metal container to Karen Laswell.

"Please verify the contents," he said to Karen.

Karen Laswell took the metal briefcase before moving forward to take advantage of the added light coming from the cockpit. From his vantage point near the open hatch, Joshua watched her carefully. She removed a key from the right front pocket of her dungarees. She put the case on the floor, opened it. The forward light bounced off the matte finish of the opened lid. It was spookily quiet for the next minute or so, with the only sound the soft slapping of the lagoon's water against the metal hull of the anchored plane. Apparently satisfied, Karen closed the case.

"The payment is correct," she said to Joshua, "and I formally accept it."

While waiting, Joshua's mind had returned to the airport at Corpus Christi and what Michael Brav had revealed to him as his final hole card, another ace, the fact which had made up his mind to accept the Jordan assignment: that the Israeli government was committed to return the Armatrex plutonium to the United States. He had been sworn to secrecy by Brav, unable to tell even Alan, or anyone, for fear that it might leak back to Calvin Price. He still did not understand entirely why that was critical, but he accepted the priority because it was apparently a necessary part of the plan. Now, he was thinking that it was nearly finished, and the score was approaching even.

Benjamin Caplan could rest a little easier.

"So let's get it moved," he said sternly, and he stepped onto the dock, calling to Alan Hunt to give them a hand. When he moved back into the plane, he noticed that Karen did not have the metal briefcase. "You're supposed to keep the money on your person," he said to her.

"It's safe here."

Joshua held out his hand to the courier, who was about to start releasing the canvas straps on the cargo containers. "The key to the wristlock," said Joshua.

The courier handed him the key.

"Lock it on your wrist," said Joshua to Karen, who showed by her disgusted expression that she disagreed with the order.

"We stick to the plan," he reminded her.

"Yes, sir," Karen replied angrily as she stepped to her duffel bag, where she lifted out the briefcase. "You know this thing weighs a ton," she complained, but she snapped the lock on her left wrist. She held out her right hand then. "The key, please."

Joshua put the key in his left front pocket. "You'll get it when we arrive at Port-au-Prince."

With all the men working, the cargo was transferred from the plane to the waiting boat. The mist had turned to intermittent heavier drizzle by the time they finished. Dressed in ponchos borrowed from the more prepared Israelis, Joshua and Alan carefully inspected the transferred cargo, making sure the containers were securely lashed to the pallet tied to the deck. Finished, Joshua pulled Alan onto the dock to squat down under the cover of the Grumman's wing. "You and Sharon will go to the trawler," he told Alan. "Brav says you can go with the boat back to Kingston."

"What about the weather?"

"It won't be a problem," Joshua assured him. "This is the leading edge of the front, and there's practically no wind. This light stuff will come and go for several more hours. Just be careful while you move the containers."

"So it's just about over."

Joshua didn't have the time to answer as Hank Koman pulled up beside them. "Let's get moving," Koman said authoritatively.

After they came out from under the wing, Joshua and Alan quickly pulled out of the ponchos, handing them to Koman. Joshua was feeling confident as he watched Alan hand Koman the oilskin packet containing the manifest instructions on how to handle the delicate cargo. He reached out to take Koman's extended hand.

"Good luck," said Joshua warmly.

"Shalom," said Koman, and he moved away to drop down the forward deck of the boat, moving quickly along the rail toward the canvas-covered bridge. Koman started snapping orders to his men, and Joshua was impressed by the Israeli's expert way of handling himself. Michael Brav obviously had his first team on the job. The courier followed next, then Sharon Iser. The two other Israelis were already aboard, waiting quietly at their assigned posts on the fantail. Koman pitched them the two ponchos. Alan stepped down to the deck, turned to face Joshua, using his left hand to shield his face against the light rain.

"Where's Brav?" he asked.

Next to him, Sharon told them, "Karen said that he had a call from the trawler."

Joshua turned impatiently away from the boat, hearing that Koman had cranked up the engine. Back in the seaplane, he passed by Karen in the cargo compartment to find Brav forward in the cockpit. Brav was shutting down the transmitter.

"What's going on?" Joshua demanded. The damp smell of their wet clothes was heavy between them, and Joshua reached up to rub his nose.

"A minor problem," Brav was saying calmly. His bald head was still wet, glistening under the overhead standby light.

Joshua studied him briefly, before commenting, "At this stage of the game, I consider any problem a major one. So, what's going on?"

"It has no bearing on the transfer," Brav insisted, and he shrugged to emphasize his point. "All I can tell you is that something has come up."

"Don't give me that *something* jazz," said Joshua suspiciously. "We stick to the plan now, right to the letter, no deviations."

"Calvin Price was right," Brav said resignedly. "There are times when you have a one-track mind."

Joshua stepped partially aside, making room for Brav to pass. "Get your tail out there on that boat, and like *now*."

Grunting once and shaking his head, Brav started moving aft. As he crossed in front of Joshua, his left hand came up in a vicious arc, so swiftly that Joshua had no time to respond.

The leather-covered sap caught Joshua just behind his left ear.

Brav did not bother to verify that Joshua was unconscious, moving instead into the cabin, where he ordered Karen forward to fire up the engines. He then hurried to the boat.

"Something has come up!" Brav yelled to Alan Hunt, who had come out from under the bridge's canvas cover. "Nothing important," Brav further explained. "I just have to go to Port-au-Prince," and he gestured for Hank Koman to come to the rail.

Behind him, the plane's port engine finally coughed into life, suggesting that Joshua Bain was at the controls.

Hank Koman pulled up to lean over the dock. "What the devil is going on?" he asked impatiently.

Brav leaned down to tell him privately, "I've got to make the bravo connection myself. Sheldon seems confused about the *Bushnell* coordinates. Otherwise, there's no change," and he terminated the conversation by standing up to move forward, where he reached down to untie the last line holding the boat to the pier. The plane's second engine started with a roar. Tossing the line in, he waved with his right hand, smiling broadly as Hank Koman throttled the boat away from the pier.

Back in the seaplane, he first went to the still form of Joshua Bain. Turning Joshua onto his stomach, he quickly tied his hands behind his back with a piece of canvas strap. He took Joshua's revolver forward with him to the cockpit, putting it in the duffel bag on the floor next to Karen Laswell.

"You sure took your time cranking up that engine," he said irritably. He leaned forward then to look over the top of the instrument panel. The boat was well on its way out of the lagoon. "Are you sure you can fly this thing?" he then asked her.

"I can fly it," Karen was telling him as she busied herself with the controls. "You already know that the Colonel would not have allowed Jordan aboard without that assurance," she reminded him, as if giving herself even more authority. She backed the yoke off then, turning to look at him. "What I want to know is why the change?"

Brav studied her before answering, "Let's just say I'm riding shotgun to protect *both* our interests." He sat down heavily in the copilot's seat.

She pondered the explanation. "You know I don't have to do this."

"You most certainly do," he said confidently. "Otherwise it's a bust for all of us," and he smiled at her, causing her to look away. "Besides," he went on just as matter-of-factly, "if I have to, I'll taxi this turkey all the way to Port-au-Prince myself. I may not be able to fly it, but I can sure make it move."

"You wouldn't even make it to deep water," she told him. "However, I will fly us to Port-au-Prince so long as we still make the connection."

Michael Brav looked at the briefcase manacled to her left wrist while he turned her comment in his mind. "Why is that so important to you?" he asked. "While it's a good cover move, bravo is not necessarily essential."

"I don't want Calvin Price chasing me for the rest of my life."

"All right," he seemed to concede, "so we'll make the connection."

She looked at him once more, as if trying to find some further assurance in his face. "What about Bain?" she asked then.

"I'll take care of him."

"I know I can fly this, but we may still need him in case of trouble."

He was smiling again. "Just get us in the air, and let me worry about any trouble."

It was pitch black on the water now, and Alan Hunt had no idea of their location. He could tell by the rolling swell action that they had cleared the lagoon. A few seconds later he picked up the roar of the seaplane's engines, revved up to their full power. He peered aft through the intervening curtain of fine rain to see the aircraft moving sluggishly across the water behind the bright glare of its landing lights. It seemed to take the plane longer than it should to finally get airborne. And, once it finally cleared the water, it started gaining altitude on a course directly toward Haiti.

Waiting a few seconds to verify the heading, Alan turned up his transceiver, calling for umpire. Several seconds passed without an answer, and he repeated the call with a more urgent note in his voice.

Sharon Iser followed his line of sight. "Something wrong?" she asked.

Before Alan could answer, the voice of Michael Brav came on the radio, acknowledging as umpire one.

"Our schedule calls for overfly at this point," Alan told him.

"We are low on fuel, repeat, low on fuel," Brav said. "What is your status?"

Alan switched the transmit button. "We are okay. Tell umpire I'll see him at Canaan." He shut the transceiver down. He put the matter out of his mind as he remembered that Joshua had complained they might run low on fuel. He realized then that the boat had slowed. The two Israeli commandos who had taken cover under the canvas stepped out aft, moving carefully around the container pallet.

"There's the trawler," Sharon said, pointing off the starboard bow.

Picking up the dark gray, almost black ship, Alan felt himself starting to unwind. It was almost over for sure. "So you'll be going home," he said to Sharon.

"Yes."

"I probably won't get to see you again," he said slowly. They were close enough to the trawler for him to make out the lines of the ship, which now appeared larger than he had expected. He saw that one of the crewmen was leaning out over the rail, motioning for Koman to come alongside. "Please give my regards to your husband. Dan, isn't it?"

"Yes," she said. "I'll tell him that I ran into one who is a lot like him."

"I'd like to write to him," Alan said. "Or, would you mind if I tried to encourage him."

"Not at all. I'll write down our address before you leave."

The smaller boat bumped once alongside the trawler at its lowest point. Koman reversed the boat's engine expertly, holding them against the larger ship's hull. The courier from Tel Aviv came up from below to stand next to Koman at the wheel, and Alan was thinking it was going to be tricky to make this the last transfer.

He was beginning to relax as he thought about Anne and the warm comfort of Rancho Canaan. It was going to be good to get back . . .

Shielding his eyes against the rain, he glanced up to see that several more figures had materialized on the higher rail of the trawler. He heard a click then, a metallic switching kind of sound—

Floodlights slammed into their faces!

The following order was harsh, "Don't anyone move!"

Hank Koman jammed the throttle wide open.

In reverse, the boat surged backwards, sending them all sprawling on the wet deck.

Several automatic weapons opened up from the rail of the trawler.

Down on his right side, Alan rolled once to his left, trying to shield Sharon Iser against the cargo pallet. He thought he could hear the men aft answering the fire. One of the two lights went out. His eyes were adjusting, and he looked up to see that Hank Koman, defenseless under the thin canvas bridge cover, was sprawled over the boat's control panel. The courier was down also, slumped lifelessly against the bulkhead. Totally confused, Alan pushed forward with his knees, trying to give Sharon Iser all the body cover he could.

The deafening heavy fire continued for several more seconds until the boat finally stopped running.

Alan's mind was now a helpless blank.

The trawler was under power, moving in closer.

Still stunned, Alan could only think that they might make it over the side. They were obviously outgunned and virtually helpless under the glare of the remaining searchlight. He looked aft to see that both the commandos there were down on the deck.

"Throw down your weapons!" said the same harsh voice.

Alan felt movement under him, and he shifted his weight to allow Sharon Iser to raise her head. Thank God, he thought, seeing that she didn't appear to be hit. There had been no more firing now for seveal seconds.

"What do you think?" Alan asked breathlessly.

Sharon had turned her head to stare at the riddled body of Hank Koman. "Oh, my God," was all she could say.

Alan measured the distance to the rail, but he knew they'd never make it.

Sharon had apparently come to her senses, for she turned out from under him to sit against the stacked containers, which still shielded her off from the trawler's rail. "They'll probably kill us anyway," she said hoarsely, and she reached down to her right side, pulling at the hand gun in her belt holster.

"Don't do it!"

Alan looked to the source of the order, a man standing over them in the glare of the searchlight. He was dressed in a black wet suit. His face, too, was black with charcoal. The pump shotgun leveled at them was sawed off, its muzzle looking like a cannon.

Sharon sighed heavily, started lifting her hands.

"Is your name Alan Hunt?" he asked Alan.

Alan delayed for a moment before nodding his head yes.

Chapter six

Michael Brav figured that by now he should be used to risking his life. He had brushed with death so many times that he had given up trying to keep score. Perhaps, he thought, the alcohol was finally getting to his brain, disrupting his memory. The seaplane was holding steady at its cruising altitude of two hundred feet, and he felt himself starting to relax. One more experience on the books, he thought laconically. Releasing his shoulder harness, he reached inside his jacket for what was left of his last pint of Scotch.

"What about Bain?" Karen was asking him again.

Brav wiped his mouth with the back of his hand. "He's tied up and probably still out." He knew he would have to take care of Bain shortly, but for some reason the task did not appeal to him.

"Don't forget the key," Karen said then, holding up her left wrist to show him the wristlock.

Brav had to resist the temptation to smile, for there was no way he would forget the key. He leaned down to jam the empty bottle under his seat, before reaching across to pull Joshua's gun out of the duffel bag. Turning up the muzzle, he noticed the male threads on the end of the short barrel. Absently then, he rummaged in the bag until he found the mating silencer, which he screwed slowly down on the barrel. Weighing the weapon critically in his hand, he sensed that he really did not want to shoot Joshua Bain in cold blood. Sighing to himself, he dropped the revolver back into the bag, zipping it closed.

Karen Laswell had been watching him out of the corner of her eye. "What's wrong?" she asked him.

"I'm starting to slip," he admitted.

"You mean Bain?"

"Who else."

"So let it go; he'll be taken care of anyway."

Brav was shaking his head slowly. "It won't look right with his hands tied behind his back. Besides, what if he comes to, starts talking?"

"It's your problem," she said pointedly. "We can always put him out right after we land."

He took a deep breath as he pushed himself up out of the seat, not answering her because it was actually none of her business. As he started aft, he reminded himself again that Joshua Bain was the only witness now who could tie him in; and if Karen Laswell was worried about hiding from Calvin Price, that would be nothing compared with him trying to hide from the Israeli Government.

He knew, because he had been one of the hunters.

So, he really had no choice.

Joshua Bain was still unconscious, face down. Brav rolled him over to his back, checking to make sure his tongue was free. The gesture was an automatic one, out of habit, for it really didn't matter if Joshua Bain might strangle on his own tongue. He first removed the wristlock key, putting it in his own left front pocket. Curious then, he started a systematic search of the limp body. He found the automatic pistol strapped high up on the inside of Joshua's crotch. As he turned the exotic weapon in his hand, he was thinking it was so typically a tool of the trade, and he tossed it indifferently to the other side of the cabin.

The plane lurched, and he sat down awkwardly, turning his back against the nearby bulkhead. The pain in his lower neck worked down his right shoulder, and he reached in what was a reflex action into his inside jacket pocket before realizing there was no bottle. Resigned to his temporary state, he leaned forward to take hold of Joshua Bain's ankles.

Joshua assumed he was dreaming. It seemed that his eyes were really open, though the images of things around him were distant, like on a reel of black and white silent film, but then he smelled the strong odor of stale alcoholic breath. He heard himself make a noise, something like a groan.

Brav dropped Joshua's legs as he pulled even with the side cargo door.

Joshua lifted his head, focused in on the man above him. He looked around then, and it all came to him in a nauseating rush. He was at once sick to his stomach, and he turned his head to gag once. His own stomach bile burned in his throat.

"So you're still among the living," Brav was saying, and there was almost a note of disappointment in his voice.

Joshua discovered that his arms were tied behind his back. He clumsily pushed himself to his elbows. With his head clearing, he began to assess the situation. "How long have we been airborne?" he asked first.

"About twenty minutes."

"Who's at the controls?"

"Karen Laswell. I thought you could've guessed it."

Joshua digested the input, trying only to figure how it might affect his chances. He noticed that Brav's speech was flat, slurred enough to show he was in some stage of an alcoholic stupor. Joshua had worked the inside of his thighs together enough to determine that the Viper was missing. "How'd you find the pistol?"

A small smile crossed Brav's face. "I survive by noticing small details. Like the alarm bell that went off when you entered the main salon of the yacht."

"I should've known," said Joshua weakly.

"You might have thrown me off with a derringer in your sock."

Joshua looked aside, and he was feeling stronger by the moment. "So tell me what's happened to Alan."

"I don't really know for sure."

"Baloney."

The plane dipped again in response to an air current, and Brav reached out to the nearby bulkhead to steady himself. "It doesn't matter whether you believe me," he said wearily.

Joshua began to sense his predicament, so he offered a verifying probe, "Why don't you untie me, since you've got all the cards."

"Can't."

"You mean like it's my turn?"

Brav nodded slowly, his expression sober.

Joshua sought desperately for a way to stall him. "So Price never intended to let the plutonium go?"

"Looks that way, although I really don't know for sure."

He looked aside then, as if he felt uncomfortable with the subject. "However," he added evenly, "I'd say the odds are good that he's hit the transfer cruiser by now. Maybe the trawler. But, regardless, all is not totally lost."

"How is that?"

Brav grimaced, reaching up to massage his right shoulder. "Let's just say that I'm not a complete traitor," he said slowly, and there was now a distant look across his eyes, as if he were occupied with something far away.

Sensing Brav's unwillingness to go on, Joshua switched subjects to keep him talking. "Does she know?" he asked quickly, nodding his head forward.

"I doubt it," Brav suggested, "since Price is smart enough to keep his plans properly contained."

"So you're going to take the money yourself?"

"You can bet your cherry tree on that."

Joshua was unimpressed with Brav's sudden bent for honesty, which was really more of a warning that his own time was slipping away. "What about her? Like she's got to keep this bird flying."

"She'll do just fine, since she thinks it's her neck too."

"So your deal isn't with Price then?"

Brav laughed hollowly. "You think I'm crazy?" and he turned toward the doorway.

Joshua wrenched futilely against the strap holding his wrists. "You can't land at Port-au-Prince," he said quickly. "Price's people will be waiting for that money, you know."

Brav hesitated, turning his upper torso to look down at Joshua. "You might think you've had a chance all along, but, believe me, the program was against you from the beginning. I tell you this now because it really doesn't matter."

Joshua closed his eyes as he tried to understand.

"And now that you've found me out," Brav went on, "you're simply forcing me to hurry up the process. Also, for what little comfort it might provide, you should know that I'm not enjoying it."

Joshua felt himself filling with anger in the wake of his helplessness. The old pro, Michael Brav, had spent all his adult life in intrigue thicker than this, and the man now had it figured again. Still, Joshua could not give up. "Alan Hunt needs my help," he pleaded. "Plus your own people if we act soon enough. I give you my word. All you have to do is to cut me loose—"

"It's too late," Brav said, cutting him off as he turned to face the closed hatch. "How do you work this thing?" he asked conversationally.

"You got to be kidding!"

Brav laughed appreciatively, before he turned to look back down at Joshua. "I could end it now, if you prefer. Although, I guess there is a kind of mathematical chance."

"Get on with it!" Joshua snapped.

Brav turned to reach up to the door release.

Joshua's only hope was that Michael Brav might not be aware of the physical forces which would come into play when he released the cargo door. But he was at once disappointed to see Brav reaching up with his left hand to grab the overhead hand rail to brace himself. Joshua nonetheless lifted his legs to rotate on his buttocks, pulling his knees up at the same time.

The hatch started out.

Caught in the slipstream, it was instantly torn from its hinges. The cabin was also instantly filled with the shriek of the rending metal, the suction of the outside air—

Joshua kicked viciously, aiming at Brav's thighs.

He missed cleanly, because for some reason Brav's heavy body was already on its way out!

Joshua watched in a kind of horror as the man who was about to be his own executioner struggled to stay in the plane. Brav's right foot was hooked on the rear jamb as his body started to rotate in the force of the slipstream. There was also an inexplicable look of surprise on Brav's face as he reached toward Joshua with his one free hand.

Involuntarily, Joshua thrust his left foot out to help, sensing that the man's great strength should save him. Michael Brav might have made it, otherwise, but apparently the turning of his body served to wrench his left hand loose from the safety rail.

Michael Brav was gone.

He had made no sound.

Joshua stared at the black void.

A few seconds later, he struggled to his feet. He looked up then to see Karen Laswell standing in the cockpit doorway, which meant the plane was now on auto pilot. Joshua also noticed that she was holding a revolver on him. The black briefcase was still cuffed to her left wrist.

"Untie me," he told her.

She took a tentative step toward him, hesitated. "Where's Brav?"

"He's gone," said Joshua with a note of finality.

She gestured toward the open doorway with the revolver. "You mean—"

"That's right," he cut in impatiently. "He went out the door the hard way, and you should be pleased, since you were to be next on his list after me."

She frowned.

"It's true," he assured her, and, seeing her indecision, he hurried on, "Do you really think you can pull this off by yourself?"

"Don't try to intimidate me," she warned him, but there was not total conviction in her voice.

"I don't know what your deal with Brav was," Joshua went on, "but it's over with now. So, what do you do with your partner gone? I mean, was it an even split with the money? Was the plutonium involved also?"

"Stop it!" she yelled at him.

"So think about it!"

She delayed a few seconds before telling him, "So we will go through with the plan as originally devised. After we land at Port-au-Prince, you'll be out of it."

Joshua was shaking his head no. "What about Alan Hunt?"

She promptly gave him the same answer as Brav had. "I don't know anything about Alan Hunt."

"So we'll go back and find out."

"You know we can't. We're already past the half-way point on fuel."

Joshua considered the truth of her statement, realizing they would have to land at Port-au-Prince after all. "As thick as you are in this mess," he insisted, "I find it hard to believe that you know nothing about Price's options on the plutonium transfer."

"You're impossible, Joshua. None of us has any evidence that the Jordan shipment isn't safely aboard the trawler."

Joshua took a deep breath. Perhaps she was right, he had to concede to himself as he recalled that Brav had also been indefinite on the same subject. "So we'll call the trawler," he said evenly.

"We're beyond transceiver range, and Brav pulled the wires on the radio."

Joshua could only shake his head. "What kind of evidence do you need?"

"I deal in facts, not intuition."

"Okay, so untie me."

She balked, taking a half step backward, as if putting some needed room between them while she studied him intently. "Only on two conditions," she finally said. "The first is that you will cooperate and allow me to finish out my end of the bargain, which should present no problem for you. Secondly, that for at least twenty-four hours, you will not tell anyone that Michael Brav is dead."

Joshua considered the two-part proposal before nodding his head. "I'll not interfere, so long as I can do what I have to do after we land."

"You're being evasive," she countered. "I'll ask you again to directly agree to the two points."

"I give you my word."

"Then I don't care what you do after we land," she said icily, and she moved toward him.

Joshua turned to let her begin untying his wrists. "By the way," he said, "why is it critical that Brav's death be kept a secret?"

"It doesn't concern you. All you have to do is to keep your word."

"That's fair enough," Joshua observed, but he could not help but admire her businesslike manner and self-control. She obviously had been in league with Brav over the money, yet here she was willing, apparently, to face Calvin Price. Joshua sensed that he could be an incriminating witness against her, which meant he would have to stay on his guard constantly. Feeling his wrists free, he turned to face her. "I might need a weapon," he said.

"This is yours," she said after a moment, turning up the butt of the .38 and holding it loosely by its silencer.

Taking the pistol, Joshua realized he was now even more perplexed. Watching her turn toward the cockpit, he also suspected there had to be more than one double cross involved. Perhaps it had been Brav who had been in over his head. After retrieving the Viper, he moved to follow behind Karen, thinking that the only sure thing he had to deal with was the safety of his friend, Alan Hunt. All the rest suddenly didn't matter to him anymore, and he resolved to let the interested parties sort it out for themselves.

After the transfer of the plutonium containers was completed, Alan Hunt was pushed roughly forward along the starboard rail of the *Arosa*. His escort repeatedly jammed his shotgun into Alan's lower back until they reached the small doorway opening below and behind the wheelhouse. Behind them, Sharon Iser, the only other survivor from the disabled cabin cruiser, was being held under guard on the fantail. Alan was shoved through the doorway to find himself in what looked like a combination galley and ship's mess. There was a narrow table in the center of the small room, and Alan was directed to sit down opposite another man, who snapped an order to Alan's escort in a language he couldn't understand.

After dumping Alan's personal effects on the table, the guard took up a position near the open door.

"My name is Kasim," the man across the table said to him.

It was Alan's first impression that Kasim had the build of a boy under his tight-fitting wet suit. His thin face was pinched in the oval opening of his head hood, looking in the bad light like a baroque cameo, made to look even more grotesque by the beard stubble which only partially covered the almost absent lower chin.

"According to your identification," Kasim went on curtly, "your name is Alan Hunt. And, I want to know what your role is in this situation."

Alan stared at him for a moment, before saying, "What do you intend to do with the woman?"

Kasim took an impatient breath and exhaled heavily through his nose, looking down at the table between them as he spoke slowly, "I am not required to tell you that one of the conditions relative to this exercise is that you be taken into custody. And, since I'm naturally curious, you will please answer the question?"

"Not until you tell me what you're going to do with her."

Kasim slammed his right fist on the table. "You fool!" he exclaimed. He relaxed then, as quickly as he had exploded. "All right. So allow me to inquire about your wife? Anne is her name, isn't it?"

Alan Hunt wavered briefly, concern etched on his brow. "What about her?" he asked quietly.

"Would you care to answer the question?"

"What about my wife?" Alan persisted.

"She is safely in our custody."

"Who are you? What's going—"

"We are members of the Popular Front for the Liberation of Palestine," Kasim told him flatly. "And, at this time, your wife is safe, and perhaps she will continue to remain so if you cooperate."

"I suppose I should ask you for proof."

"In time you may get your proof. For the moment, however, you will just have to accept my word. At any rate, I'm running short on time, and it shall be necessary—"

"All right," Alan interjected. "My role is that of an intermediary. It is, or was, my job to supervise the exchange of the plutonium and the funds for its purchase."

"Do you know how to handle this nuclear material?"

Alan eyed him suspiciously. "I know how to handle it."

"That will be helpful. You see, the packet holding the instructions was under the shirt of the Jew at the controls of the boat. My men report that it was shot up and can be of no help to us."

Alan sensed the man's fear of the plutonium, and he elected to push forward on what might be an advantage. "The material is very dangerous and needs to be in the care of an expert. While I know enough about it to help, Sharon Iser knows much more, since she's a nuclear physicist."

"But she is a Jew."

Alan Hunt turned his hand in an indifferent gesture. "Don't forget the story of the snake and the rabbit, and how it was that they shared the same quarters . . . "

Kasim felt his face turning into an appreciative smile. "You make what appears to be a worthwhile point," and he reached thoughtfully down to rummage through Alan's personal effects. He picked up the small New Testament, turned it once in his hand. "Are you a religious person?"

"I believe in Jesus Christ."

The brow of Kasim furrowed as he pushed the effects across the table. "You may keep the Book, then," he said soberly. "You should know that we, too, are a religious people. You should also be aware that Jesus Christ is one of our most honored prophets."

"Then we are both privileged, and . . . "

"And what?"

"And may we both be guided by His teachings."

Kasim stood up abruptly, warning him, "You will be guided by my orders. And, you will be killed instantly at the slightest sign of disobedience."

Standing up himself, Alan Hunt resisted the temptation to remind Kasim that he had already shown he was both willing and able to kill instantly.

At his estate villa, Calvin Price was stalking impatiently back and forth between his den and the security office. It was his opinion, despite Maurice Garand's assurances to the contrary, that the schedule was already snarled up. He pulled up once more behind Garand, who was still seated calmly before the radio transmitter. Price glanced up to the array of wall-mounted clocks, checking again the one set for their time zone. "The *Arosa* is fifteen minutes overdue. And, as of this moment, Karen is also overdue." He then turned up his Rolex, double checking the time on the clock, before going on, "I say we should call the trawler."

Garand turned his head to speak over his shoulder, "There is no standby procedure in an operation like this. It has either come off as planned, or it's been blown."

Price reached up to smooth down the hair at the nape of his neck, a nervous gesture, and he was thinking that Garand, as usual, was right. If the Arabs had failed, then they were simply on their own now. But he could not so casually dismiss the status of Karen Laswell, and he was about to order Garand to call the seaplane when the radio came to life. Garand snatched up the mike to acknowledge.

The *Arosa* reported a satisfactory catch.

"Why the delay?" Price demanded, and Garand repeated the question.

"The first group had engine trouble," the explanation came back.

The "first group" meant Brav's transfer team.

"Is umpire safely on his way?" Garand spoke into the mike, as if he was reading Price's mind.

"They departed on schedule," the answer came back.

"Ask him if Karen has the money," said Price impulsively.

Garand glanced over his shoulder, leaving the microphone closed. "We are well within the monitor range of Guantanamo, and we're already pushing our luck on an open channel."

"Shut it down," said Price resignedly.

Garand complied, getting up then to move to his desk, where he sat down heavily. He reached up idly to adjust his heavy glasses on his nose. "I doubt that we are really behind schedule," he suggested quietly as he began to arrange the loose papers on his desk. "We only allowed four to five minutes for the action phase, but that was an ideal estimate. After all, the Jews could've put up an extended fight. It's likely that Brav had something to do with the delay."

Listening thoughtfully, Price had moved to the radio,

where he cranked the frequency dial to another setting. It appeared they were on schedule, after all. He levered the transmit button, calling for Nick Villon, who was standing by in the estate launch at the harbor in Port-au-Prince.

Nick acknowledged almost immediately.

"It looks like Karen will be about fifteen minutes late," Price told him, noticing that his own voice was now subdued. "Report to me as soon as she is aboard. And, don't forget to follow your instructions to the letter."

Not waiting for a reply, he shut down the radio.

Turning back toward the desk, he realized that he was tired and definitely let down, now that they were apparently on the downhill grade for the present phase. "So now all we can do is wait," he said softly. "Do you have any guess as to how long it will take to finish?"

"Four or five days, at least."

"Karen and I will leave for Sri Lanka as soon as she returns. Nick knows how to reach us."

"I can clean things up here in a day or two."

Price thought for a moment, before answering, "Only for a day or two, unless you think Barca needs your help in making the crossing."

"There's nothing we can do now. He's on his own after Tampico. Of course, it will look better if he takes a free ride through Cuba. The more third-world witnesses we get, the better."

Price nodded that he agreed with the estimate. "So wait until you receive confirmation that he's cleared the area, just in case he needs help." He paused then, reaching up to smooth down the back of his hair. "I've been thinking about the Beirut extension . . . " and he paused more thoughtfully.

"Are you still worried about our Arab friends?"

"Not so much as I am about the Jews. They're going to be hopping mad now, especially with the casualties. And, it also occurs to me that the Kasim connection has got to make them think the plutonium is headed for an Arab buyer."

"So the Jews are going to go all out."

"Wouldn't you if you were in their shoes?"

It was Garand's turn to pause thoughtfully. "Barca has already been programmed to go through with the Beirut extension, anyway, so we're ready on that part of it. All I have to do is to get a plane ticket and alert our Beirut operative." He leaned forward to make a note on his desk calendar.

Watching him, Price suggested, "Put a question mark behind it. If all goes right on schedule with the Arabs to the final leg, then we can save ourselves the Barca fee."

Garand had jotted a pair of question marks after his note. Turning the pencil in his hand, he then suggested, "I've already figured a way to beat paying the fee. And, I think you're right in going through with Beirut to take the heat off. Like you say, the Jews are going to pull the cork now."

"Okay, so tentatively plan on Beirut. Just don't forget to get Nick on his way by Friday night."

"The Arabs won't like the nursemaid."

"Nick will be a calming influence if they start getting nervous."

"I still say we're doing it the hard way," Garand proposed. "We could much more easily make our next rendezvous this side of Africa."

"That may be true, my careful friend. However, it is my judgment that we have enough enemies already. Don't forget that we've targeted the Arab accounts, most of whom would secretly like to see Kasim neutralized anyway. We are, you might say, doing them a favor."

"But what about the Jews? You don't think for a minute that they're going to buy that Kasim hit them on his own. They'll automatically assume we were behind it."

"They've neutralized themselves because of their own betrayal," Price pointed out as he made for the door. "So what they think doesn't interest me."

Joshua Bain had assumed control of the seaplane, and he landed at Port-au-Prince without further incident. As he coaxed the aircraft into its assigned dock, he was aware that he had only two choices. The first was to find a radio which would enable him to contact the *Arosa*. The second would be to refuel and head back for the Jamaica exchange site. The latter option seemed less desirable, since if Alan and his group had been engaged, then the incident was already nearly a full hour over with. And, with such a time lapse, his chances of finding anything in the dark would be remote. As far as he was concerned, the wraps and all bets were off. Find a radio first, he thought. Get the Jamaican Coast Guard hopping. Anyone. The American consulate—

"You'll have to wait here," Karen told him.

Joshua cut the engines.

When they had turned into the channel, Karen had flashed a lantern signal out the cockpit window. Her terse explanation was that the signal was only an all-clear sign to Nick Villon, who was to escort her and the money back to the villa.

"How do I get to Price?" Joshua asked, the heavy note of a demand in his voice.

Karen Laswell pulled out of her harness. "You have to give me a couple of minutes in the back first," she said evenly; "then I'll make the arrangements."

He put his right hand on her forearm for emphasis. "You've got just two minutes." And he watched her as she pushed out of the cockpit. Waiting, he absently-mindedly shut down the remainder of the controls while he considered his next move. Several more seconds passed before he heard what sounded like footsteps on the catwalk. Curious, he pushed out of his seat and turned toward the cockpit door. He opened it far enough to see the length of the open cabin. Karen Laswell was standing near the open cargo door, and her right arm, the nearest to him, was extended. Even in the poor overhead light, Joshua could see that she was offering the black metal brief-case to someone standing outside. He pulled the .38 out of his belt, debating whether to push the door open. Per her own request, he elected to leave Karen to her business; she apparently was handing over the briefcase to Nick Villon.

Major David Sheldon had taken the briefcase from Karen Laswell. Like his companion on the catwalk behind him, he was dressed in typical night combat gear, including a black wool ski mask. He weighed the briefcase in his hand. "Is it all here?" he asked quietly.

"Of course," she whispered intently.

"Where's Bain?" he asked her.

She gestured toward the cockpit. "He's armed and will be difficult to take," she warned him in a whisper. "He's not worth it, and you'll run out of time," and she reached out to put her left hand on his right forearm. "There's been a change in plan, and I must go with you, now."

He pulled out of her grip, lifting his right hand to pull a revolver out of the shoulder holster under his left arm.

"Forget Bain," Karen hissed, and she noticed with little interest that there was a blunt silencer attached to the muzzle of the handgun.

Major Sheldon shot her once.

The bullet passed through her sternum, slightly off center.

Her executioner watched impassively as she folded quietly to the floor.

"What's with the change in plan?" he heard his companion inquiring in a low voice.

"Who knows?" said Sheldon indifferently. "She was probably getting cold feet with the order to eliminate Bain," and he lifted the revolver to the port position, levering the hammer back with his thumb.

The subdued thump of the shot in the confined silence of the cabin had caused Joshua to flinch. Watching Karen collapse, he had raised his weapon, thumbing its hammer back. A dark form now started to materialize in the cargo doorway, and he saw the revolver coming around to point in his direction.

He snapped a shot off, not aiming.

He fired twice again in quick succession. Pulling the narrow door closed, he stepped back and aside against the radio panel, and there was now the sinking feeling of anticipation in his belly.

A burst of automatic fire ripped across the door.

Joshua was not surprised.

The burst had to be more than just a cover move.

They were after him now—

Joshua fired again, through the door, finding the revolver empty after only one shot. He spun to his right, stepping over the copilot back rest, where he reached up to grab the release on the side window.

On the catwalk, Major Sheldon reached out to take the arm of his assistant, who was readying himself to fire another burst into the cockpit area.

"We don't have the time," Sheldon told him, and he reached into the black canvas bag hung over the other man's left shoulder. Pulling out an oilskin package, he ripped one end of the waterproof charge to expose its timer. Carefully counting the clicks, he rotated the time to thirty seconds. Tossing the heavy charge well into the plane's interior, he turned to lope along the catwalk to the dock, his companion following. They had moved about another twenty steps, padding almost silently on the weathered dock, when Sheldon thought he heard a splash, like a body hitting water.

He pulled up, putting out his arm to stop his companion. He cocked his head, listening.

"What is it?" his assistant hissed.

"I think Bain is going for a late night swim."

"I could've got him."

Major Sheldon realized he was smiling under his mask, remembering Michael Brav's warning that Joshua Bain was tricky and tended to be lucky. He also remembered that Brav's report included the information that Bain's parents had perished at Auschwitz.

Bain's luck was thus not inherited.

"We got what we came for," Sheldon said, and he pushed off again, now running at a quicker pace.

A few seconds later, the midsection of the seaplane was blown to pieces. The secondary explosion of its nearly empty fuel tanks came almost immediately afterwards, destroying what was left of the wings and cockpit fuselage.

At the top of the dock ramp, Major Sheldon ducked involuntarily under the hail of debris peppering the area. He turned to look down, seeing that the port engine was askance on the dock itself, burning furiously, the only remnant of the aircraft he could make out.

He pulled his head mask off, satisfied that he had adequately fulfilled his assigned mission. He turned then to move hurriedly toward the opposite pier and their waiting boat, thinking ahead to what hopefully would be their final rendezvous in what appeared to be a most successful operation.

The swell of water generated by the explosion caught the estate launch broadside. Nick Villon pushed the throttle forward, snapping the wheel to starboard, enabling him to power out of the sudden list. Startled at this, yet another unexpected development, he turned the launch toward the dock anyway. There was one armed crewman on board to help him if needed, and he now yelled at him over his shoulder, "We'll take a look!"

He eased back on the throttle, thinking frantically as he tried to piece together the report he would have to make to Colonel Price. There had been the signal from the seaplane before it docked, apparently from Karen as planned, telling him it was all clear. Then, while he had waited for Karen to emerge, two men had approached the seaplane from dockside. He had not reacted because his orders were specific that he was not to interfere, regardless of the circumstances. He had started the boat when he heard the string of automatic fire.

The smoke from the explosion rolled over them now in a brief wave.

Nick Villon realized he was holding his breath.

There was a fire on the dock now, and as he let the air out of his lungs he thought he could make out a part of the plane burning on top of the adjacent pier.

He took another breath, slower and more deliberate, as he began to understand that Karen Laswell was probably gone, and that he was the one who would have to report it to the villa.

"Watch it!" the crewman yelled at him. "The water's full of junk."

His assistant had a lantern, and as they came closer he began to sweep the area where the seaplane had been just a few seconds before. The blast had been awesome, and Nick slowed the launch, thinking it was hopeless.

Something bumped the bow.

Nick cut the engine, not wanting to foul the propeller. The launch slowed to a near stop, and he turned out of the cockpit to mount the higher bow rail. He saw lights moving on the upper dock, and he knew their time was limited before they had to get moving.

"Over here," the crewman was saying, pointing the light under the pier.

It took a few seconds for Nick to realize it was a body. He was disappointed to see it was apparently a man, floating face down between two pilings. He reached out to take the lantern. "Go get him," he said urgently, thinking that no matter who it was, Calvin Price would want him alive.

It took only a few more seconds to get the body aboard.

Nick made a last survey of the area with the lantern, before starting up the launch. By now, people were beginning to show up on the dock. He could hear a siren in the background, probably the fire department. With the crewman working on the man they had pulled out of the water, he throttled the launch up enough to work out of the area. In the main channel, he cut power, letting the launch drift for the moment. He then stepped to the aft deck, thinking he had to get on the radio fast.

"Is he alive?" he asked, bending down over the still form.

"I think so."

Nick didn't at first recognize him. He put the lantern more fully on his face, saw the blood clotting in the nostrils. And it came to him then. Corpus Christi. The man he escorted to the yacht. Joshua Bain.

The crewman turned the man's head gently. "His neck seems okay."

"Bad concussion," Nick commented, noticing the blood draining out of the left ear. He reached under Joshua Bain's rump, fishing out a billfold. He started for the radio with a measured reluctance.

Maurice Garand took the call.

Calvin Price pulled up behind him, listening in stunned silence as Nick reported the destruction of the seaplane. Noticing a lapse in the two men's exchange, he reached out to put his hand on Garand's shoulder. Among the few details that Nick had just reported was that there was no sign of Karen Laswell. "So he saw two men coming and going right before the explosion," said Price hurriedly. "Ask him if he's *positive* one of them leaving couldn't have been Karen."

Garand passed the question.

There was a pause before Nick reported slowly, "I'm sorry, sir, but I had the glasses on them most of the time. And, while I couldn't recognize them because they were masked, I am certain Karen wasn't one of them. I repeat, sir, that someone did signal me when the plane hit the channel, so I presume she was the one."

So they must've killed her, Price thought bitterly. He turned away, angrily hammering his right fist into his other palm. He straightened up then, to stare at the ceiling, trying to compose his thoughts. Behind him, Garand was routinely going about his business, asking Nick if they had identified the man they had fished out of the water.

Calvin Price listened numbly while Nick reported that the man was Joshua Bain. Price was shaking his head as he turned back to the radio. The lousy Bain luck had surfaced again, just as Price had assumed it would, which was why he had been pleased to have seen Karen scheduled to accompany Bain. There had been the presumption that the man's good fortune would extend to those near him. But, it hadn't worked. He was aware then that Garand was asking him what to do with Bain.

"Why not dump him overboard," Garand went on to suggest. "That was part of the arrangement, anyway. They'll find his body, assume he was killed in the explosion."

Calvin Price fought down the temptation to agree.

"Put him ashore," he ordered quickly. "And make sure he gets medical attention."

With Nick off the radio, Price moved quickly to his den office. Maurice Garand followed, pulling up in front of the desk.

"I want a watch on Bain twenty-four hours a day," Price told him.

Garand nodded, before asking, "Why the Bain gambit, sir? If he can help us, why not bring him here?" and he smiled thinly. "We have the means to obtain his cooperation."

"No, we don't," Price corrected him sternly. "I can guarantee you that Bain was not a part of what went down. Our choice is to either kill him or use him. Remember, the point now is that we've got to locate the money. And, Michael Brav is the obvious answer."

"It doesn't make sense!" Garand said heatedly, and he turned to begin stalking the floor in front of the desk. "We have to assume it was Karen who signalled Nick, which meant that she was all right and that the plan was on schedule. Also, Brav's people showed up right on schedule. Now, we allowed for the contingency that Brav would attempt to alter the plan at the lagoon, primarily because he would likely have second thoughts about having to deal personally with whoever was to intercept Jordan. After all, he would've been a fool not to suspect that probability. However, we figured that Bain and Karen, together, would be too much for him to contend with, especially with his need to use the aircraft as an escape means."

"We couldn't afford to spook Brav," Price reminded him.

"I know, but Brav could not possibly have been on the seaplane. Karen wouldn't have signalled, to begin with. And, Nick said that the same two men who arrived at the plane were the ones who left. I mean, after all, had Brav been on board, he surely would have left with his own people. We have to assume it was his own team that blew the plane."

"I still say that Brav's the answer."

"If he's still alive . . ."

Calvin Price pondered the remark in the following silence.

"But I can appreciate now why we must keep Bain alive," Garand finally offered. "However, I still don't understand why we didn't bring him here." He had stopped pacing to pull up in front of the desk.

"You don't know the Canaan team well enough," Price told him bluntly. "With Alan Hunt and his wife among the missing, Joshua Bain will be on the trail as soon as he can walk. All we have to do is to keep him in sight. Between him and our resources, we should find Brav soon enough."

"And the money."

Calvin Price leaned back in his chair, crossed his hands behind his head. "So we're still in business," he mused, almost to himself. "We still have the handle on the plutonium. Alan Hunt should be in custody by now," and he paused, closing his eyes. The sharply defined image of Karen Laswell crossed his mind almost at once. "Do what you can to help recover Karen's body."

"That might not be easy," Garand suggested quietly.

"Get with the port authorities right away. Use the *Swanya II*. Also, I want the best salvage crew on the island, and if you can't come up with someone high-powered enough, then go to Miami and fly 'em here."

"You want all of it?"

"Of course, every scrap. We have to. Don't you understand?"

Maurice Garand nodded that he understood.

Calvin Price felt his throat tighten up, and, as he leaned forward he had to cough to clear the obstruction. "You open up a new section on your wallboard," he said, hearing the break in his voice, "and devote yourself to finding out who was responsible for her death." He lifted his right forefinger to point it threateningly at his security chief. "And when you find out for sure, you tell me and only me." He stood up then to move away from the desk and out of the room, not wanting Maurice Garand to see what had to be showing on his face.

Chapter seven

The dream had started a long time ago, at Berkeley when he had returned to college after he had been released from confinement as a prisoner of war. The Air Force psychiatrist had told Joshua Bain that while he was asleep the stage in his mind was set because of his inner feelings of insecurity, the consequences of his lack of self-confidence, and was usually accompanied by severe depression. The dream was almost always the same and supposedly not an uncommon one with many people, especially for those who set standards for themselves which they couldn't possibly obtain. He was always running in the dream, desperate and afraid, and he could not get away. His pursuers varied from unknown persons to, once, even his own adopted father. And, they were always armed, threatening and intent, close behind, and he was running for his life, clambering over walls, down dark alleys, and into strange buildings. And always the closing footsteps behind him, until he became exhausted, turning to see over his shoulder the shadowy forms still right on his heels.

He awoke now with a start.

The dream became his consciousness.

The momentum of his pursuers was such that Joshua imagined they were on top of him, and he raised his right arm in a protective gesture—

"Are you all right, sir?"

He warily lowered his arm from his face. The cream-colored walls of the small room were not enough at first for him to recognize his surroundings, and he looked to his left for the source of the voice. The white uniform of the young, dark girl was obviously that of a nurse, and Joshua dropped his arm back to the bed beside him.

The bed sheets were soaked with his sweat.

The nurse was taking his pulse on his left wrist.

"I'm okay," he told her slowly. "I was just having a nightmare."

"That's not unusual," the nurse told him, her voice inflected with the musical Creole influence. "Your body was put to rest by the drugs," she went on to explain, "but your mind has remained awake." She carefully placed his left forearm in next to his side, looking at him with a full smile.

Joshua noticed that there was the same music in her eyes.

"You have a visitor," the nurse said.

Joshua had come around enough to remember that he was in a hospital at Port-au-Prince. He had been conscious before, long enough to make a telephone call to the American consulate. He focused on the wall clock across the room, which reported the time as two minutes before twelve. The outside light filtering in through the one window told him it was nearly noon.

"Is today still Tuesday?" he asked.

"Yes, sir."

So he had been asleep only an hour. Fully awake and more

alert now, he tried to push himself to a sitting position, but the eruption of pain at the base of his skull dropped him as if he'd been struck with a baseball bat. He bit down on his teeth as he went down. The pain was excruciating, spreading across his skull to his forehead, and he let his breath go with a groan.

"You must relax and stay quiet," the nurse told him. "I don't think you're well enough to see anyone."

The pain had passed, and Joshua opened his eyes to look at the ceiling. "Who is it?" he asked.

"It's a Mister Crofton."

"Please send him in. It's most important that I talk to him."

With the nurse gone, Joshua tried to arrange his thoughts. His phone call to the consulate had been with a Mister Crofton. He had made several requests to the man, but he couldn't remember exactly what they had been. He knew for certain that operation Jordan had turned upside down. So far as he could tell, Alan was gone. Both Michael Brav and Karen Laswell were dead. His thoughts tumbled. How, for example, did he get here? He reached out impulsively to pick up the phone receiver, asking for the business office. He hung up the phone after being informed that he had been admitted by a Nicholas Villon, and that a cash deposit of five thousand dollars had been made to cover his medical expenses. He was trying to digest that input when the door to his room opened to admit a man who introduced himself as Theodore Crofton.

Joshua gestured weakly with his left hand for Mister Crofton to sit down. His visitor was middle-aged, stockily built, and heavily tanned. Joshua was used to the clothes of a tennis player, and he saw that Crofton was ready for the courts. He had a more official looking briefcase in his hand.

Crofton did not sit down. "May I see your passport, please?" he asked in the tone of one being inconvenienced. "You see, Mister Bain, it is necessary to complete certain reports when an American citizen has been injured. According to your admission record, you were hurt in a sailing accident. Do you have anything to add?"

"No," said Joshua, and he pointed to the drawer in the table next to his bed. "I think my papers are in there."

After inspecting Joshua's still damp passport, Crofton took the chair across the room.

"Did you make the calls?" Joshua asked him.

Crofton opened his briefcase to remove a notebook. "We

tried twice but could not get an answer on the area code seven-one-four number in California."

Joshua was perplexed why Anne didn't answer the private number.

"We have not had any inquiry, nor has Kingston, from a Mister Alan Hunt either," Crofton went on. "Also, our Kingston office reports that the Jamaican authorities have impounded a foreign trawler which was beached near Morant Point."

"What about Calvin Price?" Joshua asked him.

"We have no record of that name as a resident or visitor in the Republic of Haiti."

"Okay, but what about the trawler, the *Arosa*?"

Crofton stood up. "We have been advised that the matter is under investigation by the Jamaican coast guard. Privately, our office there suspects it involves illegal narcotics."

Joshua realized that he was in the process of striking out. He had not mentioned the seaplane and the explosion for fear that would implicate him with the local police. He had made a mistake, and, as a result, he had lost valuable time. Watching Crofton start toward the door, he sensed that it was time to pull out all the stops. "Hold it," he said as sternly as he could.

Crofton pulled up, turning to face him.

"Write down the following message," Joshua started slowly. "Quote. I have vital information concerning operation Jordan, which involves the Armatrex plutonium. My contacts are Calvin Price and Michael Brav, an Israeli national. Unquote. And, sign it Joshua Bain."

Crofton looked up from his notebook. "Is that all?"

"No," said Joshua after a thoughtful moment. "Add in, quote, I prefer to communicate with Jerome Mason, unquote."

"Whom do I address this to?"

"To three different agencies. The U.S. State Department, the U.S. Justice Department, and the Israeli ambassador's office, all located in Washington, D.C. And, use the quickest method of transmission possible. While I don't care, you probably should keep this classified," and he paused before adding, "If money is a problem, you'll find adequate funds in the drawer with my passport."

Crofton returned the notebook to his briefcase. "I'm sure we can manage on our own," he said then. "By the way," he continued, stopping momentarily, his hand on the door, "is the Jerome Mason you refer to the retired director of the FBI?"

"The one and the same."

"Wouldn't it be helpful if I put the hospital phone number in the message?"

"An excellent idea," said Joshua gratefully.

Theodore Crofton pushed through the door without further comment.

Joshua took a deep breath and reached for the phone, asking for the overseas operator. The business phone number for Rancho Canaan was ready in his mind, but as he waited for the operator he had no idea what he might say to Anne Hunt. Alan was gone, perhaps even dead, a possibility so grotesque that he had no way to deal with it. There was literally no one left. To an outsider, operation Jordan could be a myth. Joshua had to admit that he was now in the middle of a nightmare worse than any he had ever dreamed before.

His depression was final, sapping both his mind and his strength, so that when the operator came on the line he gave her the number in barely a whisper. He was thinking he should just give it up when he heard the ranch's answering service distantly telling him that Anne Hunt was missing, and that he had an urgent message to call the local sheriff's office. Shocked, Joshua Bain dropped the phone to the floor, feeling as if something had turned loose in his mind, like a water hose flowing, cold and unrelenting, its pressure building until he thought his head would explode. He fumbled for the switch to the nurse's station.

The Seacliff Manors was a fashionable condo' complex set back from the beach along the north shoreline of Fort Lauderdale, Florida. Finished with an afternoon of golf, Jerome Mason passed through the security gate, as usual, without having to show his resident's pass. It occurred to him as he pulled in to park in his private garage that the Seacliff Manors was a fraudulent name devised by a promoter who was more interested in sales than in the truth. He doubted if he could see the ocean even from his roof, the ultra-modern decor of the sprawling grounds no more resembled a manor than did Disneyland, and he was ready to wager there wasn't a genuine cliff within a hundred miles.

He punched the button under the steering column to close the automatic garage door. Leaving his clubs in the trunk of the car for tomorrow's round, he entered the plush apartment via the nearer kitchen door. There was a note on the bar counter from his wife which told him she had been invited to the meeting of a club whose name he couldn't make out beyond the more legible word, "Fuchsia."

He moved listlessly to his office, a converted den, where he poured himself a short brandy before sitting down behind his desk. He had broken eighty today for the first time, and there had been a mild celebration in the clubhouse afterwards. The effects of the minor drinking he had indulged in were beginning to wear off, and he felt terrible. With nothing more to do, he picked up the phone to call his answering service. There was one message, which he didn't bother to jot down, since he already knew Les Stalmeyer's private-line number by heart. The calls from the Attorney General had fallen off during the past few months, since Jerome Mason had formally retired. But, from time to time something would come up requiring his opinion, or clarification of something left over from before he left. Now, he checked his watch to see that Stalmeyer was probably still in his Washington office, so he picked up the phone, punching in the area 212 number.

Les Stalmeyer came on his line sounding like Jerome Mason felt.

"This is Jerry," Mason told him cordially, "and how come you sound so sweet?"

"You calling from the eighteenth hole?"

"Don't knock it. I came in under eighty today."

"So you'll be turning pro soon."

"Forget it. You could break sixty on this course with your left hand."

Stalmeyer actually laughed. "You're at home, I hope?"

"Yes, sir."

"So put it on the scrambler."

Mason reached around to the back of the phone console to throw a bat-handled toggle switch. "Go ahead," he reported.

"Do you remember Joshua Bain?"

"How could I forget."

"Well, it looks as if he's done it again. Only this time he's managed to work himself into the big leagues."

"Is he in trouble?"

"I don't think so, yet. But he's about as close as he can get. While I can't give you all the details now, I can say that the Is-raeli government has turned the Armatrex plutonium, and they apparently worked out a deal with our old friend Calvin Price to get it back to us. The bulk of the action so far has apparently taken place in the Caribbean."

Jerome Mason had pulled out a yellow-lined tablet and was now scratching notes. "So what's Bain got to do with it?"

"I don't know all the facts, Jerry. Beyond what I've told you, all I can add is that Bain is in a hospital at Port-au-Prince, and he's yelling for help. He sent us a message asking for you by name."

"I'm interested," Mason said truthfully.

"Jon Malek has been handling it for us, and he'll be leaving for Miami early tomorrow morning. Interpol is also involved."

"We'd all like to nail Price."

"I'll level with you, Jerry. I've got Malek up to his ears in an operations project, and if you can find the time—"

"You've got to be kidding," Mason interjected.

"That's what I figured, so I told Malek to get Bain up to Miami as soon as possible. Malek will meet you there also to brief you completely. You will, of course, only have investigative authority."

"I understand."

"So I'll cut the papers appointing you as a special investigator, which will not only put you on the payroll but cover your expenses as well."

"Any idea when Bain will be here?"

"We're shooting for tomorrow morning."

Writing furiously, Jerome Mason could hardly contain himself. "Do me a favor," he said in the following pause. "Have your girl knock out a memo to both the Washington Interpol bureau and the Israeli ambassador's office fronting me in as your rep'."

"It's done."

"It's getting late," Mason commented, "and I need to do some thinking before I contact them."

"Help us get this cleaned up, Jerry. You're the kind of experienced operator the situation requires. Bain is obviously in over his head, and as good a man as Malek is, he's still a lightweight in the field."

"I'll do my best."

Les Stalmeyer hung up without further comment.

Replacing his phone in its cradle, Jerome Mason had to shake his head several times to assure himself that the conversation had been for real. The notes were there in front of him, a reality he could not ignore.

Unbelievably enough, it seemed he was back in the saddle again.

The yacht *Swanya II* was at anchor at the edge of the channel about one hundred feet directly outboard from the dock site where the seaplane had been destroyed the night before. Maurice Garand was in charge and had decided to use the yacht as his operating base during the salvage operation. Nick Villon, who was assisting him, was now on the dock itself and in direct contact with the salvage foreman. They were using hand-held transceivers to communicate, and Garand was standing impatiently on the port rail of the bridge when Nick made one of his routine progress reports.

"They think they found her right foot," Nick told him tentatively. "But the foreman says you might as well forget the rest. The crabs are murder around the pilings. We wouldn't have found the foot without the protection of her boot."

"All right," said Garand as quickly as he could transfer the channel. "You keep in touch with the coroner and keep a written record of everything they recover. You know how the old man feels about this."

"I understand, sir."

Garand went below to the main salon, where he pulled up at the bar counter to assess the day's developments.

Hafiz Barca had reported in from Tampico that Anne Hunt was in custody and they were about to embark by fishing boat to Cuba.

The Arab hijack team had already cleared San Juan on the first leg of their scheduled itinerary, and Garand had not questioned the impromptu decision to include the Israeli inspector as a hostage along with Alan Hunt.

Joshua Bain was recovering, apparently, and was under constant surveillance.

Michael Brav was still among the missing.

Calvin Price was well on his way to Hong Kong, an intermediate stop before moving on to his Sri Lanka rendezvous.

Turning toward the dining table and his notes, he concluded that the Jews had suffered the heaviest casualties. Alpha team had been wiped out to the man. The bravo team had escaped, as expected. The Jews had also lost the plutonium, but they at least had recovered their investment. He wondered if Tel Aviv would be satisfied with that half a loaf.

Chapter eight

Jonathan Malek set a fresh reel of blank tape on the recorder. The move was one of habit, and he hesitated a moment, wondering if in this instance it was really necessary to have the formal record. There was a light knock on the door to his hotel room, making the decision for him, and he reached down to punch the start button before he reported quickly, "Time and date of oh-nine-hundred hours, Thursday, October twelve. Location is room two-eighteen, King's Inn, Miami, Florida." Taking a deep breath, he opened the door.

Jerome Mason strode wordlessly past him, filling the room instantly with his presence. The former director looked fit, the heavily tanned skin on his weathered face in striking contrast to the great mane of white hair which he was allowing to grow even longer now that he was retired from active service. He was informally dressed for the warm weather, suggesting his next stop might be the club golf course.

"A pleasure to see you again, sir," Malek offered.

"That's a probable crock," Mason suggested tersely, a hint of a smile around his mouth as he sat down in a chair next to the small service table. He had a thin-line briefcase in his left hand, which he placed on the table next to the tape recorder. He next removed his dark glasses to stare curiously at Malek with the same cobalt blue eyes which had become his trademark.

"Are you enjoying your retirement?" Malek asked cordially, looking aside. He had been informed by his own superior, the Attorney General himself, that he was to afford the retired director the full respect due his former office.

Mason grunted contemptuously. "Down here, your options include golf, gardening, tennis, bingo, drinking, and, if you're lucky, an occasional game of poker."

Malek glanced out the window to the verdant hotel grounds. "I should think gardening could keep you occupied." He was encouraged that Mason seemed to be in a better mood than usual.

"Forget it," Mason told him. "I used to worry that the communists were going to take over the world. They don't stand a chance. It's going to be a close race between the ants, bermuda grass, and snails." He reached out then to touch the recorder. "So we're on record," he noted absently.

"That's up to you, sir."

"Are you aware that I turned down the special investigator's appointment?"

"Yes, sir, I am."

"I suppose you can let it run for now," Mason said thoughtfully. "If there are any official decisions made, they should be on file. Mostly, of course, for your protection."

"And the Department's, sir."

"Of course, so let's get to it."

Malek moved to the table, picked up a full tape reel. "This is your copy of the Joshua Bain report. It contains the details of the rough verbal report I gave you last night on the phone. I should also add that Bain told me a few minutes ago that he has already sent a copy to, as he put it, a disinterested party."

"That figures," Mason observed dryly. "He's dealt with us before, and he's getting to know the ropes." He took the tape and pushed it into his briefcase before asking, "Where is Bain now?"

"He's in a room down the hall, waiting for you."

Mason pushed himself to his feet, and when he looked at Malek his eyes had narrowed down to an appraising stare. "I presume you're not holding anything back. Like, for example, the connection with Donaldson's people."

"The only function of the CIA was to arrange the logistics and help in the transport. In fact, we brought them in the back door at the very last minute."

Jerome Mason worked his right hand in and out of a clench, as if performing some isometric exercise. "I wonder," he finally said thoughtfully. "From what I gather, Price and Tel Aviv had a fairly smooth plan laid out. Yet, it apparently went to pot at practically every turn. Bain, too, is not noted for his notorious blunders. All in all, I get the feeling of deliberate sabotage. And, it occurs to me . . ." He hesitated, then reached out to shut down the recorder. "It occurs to me," he went on, "that there are those who would like to see the Jews embarrassed, especially their secret service, and, would go to any length to prevent Israel from laying their hands on a large shipment of weapon's grade plutonium."

"The deal was to give us the plutonium," Malek pointed out.

"Oh, yeah," Mason noted cryptically. "So where is it now?"

Malek could only shrug.

"Don't you see," Mason said argumentively, "Tel Aviv could've easily been setting us up, especially to give credibility to the operation. If it ever was time to look a gift horse in the mouth, it was on this occasion. Look at it from Donaldson's point of view. Here we were, on short notice, informed that we were to receive our plutonium back, without cost, and to pick up Primo as a bonus. And all we had to do was to provide a submarine and some basic communications. And, what was the outcome?"

Malek shrugged once more. "Like you said, it went to pot."

"I have the feeling it never had a chance." He picked up his dark glasses to put them in the pocket of his knit sport shirt. "Have you told Bain about the Interpol connection?"

"You mean gardenia?"

"Yes."

"No, I haven't. We are of the opinion that we should obtain permission first, because of the chance for compromise."

Mason started toward the door. "Do you have anything else?"

Malek had already moved to his own briefcase on the bed. He pulled out a manila envelope, handed it to Mason. "This is a copy of the letter found at the Rancho Canaan office. It came in on the wire from L.A. and was delivered by an agent from the downtown bureau office a few minutes before you arrived. I expect Bain will want to see it also."

Mason took the envelope without comment.

"For whatever interest it may have," Malek went on carefully. "The Jamaican authorities have verified that Alan Hunt was not one of the bodies found on the beached Portuguese trawler. The crew, oddly enough, were not harmed."

Jerome Mason paused at the door. He sighed heavily, before asking, "Have they identified the bodies yet?"

Malek shook his head negatively. "If what Bain says is true, then they're probably from Brav's commando group. We notified the Israeli ambassador's office, and they're sending a man to Kingston."

"So what's the government's official position on all this?"

"I've been told there literally isn't any," Malek said evenly, and he glanced over his shoulder to verify that the recorder was still turned off. "There's been no criminal activity, so far as we can tell, on American soil," and he held up his hands in a definitive gesture. "Whatever case there may have been can be classed as closed."

"Including the kidnapping of an American citizen?"

"If you mean Anne Hunt, there is no direct evidence that she didn't leave voluntarily."

"That is a definite crock, and you know it."

Malek realized he was smiling, and he was briefly surprised by his own affrontery. "Then all someone has to do is to produce the evidence," and he noticed that Jerome Mason was also smiling thinly.

"Which leads to my last question," said Mason. "How far can I go, in my unofficial capacity, and still expect to be backed up?"

"I was told, sir, to advise you to use your own judgment in that regard."

Mason glanced over his shoulder to the tape recorder. "I wish you'd had the machine on for that comment."

"I couldn't have said it then."

"Just remember that when I file my expense reports."

Malek followed him into the hallway, where he pointed to his left. "Bain's room is the second door down."

Joshua Bain returned to the edge of his bed, sitting down gingerly. The exertion of crossing the room to answer the door had made him light-headed, and he reached up to feel the dampness on his forehead.

"You look terrible," Jerome Mason told him as he sat down next to the small table near the bed, putting his briefcase on the floor next to his feet. He pushed back in the chair to study Joshua carefully.

"You are indeed a sight for sore eyes, sir," said Joshua slowly.

"Drop the 'sir' business. I'm a private citizen now, remember."

Joshua tried to smile, but even that simple an effort brought pain to the base of his skull. He reached out to the night stand to pick up one of the several capsules lying loose.

Watching him swallow the capsule without water, Mason commented, "I recall that the last time I saw you, the circumstances were similar."

Joshua nodded slowly, admitting to the accuracy of the

statement. "I do seem to have the knack," he proposed hoarsely, "of being around when the bombs go off."

"Which reminds me," Mason said, "how did you permit yourself to get so badly burned this time? This is what, the third time around?"

"Have you listened to the tape?"

"Not yet," and Mason glanced across the room to the recorder on the dressing table, "but Malek gave me a rough report last night." He reached down to open his briefcase, pulling out a yellow-lined tablet and a manila envelope. "We can go over the tape in a few minutes." He had a pencil and started writing something on the pad.

"I can't really say why I let it get away from me," Joshua started to explain. "I was confident of the Tel Aviv end, and I still am, excepting Brav's performance. I naturally figured Price might pull something, but there was heat on him to play it straight. After all, he makes his living by delivering."

"But Price was emotionally involved," Mason pointed out, "and that should've alerted you. He had a score to settle with you and Alan, remember."

Joshua was shaking his head slowly. The pain killer was starting to take effect. "That doesn't make any sense either. Price could've hit us at the ranch at anytime he wanted."

"That's not his style, and we both know it. How much more sweet it is to him now, Joshua. It's obvious, at least to me, that disposing of the Canaan team was an integral part of the exchange."

Joshua allowed his eyes to close again, and the cold chill started up his back again, working up across his shoulders. He shivered once, involuntarily. "We've got to find them," he heard himself saying. He opened his eyes to stare at Jerome Mason. "What do you figure their chances are?"

"Impossible to even guess at this time. Malek told me a few minutes ago that Alan wasn't found on or near the trawler." He picked up the manila envelope, tossing it to Joshua. "This came in from L.A. this morning also."

Joshua removed the single sheet of paper from the envelope. It was a copy of some kind, and he immediately recognized the letterhead stationery from Rancho Canaan. The brief note was typed and dated Sunday, October 8:

Dearest Alan:
What you are doing is too much for my conscience to
   bear. I'm returning home, where I realize I really be-

long. Please forgive me, but I'm sure you will understand in time.

The note was signed with the typewritten name of Anne Hunt.

"They must not have had the time to force her to sign it," Joshua said thoughtfully as he refolded the paper.

"It doesn't matter, really. The point is that it takes Price off the hook for the hijack responsibility. When the Jews start yelling foul, all Price has to do is hand them a copy of this note, reminding them that Anne Hunt's maiden name was Anne Delemar, alias Sheila Vardi."

"Which suggests the hijackers were Arabs."

"I'll give you ten-to-one odds, plus points."

"Okay, so we prove that Anne was kidnapped," Joshua reasoned.

"Malek agreed last night to push for a full investigation. We should get some input by this afternoon." He got up to move toward the dresser and the tape recorder. "Do you have a copy of the tape?"

"It's on the machine."

"What's the time frame?"

"From the beginning, at Corpus Christi, to the seaplane explosion."

"What about since the explosion?"

"Not much to report," Joshua reflected. "I came to yesterday morning in a hospital at Port-au-Prince." He paused for a moment, trying to renew his thoughts, and when he started again, there was a tremor in his voice. "You can't imagine how helpless I felt. It was worse than a nightmare."

"I can imagine," said Mason softly.

"There was no one to turn to," Joshua went on, struggling to control himself. "Price wasn't available, and I had no way to reach him. Brav and Karen Laswell were both dead. I couldn't get Anne on the phone at the ranch. And, of course, Alan was gone." He had to stop because of the constriction in his throat.

"How did you get to the hospital?" Mason asked after a respectful wait.

Joshua cleared his throat. "Price must have arranged it via one of his men, a Nick Villon. I met Villon at Corpus Christi, so Price knew I would recognize the name. They even put up the money to cover the expenses."

"That doesn't strike you as strange?"

"Not at all. It shows that Price was probably ripped off along with the rest of us. Villon was obviously Karen's contact at the seaplane dock, so he was there to pull me out of the water."

"So Price now wants you alive?"

"From what I can gather, he's out the money, and, possibly, the plutonium as well." He paused then, realizing he was feeling better. "Although I have to admit the last guess is the purest of conjecture. There is, however, one fact out of Port-au-Prince, and that is I was followed from there to here."

"One of Price's men," Mason theorized.

"No doubt, and, as soon as I'm well enough, I'm going to nail him."

"Forget it," Mason told him. "The odds are the tail has no idea where Price is. At best, you could only force his contact out of him." He reached down to trip the rocker switch starting the tape recorder.

Joshua had made the tape earlier in the morning, and he heard in the recording the strain and weakness that he could not otherwise recall; it was like another person speaking, distant and removed. He leaned back on the bed to rest while he waited, his thoughts confused and running together.

When the tape finished running, Jerome Mason got up to shut off the recorder. He had compiled over three full pages of notes on his legal-sized pad. "Do you have anything to add to the tape?"

"There's something about the gun that Karen gave me on the plane," Joshua said reflectively. "She said it was mine, and I thought it strange at the time that she would have the gun. You know, like Brav had commandeered the aircraft, was really forcing her to fly it, so why had he allowed her access to my weapon?"

"But you said on the tape that they were in cahoots to divert the money."

"So that makes sense," Joshua admitted, "but after we landed, and she was shot, I tried to cover myself with the same gun. I remember now firing twice quickly. No, once first, then twice quickly for insurance, before turning back into the cockpit, figuring I had at least a couple shots left. There was a burst of automatic fire, then I decided to try for the emergency hatch. I turned to cover myself again, but there was only one round left. I remember, because I thought at that moment that I had really bought it."

"Maybe the gun jammed."

"No, it was a revolver, and when the chamber turned it was hitting on empty." He took a deep breath, before going on, and there was the first note of enthusiasm in his voice. "That's it; that's got to be it!"

Jerome Mason waited, pleased to see that Joshua was finally starting to come around.

"Brav had me cold turkey," Joshua went on. "When he opened the cargo door, the wind almost got him, but he pulled out of it. He was strong as a bull. Then, for no apparent reason, he just started out the door. I was stunned. It was like a miracle." He snapped the fingers on his right hand. "Don't you see. Karen shot him. She had to, because that accounts for the missing round."

"How come you didn't hear it?"

"The revolver had a silencer on it. Plus, there was the wind noise."

"That makes only five, by your count."

"That's right. I loaded my revolver with only five rounds, leaving the hammer chamber open for safety, a habit I picked up in the service."

"So what does that tell us?"

Joshua felt himself starting to slip into a slouch again. "Not a whole lot, I guess, but it at least shows that she probably saved my life." He paused again, trying to remember. "There's something else about her that seems to be bugging me, but I can't put my finger on it."

"You need more time to sort it out," said Mason, and he made a final note on his pad before returning it to his briefcase. "I'll be back in a couple hours, which will give you the chance to get some more rest."

"I'll be able to travel by tomorrow morning."

"Plan on Kingston first," Mason suggested. "You can meet with the authorities and whoever Tel Aviv is sending over to identify their people. All we've got to go on now is that trawler and her crew."

"What about Price's villa?"

"You know where it is?"

"I can find it. Alan and Sharon Iser were on the inspection team, and they were moved by power launch both to and from the villa from Port-au-Prince. On Monday, before we took off, Alan briefed me on the timing and his estimate of the distance. He also had free run of the estate and gave me a good description of it."

"Price has got to be long gone."

"But the plan probably came out of there."

"It's worth pumping in," Mason noted after a moment's thought.

"And that reminds me of another reason why it got away from me," Joshua said under his breath. "When I went to refuel the plane on Monday morning, the pumper on the dock was low on aviation fuel, and the operator wasn't going to give me any because I wasn't a regular customer."

Mason laughed. "The Arab nemesis again."

"Yeah, but I got the charter pilot on the phone, and he came down to the dock and was able to get us a hundred gallons. Alan gave me the report on the villa while we were waiting." A small finger of pain probed at the base of his skull, and he tried to relax before going on. "My calculations indicated the fuel load was more than adequate. But, I made a mistake, the most basic kind of error, because I neglected to remember that low-level flying consumes as much as twenty percent more fuel. So, as it turned out, when I got control of the plane again on the way back I couldn't return to the trawler."

"It's a good thing you couldn't," Mason suggested. "You know that the hijackers would've killed you for sure. In fact, I would have to say your negligence, if that's what you want to call it, will probably help more than hurt Alan Hunt in the long run."

Joshua didn't respond, choosing instead to watch the older man closely, until he felt the weight of his eyelids reminding him of his weakness and present vulnerability. "Thank God you're here," was all he could say.

Jerome Mason removed his dark glasses from his shirt pocket, along with a small white card, which he handed to Joshua. "I have my own contact with the Justice Department, as you know, and I'll operate out of my home for the time being. You can reach me at the phone number at the top of this card. If I'm not in, there's an answering service which can find me twenty-four hours a day. Jordan is our code word, naturally."

Joshua took the card, studied it briefly before placing it on the night stand.

"How're you fixed for cash?" the older man asked him.

"I've got the better part of fifty grand."

"I hope you're prepared to blow it all."

"I just hope it's enough. If it isn't, then I'll borrow on the ranch."

"Malek says you've sent a copy of the tape to someone."

Joshua looked aside, before telling him, "That has nothing to do with you, sir."

"Okay, and I appreciate your confidence, but I wanted to hear you say it."

"I did it on impulse. The season's about to start at the ranch, so as soon as I got here I contacted our attorney in Riverside to take over until . . ." and he paused, sensing his feeling of helplessness, "until whatever."

Jerome Mason came to his feet. "That's a good sign, Joshua."

"I sent him a letter of authorization with a money order," Joshua went on, "and I went ahead and included a copy of the tape."

"So I'll see you in two hours," Mason told him, walking out of the room without waiting for a reply.

Joshua Bain sat still on the edge of the bed for several seconds, staring at the closed door. His mind tumbled again. He sensed he was still in the pit, despite Mason's apparent optimism, and he knew he had a long way to pull before he would glimpse daylight again.

In the elevator, Jerome Mason concluded to himself that the Jordan angles were definitely tetrahedral. He had already identified at least two obvious double crosses, with a probable third, which meant the count could even go higher. It was a Calvin Price script, unquestionably. As the elevator bottomed on the lobby floor, he was aware that he had misled Joshua into believing that the government was the obligated reason for his being there. Jerome Mason knew better but would have been embarrassed to admit that he was involved because he was a willing volunteer.

He had called Les Stalmeyer at the crack of dawn to decline the special investigator appointment. While he would lose the active duty pay, he still had managed to wrangle expense money, which could be funded out of any one of several contingency accounts. The loss of pay was a minor trade-off, because this way there would be no skeptical judges or warrants, no recalcitrant prosecuting attorneys. No indictments or delays, and, not a single oversight committee on the agenda. He pushed through the elevator door with a decided bounce to his step.

At the desk, he asked the clerk for a piece of hotel stationery and an envelope. Quite casually then and with a flourish he wrote out the message, "Praise the Lord," putting the paper inside the envelope, which he addressed to "Joshua Bain." Handing the envelope to the clerk, he turned and moved quickly to the nearby magazine stand, where he pretended to shop the racks. There were about a dozen people in the lobby, but it took only a few seconds for him to spot the man who was showing a special interest in the clerk's move to place the envelope in the key box for Joshua Bain's room. In one glance, Jerome Mason catalogued the man's description. Finished with that brief chore, he strode out the front entrance with the same show of energy, thinking that their first ploy had been a success, and, hopefully, a harbinger of things to come.

The small boat reduced power as it entered the shallows. The windows on the wheelhouse were so filthy that Hafiz Barca had to step out to the deck in order to make out the shoreline. He spotted the wooden pier then, estimating it to be about two hundred yards away. There was the sound of a surging engine behind him, and he turned to see that the Cuban patrol boat was on its way back to the open sea, its red and blue ensign snapping a kind of farewell salute in its fantail slipstream. The sudden departure of their escort vessel suggested to Barca that the rendezvous was set and they were at the right place, so he stepped back into the cramped wheelhouse, gesturing to the man at the wheel to steer toward the pier.

He immediately returned to the deck to move aft, thinking it was all so absurd. They could've just as easily disembarked at Havana, but apparently Castro's security people were given to both melodrama and excessive caution, so that now they would be coming ashore at some isolated point probably miles away from the nearest city.

Aft of the wheelhouse, he stooped down to push aside the canvas flap on the makeshift tent that had sheltered them during the nearly day and a half it had taken to cross the lower Gulf from Tampico. While it was only midmorning, the heat had already started to build, and Barca folded the canvas flap back to give him both light and ventilation. Anne Hunt was still in her place, huddled into a burrow of rotting fishing net. Barca took a deep breath, almost gagging on the stench. His captive had been kept drugged for the crossing, and she had thrown up many times. Holding his breath, Barca leaned down to check the pupils of her eyes. He backed out then, checking his watch. It had been several hours since her last injection, and he figured she should be coming around in a few more minutes. As he started forward to oversee the landing, he decided that it would not be necessary to keep her drugged, at least for the time being, since they were about to enter safe ground.

Anne Hunt had been measuring her own breathing, with no other purpose than to verify that she was still alive. She had pretended unconsciousness while someone checked her eyes. Experimentally then, she began to move certain parts of her body slowly and deliberately. After a few seconds, she was able to assume she was not injured. A familiar and painful wave of nausea rolled over her again, and she gagged once before retching uncontrollably. Nothing came up, only the acid of her empty stomach, and she swallowed the bile while trying to relax her stomach muscles. She desperately tried to sort out her predicament, about which she knew practically nothing. She could recall enough to guess they were still on the same fishing boat they had boarded at Tampico. She had not been drugged during the embarkation; probably, she now guessed, because it had been easier and safer to move her on her own two feet.

The engine of the boat had now slowed to an idle and she flinched as the boat bumped something before coming to a standstill. With its wind draft gone, the diesel exhaust settled over the deck, and enough of the rich greasy fumes reached her to start her retching again. The air seemed to clear after a few seconds, and she realized that the engine had been turned off. Noticing the flap to the tent was open, she tentatively lifted her head to squint through the angular opening. She blinked several times against the indirect light before she could make out the outline of a wooden pier running about two feet higher than the rail of the boat. The image of a man came into view, and she shrank away. She had seen enough of the man's profile to recognize the one who had called himself Barca.

Exhausted with the brief effort, she let her head drop back into place. There was the guarded sound of a hushed conversation coming from the nearby pier. She realized that her life was in the process of turning full circle. The bits and pieces of what was happening started to flow across her clearing mind. She had been drugged for a long time, at least one or two days now, not to the complete point of unconsciousness but only enough to keep her immobilized, she presumed, to prevent her from trying to escape. So that she had been able to pick out the familiar signs filtering through the curtain of mist drawn across her mind, the dim yet recognizable trappings of being on the run again.

She suspected a link with the code name Jordan.

The image of Alan crossed her mind.

She felt her eyes starting to burn.

Don't let them see you cry.

She reached up to wipe her eyes, noticing then the steel handcuffs.

Oh, my God, she implored as she felt herself starting to shiver, another sign that she was starting to withdraw. After the spasm passed, she formed the image of Alan again in her mind, and she felt herself starting to breath more evenly. The scene in her mind now shifted to the higher ground above Rancho Canaan, and the warm spring rain coming down, and his breath close on her cheek. And he told her that the spring rain was like Jesus, who came to renew life, so that which was dead might live. And, that which lives, loves . . .

That which lives . . . loves.

The words began to repeat themselves, over and over, until they became a refrain of hope, a point of focus for her rising determination. She pushed herself to her right elbow, struggling clumsily in the web of fish net.

"Go slowly." The voice was calm and gentle.

"Do you remember me?" Hafiz Barca asked, squatting down near the canvas opening, his elbows on his knees. The morning sun was on his face, and he was smiling.

Anne tried to tell him yes, but she began coughing instead.

"My name is Hafiz," he said.

She nodded once weakly, indicating that she remembered.

"We must leave now," he continued, as he reached out with his right hand to help her. "We are the guests of the Cuban government," he added, "and in case you've forgotten, I must warn you not to try to escape." He took her wrists to pull her to a sitting position, waiting then as if to give her a chance to catch her senses.

"I am dirty," she said hoarsely.

He laughed, sounding like a man for whom things were obviously going well. "You are in fine shape," he proposed after a moment, "if all you need is a bath to make things right," and he leaned forward to take her elbows.

She fell forward against him, her hands crossed over her stomach. She felt an object against her wrist, and it took only a fraction of a second for her to realize it was a shoulder holster. The hard butt of the revolver pressed into her right breast. She tried to reach it with her right hand but couldn't because of the restraining handcuffs. He turned her sideways to lift her up bodily. She realized now was not the right time anyway. She was much too weak. She would have to wait, and use the time to get to know Hafiz Barca, who to this point showed signs of carelessness.

Anne Hunt, formerly Anne Delemar, knew she had just made a classic mistake—that of underestimating the enemy.

She was out of practice.

The discipline was in need of repair.

Part Two

THE CHASE

Behold, the days come, saith the Lord, that I will make a new covenant with the house of Israel, and with the house of Judah: not according to the covenant that I made with their fathers in the day that I took them by the hand to bring them out of the land of Egypt; which my covenant they brake, although I was an husband unto them, saith the Lord:

But this shall be the covenant that I will make with the house of Israel; After those days, saith the Lord, I will put my law in their inward parts, and write it in their hearts; and will be their God, and they shall be my people.

And they shall teach no more every man his neighbor, and every man his brother, saying, Know the Lord: for they shall all know me, from the least of them unto the greatest of them, saith the Lord: for I will forgive their iniquity, and I will remember their sin no more.

—Jeremiah, chapter 31

Chapter nine

As his taxi cleared the outskirts of Kingston into the commercial part of the city, Joshua was reminded of an operetta he had seen at an outdoor theater when he was young. The gingerbread houses along the neat and clean streets were giving way to the buildings of the main part of the city, and everywhere, still, the madness of color. The colonial fronts, the traffic police in starched colonian uniforms, and the people, overwhelmingly black, dressed in prints and paisleys, against the contrast of the British influence in the more somber architecture. He was en route from Norman Manley airport, having ordered his taxi to hurry to the address of the government building containing the office of the coroner. To make an already dreary situation worse, the weather was turning bad with heavy rain showers predicted for most of the day.

He still had very little to be encouraged about. Before he had left Miami, Jerome Mason had received the report that on the morning Anne disappeared, a small plane had been seen taking off from the ranch's private strip by Antonio Flores, their resident foreman. Flores was able to get enough of a partial on the plane's ID markings to enable the bureau to identify its registration. The plane was next reported on Tuesday by the Mexican authorities, who had found it abandoned at an oil field landing strip near Tampico. Its pilot had been found shot to death. Among the evidence found on the plane was a CO_2 air rifle and a supply of tranquilizer darts. Bureau agents also confirmed that the rear kitchen door to the main ranch building had been forced. By yesterday, they had checked the motel in Palm Desert where the pilot and a man seen associating with him had stayed for several days.

He once again reminded himself that it was entirely his fault. The two people he loved most, if they were still alive, were in the worst difficulty imaginable—all because of him. The cab stopped at the curb and he climbed out.

Inside the colonial-faced building, he was directed to the

coroner's office, where he was promptly ushered into the office of the man in charge. The coroner was a tall black man with a full afro haircut. Joshua quickly introduced himself.

"You were expected, Mister Bain," the coroner said with an accent suggesting he might have been educated at Oxford. "Will you please follow me."

Joshua was pleased to see that Jerome Mason had put the word out. They dropped down a short staircase to the morgue. Joshua was not prepared for the stark sterility of the large room flanked on both sides by the double rows of tell-tale rectangular doors.

"This is Mister Sheldon," the coroner stated flatly.

Joshua turned to his right. David Sheldon had been behind the tiled block wall beside the door. He now stepped forward, his right hand extended. Taking it, Joshua saw that the Israeli was about his height and similar in build. His hair was cut short in a military way, over a face that appeared at first glance to be more squarish than round because of his full moustache. After a firm exchange, Joshua said soberly, "My name is Joshua Bain."

"A pleasure to meet you, Mister Bain," said Sheldon, and he didn't try to hide his own appraisal of Joshua either.

"May we begin, gentlemen?" the coroner asked.

"You may proceed," said Sheldon.

The sheet came back on the first body, and Joshua recognized the young Israeli leader of team alpha. The face was relaxed and intact, but there were exit wounds showing on his arms and chest. It was one thing to talk about death, to plan it or even prepare for it, but it was something else to meet it face to face.

"His name is Henry Koman," Sheldon told the coroner, reaching up to cover his mouth.

They worked down the next three, and in each instance Sheldon reported the names in the same somber monotone: Hirsh Joseph, Nathan Hadar, and Dov Mellman. He closed the last metal door himself, staring vacantly down the length of the long room. "Doctor Mellman was the courier," he added quietly, more to himself and almost as an afterthought.

"He was a doctor?" said Joshua without thinking.

"Doctor Mellman was head of the foreign language department at the University of Tel Aviv," Sheldon explained. "He was a noted authority on Indo-European languages, with many books published on the subject. You see, he was especially valuable to act as a courier to many parts of the world since he spoke all the Romance languages fluently."

"An incredibly tragic waste," Joshua stated.

"Yes, it is," Sheldon agreed. "For all of them."

The tall coroner broke the following silence, "You gentlemen are now requested to meet with Inspector Bradford, who is waiting in the foyer."

"May I see the first one again?" Sheldon asked quietly.

"Of course, sir," said the coroner, and he moved to remove the body from its enclosure.

Sheldon lifted the edge of the sheet to expose Koman's right side. "Look at this," he hissed under his breath, and he lifted the lifeless right hand.

Joshua moved closer to see that the little finger had been removed. He had to clear his throat before commenting, "You mean it was cut off?"

Sheldon didn't answer, turning instead to stalk away toward the exit.

"What about disposition?" the coroner asked after him.

Sheldon turned to speak over his shoulder. "There will be a member of the Israeli diplomatic service here before the day is out to claim the remains."

Joshua followed behind the swiftly striding Israeli until they reached the building's lobby, where Sheldon finally pulled up to stare out the double glass entry doors.

"Why are you so angry about the finger?" Joshua asked him slowly. "It seems to me it could've been shot off."

Sheldon shook his head resolutely. "It was a clean cut, as usual," and he turned to look squarely at Joshua. "It is the trademark of the one who calls himself Kasim."

"That's rather bizarre," Joshua commented.

"Not really. You see, it's not altogether because he's simply a sadist. In this maniacal act, he multiplies the casualty rate tenfold." He paused a moment before adding, "Can you imagine the grief of the Koman family burying their loved one, for example, who is not complete, especially knowing that the missing part is in the hands of a despised enemy?"

Joshua considered the statement before suggesting, "If that's true, then you're letting this nut get to you. He's dealing the hand, and you're picking up the cards and playing them."

"Would you feel the same way, Joshua Bain, if the little finger belonged to Alan Hunt?" he retorted quickly.

Joshua was unable to answer, totally unprepared by the remark. His first thought was to question how this man even knew of Alan Hunt. And he was about to ask that question when they were confronted by another tall black man.

"I am Chief Inspector Bradford," the man was saying. Unlike the coroner, his hair was moderately shorter, and he was dressed in a brown seersucker suit. "Which of you gentlemen is Mister Bain?" he added in the same polite tone.

Joshua introduced himself first, then Sheldon.

"I have been instructed to tell you, Mister Bain," the inspector went on, "that the Jamaican government will cooperate to any reasonable extent in your investigation."

Joshua was at a loss for words.

"I'm surprised," said Sheldon, "that no members of the press are present."

"That was resolved quite handily," said Bradford proudly. "We simply released the information that the trawler had been involved in a narcotics exchange that apparently went awry," and he lifted his hands in a definitive gesture. "The local press no longer shows an interest in such common events."

"Even if the casualties were four Israeli nationals?" Sheldon questioned.

"That's our little secret, at least for the time being. I figure, at best, that you have twenty-four hours before that leaks out."

"That's time enough," Sheldon told him.

"I'm at your disposal, gentlemen," Bradford told them.

"We'd like to see the trawler," Sheldon said.

"Did the crew positively identify the hijackers?" Joshua asked.

"Oh, yes," said Bradford. "The leader was Kasim, and he openly identified himself and his association with the PFLP."

"Does the captain know where Kasim is going?" Sheldon asked.

"Oh, no," answered Bradford, smiling broadly. "The only other information divulged was that Kasim wanted the world to know that he had spared the crew for humanitarian reasons."

David Sheldon grunted disgustedly.

"Shouldn't we talk to them, anyway?" Joshua suggested.

"We'll pass on them for the moment," Sheldon answered quickly.

"So to the harbor then," said Chief Inspector Bradford. "There is a car at the curb."

Twenty minutes later, Joshua Bain stood on a dock looking down at the Portuguese trawler, the *Arosa*. The rain now was a fine mist, not unlike the weather at the lagoon on Monday night, and the dark gray cloud cover gave to the ship a certain forlorn look, one which he had not anticipated.

"I'll leave you now," said Inspector Bradford, and he handed Joshua a business card. "You can reach me at this number anytime. In the meantime, I've dispatched a jeep and a driver for your convenience."

"I'm sure," said Sheldon, "that we'd like to visit both the abandoned mine and the site where the trawler was beached."

"Your driver is one of my assistants. He has equipment in the vehicle which you may need in the back country."

"You're certain they didn't switch ships?" Joshua asked him.

"As positive as we can be, Mister Bain. As I told you in the car, they moved inland to the abandoned bauxite mine, where they used an aircraft to make good their escape from the island. The physical evidence is available for you to investigate yourself."

As if satisfied that the following brief silence had marked the end of their questions, Chief Inspector Bradford turned to walk away along the dock, hunched over and using his right hand to shield his eyes against the fine mist.

The two men swung over the wooden rail to drop to the higher and forward deck of the small trawler. Joshua worked his way slowly aft, carefully inspecting the ship. At amidships, he noticed minor damage to the port side of the bridge structure, a single string of bullet holes apparently inflicted by an automatic weapon. Two searchlights were clamped with temporary fittings to the same rail. He lined up the bullet holes in the wheelhouse, determining that the single stream of automatic fire had knocked out one of the searchlights.

Sheldon, who had been below, came up beside him.

"Somebody got off one burst," Joshua told him. "Whoever it was made it good, because he got at least one of the lights."

"What can you tell me about it?" Sheldon asked as he took one step to the rail to stare down at the quiet harbor water.

"Not a whole lot, I guess. The transfer craft was about a twenty-eight to thirty-footer. A cabin cruiser with a moderate bridge, canvas covered."

"Koman was at the wheel?"

"Yes."

"That explains why he got it in the back, because they had to take him out first."

"The cargo was battened down on the open deck aft," Joshua continued, turning away then to look out across the harbor. "And that's about it. When they came in, two of Koman's men were on the fantail, so I guess they took up the same position when they left. The courier was probably below to get out of the weather."

"The weather was bad?"

"The rain was starting to come down."

Sheldon took a deep breath, shaking his head sadly. "So that explains it," he said slowly. "I couldn't figure why there was no grenade damage."

"I don't understand," said Joshua after a moment.

"They had on their ponchos, didn't they?"

"I suppose they did. After all, it was raining."

"So they kept dry, and they died," and he turned to look at Joshua, the brown in his eyes a shade darker. "Would you rather be wet or dead?"

Joshua looked away, taking the question as a rhetorical one.

"I found nothing below," Sheldon told him.

"So why don't we talk to the crew?"

"I can't."

"Why not?"

"Because they will recognize me. How would you like to explain that to Inspector Bradford?"

"So that's how you knew the name Alan Hunt."

"What do you mean?"

"You were on Brav's team, weren't you?"

"I figured you'd pick up on that."

"Because you want me to, right?"

"It had to come out, sooner or later," Sheldon said evenly, and he reached into his hip pocket to pull out a thin wallet.

Joshua studied the ID briefly. "What does this mean?"

"The *Agaf Modeyin* is the intelligence branch of the Israel Defense Forces, or IDF. You may have heard *Agaf Modeyin* referred to as *Aman*, the short version."

"I figured you to be a member of the Mossad."

"I am presently working under Ha Mossad. Unlike in your country, our various intelligences branches cooperate with each other."

Joshua returned the ID. "So you must've been in charge, right, Major?"

"Not exactly. It was a Mossad mission, and Brav was actually in charge, at least to the extent that I had to obey his orders. My authority was over the field unit."

"So what about now?"

"We're going to hunt down Kasim."

"What can you tell me about him?"

"There's not a whole lot to know. Kasim is really a small-time butcher with ambitions. He splintered off with his own small group of followers after his idol Fawd Al-Shaer was killed. He stays buried underground constantly, surfacing only for an occasional operation."

"If he broke with the PFLP, where does he get his support?"

"He's still tolerated by the PFLP, because they can't disown him entirely without risking the loss of their fringe support. Our best estimate is that he's backed by Iraqi intelligence, which uses renegades like Kasim to spy on the Syrians in Lebanon. Regardless, we've got to get him quickly."

Joshua assumed the collective "we" included himself, but he spoke up to make sure. "You don't mind my tagging along?"

Major Sheldon looked away, before explaining, "I'm under orders to cooperate with you, despite my strong objections."

Joshua noted that the major was no longer resorting to subterfuge.

"You are at best a bumbling amateur," Sheldon added, "and I want you to know how I feel right from the beginning."

Joshua held his temper, because there was a certain element of truth in what the major was saying. Sheldon was also a professional backed up by an organization with a proven record of tracking down fugitives.

"I'll grant you the advantage, for the moment," he said slowly. "And I'm also willing to go along with you giving the orders—at least for the time being."

"That's charitable of you."

Joshua could no longer contain himself. "You've schooled yourself well in the art of being an idiot, Major."

Sheldon turned away from the rail to stand facing Joshua with his legs apart, one foot behind the other.

Joshua moved more casually away from the rail, but inside

he was also tensed and ready. "Unless your G-2 is the world's worst," he said carefully, "you should know that the two people I care the most for in this world are out there, probably with the same sadist who slaughtered your people. And, if you can't come to grips with that fact, then you can take a walk, Major, and the sooner the better."

Sheldon dropped his eyes down to the deck between them. "I'm sorry," he said after a moment. "And I apologize." He stuck out his hand. "If it's all right with you, I suggest we jointly make the decisions."

Joshua took his hand, sealing the agreement.

Finished on the trawler, they lifted themselves to the pier. Joshua looked up to the top of the dock to see a military jeep parked with a driver behind the wheel. "What about the abandoned mine?" he asked as they moved out quickly along the pier.

Sheldon glanced up to the overcast sky. "Let's hit it next, since we've got enough daylight left."

"Did you get my report?" Joshua asked.

"Our Washington resident gave me a one-page transcript this morning when I passed through. I also talked to your friend, Jerome Mason, on the phone, which, by the way, was the second time I heard the name of Alan Hunt."

"Do you agree with my suspicions about Brav?"

"Very definitely. There's no question that he was working with Karen Laswell to steal the money. After my first meeting with him, I warned the home office that Brav could become unstable for reasons other than his heavy drinking. He had become extremely cynical, and I felt he had lost confidence in his country. While Brav didn't know it, I had orders to not turn the money over to him once we got aboard the *Bushnell*."

"You mean he was finished?"

"More than likely after Jordan, but he had too important a role already established to let him go any earlier. One thing you don't know is that Brav had been put in charge of the search for the Armatrex plutonium."

Joshua was surprised. "You mean you've been after it all along?"

Sheldon smiled as he looked aside at Joshua. "Israel never closed the book on Rahab. And Brav has been chasing the plutonium ever since."

"Brav told me that you were going to return the plutonium to the United States. That was why you took back the money, wasn't it?"

"It was integral to the plan. After all, you couldn't expect us to pay for something that expensive and just give it away."

"Of course not," Joshua chuckled.

Sheldon gestured toward the nearby jeep. "We better head for the mine. You can give me the details of your end while we're en route. And, from here on, bear in mind that we must hurry. Price's involvement with the plutonium makes it doubly important that we find Kasim quickly."

"So let's get moving," Joshua said. Climbing into the rear of the vehicle, he felt his spirits rise. The quiet confidence of one Major David Sheldon appeared to be contagious.

Alan Hunt estimated that the temperature in the cargo compartment of the DC-3 had climbed to over 110 degrees during the few minutes since they had landed. It was midafternoon, and even in the good light all he could tell about their location was that they had put down on just another in a series of isolated and private landing strips. This time they had been left alone, except for a single guard stretching his legs outside the open doorway. Alan turned away from the small window opening to see Sharon Iser staring listlessly, her dejection again showing in her face. The Jordan containers were lashed down forward and appeared to have thus far weathered the trip without damage.

"What's your guess?" he whispered, and he coughed once. For three days they had not been allowed any water, except to drink. The skin around his mouth was chapped and irritated, and it hurt to talk even in a whisper.

Sharon looked at him through the glaze across her eyes. Like him, she was chained to the aluminum support rail of her canvas seat against the hull of the fuselage.

"Come on," he implored. "Look outside at the terrain. It's sandy and flat. There're some low hills three to four miles out. I saw tents when we came in."

She turned her head to look out the nearby window.

"We're only a couple minutes from coming in off the water," he went on. "You remember, because you said it couldn't be the Suez."

"I have no idea," she said hoarsely, and she turned her head back to stare down at her knees again.

"That's great," Alan commented, trying his best to sound enthusiastic. "Now we're going to start talking to each other, so you say the first thing that comes to your mind."

She looked up at him. "You are the most transparent man

I have ever met. You are totally without subtlety or finesse. In short, you remind me of my husband."

"Is that good or bad?"

"It is both, always has been, always will be."

"Jesus Christ, the same yesterday, today, and tomorrow."

"You are impossible."

"If a prisoner could convincingly pretend insanity, the Chiricahua Apache would almost always release him unharmed."

"So what are you trying to say?"

"We must do two things. We first trust in the Lord, then we use our wits."

"This isn't the movies, and there's no cavalry just over the next hill."

"Of that I'm more than aware. In the movies they don't tell you how you smell after three days in the heat, or, that your ankles are twice their normal size, your gums hurt, and you're practically paralyzed from your waist to your knees. I wouldn't be surprised if my hair started falling out."

"It still could be much worse, and it probably will be."

"No doubt, but it is said that when you stop complaining, it is a sign that you no longer care about living."

"That sounds selfish."

"Which reminds me, do you know what first came to my mind a minute ago when I said to start talking?"

"What?"

"A root-beer float."

"That surprises me. I should've expected the Sermon on the Mount."

"So you condemn me because I think of my flesh before the welfare of my soul."

"I cannot judge you."

"Is that an echo of husband Dan?"

"Perhaps."

"We are both saved by the shed blood of Christ, but we are still human."

"Dan does not echo very well. You see, he has less than half a tongue."

"I'm sorry. I didn't know."

"And he carries a pocketfull of small smooth stones, so when someone begins to rave, he says nothing, which is appropriate for his condition, handing them a stone instead."

"He who is without sin, you mean."

"The stones of Dan Iser are revered by his friends."

"And his wife?"

"He says I am sanctified."

"Right now he is probably our best ally. Remember, the fervent prayer of a righteous man availeth much. Which means, of course, that our friend Kasim is really the one who's in trouble."

He saw then that she was smiling, with the perspiration running down her cheeks, and he took a deep breath as he offered up a brief and private prayer of thanks. Don't stop now, he told himself. "What about our location? We've got to make a guess now while the details are still fresh in our minds."

"All right. So we came in over water. How long did it take us to cross the water?"

"A little over thirty minutes, which means about a hundred miles or more. You're sure it couldn't have been the Suez Canal?"

"The Suez is much more narrow. Besides, Kasim would not risk flying through Egyptian air space. It's either the Red Sea or the Persian Gulf."

"We're definitely going east, remember, and we figured Africa yesterday and last night, and we haven't crossed any other water recently."

"So it has to be the Red Sea, which means we're in Saudi Arabia, or possibly South Yemen. But I can't say for sure, because my geography isn't that good."

"If we're not stopping here, where do you figure we're heading?"

"Depends on our direction when we leave. I would guess north, either by plane or boat."

"Why north?"

"Remember what I told you the night we were captured, when you asked me where we might be going?"

"You said either Lebanon or Syria."

"I still think so. With us and the cargo, he's almost got to get on his home ground as soon as he can. Which also explains why he's using the private landing fields."

"Explains what?"

"Well, the PFLP is still a threat along with its influence even among its friends."

"You mean like a scorpion in its own habitat?"

"Something like that. However, if one of his hosts actually knew what was in these containers . . . don't you see?"

"They might confiscate it?"

"What do you think?"

"I don't like the possibility. Do you realize that if the plutonium goes, so does Kasim's need for us?"

"I know, which is why I bring it up now," she said softly, and she held her hand up for quiet.

Alan could also hear the voices coming from outside the plane, but the Arabic was just gibberish to him. After a few seconds, there was a lull, and he whispered, "What's happening?"

"I'm not sure, but it's an argument." She held up her hand again.

Alan could now easily hear Kasim, who appeared to be yelling angrily at someone. The conversation ended abruptly when a vehicle started up. As it pulled into gear to roar away from the plane, Alan could tell by its sound that it was probably a jeep. There was a following silence, and he glanced at Sharon, who was now frowning and shaking her head.

"What do you make of it?" he whispered.

"Not much, except that Kasim was refusing to allow whoever it was to come aboard the plane."

The implications of Kasim's apparent problem were becoming evident to Alan when he heard someone climbing up the metal ladder to the side doorway.

Kasim entered the plane first, followed by one of his men. He stalked past Alan to pull up in front of Sharon. It was hard for Alan to see his face because of his dark glasses and the folds of his headscarf.

"We are being delayed for several hours," Kasim said brusquely. "The local military commander is an idiot who refuses to allow us to proceed without the approval of his superiors." He gestured toward the cargo. "So I must know how the material will react to this heat. We may have to be here for some time."

"I was about to warn you about that," Sharon said evenly. "It becomes very unstable at high temperature. A hundred and twenty-five degrees is a critical point."

"What can we do? It is a hundred and eighteen degrees in the shade now."

"Get to higher ground, where it is cooler."

"That is a stupid answer for this area," Kasim snapped, "even if we could move."

"It's still cold from the flight in," she pointed out, "so you should insulate it to keep it as cool as possible."

Kasim put his hands on his hips to lean forward slightly. "And where in the middle of the desert do I get insulating material?"

"We saw tents coming in," Alan offered. "Can't you bargain for their blankets?"

"The Bedouins only want guns."

"Well, there's no shortage of those around here."

Kasim started toward the doorway.

"I must ask you again," said Alan with an insistent tone, "about my wife."

Kasim turned in the doorway, his upper torso exposed to the unrelenting afternoon sun. "I warned you not to mention that again. I remind you that you are alive only because I don't know what value you may have. However, your mouth is close to settling the issue against you," and he gestured to the man he was leaving behind to guard them, "Gag him."

"Stop it!" Sharon yelled at him.

Alan was as surprised at the outburst as was Kasim.

"You will leave him alone," Sharon commanded, "or else you will go without my cooperation. I remind you that you still have a ways to go before you can consider this material safe."

"What does this man mean to you?" Kasim asked her, his voice curious.

"We've formed a mutual defense treaty."

"Against the common enemy?"

She looked aside at the implied and intimate tone in Kasim's voice.

"You are an incredibly cruel man," Alan said.

Kasim laughed briefly as he turned to start down the metal steps. "So you continue to think about your wife, Alan Hunt," he said before he dropped from sight into the broiling afternoon heat.

The abandoned bauxite mine was guarded by uniformed soldiers of the Jamaican Defense Force, and the corporal in charge directed them without delay to the site where the suspects were presumed to have spent their time while waiting on Monday night. The ribbed hull was all that was left of the metal quonset hut, and as Joshua Bain dismounted from the jeep, he noticed the steel cables the size of his thumb spaced evenly over the metal shell of the circular roof. Sheldon paused beside him, following his line of sight.

"Hurricane protection," the Major said impassively.

It was late afternoon, and the cloud cover had been building since they left Kingston, so they moved quickly into the
hut. Turning on his flashlight, Joshua led the way to the more
sheltered middle area. He already had seen enough to guess the
hut had been a maintenance and storage shed for the nearby
cement landing strip. There were several rusty oil and fuel
drums, broken-down workbenches, and a metal rack of some
kind cocked off at an angle.

"Over here," said Sheldon, who was standing beside the
remnants of a wooden packing crate. Sheldon kicked at the
layer of dirt packed on the decaying cement floor. "Cigarette
butts," he muttered.

"Could be from the soldiers."

"Not this brand," said Sheldon under his breath. "One of
them is Turkish."

"The crate could've been used for a table," Joshua suggested, stooping down to aim his flashlight into the area between it and the nearby metal wall. The opening was littered
with debris.

Sheldon looked around before gesturing with his hand.
"Get me that small tin over there," and he reached down to
push the crate aside.

Joshua whacked the square metal can several times to
make sure it was empty before handing it to Sheldon. He stood
back then while Sheldon used a wooden stake to scrape something away from the wall.

"Candy wrappers," Sheldon said quietly. "And an empty
box for alcohol tablets." He reached down to pick up what to
Joshua looked like the fragment of a small vinyl bag. Sheldon
lifted the plastic bag to eye level, backlighting it against the
open end of the hut. "There're a few grains of rice left," he told
Joshua.

"What do you make of it?"

"Arab field rations."

Watching, Joshua felt his disappointment with the meager
findings. He followed behind as Sheldon moved to the open
end of the hut next to the parked jeep. Sheldon dumped the tin
on top of a 55-gallon drum. "Unfold the wrappers and smooth
them out," Sheldon told him, and they both went to work.

Joshua picked up the last wad of paper, unfolding it slowly
to see it was another candy wrapper. He inspected it carefully,
turning it several times in his hand before dropping it. "Nothing," he said. There was a piece of thin black heavier paper

glued to the wrapper used by the manufacturer to stiffen the package. Sheldon picked up the wrapper and began peeling it away. He studied the paper briefly before handing it to Joshua.

Joshua took the narrow black strip of paper, looking at the side that had been next to the wrapper. In between the two outside lines of glue, there was a postage-stamp-size piece of thin paper with printing on it. He turned it to the light, reading the words to himself slowly, his lips moving with the effort. When he glanced up, he saw that Major Sheldon was grinning.

"It's a piece out of the Bible!" Joshua exclaimed.

"What does it say?"

Joshua read it out loud, "*And from thence he arose, and went into the borders of Tyre and Sidon, and entered into an house, and would have no man know it.*" He paused after he finished the brief fragment, reaching up to pull on his lower lip. "It has to be out of Alan's Bible."

"He carries a Bible with him?" Sheldon asked.

"You don't understand," Joshua explained excitedly. "He has a compact copy of the New Testament that he carries around in his pocket." He took another closer look at the scrap. "This is exactly the right size."

"It might be a deliberate plant to mislead us."

"I was just thinking the same thing; however, it would take someone familiar with the Scriptures to locate such a passage. Plus, we came close to not finding it because it was so well hidden. You'd think Kasim would leave a deliberate plant in a place that would be more likely discovered."

"You could be right," Sheldon conceded. "So what does it tell us?"

Joshua studied the scrap again. "Looks like two things. First the location of Tyre and Sidon. Plus, if it means anything, that they will be hidden."

"Tyre and Sidon," Sheldon repeated to himself. "Ancient centers of Phoenicia, if my history is correct."

"What's the modern nation now occupying the seam area?"

"There are two of them, Syria and Lebanon."

"Of course. Alan's probably trying to tell us their destination."

"Makes sense, since Kasim's base of operations is in that area."

"But we don't know exactly where."

"And that's the problem. We're looking at tens of thousands of square miles, and we don't even know where to start."

Joshua looked at the scrap again, fingering it in his hand. "At least we know that he's alive."

"And Sharon Iser, hopefully."

Joshua looked out to see that darkness was not too long away. "Do you want to try the beach?"

"My only interest there would be to look for Sharon's body, but the army boys have gone over the site pretty thoroughly and couldn't find anything. It's apparent that Kasim came right off the trawler and went directly on the truck."

"What about the truck?"

"You heard the corporal. It was burned right down to the ground."

"So what now, Major?"

"We hit Price's villa, and the sooner the better. It's the only shot we've got left; otherwise, we're off looking for a needle in a sandy and rocky wasteland."

Joshua pulled out his billfold, inserting the Bible fragment for safe keeping. "It'll take a couple days to put it together."

"We move within twenty-four hours."

"You mean by ourselves? According to Alan's report, there were a half dozen guards on the villa perimeter."

"I have two people arriving at Nassau late tonight. All I have to do is route them on to Port-au-Prince."

"So you've been figuring on the villa all along."

"I'll supply the muscle," Sheldon said, "and you take care of the rest."

Joshua contemplated the offer.

"Well . . ."

"One more thing first," Joshua said, and he braced himself for what he had to say. "At our last briefing in Miami, on Sunday morning, Brav told me that he had five people involved in his back-up group. Taking out the transfer people leaves two, and I'm not counting Doctor Mellman, the courier."

"There was a bravo team," Sheldon told him. "And I was on it."

"The seaplane?"

"Yes."

Joshua wanted much more of an answer. "Were you the one with the handgun or the automatic weapon?"

"I shot the woman, if that's what you want to know."

"Short on time or not," Joshua said evenly, "you're going to have to explain that."

"What's to explain?" said Sheldon with the same indifference. "Brav's orders at the time were specific. It might be of interest that you were also included."

Joshua could only shake his head sadly. "And you just did it—on orders, that is. It seems to me that I recall a similar defense at Nuremberg—"

"I need no defense," Sheldon snapped.

"Oh, I see," Joshua went on. "So back there at the morgue you tricked me with your display of grief and sensitivity," and he grunted with a note of disgust. "And you said that Brav had become a cynic."

"All right," said Sheldon. "So it's a rotten inexplicable business. Perhaps I could've changed things by going against my orders, but I doubt it. You should know that I questioned Brav about it myself, in the case of the woman, but he insisted that it had to be done in order to guarantee the mission."

"Brav conned you, and you know it. He wanted all the money for himself, and he used you to take out his partner."

"We know that *now*," said Sheldon pointedly.

Joshua insisted, "It doesn't make any sense. With Brav out of the way, and with me still tied up, all Karen Laswell had to do was to land anyplace. She had the money and the means to get away with it all, scot-free, but she still insisted on making your connection."

Sheldon threw up his hands. "So what do we do now, Joshua?" he said impatiently. "Maybe we should appoint a blue-ribbon panel to perform a post mortem."

"No," said Joshua evenly. "We've got to get moving, because I've got to reach a phone to line up what we need to hit that villa."

At the Port-au-Prince seaplane anchorage, the salvage foreman had strung a canvas cover over the section of the dock to protect the air compressor and a a small working area from the intermittent rain. There was room under the tarp for an army cot, a small worktable with two heavy stools, along with random piles of equipment accumulated during the two-day operation. The foreman was a working manager, and he had just finished his shift, the worst of the day, since it had been dark now for nearly two hours.

Nick Villon watched with a rising sense of indifference while one of the crew removed the foreman's helmet. The single overhead light continued to dance on its line, agitated by the wind moving across the dock from the bay, and Nick realized he wanted to get into the city to see his girl. Tomorrow night would be his last chance for a long time.

With his helmet removed, the foreman was still breathing hard as he sat down awkwardly on one of the work stools.

"Any luck?" Nick asked him at once.

"Forget it," the foreman said haltingly but emphatically. "All we're doing now is stirring up the mud," and he tried to wipe the sweat from his face, but his hands were still wet, and he cursed, revealing that his temper was also short.

Nick picked up a rag from the worktable and handed it to him. "So what do we do now?"

"We knock off for the rest of the night," the foreman told him. "The metal detectors will be in from San Juan tomorrow morning, and we can get a fresh start."

"The boss isn't going to like that."

"Then he can suit up and go down himself."

"What about the crane?"

"It should've been moved out two hours ago. I made a sweep all the way out to the buoy line, and I can guarantee you that anything we find now we can pick up and carry."

Nick Villon pulled the transceiver off his belt.

"While you're at it," the foreman said, "ask him what exactly we're searching for."

"I already have, and he just tells me to keep looking."

Jonathan Malek was preparing to leave his office when his private phone rang. Checking his desk clock to see it was eight-thirty, he suspected the call was from his wife, so he picked up the receiver not knowing how he was going to explain that he was already over three hours late.

"You better get home," Jerome Mason told him.

"You tried there first," Malek guessed.

"Yeah, and Momma isn't too pleased with your oil burning."

"Goes with the job."

"I'm glad you're philosophical, because your day isn't finished yet."

Malek leaned forward in his chair to pick up a pencil.

Jerome Mason gave him a phone number, which he jotted down.

"I've arranged for some confiscated material out of Atlanta storage," Mason went on hurriedly. "For what I need, it's the closest location to Miami I could come up with."

"What kind of material?"

"Don't worry," Mason said evasively. "It's going out of the country. But, Dave Appleton needs your official release before he'll let it go."

"I'll get to it first thing in the morning—"

"No, no. You must do it right now. Dave is standing by waiting for your call. He's all ready to have the material loaded on a truck for transfer to the airport."

"You mean you're going to take it out tonight?"

"That's right; which brings me to my next request."

Malek almost laughed at the term "request."

"There will be a twin-engined Cessna arriving at Port-au-Prince early tomorrow morning with a small shipment consigned to Air Antilles," Mason told him, "and we need influence to get that cargo cleared without opening it. The crates will be on a bill of lading addressed to an antique dealer in Cap Haitien."

"I'm afraid to ask what's in the cargo."

"Antiques, of course," said Maston matter-of-factly. "Any more word from Los Angeles?"

"Have you checked with the Miami bureau office this afternoon?"

"No, I haven't, come to think of it."

"There's a courier package there for you, which has the latest from Los Angeles. Also a dossier from Interpol on Price and his operation."

"Anything else?"

"Only that Interpol now considers gardenia terminated. Since there's no peripheral or support agents involved, it can be discussed on a need-to-know basis."

"Okay, and thanks."

The line went dead.

Chapter ten

At midmorning on Friday, Jerome Mason arrived at Port-au-Prince's international jet airport via Pan American Airlines. After clearing customs, he hired an airport limousine to take him to the Air Antilles hangar, which turned out to be a rundown structure on the opposite side of the airport. As arranged, the Cessna charter had already arrived and was parked in the hangar ostensibly to get it out of the bad weather.

The charter pilot informed him that the plane's cargo had cleared customs following a cursory inspection.

After checking over the cargo, Mason returned to the open door of the hangar while he waited. The wind pushing the rain was gusting and uneven; and as a squall line rolled across the airfield, he watched the water arriving in sheets, rolling in like giant swells on an angry sea. Despite the rain, it was still hot, and he was thinking that it wouldn't be long before he would be stewed alive in his plastic raincoat. His eyeballs ached, and he needed a shave. A short nap on the plane was the only sleep he'd had in the past thirty-six hours. He was standing still, but inside he was still running at sixty miles per hour.

Mason had no word from Joshua, nor from the two Israelis supposedly en route from Nassau. He was wondering again what had happened to their hurry-up program when he spotted a black limousine moving along the apron toward him.

The limo moved in to park under the protection of the hangar. The two passengers got out on his side. Mason was mildly surprised that one of them was a woman.

The man walking toward Mason was about his size, of medium height, but heavier across his chest. His gait was crisp, almost military, with his arms moving rhythmically.

Mason stepped forward to identify himself.

Taking his hand, the man reached up to his throat with his left hand, and when he spoke the words were paced as if on a computer recording, "My name is Daniel Iser."

It took a second for Mason to realize that the voice was coming from a speaker, that the man was talking to him through a special electronic voice transmitter. "Welcome aboard," Mason finally told him.

"Don't be embarrassed," Iser told him frankly, and there was a positive, almost cheery look in his dark brown eyes. His face was handsomely full, under a close crop of the waviest dark brown hair Mason had ever seen. Iser made a quarter turn to his left, introducing the young woman who had come forward to stand next to his elbow. "This is Shira Elazar."

"Pleased to meet you," said Mason, gripping her hand firmly. "Is it Miss or—"

"Please call me Shira," she told him. Her voice was an octave lower than he had expected, which seemed appropriate, he thought, for she seemed as businesslike in her ways as she was in her appearance. Her hair was cut short, so that most of her ears showed. She wore no makeup that he could see. She was taller than the average and slender, yet filling out her military styled khaki shirt and pants in a way causing him to stare at her for a moment. "Well, then," he offered, "I presume you are from Nassau."

"That is correct," said Dan Iser.

Jerome Mason was wondering what Joshua Bain might think of the reinforcements; a young woman who could probably qualify for a beauty contest and a man who was practically a mute. Either Tel Aviv was desperate for help or they had elected to use operation Jordan as an experimental exercise for diversified and nonstandard personnel.

"Have you had contact with David Sheldon?" the electronic voice asked.

"Yes, I have," Mason confirmed, and then it began to dawn on him. "Are you related to the Sharon Iser involved here before?"

"I am her husband."

Jerome Mason was grateful that the pilot had come forward, advising him that he was going mainside with the limousine. Using the time to think, Mason followed him back to the car, handing him a fifty-dollar tip before he climbed in beside the driver. The rain had slackened, and as Mason turned he heard the sound of a second vehicle stopping in front of the hangar. It was a taxi, and he spotted Joshua Bain getting out, followed by another man who he presumed was David Sheldon.

The two cars pulled away one behind the other, and Mason came out in the open to meet Joshua before he could get into the hangar. Joshua introduced him to Major David Sheldon. Since they had already talked to each other on the phone, the two men merely exchanged brief amenities before Sheldon moved on quickly into the hangar.

Joshua started to follow, but Mason pulled him aside to the cover of the nearby hangar wall. The last of the squall was down to a fine drizzle.

"Did you get everything?" Joshua asked him, looking curiously around the corner of the door opening.

"We've got enough arms and explosives to lay siege to Port-au-Prince," Mason told him in a guarded whisper. "But wait'll you see who we've got for help."

They both turned into the hangar door. "One's a woman,"

Mason went on hurriedly, "and the other one's the right sex, but he has to talk with a voice box. And, to top that off, he's Sharon Iser's husband."

Mason watched Joshua carefully while he was introduced to Shira Elazar and Daniel Iser. Joshua was cordial and otherwise normal while he chatted with the two Israelis. Sheldon then suggested they all move to the plane for a briefing. Lagging behind, Mason signalled privately to Joshua, who fell back to join him.

"What do you think?" Mason asked worriedly.

"Don't sweat it," said Joshua confidently. "Sheldon gave me the word coming in. Shira Elazar is both a communications and explosives expert. She's already been on several missions, all of which, by the way, have been successful. Daniel Iser is no less experienced and obviously is in a highly motivated position. He's had front-line infantry experience in two wars and holds a commission in the IDF reserves on a special waiver for his handicap. He also holds an award for valor under combat conditions."

"Why didn't you tell me?"

"You didn't give me the chance."

Joshua helped him up the short ladder leading to the Cessna cargo compartment. Jerome Mason was feeling better as he scaled up the narrow incline of the cabin. Major Sheldon and the two other Israelis had already grouped themselves forward. As he and Joshua joined them, Sheldon went right to work. "The reason we were late," he explained, "was because we couldn't find a helicopter large enough to accommodate us all."

A setback already, Mason thought.

"So we've got two choices," Sheldon continued. "We either use a boat or go in on Price's private strip with a conventional aircraft."

"Which way gives us the best advantage?" Shira asked.

"We're at a disadvantage with a conventional plane," Joshua reported. "Even by coming in low without a one-eighty, we'll be vulnerable for several minutes just getting on the ground. One man with an automatic weapon could chop us up before we could even get stopped. Plus, we would probably alert them because we still don't know exactly where the villa is located, which means we'll have to overfly the area first just to find it."

"Time is killing us," Sheldon complained.

"The explanation is simple," Dan Iser told them, and Mason figured that the man had no choice but to be so direct, since he didn't have the normal voice inflections to assist him.

"We rent a light plane," Iser went on to explain, "to both locate the villa and reconnoiter the area. At the same time, the main party will advance to the area by boat."

"An excellent idea," Sheldon observed thoughtfully. His briefcase was open on the wooden crate before him. He opened a map of the area where Price's villa was known to be located. "According to Alan Hunt's estimate, the villa is about here," and he pointed to a location west of Port-au-Prince along the coastline. "We know there's a cove with a private dock, as well as an airstrip able to handle an aircraft of the Lear jet class. There's also a radio antenna approximately one hundred feet tall. The house layout and the immediate grounds are distinctive in both size and shape. So, spotting it from the air will be easy," and he looked to Joshua. "Could you do it while flying the plane?"

"No problem."

"Okay," Sheldon went on reflectively. "I can handle the boat. Shira, you and Dan work out a ruse plan, perhaps as husband and wife."

"I'll arrange for the plane," Joshua said.

"You take care of the boat," Sheldon said to Dan Iser. "We'll need a minimum twenty-two footer."

Mason pulled himself erect. "What can I do?" he asked Sheldon.

"You get on the phone," Sheldon told him, "and line up a car for Dan. In fact, get a couple sedans. After that, locate a sportfishing rental at the docks, and don't forget to offer a bonus payment if necessary."

"Why the bonus?"

"Because we need the boat this afternoon."

"You mean we're going in today?"

"Of course, and we've got to get moving to make it before dark."

With the others gone, Mason turned to face David Sheldon, who was busily engaged in prying open one of the crates. "Would it be of any help," Mason said loudly, "if you had a complete dossier on Price and his organization?"

"Of course it would," Sheldon answered.

"Mason hurried forward to the cockpit area to get his briefcase, which he opened quickly. As he pulled the bulky folder out, he saw out of the corner of his eye that Sheldon had followed him into the forward cabin.

"Please take your time," Sheldon told him.

Mason took a deep breath before sighing heavily. He then handed the heavy folder to Sheldon without saying a word.

"I must apologize, sir," Sheldon said as he took the dossier. "You see, we operate most of the time with strings and mirrors, and, especially, with a minimum amount of time. And, strangely enough, it usually works very well for us. We are uncomfortable with the slow, methodical way, which, to us, only serves our enemies."

Jerome Mason felt himself settling down in response to Sheldon's conversation. He pulled a piece of onion skin paper out of his briefcase. "Here's the cargo manifest."

Sheldon took the flimsy piece of paper, scanning it briefly. "You've done remarkably well, sir, in a short period of time. Flak vests, smoke grenades, medical supplies."

"I have a few due bills out," Mason admitted. "One of my closest personal friends is the Miami SWAT commander, for example. The Justice Department also came through with confiscated wares out of their Atlanta storage depot."

"Atlanta, Georgia," Sheldon remarked to himself. "So some of these arms might have been used by the KKK. That somehow seems ironic, to say the least."

"I have found that irony is the stuff that makes life interesting. For example, the crate of frag grenades came from a JDL raid."

Sheldon laughed under his breath.

"Please try to get all of it back if you can," Mason said as he turned to leave. "We either have to return the material or pay for it."

Sheldon followed behind him to the cargo doorway, where he reached to Mason's shoulder. "You are planning to stay here, of course," he said quietly.

"I was thinking about that while listening to your plans. You could use a coordinator, like someone to monitor things."

"Not a bad idea, since we'll be split into two groups."

"I could go for a smaller second boat, lagging back for a couple miles."

"Then get to it," Sheldon told him, and he turned back to help unpack their equipment.

Just like that, Mason was thinking. No discussion, no pros and cons, just get to it. So, why not? Making his way carefully down the metal ladder, Mason realized the adrenalin was starting to flow, and he was in fact getting caught up with the rest of them. So it was now strings and mirrors, he noted to himself, for he remembered back to his early days when he was a fledgling agent in a bureau always short on funds, when their watchword had been gum and bailing wire. And he figured that things never really changed, only the names people gave to them.

With the squall line passed, Maurice Garand came onto the bridge deck of the *Swanya II*. He was pleased to see that the heavier rain had not interfered with the salvage divers, who were still submerged, but he was otherwise discouraged because it appeared they would have to go right down to the wire. His report to Calvin Price at noon, two hours earlier, had been the same negative news. The only remains they had found were definitely those of Karen Laswell, which meant that Michael Brav must not have been on the seaplane. Squinting through the thick upper lens of his glasses, he spotted Nick Villon on the dock. He called him at once on his portable transceiver.

Nick reported that with the efficiency of the metal detectors, their production was now down to tin cans and other similar type debris. Putting him on hold, Garand again contemplated their progress.

Calvin Price had agreed with him that the verification of Brav's absence from the site meant they were probably wasting their time. But there was that element of chance, made more mysterious and probable because of Karen's all-clear signal, which required that they keep looking.

He punched the transmit button to tell Nick, "Extend the perimeter on this side another twenty feet," and he glanced down to the water between them. Their search perimeter had been marked off by buoy floats tied together with rope on the nearer channel side, a semicircle extending away from the dock about sixty feet. The extra footage would push the search zone almost to the yacht.

After Nick acknowledged, Garand returned below to the main salon, where he sat down next to the bar counter. The search operation would consume another four to five hours, which meant he could depart for the villa about dark or a little later.

He reminded himself that he had to be in Beirut by Sunday night.

Nick Villon also had to be on his way no later than tonight. The scheduling was tight but workable.

Because of the poor weather and the slow tourist season, Dan Iser had little trouble in finding the cabin cruiser he wanted at the right price. With Jerome Mason acting as their ground coordinator, each member of the team had arrived at the selected boat anchorage by the deadline of 3:00 p.m. Knowing they had thirty minutes before departure time, Mason had stopped by a delicatessen in the city to buy an armload of sandwiches and cold salad. The rain had lightened but was holding steady, so Dan Iser arranged with the boat's owner to use a back storage room in his maintenance building next to the dock.

Major Sheldon conducted the briefing while they ate. Coming in, Joshua had spotted the *Swanya II* and had verified the salvage operation in progress. They had all agreed that while the yacht was too defensible on the open water, it could still be held as a reserve target if they failed to score at the villa site. Their ruse for moving against the villa was simple. With Sheldon below to back them up, Shira and Dan would enter the cove on the cabin cruiser as husband and wife in need of emergency help. Joshua's function was to land on the villa's airstrip, upon radio signal, to further divide and perhaps confuse the villa's security force.

Jerome Mason was not exactly enamored with the plan's simplicity.

Major Sheldon took several minutes to go over their weapons' assignments, timing schedule, and what they would do if stopped by the Haitian Coast Guard. After checking all their watches, he turned to Mason. "Do you have our code names worked out?"

"Per Dan's suggestion, the aircraft will be Matthew, the main boat will be Mark, and my launch will be Luke. The sequence is deliberate to help us remember, based on our arrival order at the villa."

Joshua smiled as he stood up. He noticed that both Sheldon and Shira were smiling also. "I should think the home office would prefer Genesis, Exodus, and Leviticus."

"So you know your Bible, Joshua Bain," Dan said mechanically.

Jerome Mason watched with a certain amusement as the standoff continued, noticing too that neither Sheldon nor

Shira were willing to interfere as they went about finishing their food.

"My best friend knows it much better," Joshua replied then.

"Then he is richly blessed," said Dan.

"His name is Alan Hunt," Joshua went on slowly. "And he is one of the captives we're searching for and hope to find."

"Please allow me to recommend," Dan told him, "that you try praying instead of hoping."

Joshua dropped his eyes, not answering.

"Let's get moving," Sheldon said abruptly.

On his way out, Dan Iser pulled up next to Joshua's shoulder. He put out his right hand to take Joshua's. "I've already been praying for you and your friends. Mister Mason told us a little about you before we left the hangar."

"I appreciate it," said Joshua sincerely. Watching Dan moving away through the doorway into the rain, he felt something in his right hand. Turning his hand up, he saw that Dan Iser had given him a small, smooth rock about the size of a dime. It took a moment for the significance of the small stone to register, or, at least, what he thought it probably meant.

"I see you've been honored."

Joshua looked up to see that Shira was standing in front of him. This was the first time they had been so close face to face. The harsh light from the single overhead bulb revealed that she was lighter skinned than he had thought. There was a patch of hardly discernible freckles across the bridge of her nose, and as she smiled he also noticed that her full mouth turned a certain way, reminding him of someone he had once known. He saw too that her eyes were really more hazel than brown, with a faint touch of green. "I'm sorry," he said then, realizing he'd been staring.

"I said you've been honored," she repeated.

"You mean this?" he asked, holding up the small stone.

"Oh, yes. I've known Dan and Sharon for many years. Sharon is a Sabra, like me, and we were raised on the same kibbutz. Our parents are close friends. In fact, Sharon and I were born within hours of each other. You may have noticed the similarity in our first names."

"I hadn't thought about it."

"Our parents did it deliberately, a kind of gesture to show their love and affection for each other." She paused, looking aside with an expression suggesting that what she had to say was a description of a scene she was forming carefully in her mind. "Anyway," she went on slowly, "Dan started carrying the stones around after they worked over his tongue."

"How did it happen?"

"Dan was converted to Christianity in '67, during the war, and when he came home he was excited and fired up, wanting to be a missionary, I remember. Sharon worships the ground he walks on, and she would do anything he asked her, but she convinced him that they shouldn't leave Israel. So, he took to street campaigning."

"You mean witnessing?"

"That's right, but he felt led, as he put it, to try to reach everybody, including the orthodox Moslems who lived in a neighborhood not far from their apartment. He was warned, even by the police, but that only seemed to goad him on. He would work the streets during his time off, and they got him one night on his way home." She paused again, looking up at him. "Dan refused to identify anyone, or even say he actually knew who did it."

"That's understandable for a man like him," said Joshua sympathetically. "He probably felt that he had asked for it, or something like that."

"The police tried to find out who did it, anyway. Dan was well known and respected, as he still is, and the police did their best. But they couldn't prove anything without Dan's help. The man in charge of the investigation finally told Sharon that they suspected a punitive squad of one of the more militant Shi'ite sects had done it to teach Dan a lesson."

"Some lesson."

"Dan was lucky to have survived."

"Perhaps," said Joshua, who was tempted to elaborate on the term "lucky," but he saw that Sheldon and Mason were preparing to leave. "So what about you, Shira Elazar? For example, is that your maiden name?"

She smiled broadly. "You have an oblique way, Joshua Bain, of asking a woman if she is married."

Major Sheldon, looking preoccupied and serious, pulled even with them on his way out. "We're getting close," he reminded Shira, who turned without further word to move out the door.

"Good luck," Joshua yelled after her, and she waved an acknowledgment.

"Mason says you'll be taking off in an hour and twenty minutes," Sheldon said to him.

Watching Shira until she turned the corner of the building, Joshua finally looked at Sheldon. "I'm sorry," he said slowly. "What did you say?"

Sheldon studied him for a moment. "Is there something wrong?"

"Not exactly, except that I have to say the situation stinks."

"If the smell gets bad enough, Joshua, then try breathing through your mouth."

With that advice, Major Sheldon turned and walked out of the room.

Waiting behind Sheldon, Jerome Mason had stepped forward.

"So what do you think?" Joshua asked him frankly.

"It's hard to say. One minute I'm thinking I'd hate to have this bunch after me, the next I'm worrying because they seem so relaxed, almost blase. They could all be dead within two hours."

"I was just thinking the same thing," said Joshua. "But now I've got the hunch we'll make it because we have to."

Mason briefly considered the statement. "I hope you're right, Joshua, for all our sakes."

As Joshua watched the older man hurry across the wooden dock, he reached into his left front pocket to touch the small stone. Jerome Mason's last words moved across his mind, and he remembered Dan Iser's advice to try praying instead of hoping. He stood near the open doorway, staring at the rain falling on the wooden surface of the dock. He admitted that he had the time, and he turned to look self-consciously around the empty room, feeling the tug of war starting inside him. Taking a deep and resolute breath, he stepped forward to swing the door closed, locking it carefully and deliberately. Standing alone in the empty room, listening to the rain pelting the roof reminded him of the wind which sometimes passed over the promontory above Rancho Canaan with the same intensity of purpose.

The moment seemed right, and the need was there.

The knock on the door startled him.

He moved quietly to the left of the closed door, reaching inside his right trouser pocket to palm the Viper. He reached out then to slowly turn the latch on the door.

Dan Iser stepped into the room.

Joshua relaxed, sighing with relief.

"Did I disturb you?" Dan asked him, his left hand at his throat.

"Not at all; I was using the time to think."

Dan unzipped his nylon jacket to pull out a book, which he handed to Joshua. "I had this on the boat, and I thought you might like to have it."

Joshua turned the Bible in his hand. "Did Mason tell you I'm Jewish?"

"Sheldon told us that."

Joshua handed the Bible back to him. "I want to thank you for your concern, but I already have one in my kit back at the hangar."

Taking the Bible, Dan glanced around the room before commenting, "I also suspected I might find you praying."

"You almost did."

"Have you accepted the Lord, Joshua?"

Joshua took a moment to reply, "I have not yet accepted that Jesus Christ is the Messiah."

"Your skepticism is not complete, since you refer to Him in the present tense. However, be that what it may, please allow me to give you some advice," and he paused.

Joshua was thinking that it all had been planned out, that with Alan gone this man had been provided as his replacement. "So go ahead," he said, not trying to hide the resignation in his voice.

"The moment is especially blessed," Dan Iser told him, "since we are short on time and I will have to be brief," and he held up the Bible in his right hand. "It says in here that we all have sinned and come short of the glory of God." He lowered the Bible slowly.

Waiting long enough to realize it was his turn to speak, Joshua finally asked him, "You mean you're telling me I'm a sinner?" He was frowning as he went on, "This hardly seems an appropriate time."

"Anytime is appropriate, Joshua, because God reminds you that you're a sinner for a specific purpose. He takes no delight in degrading you, in pointing out your faults. Rather, He does it to show you your deep need, to make you aware of the gulf between you and Him. I'm sure you are already aware of the need, but I'm not so sure you're aware of the gulf."

Joshua had removed the small stone from his pocket, holding it between the thumb and forefinger of his left hand. "Is that why you gave me this?"

"I gave it to you on impulse. However, it has turned out to serve a purpose which is proper for this moment. You stand there with all your pain and grief, the weight of which has become so great that you consent to ask your Maker for help. Which is contrary to the truth, because as it is said, 'Now we know that God heareth not sinners.' Joshua, you might as well be praying to the wind and the rain, for all the good it will do you."

"If He doesn't hear sinners, how then can He hear any of us?"

The eyes of Dan Iser narrowed down appraisingly. "Someone has been too careful with your feelings, Joshua Bain."

Joshua tried to deal with his rising irritation by looking at his watch. When he looked up, he saw the same reaction in Daniel Iser's face. "You still didn't answer my question," Joshua reminded him.

Dan lifted his Bible again. "If you've read this, then you already know the answer. The question should be, do you want to admit it?"

"You mean the Messiah, of course."

"The time is appropriate, after all."

Joshua looked aside.

"Oh, Joshua, you are so much like my people . . . "

The voice moving across the room had the same unchanged tone, rasping and metallic, the syllables evenly spaced and lacking expression, so that Joshua had to again look into Iser's face to verify the deep emotion behind the words.

"To this very day," Dan was saying, "we find it so difficult to accept that God could simply acquit us, a guilty and sinful people. It is apparently as incomprehensible today as it was two thousand years ago, that a sinful man can somehow be made righteous."

"Just like that . . . "

There was a hint of a smile around the mouth of Dan Iser, who was also nodding slowly, as if Joshua had just confirmed some inner thought. As he moved toward the door, he lifted his hand once more. "Why is it so hard for us to accept it, Joshua?"

"You mean the redemptive role of the Messiah?"

The surprise was brief in Dan's eyes.

"So maybe I'm closer than you realize," Joshua added.

Dan had lowered his left hand to open the door, and, as he returned it to his throat, Joshua sensed the gesture was more tentative than usual.

"We were warned before we left Israel," Dan said mechanically, "that we would be working with an amateur, and I see now that the estimate was only partially correct."

"I'm trying my best."

"It's not good enough, because you're in worse danger of becoming a fool."

Joshua took a deep breath as he struggled to keep his temper.

"You recognize your position," Dan went on quickly, "but you incorrectly deduce some degree of safety or acceptance because you think you've moved closer. Salvation does not detonate by proximity fuse, Joshua. As the Lord pointed out, you're either for Him or you're against Him. There's no middle ground, no negotiated peace, and especially no truce while you agonize over what could be right or what could be wrong. In short, you're either in or you're out."

Joshua could restrain himself no longer. "I'm beginning to understand why someone took a knife to your tongue."

A smile crossed Dan's face. "My wife recently threatened to short-circuit my batteries . . . "

Joshua's anger faded as quickly as it had come. "I'm sorry," he said then.

Dan appeared to ignore his apology. "Just remember, Joshua, there can be no compromise in your relationship with the Lord, and all I'm trying to do is to set the record straight." He made a quarter turn toward the open door. "So I'll leave you to address yourself to the wind and the rain, unless, of course, you'd like to take the step to talk to the One who can help you."

Joshua averted his eyes again.

Dan Iser moved out into the rain, stooped over and hurrying.

The small, sparsely furnished room was in the transit quarters used by the Cuban replacements assigned to the military airfield. There were two metal cots with stained bare mattresses against one wall, below a faded poster picture of Fidel Castro which had been nailed up without a frame. It was nearly dark outside and cooler than when they had arrived several hours earlier, but the wooden hut was still uncomfortably hot and stuffy. Anne Hunt rubbed her nose again, trying to erase the pungent odor in the closed-in room. Like most of the rest of it, even the odor was a familiar one. It was the smell of men who hadn't washed or changed clothes in a long time. And, it was the sure smell of guns, because the table between her and

Hafiz Barca was heavily stained with what she knew was Cosmoline, Lubriplate, and bore cleaner. A small canvas knapsack was on the cot nearest to her, next to a small Bible, both of which had been obtained for her by Barca while they had waited in Havana.

"It's your pick," Barca reminded her harshly.

She reviewed the discards, thinking that Barca's mood had grown progressively worse during the two days since they had left Cuba. He had become tight-lipped and brooding, which she figured had to be a warning. Anne Hunt had no choice but to suspect that Hafiz Barca was getting close to something which he obviously was worrying about or didn't like.

"Will you play," he insisted.

"All right," she said quietly. The gin rummy was a part of the program, too, something which she hated because it reminded her of the past. Not wishing to antagonize him, she picked up a totally unneeded deuce, discarding a face card she knew he wanted.

"Gin," he said at once, and he allowed his face to relax only enough to break his scowl.

Jotting down the score, she suggested, "We're on friendly ground now."

"So," he remarked tartly, and his face began to cloud over again.

"So why don't you relax?"

He quickly shuffled the cards, started to deal, before he finally replied, "We're still a long way from home."

The answer told her one thing, but Anne Hunt suspected it was time she had to try for more. All she knew to this point was that they were at a military airfield near Addis Ababa, the capital of Ethiopia, after a two-day flight on a Russian T-27 transport. The other passengers on the military plane had been a contingent of Cuban nationals, a mixture of military and civilian advisors who had been talkative enough to reveal their itinerary. They had refueled and laid over for several hours in Angola last night.

"Turn the knock card," he told her.

She obliged before picking up her hand. "I realize there isn't much you can tell me about what's happening," she said then, "but I am concerned about my husband."

He looked at her over the top of his cards, suspicion showing in his eyes. "I don't know myself. Even if I did, you know I couldn't tell you."

She dropped her first discard.

He drew his first card from the top of the deck. "You were in the movement before, weren't you?" he asked.

She was at once on the alert, because this was the first time he had offered an interest in conversation. "Yes, I was."

"With what group?"

It was her turn to study him suspiciously. "Don't you already know?"

"Only that you were one of us."

She elected to tell him the truth. "I was with Fawd Al-Shaer."

He grunted appreciatively, folding his cards as he looked up to study her. "Were you with him at the end?"

"Yes."

"It is said that he was betrayed."

She swallowed once before replying, "Fawd betrayed himself in what he was trying to do, and the record is clear on how it happened."

"He almost made it."

"Oh, yes. Despite himself. But I'm convinced now that he never really had a chance."

"Why is that?"

"Because he only believed in himself."

Barca grunted again, but not so much in appreciation. "That we believe in ourselves is the backbone of our movement."

"Then, like Fawd, you will never find real satisfaction or resolution. There is never a finish line in your race. You run, and you will keep on running, until one day you will fall down exhausted."

"That is defeatist talk."

"It's as much the truth as the fact that metal must expand when heated."

"We're not rods of iron. We have brains, a will, a mind to use."

"A further disadvantage the rod of iron does not enjoy. However, you help make the point yourself, because even the conduct of the iron rod is governed by a law higher than itself."

He shook his head then. "Your talk is typically female, for it runs in circles."

She resisted her impulse to laugh.

He squared up his hand on top of the deck, signalling an end to the card playing. "Was it hard for you to quit?"

"Yes, in fact, it was."

"And what about your conscience now? Like the struggle still goes on, you know. Our people are still without a country. How do you face that each day, knowing that you turned away from your brothers and sisters?"

Anne Hunt took a deep breath as she tried to compose as honest an answer as she could provide. She wanted to keep him talking now, because in his questions there were answers about himself she desperately needed. "In looking back on it," she started slowly, "I see where I was dangerously close to becoming hardened. It's like there's a point you pass where nothing seems to matter anymore. Fawd had passed the point. I was lucky enough to have had an opportunity to get out when I did."

"So you run a different race now?"

"The difference is in the prize . . . " She hesitated, praying inside for the right words to go on. "The reason there is no finish line to your race is because the prize you seek has become a dishonest one. What got you started was perhaps right, but as you run and begin to fall behind, the terms and conditions change so that in time you begin to use the cause to justify just about anything you want. After all, it takes a certain kind of loser to turn away with indifference after having just machine gunned a six-month-old baby."

Anger showed in the upper cheeks of Hafiz Barca. "Your sympathy for Jewish children somehow seems misplaced. What about the torn bodies of Arab babies?"

Anne Hunt looked aside. "You should know that I am the only survivor of my family."

He followed her line of sight to see that she was staring at the Bible on the cot. "So you forgive and forget," he said acidly.

She took a deep breath before sighing heavily. "We occupy only a fraction of an inch on the yardstick of history," she said slowly. "We are the direct descendants of Ishmael, you and I, and now we fight against the bloodline of Isaac for the first time in these many thousands of years. It is a special kind of irony that we are all brothers and sisters under the common father, Abraham, a fact which makes us unique among the nations of the world which have sought mutual genocide in the past."

"That's enough!"

"It's not nearly enough, because the one God we all share

sits on His throne, shaking His head in wonder at the antics of Abraham's children who just keep on playing out their selfish little games. Don't you see, both you and the people you hate are on the same treadmill? Your more radical ones want Israel pushed into the sea, while there are Jews who want to colonize right up to the gates of Damascus. And, if the truth were really known, those two objectives are probably on the minds of far more than just the extremist minority who are willing to openly admit them!"

The following silence was heavy in the room.

"I suppose," Barca finally proposed, "that you will now suggest your solution to the problem."

"No, not at all," she told him quietly, and she looked down to the table between them. "During the past few days I've come to believe that you are most likely under orders to eliminate me. I seem to be serving a purpose now, but I suspect that once we reach our destination you'll have no further use for me. You see, I've been this route before. So, if and when you do pull the trigger, I want you to be aware of the real reasons why."

"I see I will have to be more careful," she heard him saying after a moment, "because I was not aware you were arguing for your life."

"If I argue, then I pray you understand it's for all our lives, Hafiz."

He laughed lightly, perhaps self-consciously, she noticed.

"I understand one thing for sure," he said evenly. "It is an obvious drawback to Christianity that it allows its women to voice their opinions."

She felt encouraged by his apparent improved mood as he pushed himself away from the table to stand up. He reached behind his back to pull the handcuffs out of his belt. He studied her briefly, before commenting, "I've got to go get our food. I won't use these if you give me your word you won't try to escape."

She shook her head after a moment. "You know I can't do that."

He laughed again. "So there's a little bit of Ishmael still left in you, after all."

Chapter eleven

Jerome Mason checked his watch to see that an hour and twenty minutes had passed since the two boats had left the harbor at Port-au-Prince. It was nearly ten minutes to five, the time for their contact, and he reached for the radio. He was in the back-up power launch, now about a hundred yards behind the lead boat. He levered the mike switch, "This is Luke calling Mark."

Sheldon acknowledged at once.

"I'm breaking off," Mason told him, and he throttled the launch back. Sheldon did not respond, per plan, because from this point on the radio channel on the lead boat would be left open until it broached the cove. They were supposedly about five minutes away from the villa location, and it was now up to Joshua to lead them in. He saw then that Sheldon was veering in closer to the coastline, a dangerous but necessary maneuver to enable him to identify the landmarks reported by Joshua.

Jerome Mason glanced nervously over the cabin cruiser to the eastern horizon. The weather report was for continued intermittent showers, and the cloud cover was still dense and threatening.

In the eighteen minutes since he took off, Joshua had already flown through two rain showers. The Piper was old, the best he could get on short notice, and he was occupied constantly with the controls and the instrument panel. It was impossible to keep the small plane in trim for more than a few seconds, especially with the erratic air currents. On visual, he had to stay low, using the coastline as his only available landmark.

At twenty minutes out, he dropped the left wing and pushed the nose down to level out about a hundred feet above the beach. Timing was critical now, and he began to scan the water for the two boats, intending to use the lead boat as a reference point to begin his shoreline search. He spotted the launch in his forward starboard quarter, and he reached to turn on his radio.

Jerome Mason verified he was in sight of the launch.

Joshua reported the villa in less than a minute.

Dan Iser nodded his head that he understood as Sheldon secured the radio. All they had to do now was to spot the giant antenna servicing the villa, which, according to Joshua, was the first and only one north of their present location. As Sheldon pushed the throttle forward, Dan started aft to help Shira set out the fishing equipment, a necessary supporting ingredient in their ruse to gain at least the cove without a firefight.

With his first phase completed, Joshua started a slow turn out over the water, gaining altitude carefully. At fourteen hundred feet on the altimeter, he began to pass through the power fringes of the cloud cover, then turned again in a ninety degree swing to a heading taking him parallel to the coast. He checked his watch and was tempted to call Mason, but he knew there could be no progress report.

It was either going to work or fail, simple enough.

The guard assigned to the villa dock area was in the small maintenance building which also served as a guard shack at the head of the small wooden pier. He heard the sound of the boat engine first, thinking that it was the yacht returning from Port-au-Prince. He got up from his chair, where he had been reading, taking his time as he moved to the door. The old man had been gone for several days, and, with Garand and Nick Villon at Port-au-Prince, the villa was deserted except for its standby servants and four-man security force under the charge of the resident secretary.

It was raining lightly again, and he squinted across the cove to see the slowly moving boat, a small cabin cruiser. Alerted now, he reached inside the door jamb to pick up his carbine. It was not unusual for an occasional curiosity seeker to enter the private cove, and a stern display by an armed guard would normally move them out in a hurry. The boat had moved close enough for him to make out a woman at the wheel. He moved quickly to the telephone which was on a direct line to the house. Colonel Price's secretary answered the phone.

"We have a visitor in the cove," he told her, and he looked out the nearby window. "It's a rigged sportfisher and looks clean. So far as I can tell there're only two aboard. One's a woman."

"Should I alert the other station?" she asked him.

"Let me talk to them first," he told her. The other station was the post on the airstrip side of the villa, also manned by one man. The other two guards in relief were in their quarters.

"So let me know if you need help," she told him, and she hung up.

He walked out onto the pier after slinging the carbine muzzle down over his left shoulder to protect it from the rain. The boat was close enough now, and he lifted his right hand in a gesture to stop, while yelling, "This is private property! You must leave now!"

The woman at the controls shook her head frantically, gesturing over her shoulder to the other passenger, a man who the guard could see was slumped over in a deck chair aft.

Sheldon waited below, behind the partially closed door to the cramped sleeping quarters. Their ploy was predicated on the reasonably good gamble that the villa security would be both lax and short-handed. The weather was bad, a point also in their favor. He tensed as the boat bumped the pier, and he peered anxiously through the narrow crack between the door and its jamb.

Shira tapped the door once lightly with her foot, and he pulled it closed on the signal that she could handle the situation. The single tap indicated there was only one man visible in the area.

Major Sheldon calculated that the early odds appeared to be in their favor.

With the boat holding against the pier, the guard reluctantly took the aft line from Shira.

"You must leave at once," he commanded.

"Can't you see," said Shira, trying her best to sound like a panicked and frightened woman, "my husband is critically ill!"

"This isn't a hospital."

"We called the authorities at Port-au-Prince, and there's a plane due here any minute to pick us up. They said this was the closest place they could reach us."

"That's impossible. This is a private—"

"We were told to come here, you idiot!" she shrilled.

Sheldon winced at the outburst, hoping she wasn't overplaying it.

"Besides," Shira went on less excitedly. "We are the friends of Mister Price, and I demand that you call him right now."

Sheldon liked the timing of the bluff, but then it occurred to him that Price might still be there.

"The Colonel is not here, ma'am."

Sheldon knew they had broken through.

"Then get Mister Garand down here," Shira said authoritatively.

Sheldon held his breath again.

"He's at Port-au-Prince, ma'am."

"Then who's in charge?"

"The Colonel's secretary, Miss Ferguson, but—"

"There'll be no buts," Shira said threateningly. "Either you get moving or I will go to the house myself."

The guard moved to board the boat. "I will look at your husband first."

Sheldon opened the door a crack, bracing himself. It was stifling and damp in the small quarters, and he felt his sweat running down his sides. The .38 revolver in his right hand had a silencer on its muzzle.

Dan Iser heard the guard come over the rail, and he continued to hold his breath while he forced his diaphram against his lower throat. The guard lifted his head carefully. Dan's shirt was open, revealing the wires leading to the voice-transmitting disc next to the small of his throat. The area around his mouth and nostrils was turning blue. It was a final kind of touch that there was an open Bible on his lap.

"What's all that?" the guard asked, pointing to the wires.

The question told Shira that the man had little medical knowledge.

"It's a part of his heart stimulator," she told him sternly. "It's not operating properly, and he's dying. Are you blind?"

The guard let Dan's head drop back to his chest. "I'll call the house," he told her as he mounted the pier.

"And we need help to move him," Shira said after him. "And tell that secretary that the Letourniers are down here. We're from Monte Carlo, and Colonel Price is going to hear about this."

Sheldon opened the door after Shira tapped an all-clear.

"We shouldn't use the flare," she whispered while she stayed upright. "I figure we can make the house without any trouble."

Sheldon conceded the point without comment. The flare would likely alert the house. He reached up to take the radio mike she was now holding by her side. After Luke had acknowledged, Sheldon told him tersely to order the plane in at once.

Shira moved aft, bending over Dan Iser, who was smiling as he placed the disc sensor against his larynx. "How'd I do?"

"Magnificent," she told him. "You better hide that thing; someone up there might not go for the stimulator business."

"What's with the fancy French name?" he asked her before removing the disc from his throat.

"He'll have trouble remembering it, let alone repeating it accurately to the secretary." She helped him button his shirt. She turned then, toward the top of the pier. "Here he comes," she said softly, and she looked forward to see that Sheldon had closed his door again. She spotted movement above the bridge; a second man was moving hurriedly down the long flagstone stairway leading up to the higher ground and presumably to the house itself.

Absently then, she reached down to pick up Dan's Bible. As she took a deep breath, she was trying to prepare herself for the more critical role she still had left to play, one of being in a rush and overly concerned, enough so to prevent a personal search. They could check her bag, but not her person, because she was going up the stairs with a 9mm automatic taped to the inside of her ankle.

Sheldon had holstered his revolver in exchange for a grease gun. He waited now, an extra clip taped to the inside of both his forearms.

Joshua felt a rush of relief as he took the call to land immediately. He dropped his right wing to go into a heading bringing him in behind the villa, knowing he had to land into the wind.

Jerome Mason was unsure about what he should do next. His strongest impulse was to wait, figuring that if the Mark team needed him, Sheldon would call. Confused and unsure, he tentatively pushed the engine's throttle ahead just enough to start the launch moving.

Shira Elazar took stock of their situation. The two guards, obviously under orders, had cooperated fully from the time they showed up dockside. They had picked up Dan Iser bodily to carry him along the dock and up the flagstone stairs. But now they stopped to rest and catch their breath.

A few seconds earlier, Shira had heard the sound of a small plane's engine whose tone suggested it was landing. Her party was now on the deck next to a swimming pool. Beyond the pool was a patio, then what looked like the main house. She noticed a side door open across the patio with someone standing in the door opening. It was time, she thought hurriedly, to pretend near hysteria.

Keeping the lowest profile possible, Major Sheldon peered

through the lower edge of the rain-streaked bridge windshield. The four figures in Shira's group had reached the top of the stairs, where they had stopped for some reason. He saw Shira then, her arms waving wildly, and then he heard her voice, sounding shrill and excited, but he could not make out the words. The two guards, with Dan Iser between them, then disappeared.

He moved out of the boat quickly, vaulting to the pier. The rain was coming down heavily at squall strength, and he dashed along the pier running full tilt. He was exposed now, and as he hit the first flagstone step he stopped to crouch down, waiting and watching expectantly.

There was no challenge.

There was only the sound of the rain, dense and coarse, pelting the flagstone in front of him. The thick undergrowth bordering the stairway gave way to the heavy rain, sagging under the weight of the water. For an inexplicable fleeting second, he thought about Hank Koman and his men, now gone, because of the rain. He shook his head to clear it. Still crouched over, he started up the stairs, his weapon ready in front of him.

Joshua cut the Piper's engine. Because of the virtual deluge that had started while he was landing, he had decided to taxi as close as he could get to the building located at the end of the strip nearest to the house. He had on a thin nylon windbreaker, and he checked under his left arm to verify that the revolver was still in place. There was a zipper bag beside him on the floor with an automatic weapon, several frag grenades, plus two smoke grenades. He realized the smoke would be worthless in the heavy rain. On impulse, he opened the cockpit door and pushed his feet out. Picking up the bag, he turned out from under the wing to run for the small building.

He was wondering if he was early or late.

So far he had heard no shooting.

Perhaps the sound of the rain—

He remembered then that he'd left his flak vest in the hangar.

The door to the small building opened up.

With water running off him from head to toe, Joshua stepped inside.

The man was smiling at him. He was a big and tough looking native, his heavily muscled upper arms and chest bulging against his striped tank-top shirt.

"You here to pick up the sick guy?" he asked Joshua.

"That's correct," he replied. Wary of the man's size and nearness, he took a step to the side, putting some space between them. He quickly checked out the room, which was apparently used as a guard shack. The only weapon he could see was a military carbine leaning against the opposite wall. There was a telephone on a wall shelf. The man looked aside, gesturing toward the phone.

"You can call the house from here," he told Joshua cordially.

With that, Joshua pulled the revolver and stepped back.

The big man looked at him blankly for a passing moment, then he started to smile slowly. "How would you like to eat that popgun?" he asked, his voice still polite, but Joshua could see the muscles in his arms starting to move.

Joshua lowered the revolver slightly while pulling the hammer back with his thumb. "I'll take both your kneecaps out first," he said evenly. "If you're still coming after that. . ." and he paused, shrugging his shoulders.

"I guess you would," the big man said, and he lifted his hands to put them on top of his head.

Still watching him warily, Joshua was hoping that the opposition wasn't all like this one.

Major Sheldon used the bordering underbrush as a cover to skirt the huge swimming pool. Hesitating only briefly at the edge of the patio, he saw that one of the side doors to the house was ajar, with a light behind it, and he quartered across the patio, pulling up next to the door. Flattened against the wall, he took a deep breath and held it before turning slowly to peer through the door opening. He let his breath go as he saw Shira standing across the room with an automatic in her right hand. He pushed through the door with his weapon ready.

"It's about time you showed up," Shira told him calmly.

The room appeared to be an office, or type of den. Dan Iser was across the room, apparently shaking down the several people lined up facing the wall. Sheldon counted three women and three men before he moved next to Shira.

"What's our status?" he asked her breathlessly.

"According to the secretary," Shira told him, pointing to the end woman in a black dress, "this is it, except for one guard at the landing strip."

"Joshua may need some help," Sheldon said, and he started back toward the door. "As soon as you finish, Dan, you check the rest of the house."

He nearly collided with Joshua as he turned the first outside corner of the house. The rain was starting to subside, and he pulled Joshua under the roof overhang.

"What's happening?" Joshua asked concernedly.

"You can't believe it! It looks like we've taken this place without firing a shot."

"You mean nobody's hurt?"

"Not a scratch, aside from a good drenching for most of us. And you should've seen Shira. Like she deserves an award for the performance—"

"What about Mason?"

"Oh, no," Sheldon moaned. "I forgot him."

"There's got to be a radio inside."

"So let's get the old boy up here," Sheldon said cheerfully. "Because now we've got to go to work."

It took about ten more minutes for Sheldon to be satisfied the villa was secure. Jerome Mason arrived, breathless from climbing the flagstone stairs and looking a little bewildered, a decidedly out-of-character expression. Sheldon put him to work immediately running an inventory on the files discovered in the office next to the den. Sheldon, with Joshua helping, made ready to interrogate the prisoners, who were being held by Shira in the adjacent dining room. Dan Iser volunteered to patrol the outside area after bringing them all fresh coffee from the kitchen.

The resident secretary was selected by Joshua to be the first one questioned. Following his instructions, she took the chair in front of the desk occupied by Major Sheldon. Joshua stood against the wall, his arms crossed over his chest. The woman was in her early forties, by his estimate, and she was still thoroughly frightened.

"Where is Calvin Price?" Sheldon asked her first.

"I don't know for sure, sir."

"What do you mean? You're his private secretary, aren't you?"

"Yes, sir. But all I can tell you is that he said he could be reached through our Hong Kong office."

"All right, then," said Sheldon, "when did you last hear from Mister Garand?"

"He called just a few minutes before you arrived."

Joshua pushed away from the wall. "Is he on the yacht at Port-au-Prince?"

"Yes, he is, sir. He's in charge of the salvage operation there."

"What did he want?" Sheldon asked.

"He said he would be here in two hours, and that I was to have dinner ready for him and the crew."

"Is Nick Villon on the yacht?" Joshua asked her.

"Yes, sir, but he won't be returning tonight. You see, his family lives in Port-au-Prince. And, he has a girlfriend there too."

"Now Miss Ferguson," Sheldon started slowly, "what I have to ask you is extremely important. It doesn't matter what you think of us, but your answer could affect the lives of many people. Do you understand?"

"Yes, sir."

"What can you tell us about the name Kasim?" and he spelled out the name, spacing the letters carefully.

"I have heard the name," she admitted, frowning.

"And?"

"But not in connection with anything I can recall. You see, the Colonel and Mister Garand talk so much and use so many names. And all their important conversations are usually in private."

"Try to remember," said Joshua. "What we're after is the name of a city or a location. You must try, please."

"I'm sorry I can't help you," she finally offered.

Joshua slumped against the wall.

After showing Miss Ferguson out of the room, Sheldon returned to the desk.

"What about the others?" Joshua asked.

"Forget it. The only one who can help us is Maurice Garand."

"You want to try for the yacht when it arrives?"

"I've been kicking it around. We're beat, Joshua, and we've already used up a year's supply of luck. We'd have to get our two boats out of the cove first. Who knows, they might even have a password system or signal as a matter of routine. Regardless, we'd have to take them head-on, and it would be a real fight."

"Okay, so let's see what Mason has turned."

"Wait a minute," Sheldon said, and he reached up to rub his forehead, before he went on slowly. "If we don't score on the records, then we're going to have to hit the yacht."

"We're running out of time," Joshua reminded him.

"You help Mason while Dan and I go down to the cove to scout it out."

Jerome Mason looked up as Joshua entered the office.

"I hope you've got something," Joshua told him.

"Maybe," Mason reported. "I've been able to just skim through most of the files. If nothing else, our Mister Garand is thorough and a virtual master at details." He gestured toward a four-drawer cabinet. The top drawer was faced with a three-dial combination lock, which had been pried open. "The best of what we have was in there," Mason went on. "But no operational files on Jordan. This place is obviously more a branch office. And, if there are any other files around, then Garand must have them on the yacht." He held up a thickly packed manila folder. "This is for a man named Hafiz Barca."

"So?" said Joshua, noticing that Mason looked as if he were one step away from collapsing. Like Sheldon had suggested, they were all beat.

"I haven't had a chance to talk to you since we got started this morning," Mason replied. "Late last night I received a routine follow-up report on the L.A. investigation. And, the man who stayed at the Palm Desert motel used the name Hafiz Barca."

"You mean the one who kidnapped Anne?"

"We can safely assume that now."

"And he used his real name?"

"Oh, yes, because that was part of Price's little scheme. Remember, he wanted to clearly defined trail pointing to the Arabs. After all, it would hardly be incriminating for Anne if she had absconded with someone having an all-American name like Jack Armstrong."

"So what's with the folder?"

"Plenty, and it's the only file I've taken the time to go over in some detail. For example, there's a bank draft receipt here for fifty thousand dollars made out to Barca."

"That's not unreasonable for what he did."

"But there's more. Garand's notes on his negotiations with Barca report an offer of an additional one hundred thousand dollars. And that, my impetuous young friend, is decidedly unreasonable for a kidnapping gig."

"So he's getting paid for something else. But what?"

"He's an informer, for sure. Which is precisely why Price allowed, or arranged for, Kasim to pull his heist. Barca is Price's inside man."

Now interested, Joshua leaned over the desk. "What else?" It was getting close to decision-making time on whether they would have to hit the yacht.

"Maybe something," Mason mused thoughtfully as he pulled a memo-size piece of scratch paper out of the folder to hand it to Joshua. "What do you make of this?"

Joshua scanned the brief handwriting. There was a line of numbers over the statement, "Monday noon, 10/16." He handed the paper back. "The numbers look like radio frequencies." And it started to dawn on him the same moment Mason started to smile.

"Barca's going to transmit a message," Joshua exclaimed.

"At noon on Monday, the sixteenth."

"That's this Monday," Joshua went on.

"I also found a note on the desk calendar for last Monday," said Mason. He turned the calendar, handing it to Joshua.

The handprinted note said simply, *Beirut XT re HB—??*

Returning the calendar, Joshua commented, "The HB probably stands for Hafiz Barca, but what about XT?"

"Could stand for extension," Mason suggested. "The question marks no doubt mean that there is some question involved. I'd say that Garand was reminding himself to deal with some Beirut connection, if it would be necessary. And, apparently Hafiz Barca is somehow involved."

Joshua frowned, disappointed at all the speculation. "Anything else?"

Mason gestured toward the nearly empty bulletin board. "You can see for yourself. We've got a few photographs, which appear to be the transfer sites you went over. Otherwise, we've got a voice-activated tape on the radio, but I doubt it will tell us anything beyond the details on the operation up to now."

"I'll tell Sheldon," Joshua said, and he started for the door, stopping short after only two steps. "Wait a minute. When Garand finds out we've been here, he'll either know or at least suspect we've seen that file and his calendar pad. So he'll be aware that we probably know about the Beirut connection."

"I've already thought about that," Mason said. "Sheldon agrees with me that we should destroy this place before we leave. We can burn the rest of the house, but we'll set heavy explosives in here, enough so Garand will never know whether we removed any files."

"He's not that stupid."

"Come on, Joshua. All we're trying to do is put an element of doubt in Garand's mind. Besides, after going over this file I'm positive there's no way he can contact Barca anyway."

"That sounds better," said Joshua, and he turned again toward the door.

"Wait a minute," Mason called after him. "Before we set charges in here, I want all the key records removed so we can turn them over to Interpol."

Joshua stopped in the doorway. "Just take the ones we need, because we're running out of time."

"We owe Interpol, Joshua."

"We don't owe them our lives."

"Perhaps *you* do," Mason said sternly. "You see, it's time you were told that Karen Laswell was an Interpol agent."

Joshua stood stunned in the open doorway.

"Her code name was gardenia," Mason went on, "and she'd been after Price for nearly two years. And, if you're correct in your guess that she shot Brav, then she probably saved your life twice, because Sheldon told me this afternoon that she tried to talk him out of hitting you on the seaplane." He dropped the Barca file on the desk. "So would you like to get me some help to transfer these records to the boats?"

Joshua had to clear his throat before he said, "I'll help you myself when I get back," and he turned to head for the cove.

Chapter twelve

It was warm and comfortable in the back seat of the official sedan, and Major David Sheldon had slept soundly for most of the trip from the Israeli Embassy to the main gate of Andrews Air Force Base. He had long ago learned to catch rest when he could, and when the uniformed sentry asked for his ID, he was fully awake and alert as he flashed his passport. He then waited impatiently while his driver was given instructions to the base BOQ. The lingering false dawn over the eastern seaboard reminded him of the certainty in the passing of time. On Friday, time had worked in their favor; now, time was in the process of turning against them. But it couldn't be helped, because they had to stop at least for a few hours.

They had to rest, regain their strength.

It was also a time for assessment by all of them.

The more official Tel Aviv conclusion was as chilling as it was final.

As the sedan moved slowly across the darkened base, Sheldon was also aware that it was already early afternoon in Beirut, which meant they had less than twenty-four hours to prepare to intercept the radio transmission. His briefing in the embassy had taken nearly an hour longer than he had anticipated, and he was beginning to wonder if they could make it in time. The earliest El Al flight out of Washington was at eleven o'clock, over five hours away. The next international carrier departure wasn't until noon.

Jerome Mason was waiting at the curb in front of the BOQ.

Sheldon climbed out of the sedan, pulling his duffel bag out behind him.

"You're almost late," Mason told him, the remark sounding more cordial than the complaint Sheldon expected.

"We'll never make it now," Sheldon proposed. He automatically glanced up and down the street. His own sedan pulled away from the curb, and he noticed a second car parked a short distance beyond. It was light enough for him to make out the silhouette of someone sitting in the passenger side of the front seat.

"We'll be in Ankara this afternoon," Mason stated.

It was falling into place for Sheldon, who asked quietly, "Courtesy of the U.S. Air Force?"

"Yeah," Mason confirmed, and he reached up to smooth down his hair at the back of his neck. "It took Jon Malek most of the night, but it appears he finally got the message across to the right people." The older man turned to start for the BOQ entrance.

"Who's your friend in the car?" asked Sheldon as he followed behind.

"One of Sam Donaldson's people. It seems we're no longer a private expedition, so the CIA feels obliged to provide me with a protective escort." He led the way down a carpeted hallway.

"Why Ankara?" Sheldon asked curiously.

"No special clearance needed for an unscheduled courier," Mason said as he pulled up in front of a numbered door. "Beirut itself is out because of diplomatic complications. DOD suggested Tel Aviv, but I figured you'd rather come in the back door if the timing was similar."

Sheldon nodded that he understood. "What about the Ankara-to-Beirut leg?"

"A private charter is being arranged."

Sheldon followed him into the room, which was small but well furnished. There was a double bed against the wall on his left, which showed signs of having been slept in on one side. Joshua Bain, who obviously had spent his part of the night there, was seated at a table across the room. Sheldon dropped his bag near the door.

"Where are the others?" he asked.

"Dan and Shira have rooms down the hall," Mason told him as he moved to sit down across from Joshua. "They're both still asleep."

There was the smell of fresh coffee in the room, and Sheldon glanced aside to notice a pot and cups on a wall-mounted service counter.

"Help yourself," Joshua told him.

At the counter, Sheldon noticed that several of the cups had been used. "Where's Malek?" he asked as he poured himself a cup of coffee.

"He had to leave about ten minutes ago," Joshua told him.

"Sorry I'm late," Sheldon apologized, "but we have several stations which normally report in by noon, their time. And, I wanted to get the best and latest input."

"Any luck?" Joshua asked quietly.

Electing to remain on his feet, Sheldon leaned against the counter. "Not a thing on Kasim, I'm afraid." He saw the disappointment in Joshua's face, so he added quickly, "But we're sure Anne Hunt and Hafiz Barca were in Aqaba yesterday morning."

"That's southern Jordan!" Joshua exclaimed, and he stood up. "Where are they now? I mean, can you pick them up?"

Sheldon shook his head slowly. "No, my friend. It was just a sighting by a second-hand contact. Two people matching their description were spotted getting off a military aircraft. It was a routine report filed through Aman channels."

Joshua sat down dejectedly. "What about Kasim? If you've already had a sighting on Barca, then it seems to me you should've scored on Kasim's group by now. By your own estimate, he should already have crossed the Syrian border and entered Lebanon. After all, he's supposed to be a full day ahead of Barca."

"That estimate still holds," Sheldon admitted. "But neither

he nor his original group has been located yet."

"We've got three trails to deal with," Mason said to Joshua. "Barca is still on a kind of schedule, and he's probably heading north. Maurice Garand is in Nassau now, and he's ticketed through to Beirut, scheduled to reach there late today. They're all converging, hopefully."

"There's something else you both should know," Sheldon said carefully. "A part of my briefing this morning was an analysis of the impact of the Jordan shipment getting into certain hands in the Middle East. We are now well beyond simply tracking down a terrorist. Assuming that the plutonium is now in the Middle East, that quantity of weapon's grade material could easily turn out to be disastrous for the State of Israel. The French, as you may be aware, have already tried, unsuccessfully, to supply enriched uranium to one of our Arab neighbors. Only a most fortuitous accident prevented the delivery."

"Fortuitous indeed," Mason remarked knowingly.

"I've been asked to convey to you that Israel will go to any extent necessary to protect herself from such a possibility. And, I was also officially informed this morning that we are proceeding on the assumption that the Jordan plutonium is destined for just such a government. So, this is an all-out effort on our part until we are able to determine otherwise."

"That's encouraging to know," Joshua told him.

"What else came out of the briefing?" Mason asked him.

"Tel Aviv is concerned with Price's apparent timing," Sheldon went on slowly, and he reached up to finger his mustache. "He's letting this drag out, giving us the time to react."

"Maybe he doesn't have any choice," Joshua suggested. "After all, as you pointed out, Kasim can ony proceed at a certain pace. He might even be stalled right now, which could be why you haven't spotted him."

"That's the only reason the timing makes sense."

"I'm more concerned with the obvious trail of this Garand character," Joshua added, his tone suspicious. "Even without the villa lead, we could've picked him up at the Port-au-Prince airline counter. Like, doesn't it strike you as strange that he could be heading for an important rendezvous so much in the open?"

"It tells us that they figure they've got a lock on the situation," Sheldon suggested. "Option one is that they've got things so much under control that they don't care we know."

He paused then, again fingering his mustache. "Option two is a worse troublemaker, because we could be in the process of being drawn along deliberately. If we are being sucked in, then we'd like to know the reasons why."

"So why don't we just take Garand and make him talk?" Joshua asked.

"To take Garand is a tempting prospect," Sheldon told him. "However, he is as much aware of our ability to do that as we are. So, he's taking a calculated risk in exposing himself. The magic question is still why? We thus have to determine accurately the best time to take him, if we ever do."

Joshua was shaking his head wearily. "Why do I feel like a rat in a maze?"

Jerome Mason chuckled. "You can thank your friend, Calvin Price, for that. You see, the money really doesn't matter that much to him. His profile is obvious. He loves the gamesmanship, the ploy and counterploy. So that he's laughing at us right now, knowing we feel like rats in a maze, while all the time his plan is plodding along on schedule."

"You make it sound hopeless."

"Not by any means," Sheldon insisted. "It's also characteristic of Colonel Price that he has an ego and an immoderate sense of pride. He almost has a sense of overkill when it comes to flair and accomplishment."

"Is that supposed to help us?" Joshua asked skeptically.

"While it's a colorful way to go it's also impractical. For example, in plotting out the scenario to date, it appears more logical that Price should've brokered the hijacked plutonium in the Caribbean area, or at least definitely this side of Africa. Instead, he's arranged to have it carted halfway around the world."

"I see no elaborate staging involved," said Joshua. "The Kasim connection has to be responsible, since you could hardly expect him to expose himself at such a great distance from home just to be a local delivery boy."

Sheldon had started pacing to and fro in front of the table, and he now stopped in front of Joshua. "And that's the crux of the present plot. Kasim is the key. He must've consented to the plan because the plutonium is destined for one of his Arab sponsors." He paused then, before deciding to divulge the rest of it. "You might as well know that we have confirmed Kasim's splinter group is receiving support from an Iraqi intelligence source operating in Lebanon."

Joshua looked totally bewildered.

"I know it's difficult to understand," Sheldon said sympathetically, "but the Arabs are as preoccupied with themselves as they are with us. For example, Syria's intervention in Lebanon is motivated by many reasons, not the least of which is the traditional Syrian view that Lebanon is a part of its own territory stolen away by Western imperialism. So, her neighbors, especially Iraq and Jordan, are concerned with Syria's apparent expansionist tendency. At the same time, Syria is worried that Lebanon may be taken over by radical Arab forces, who would no doubt quickly form an alliance with a similarly radical regime such as is presently in control in Iraq, in which case Syria would then be caught in a hostile pincer."

Joshua finally held up his right hand to stop him. "Please, I'm already confused enough as it is."

"Oh, there's much more," Sheldon went on. "In Lebanon, you've got the left and the right, the PLO against the Christians. And, Israel is also heavily involved for obvious strategic reasons. However, it is Kasim's Iraqi support that concerns us the most. It is unlikely that he is operating without their knowledge. Also, no matter how much of an outlaw he may be, Kasim is still sensitive to the cause."

Mason offered the comment, "So it looks like the plutonium is going Arab."

"Now you can understand our concern," Sheldon said. "Kasim was probably approved by both Price and the ultimate buyer of the plutonium. The evidence is too strong for us to ignore."

"In the beginning," Mason said, "I was curious at how Price had managed to entice Kasim to join him. Now, it makes sense."

"Unfortunately for Israel," Sheldon added.

"Why the need for Barca?" Joshua mused half aloud.

"Insurance," Mason suggested.

"Exactly," Sheldon confirmed. "The fee Price paid is a small cost for the aid and comfort of an informer. Besides, Barca was needed to carry out the Anne Hunt ploy."

"Your plot makes sense," said Joshua after a moment, "but I don't view the Garand move to Beirut as any kind of special ploy. I'm convinced he's moving in the open because he's aware that we already know his destination. Even though we destroyed the villa, he has to assume we found the Barca note."

"So he's running a bluff," Sheldon said. "It's been done before, you know. But we're persuaded that the radio transmission could be a valid lead, which is why we're not taking Garand now. It's highly possible that Barca has no other way to report in, and Garand has to make the radio connection. Garand could very well be gambling that we did not find the memo, or, if we did, that we might not have correctly translated it. Remember, there was no mention of Beirut on the note itself."

Joshua exhaled heavily, showing his doubt. "The radio transmission is a mighty thin thread to hang our hopes on."

"Might even be more than we think," Sheldon mused. "It was suggested to me this morning that it could be a Kasim contact. There was no name of any kind on the memo, you may recall. The potential is there, since Tel Aviv is also of the opinion that Hafiz Barca could be a thin thread for Price to hang his contingency plans on."

"So why wasn't the note in Kasim's folder?"

Jerome Mason was chuckling under his breath. "Because there was no Kasim folder in the villa files."

Joshua glanced at him sideways.

"That means nothing," Sheldon insisted. "Both your and Brav's dossiers were also missing, and we're sure they were on the yacht with Garand." He noticed that Jerome Mason was checking his watch. "Are we about ready?" he asked then.

Jerome Mason stood up to look at Joshua. "The Major and I leave in forty-five minutes."

Sheldon watched the quick frown form on Joshua's face.

"And we've got a CIA rep' riding shotgun," Mason added.

"What about me?" asked Joshua as he stood up.

"You're going with Dan and Shira to Tel Aviv."

"Why not Beirut?"

Jerome Mason looked to Sheldon for help.

"Forget it," said Sheldon flatly. "Beirut is not only too dangerous, it's also no place for an outsider. The city contains one of our most complete networks, and I need the freedom to operate without having to . . ." and he paused.

"Without having to play nursemaid," said Joshua.

Sheldon shrugged. "Please be content to know that I've arranged for you to be on the strike team—if and when we need it. Your military background better suits you for that assignment."

Joshua sighed heavily, nodding his head in agreement.

"And what about you, sir?" said Sheldon to Jerome Mason. "Is it really necessary for you to go to Beirut?"

Mason smiled thinly. "Malek figures you can give this situation until tomorrow morning before it becomes a major flap. After that, the CIA is going to be all over it."

"I remind you that we will maintain operational control," Sheldon said carefully.

"Of course," Mason consented. "But whom would you prefer for your liaison, like the Tel Aviv CIA resident and all that he has to deal with? Or, would you be better off with an independent representative having a more direct line of communication? After all, I've already got a desk reserved in the American Embassy in Beirut, which means you won't have to play nursemaid; however, unless I get over there today you can forget it."

"Welcome aboard, sir," Sheldon said laconically.

Anne Hunt was beginning to realize that her life had finally turned full circle. The process was complete. Until today, it had only been the circumstances which had grown progressively more familiar; now it was the very country itself. It was mid-afternoon, and they had been travelling steadily since leaving Aqaba at dawn. They had crossed the treacherous Arabah desert during the day, a feat in itself made a little more bearable because of the lateness in the season. It was not only the intense heat but the monotony of the persistent threat of the land that also took its toll on the traveler who dared venture across a land that simply belonged on another less inhabitable planet.

They had turned northeast at Jiza, leaving behind the Hejaz railway, which once ran south from Damascus carrying the Turkish trains blown up by Lawrence of Arabia.

The white GMC van was fairly new, in good mechanical condition, and Hafiz Barca had pushed it mercilessly, wending his way expertly through the much slower moving traffic. As the day wore on, he swore more angrily and frequently at the drivers of the slower vehicles, causing Anne to suspect his mood had reached even a worse low point. A few kilometers out of Na'ur, Hafiz pulled off the asphalt road on a sandy trail.

"We need water for the engine," he told her.

Anne had been reading her Bible, and she closed it to put it on the dash in front of her. She was thinking suspiciously that they had not had any cooling problems with the van while they were crossing the much warmer desert.

Hafiz pulled in to stop behind a sand mound which hid them from the road.

Anne Hunt sat still as Hafiz climbed out to move around to her side. She saw that there was a nearby stream bed, but it was dry. She was not surprised.

Anne closed her eyes.

I come as the warm spring rain, and that which was dead lives, and that which lives . . . loves.

She heard the door coming open, and she opened her eyes to see that Hafiz was looking up at her. He had a revolver in his right hand.

"So it's time," she said slowly.

He gestured for her to get out.

As she climbed down, Anne tried to calculate her chances. They were still close enough to the road so that she could hear the sounds of passing traffic. The immediate area around them was apparently deserted. She moved to her right into the shady lee of the van, putting the strong afternoon sun in his eyes.

"Don't try anything foolish," he warned her as he stood aside to cut down the angle of the sun. "Because you're correct in guessing I'm under orders to eliminate you. And you're also correct in assuming that now is the time."

Anne Hunt closed her eyes again.

That which lives . . . loves.

And her thoughts broke, tumbling one after the other, without order, so that she had no notion what she should say in the following silence. She had stood on the threshold of death before and had not cared, but now she sensed that she did not want to die.

"You said you've been in my position before," he was saying.

"Yes," she whispered.

"Then you can understand."

She could not detect whether there was hope in his voice. "It is far more important that *you* understand," she heard herself suggesting, "because it doesn't matter now what I think or feel. You see, you're the one who will have to go on living, and thinking, and feeling . . . "

"So you think I'm only a rod of iron, after all," he said slowly.

"I've hoped and prayed that you've not become hardened."

He kicked angrily at the sand, startling her. "I ask you to understand," he snapped at her, "and you judge me instead!" He looked away across the wash bed, shaking his head in a gesture of disgust. "But I guess there's no way you can understand, because you have no idea what I'm having to go through now."

Anne grasped at the opportunity. "If nothing else, Hafiz, you owe me the truth now."

He turned to stare at her appraisingly.

"I have the right to know," she went on, and she was desperately trying to determine why he appeared to be indecisive. She continued with the initiative. "I can understand that if you must exchange your life for mine, then you must kill me."

"It's not just my life, which might be worth risking, but it's the lives of my family too."

The impressions were beginning to fall into place. "You're trying to get out, aren't you?" Watching for his reaction, she went on, "That's why you've been asking me all the questions about how I was able to do it."

He didn't answer, shaking his head slowly instead. Encouraged, she hurried on, "Hafiz, please. I got out, and I have no regrets, believe me," and she took a half step toward him.

He aimed the revolver at her stomach, levering the hammer back.

Anne Hunt felt the chill start up her spine.

"You have given me much help," he told her, "which is why I'm not so sure that I should kill you now. However, while I can see how you were able to start over again, I'm not so sure it will work for me. You see, the difference between us is that I may be betraying someone to carry out my end of the bargain."

"Then don't do it," she said flatly.

He took a half step away before lowering the hammer on the revolver.

"Is it too late?" she asked him.

"It's worse than that. Arrangements have been made to get my family away too; and unless I go through with the plan, we will all be in grave danger."

Anne began to understand. Hafiz Barca had gotten himself trapped into a situation where unless he performed, his family would be threatened. "Isn't there something I can do?"

"Forget it. I could never live down accepting help from the Jews."

"How are they involved?"

"I don't know that they are, but in this land they're the only ones an American could turn to."

"There must be Americans here who could help."

"It's all the same," he interjected bitterly.

Oh, you proud, stubborn man, she thought angrily. "Your loyalty somehow seems misguided," she snapped.

He glared at her. "How can you ignore your refugee brothers and sisters? Has it become so easy for you, since you've escaped to the land of milk and honey?"

"Please *try* to understand, Hafiz. I went from uncertainty in the cause to utter confusion. Then, for what reason I can't explain, I started reading the Bible, and it all started to make sense."

"Don't try to convert me," he warned her sternly. "We are right now concerned with whether you shall live or die, not the welfare of my soul."

"I'm not trying to convert you, Hafiz. I'm simply talking about biblical history and the facts that are emerging. It is the irony of Islam that the prophets you supposedly esteem predicted this same new Israel you're so determined to destroy. The Jews have come home, Hafiz. And, if that pill is indeed so bitter, then it should've been swallowed quickly and been done with. But you've been persuaded to hold the pill in your mouth, so that every day you gag on it."

"You sound more like a Jew than an Arab."

"You mean I sound stiff-necked and proud, and who does that description really fit?" She bit on her lower lip before she added, "Most of all it applies to our leaders, because it is they who promote the war that we have to endure, like you and I are doing right now."

"Our leaders do what they have to do," he insisted.

"Sure they do," she agreed with a distinct sound of disgust. "Like they form themselves into a petty cartel and wreck havoc and sorrow on the world. They've become tyrants! Allah mourns for them. The descendants of Ishmael were once worthy and mighty men, but they horde gold now and grow fat in the sanctuary of their palace halls while they scheme at the ways to destroy an enemy they already outnumber a hundred to one."

"The One God may be mourning for you shortly."

Anne nodded vigorously. "You see how far the deception has gone. You can even invoke the name of Allah to somehow justify your intent to kill."

Hafiz Barca reached up to push his dark glasses further up the bridge of his nose, as if to shield his eyes away from Anne's accusing glare.

"You realize," he finally offered, "that you're asking me to admit that I have been wrong all along, that our brothers and sisters are also in error in seeking justice—"

"Absolutely not," Anne interjected. "I am not nearly wise enough to know what the solutions are to our grievances. As you know, I was a part of a scheme to destroy an entire city with an atomic bomb. The very shock of that understanding was what first turned me to an appraisal. I thank God every night that the bomb was disarmed in time. Yet, deep down, I am still in sympathy with and fully understand the anger that pushes you. So, I cannot condemn you for feeling the way you do." She carefully selected her next words. "The truth is, Hafiz, that you are now at a turning point. While neither of us may know the solutions, I'm sure we can at least stop for a moment, hoping and looking for another way, *without* admitting we are wrong in what motivates us."

Hafiz pondered her argument, before he suggested, "So last year you came to a stop, hoping and looking for another way."

"Yes, that's exactly right."

"And an entire year has passed, hasn't it?"

"Yes, it has, but I haven't given up. Which makes a point. It's our impatience, most of all, which seems to keep prodding us."

"Thirty years is a long time, even for the most patient of men."

"Perhaps you are right," she admitted after a moment.

He finally broke the following lull. "Regardless, I've already been trying to find the way to spare you. It would be different if I were not trying to get out myself. However, since I will be finished by tomorrow, it does seem senseless to take yet another life." He paused then, studying her closely. "It seems you've finally run out of something to say . . . "

Anne had to clear her throat, before telling him, "I'm sorry, but I was just thanking the Lord."

He pushed the revolver into his belt. "You can thank your Lord all you like, but you will cooperate fully with me."

"I still say you should let me help."

"Not now. It would be too risky. I have a contact this afternoon, and it must appear that I have disposed of you on schedule." He glanced aside in what appeared to be a nervous gesture.

"Why not let me go now?" she suggested.

"I said it's too risky," he growled at her, and he was frowning as he went on, "because if they just suspect I'm not complying with their orders, it could blow up on all of us."

"I promise I'll cooperate," she assured him.

Maurice Garand went directly by cab from the Beirut airport to the eastside neighborhood of Ashrafiyeh. His cab driver spoke enough broken English to convey the message that Beirut was still a dangerous city to be about. Unaffected by the man's obvious attempt to increase his tip for alleged hazardous duty, Garand watched curiously as they turned onto Qadisha Street, their destination. He felt relived that they were now across the green line and in the safest sector, which was under the control of the Christian militia. The Syrian army was really in charge of the city, policing the current civil-war armistice.

The driver slowed as he searched for the street number.

Garand checked his watch to see it was a little past 7:00 p.m., local time.

The neighborhood was old and residential, termed by Western standards as middle-class, existing in that belt surrounding the less affluent and commercial part of the city. There were a few newer apartments spotted in among the rows of old double flats made of stone which stood so close together there was hardly room to walk in between. At this time of the early evening, the curbs were packed solid with the cars of the residents. When the cab stopped, the driver had to double park.

As Garand crossed the narrow sidewalk, he noticed discreetly that the same Peugeot sedan following him from the airport was stopped about half a block behind.

He knocked twice on the front door of the lower apartment marked "B." The door was on the right and under an alcove running under the balcony of the two units above. The man who opened the door nervously introduced himself as "Rashid Takla." He was short and stocky with a round and fleshy face, dressed in the summer shirt and wrinkled slacks of the typical hustler working any public place where there might be found the infrequent tourist brave enough to visit the troubled area.

Briefly disappointed, Garand put his right forefinger to his mouth in a gesture directing the other man to remain silent. He then pushed on through the doorway into the living room. The apartment was sparsely furnished, just enough to get by, and he moved quickly on through the kitchen to walk out the back door. The yard behind was narrow like the front, between the building and the cluttered alley, and Garand pulled up a few steps into the yard.

"Is the work finished?" he asked brusquely.

"Yes, sir. Two days ago, per your instructions," Rashid answered quickly. His demeanor was openly patronizing. "The equipment is the finest in all of the Middle East."

"We'll see in time," Garand told him tartly. "What is more important is the way we act from this point on. We will leave for dinner in a nearby restaurant in a few minutes. That will give the Jews the time to wire the phone and the house itself."

"There is an eleven o'clock curfew."

"We will return long before that. Tomorrow morning by ten o'clock, you will bring a short-wave receiver here, along with an extension ladder and fifty feet of aerial wire. Do you have the plastic explosive and detonator?"

"Yes, sir, stored in my truck, along with the sabre saw."

"The only thing left is the car."

Rashid Takla grinned broadly. "A 450-SL is ready and waiting in a garage less than twenty meters from where you now stand."

"For the car, noon tomorrow is critical."

Rashid smiled smugly. "I will be driving it myself."

"Is that a special recommendation?"

The eyes of Rashid Takla narrowed down. "Do not let my appearance and attitude deceive you. I am a professional, and I do my job well."

"So far, only your price recommends you," Garand said just as grimly.

The face of Rashid Takla relaxed, as if he had satisfactorily established himself with his employer. "Do you have anything else, sir?"

"While we are at the restaurant, we will talk, for at least an hour. I want your opinions on the politics of Lebanon, your family, enemies, girlfriends, whatever comes to your mind."

"I don't understand."

"I want to tape-record our conversation, and it isn't necessary for you to understand why."

Rashid shrugged indifferently.

At the dinner hour, the yacht *Swanya I* was at anchor in open water near the marina of the port city of Colombo, Sri Lanka, the former island of Ceylon. The only guest on the luxury vessel was a man whose Libyan passport reported the name of Phillip Maktoum. Below in the main salon, Calvin Price had just taken his own chair at the opposite end of the teak dining table. He had already critically surveyed the table's service, finding it in perfect order. He gestured for his guest to begin eating.

Phillip Maktoum looked to be somewhere in his middle forties. His face was thin and swarthy under his headscarf, and he had a thin and carefully trimmed mustache which reminded Price of the type worn by William Powell. Both men were formally dressed in dinner jackets, and the gold thread in Maktoum's head braid was interlaced with an expensive velvet. Maktoum used his fingers to pick up the large maraschino cherry from the center of his grapefruit.

The meal was Texas bill of fare, the specialty of the ship.

"Excellent," Maktoum commented after he had tasted the grapefruit.

"I thought you might like it," said Price. "It's a special pink hybrid I fly in from a grove near Laredo." He was tempted to tell his guest that with air freight and handling each grapefruit cost roughly twenty-five dollars. Instead, he pointed to a narrow velvet jewelry box in front of the Arab's water glass. "A gift from the ship," he said, nodding his head.

After pretending surprise, Maktoum picked up the velvet box to open it. His eyebrows lifted in apparent appreciation. It was a solid platinum necklace with a cat's eye the size of a marble. Maktoum turned it in the light. "It's marvelous," he commented. "I've never seen one so large."

"It's from the pits at Ratnapura, here on the island. Their overseas manager is a friend of mine. Once in a while they get a big one, and I have a standing order to get what I can." He was lying to the Libyan about the standing order business, because he had commissioned the stone from Ratnapura several months before to give to Karen Laswell on her next birthday. Now, he was trying to make the best of the loss. The gift was extravagant, but he had been trying to break into the Libyan market for a long time.

"I shouldn't take it," commented Maktoum.

Price made a shushing gesture with his right hand. "It is a personal gift. You have been patient because of the delay in the shipment, and I'm grateful."

"You have news?" Maktoum said expectantly.

"The occasion for the dinner. Less than an hour ago, my employee in Ismailia cabled me that as of this afternoon the material is en route again."

Maktoum smiled broadly as he closed the velvet case to put it on the table next to his right hand. "Your gift is accepted with great pleasure."

A minor write-off, Price thought to himself, considering that the Arabs were coughing up an extra half million to purchase the Armatrex plutonium.

"This country is most remarkable," said Maktoum as he started to finish his appetizer. "They seem to have profited from their Marxist experience."

Price resisted his impulse to chuckle. "They'll make it because they are now offering tax advantages to wealthy capitalists."

Maktoum chuckled without delay. "I remind you, sir, that in Libya we follow a way of life definitely left of center. And, we're making it work quite well without the benefit of wealthy capitalists."

Calvin Price dismissed his own protocol. "Sir, please allow me to suggest that so long as you have the wealth of the world at your fingertips, in your case, oil, then you can make any system work. Sri Lanka is not so fortunate." He smiled politely, noticing that the chill in his guest's eyes was close to that of the grapefruit he had just finished eating.

The head steward cleared their place settings, affording Maktoum the time to prepare his response, which, to Calvin Price was a challenge he could not turn down. "I'm sure, Colonel," Maktoum said evenly, "you are aware that great wealth does not automatically endow one with the wisdom to know how to rightly spend it."

"I am expressly aware of it. There is a Yankee expression which says, 'Shirtsleeves to shirtsleeves in three generations.' It's an axiom, a sort of truth really, which says that great wealth in the hands of a family is usually lost by the succeeding two or three generations of heirs. The backbone of the matter, of course, is that the heirs, by inheriting their money instead of having to earn it the hard way, are prone to squander away the wealth. For example, if you have a thousand dollars, it's easy to spend a dollar simply because you've still got nine hundred and ninety-nine left. On the other hand, if you've only got one buck to start with, you tend to be more careful in how you spend it."

"I suspect you're trying to tell me something," Maktoum mused.

The ship's stewards had started to set the main course,

which consisted of barbecued beefsteak of several different cuts, along with heaping side dishes of chili, potatoes, asparagus, corn on the cob. There was the added touch of chilled caviar within a nest of chopped sweet onions and slivers of hard boiled eggs.

Maktoum politely declined the offer of wine, asking instead for a small cup of black coffee.

Watching, Calvin Price wondered how far the necklace entitled him to go. He plunged on as he started cutting into his steak, "You oil sheiks are like the second generation heirs. In your own country, for example, you are subsidizing a socialistic system at enormous cost. I know your hearts are right, but you are still squandering millions of dollars a day. And, in the eyes of your own people, not unlike the Russians, you are already in the process of writing your own epitaph. Which will go something like, Here lies Libya, who promised too much to too many for too long and who gave too little to too few for just long enough." He paused then to take a bite of his meat.

Maktoum countered with, "Your shirtsleeves theory has foundation, I'm sure, but I'm not convinced our expenditures to improve our country's living conditions can correctly be called squandering."

Price finally had to chuckle. The man's naivete was just too amusing. "You already know how people who have nothing will revolt. However, wait until you have to face the masses when you start taking their goodies *away* from them. Then, you're really going to learn about mob behavior. And, you and your kind must eventually go bankrupt. Your oil supply is not limitless. The axiom gives you no more than three generations, and I tend to agree."

"Your remarks suggest a paradox, since you have built an empire based on sheer wealth."

"Forgive me for saying so, but if I ran my outfit the way you run your country, I'd be broke in two weeks."

"Perhaps we should hire you as a consultant."

"You can't afford me."

Phillip Maktoum laughed outright. "Within twelve hours I could put enough gold on this ship to sink her."

"I have no doubt. But, you see, I succeed because of the certain functions of the four cornerstones most affecting human conduct: greed, hate, fear, and pride. Greed is thus only a fraction of what you'd have to deal with in bidding for my time."

Maktoum frowned for the first time. "I think you are too much a cynic to persuade me."

"Aha, so you are a man of deep insight." Calvin Price's gambling instinct pushed him on. "You will *positively* fail for another equally historical truth, perhaps one even more absolute in its certainty. That is, of course, the certain consequence of your rejection and persecution of the Jews."

He was disappointed in Maktoum's mild reaction.

"The rest I have expected," Maktoum replied. "However, I am surprised to hear you defending the Jews." He frowned as he continued to work over his food. "Can it be that underneath you are religious?"

"I am not defending them, nor am I religious, as such. I am simply reminding you of a historical fact. There has never been a regime able to survive, let alone prosper, after condoning Jewish persecution."

Phillip Maktoum briefly contemplated the point, before admitting, "There is truth in what you say. It may sound strange to you to hear me admit that I respect the unique position the Jews have held in history. And, really, prior to the Zionist activists, we've all generally lived in peace with our Jewish cousins. And, in fairness to the same history you quote, you also must admit that there has never been an example of Jewish persecution against another people."

"I haven't thought about it, but I expect you're correct."

"But the situation, especially since '48, shows increasing signs of being different." He paused then to put his knife and fork down, folding his hands under his chin. "I shall not bore you with an Arab overview. Rather, I'll cite you a smaller example which is in microcosm to the larger issues. Right now, in Jerusalem, the rocks are crashing through the windows of Christian churches and retail stores. Swastikas and slogans are painted on the walls at night by Jewish fanatics. The hatred and lust for violence is thickening ever so slightly in the air of the Holy City. Imagine, if you can, what it might be like if these people were in power in Israel." He spread his hands for emphasis. "That in itself is not so earth shaking. It's been reported in the papers, which we monitor very closely, that some Christians have objected and have asked for protection."

Listening, Calvin Price had also put down his eating utensils.

"Now we get to the real point," Maktoum went on. "A Jew in Boston writes a letter to a Jerusalem newspaper saying that he is disgusted to hear that Christians are seeking protection in the Holy City, dismissing the violence of the Jewish gangs as merely isolated acts of vandalism. The letter, of course, is printed in the paper to be enjoyed by its Jewish readership, both in Israel and abroad. Now, if you dig back into the archives of the German press during the thirties, you will find the same comments by Nazi sympathizers in response to the desecration of synagogues by the brown shirts," and he waved his hands in an indifferent gesture, before he stared thoughtfully across the long table. "You'd think the spectre of a swastika would enrage any Jew anywhere, so condoning the symbol now suggests an even deeper radicalism than I had even supposed."

Calvin Price chuckled under his breath.

Maktoum asked him, "What do you find so amusing?"

"I'm sorry," Price apologized, "but I was having trouble conjuring up the vision of a Jewish nightrider. I wonder if they wear their skull caps under their sheets or on top."

"What they wear is unimportant. It's the sympathy and underlying support of their own people that is frightening."

"Maybe they're entitled. So now the Gentiles are getting desecrated for a change."

"Perhaps, but as you would say, let us call a spade a spade. It's symptomatic of the Zionist thrust in the Middle East. The Torah is their mandate. But, after all, lebensraum is still lebensraum, whether it be for Samaria or the Sudetenland. The Jewish colonizers argue that they need security corridors. Once the presently occupied lands are filled with Jews, then they will require security corridors to buffer those zones. Where will it all end? Perhaps at the Persian Gulf?"

"They have returned the Sinai, a nice chunk of lebensraum."

"An unpopular concession denounced by the Zionists. The Sinai issue is still hotly debated in the halls of the Knesset."

Calvin Price could only shrug.

"Why do you think we're really buying weapons-grade plutonium?" Maktoum asked quietly. "To use in offensive weapons? Is that really our concern? It is perhaps prophetic to you, a man of Christian background, to suspect that several years from now this material may be expended in *defensive* weapons. You see, the nationalism of the Zionists is now too deeply rooted in Jewish consciousness. The infectious strains of it run through the letter from Boston, and are shared by the tens of thousands of Jews who read it and nod approvingly. And, their mandate is not only the Torah, but it is the Holocaust as well, an inspirational combination unparalleled in the history of mankind."

"It seems to me that you've both got your hands full."

Phillip Maktoum smiled broadly. "Your expert neutrality is profit-inspired. However, allow me to remind you of an old Bedouin saying, that the man who refuses to take sides winds up the enemy of everyone."

Calvin Price was also smiling. "Speaking of profit reminds me of a cable I received from our Munich source this morning. It seems that Libya in the past few days has cancelled a sizeable contract with a West German firm for a certain centrifuge system, one which is used to enrich uranium."

Phillip Maktoum looked down to his plate. "Have you noticed, sir, that our food has turned cold?"

Price laughed at once. Clearing his throat, he offered, "Now I understand why you abstain from alcohol."

"Because it is forbidden."

"I suspect the reason why Mohammed spoke against it was because he knew it took a clear head to wield a scimitar."

Chapter thirteen

The subtle loss of power in the engines of the 747 was enough of a change in the feel of the aircraft to bring Joshua Bain out of his light sleep. He had been running again in the same recurring dream, and he awoke with a start. He involuntarily lifted his left hand to shield his eyes. Several seconds passed before he remembered he was on an El Al flight, destination: Tel Aviv, Israel.

"Are you all right?"

Joshua looked to his right to the source of the question. Shira Elazar was staring at him, a slight frown of concern around her eyes. She was in the window seat next to him. He looked past her to notice that the southern horizon was turning black.

"I'm okay," he told her after clearing his throat. Then he glanced to his left noticing that Dan Iser was not in his assigned seat. Dan's Bible, however, was on the cushion, an irrefutable sign of occupancy. "Where's Dan?" he asked idly. Their seats were adjacent to the mid-cabin galley, and he noticed that the flight attendants were busily securing the area.

"He was called to the radio," Shira answered him.

So the El Al radio was a handy IDF extension, a tactical convenience, and he was willing to gamble that the 747 could be converted to a troop carrier within an hour after landing. He checked his watch to see that they were about due to land. The flight had been an experience, best described by their young stewardess as being the same as the New York to Miami run in season, only longer.

Joshua was feeling a little guilty that he hadn't been able to share in the enthusiasm of the rest of the passengers. Following Dan's lead, he had ordered the kosher lunch, but even the bland chicken still sat in his stomach with the same sour distress as had all his meals for the past week. So much for the purification rites, including Dan's personal blessing. He turned to look at Shira. She was smiling now, looking at him with a three-quarter turn of her head, and Joshua realized this was the first time they had ever been together alone. "Would you believe," he said, "that my mind is so upside down right now that I don't know what to say." He swallowed then, watching the soft turn of her smile work up to the corners of her eyes.

"I don't understand."

"Neither do I," he admitted. "But I guess what I'm trying to say is that while I've known you for several days now, I still know practically nothing about you."

"You found out the first day that I wasn't married," she reminded him.

"That was on impulse, and I apologize for prying."

"You mean it's not on impulse now?"

The nose of the 747 had gone down, and Joshua knew the plane was now on its descent angle. Their time was running out. "No, it isn't," he assured her. "In fact, my curiosity is most deliberate. But, it's been a long time since I've talked to someone like you. That is, someone whose company is important, and you'll have to forgive me if I seem awkward."

She laughed lightly, shaking her head. "Oh, Joshua, how careful you are with your words," and she leaned back to stare up at the radius of the overhead storage compartment.

"There's very little to know about me, which may be of importance to you. I'm a widow, and I have a son. He just turned seven last month, and when I look at him I see his father in his eyes. And, I tell you that because I want you to know it all."

Joshua was thinking that little in life was ever really simple.

"Otherwise," Shira went on, "there's little else to report. I'm a graduate engineer in electronics, and I work for a company called Tadiran, where I'm presently involved in R&D on a classified military system. About all I can tell you is that we're working on the problems of integrating individual equipment into the complete system."

"You best stop there," Joshua advised her, "because I'm the world's worst security risk."

She smiled back at him. "Anyway, I like my work, and I'm in the field most of the time, so what free time I have I spend with my son and family. And, to avoid any misunderstanding, you should also know that I tend to be on the old-fashioned side."

Joshua sensed the drift of her conversation. "It sounds like you're content with the way things are."

She looked down to the arm rest between them. "There are thousands of widows in Israel like me. You might say we've become a kind of minority group, but I'm determined to lead my own life." She looked up to him again. "But what about you, Joshua? Sheldon told us that your entire family perished in the camps."

"So far as I know, only an aunt survived."

"There is the center in Jerusalem where you might be able to trace down your family."

"I know, and I've thought about it. But it's been such a long time now. I was raised by a Gentile family, and my adopted parents treated me with all the love and attention they might have given their own true son. My father explained it all to me on the day after I graduated from high school . . . "

"It must've been a shock," she finally offered.

"Not really, at the time. You see, as far as I was concerned, I was their son, and that was that. In fact, until about a year ago, it was no problem for me at all."

Shira Elazar raised a knowing eyebrow. "You mean it might have been simpler had you been born Irish instead of Jewish?"

"Perhaps," Joshua consented, "but I wouldn't change it if I had the choice."

She reached out to touch his right forearm.

Dan Iser sat down heavily next to him, abruptly ending the conversation.

"We're landing in a few minutes," Dan told them. He dropped his left hand to fasten his seat belt in compliance with the lighted overhead sign.

"Any news?" Joshua asked him when he saw he was finished.

"Not really. I was only told that we will be met at the airport for further transfer by military aircraft."

"What's your guess?"

"We'll probably be airlifted to a staging point close to the Lebanese border, maybe into the Christian sector itself," and he glanced around the cabin's interior, as if to make sure no one was listening to them. "We're already short on time, and we have to be briefed and equipped." He tipped his head forward to address Shira, "I was also told that you should prepare yourself to assist in the triangulation team."

Shira nodded that she understood.

Joshua felt encouraged that they were at least moving into action again. It was apparent that he and Dan would be a part of the strike team, if and when a target location could be pinned down. The Israelis were obviously not just content to wait for the radio transmission and what message it might contain; they were also setting up the means to fix the point of the transmission itself.

"So how do you feel, Joshua?" Dan asked him.

A distant hydraulic thump told Joshua that the landing gear was down and locked in place. "I'm still worried," he answered.

"I mean about coming to Israel," Dan explained. "Look around at the people. Look at their faces. Christians, Jews, even the Moslems. For many of them, this is the trip of a lifetime."

Joshua didn't know what to say. He was acutely aware of the question and what it should involve. He was, after all, a Jew himself. Yet, he could not find within himself the same excitement that was so common on the faces of his fellow passengers.

"If nothing else," Dan said to him, "you should find this an occasion to renew your hope."

The plane landed.

"Welcome home, Joshua," Dan said.

Joshua closed his eyes. Remarkably then, for just a passing

few seconds, the passengers fell silent as a group. And, Joshua Bain realized that there was one feeling he could not ignore, one which he sensed he shared with the others, and that was the very fact of Israel itself, that there was a home, finally, where a Jew could return if he or she wished.

The revelation was absolute.

The white van was parked behind the one-room adobe house occupied by the family of Hafiz Barca. Like the rest of the shanty homes jammed into the refugee camp, the house was built of mud brick, its walls thinly covered with decaying plaster. The sagging roof was an overlapping mixture of cardboard and corrugated plastic weighted down by scrap iron pipe. The Barca home was a squalid cell in a long row of others of the same size and shape so close together they almost touched.

Anne Hunt, nee Anne Delemar, recognized the smells and sounds.

Still covered by a heavy tarp in the rear of the van, she struggled with the temptation to drift into depression. It had been dark outside now for about three hours, and the temperature inside the van had finally started to decline enough for her to breathe a little easier. Huddled under the canvas, she had dehydrated enough to make her sick to her stomach again. Hafiz Barca had left her with a single pint of warm water stored in a plastic orange juice container they had purchased in Aqaba, but she had used up the water over two hours ago. She swallowed dryly. Carefully then, she lifted a corner of the canvas to allow at least a part of her body heat to escape.

She prayed again for the strength to go on.

The camp was beginning to settle down for the night, and with most of the children indoors, it was starting to turn quiet around the van. She did not know the exact location of the camp; however, based on their travel time and direction, she figured they were east and north of Amman, Jordan. Turning slowly to relieve the pressure on her hip, she began again to pass the time by thinking about Alan and Rancho Canaan. This time, her first thought was to realize how really fragile was their life together. It was perhaps a truth, after all, that all life, no matter how joyful or fulfilling, was in reality only a vapor, a passing thing. The ranch was now nothing more than a memory, if even that, for with each passing day the images stored in her mind became more obscure, more difficult to recall in detail. She felt the tears forming in the corners of her eyes.

Oh, Lord, please come quickly . . .

The soft sound of footsteps in the sand intruded into her consciousness.

She tensed involuntarily.

The rear door latch turned mechanically.

"It's nearly time," Hafiz told her in a whisper.

She pushed the canvas away from her head.

He handed her a small canvas-covered canteen. As she drank hungrily, she noticed over his shoulder that the night sky was free of clouds, the stars distinct and bright. The now cold desert air flowed into the van, and she started to push the rest of the canvas aside.

"Not yet," Hafiz warned her, and he replaced the canvas. "We are due for company any minute. We must leave the van here to avoid arousing suspicion, and you must be absolutely still and quiet." He closed the door.

Anne waited, listening to Hafiz as he began to walk back and forth at the opposite end of the van. She assumed that he was waiting for his contact to arrive from Amman. For her, the meeting was a crossroad, one which would verify whether Hafiz Barca had been telling her the truth. She realized that the van door could come open again, and that she could be shot where she lay. She once again considered the chances she might have by trying to escape, especially now that it was dark. She was still handcuffed. She had no papers.

She tensed at the sound of a vehicle closing from the front.

The vehicle stopped, sounding like it was near the front of the van. She then heard a car door opening and closing. The voices coming to her were at first muffled, before the exchange became louder, enough for her to realize they were speaking Arabic. There was a brief lapse, then she recognized the voice of Hafiz. He was shouting angrily, causing her to flinch. She picked up enough of the outburst to understand he was accusing someone of breaking a promise. Concerned now, she was thinking she should try the rear door, when she heard a car door slam.

She braced herself, holding her breath.

An engine revved, followed by the sound of tires digging into the sand.

Anne let her breath go after several more seconds had passed. Still braced, she could feel her heart pounding in her throat. A baby began to cry in one of the nearby stone cubicles, a baby whose small voice was not yet so urgent, like the first complaint of hunger perhaps, and it inexplicably came to her that when people cried they did so in a universal tongue, without the barrier of language.

The passenger door came open.

She peered out from under the forward flap of the canvas to see the silhouette of Hafiz Barca. She tentatively pushed the flap aside.

"It's safe now," he finally offered over his shoulder. "You can sit up if you like, but stay below the seat line."

She crawled forward to pull up behind the passenger seat. "Is everything all right?" she asked quietly. She had detected in his voice a tone of resignation which concerned her.

"Things could not be worse," he told her. "They have changed the payoff procedure, and I'm beginning to wonder if they really intend to carry out their end of the agreement."

"Can't you tell me what's going on?" she pleaded with him. "My life is still at stake, so if I can help you, then I'll be helping myself as well."

He turned to look at her, and she could see enough of his face to see he was smiling. "I wonder," he finally offered, "whether you are a source of great pleasure or the worst of irritation to your husband."

"Perhaps a little of both."

"All right," he said, looking away. "Tonight they were supposed to deliver my family's papers, including steamship tickets and passports, along with one half my final payment." He reached out to slam the dash with the flat of his right hand. "Instead, they gave me travel papers and visas enabling us to get to Beirut. And, only ten thousand dollars instead of fifty thousand."

Anne understood that someone was holding out on Hafiz Barca. "Who are you actually working for?"

He shook his head. "I don't really know for sure. The highest face-to-face contact I've had has been with a man who called himself Maurice Garand."

"So how were you recruited?"

"What difference does that make now?"

"It might help if you knew who you're working for."

"About a year ago, I was on an assignment in Algeria. I was a marksmanship instructor at a clandestine training camp, and I was working with a contingent of volunteers from Puerto

Rico sponsored by the FALN. I was initially contacted there. The original proposal, which I accepted, was the kidnapping assignment."

"Did the payoff involve your family?"

"Not originally. That came later, when Garand added in the rest of what they wanted."

Anne realized that Hafiz had been double-staged into his present predicament. Once they had found his weakness, his family, it had been easy to escalate the program. "Was there ever any mention of plutonium or the code word Jordan?"

"No," he answered after a moment. "Why?"

"I'm only guessing now, but it's possible that all this has a connection with a shipment of stolen plutonium. The chances are good that your Mister Garand is an employee of a man named Calvin Price."

"How do you know this?" he asked skeptically.

"Because my husband and a friend of ours were hired by Calvin Price to handle the exchange of the plutonium between him and Israel. That's all I can tell you for sure."

Hafiz chuckled derisively. "So it's the Jews, after all."

"I'm only guessing, Hafiz. Assuming a connection, then the motive behind my kidnapping would likely be to suggest an Arab involvement." She closed her eyes as she tried to produce an answer that could help them. "Who is the person you said you might have to betray?"

"Our group leader, Kasim."

The name registered at once. "The same Kasim that was with Fawd before he was killed?"

"Yes."

Anne felt even more convinced there was a connection. "All right, so how are you to do it?"

"I'm supposed to radio Kasim's location at noon tomorrow. The how of it is simple; all I have to do is to verify where he is hiding."

"So you already know where he is."

"Of course I know."

Anne turned the information in her mind. If Kasim was involved with the plutonium, then the radio report by Hafiz could be nothing more than a rendezvous contact. "Are you sure you'll be betraying him?"

"What do you mean? I'll be reporting his location."

"What I mean is, if Garand and Kasim are scheduled to meet, then you might not be anything more than insurance for

Garand, who simply might not trust Kasim enough to reveal himself on his own."

"That's exactly what Garand claimed. While he refused to tell me what was involved, he said it was absolutely essential that he meet with Kasim on Monday afternoon."

"So maybe it's true, especially if the stakes are high enough for Garand. And, if it is the plutonium, I can guarantee you the stakes are more than high enough."

"Enough to pay me a hundred thousand dollars?"

Anne had to admit to herself that the fee was high. "But they've only paid you ten," she pointed out.

"So you think I'm right in being upset."

"You have reason to be about the payoff. What was the explanation from the contact a few minutes ago?"

"He said that Garand was afraid that I wouldn't make the radio transmission, that they needed to hold out more to guarantee I'd perform."

"Is it possible they're more right than wrong?"

He glanced at her again. "Does it really matter?"

Anne realized it didn't. "So what's the new arrangement?"

"After I make the transmission at noon tomorrow, I move on to Beirut, where I have an address to pick up the rest of our papers and the final payoff."

Anne used the following silence to decide that Hafiz Barca had little to no chance of ever seeing his final payoff. She also sensed that it would be useless to argue the point, since Hafiz would suspect she was putting her own interests first. "So what are you going to do, Hafiz?"

"You know I must take the gamble. I've already spent most of the money I've received so far on a new home, so that we'd have a place to move into."

"Where?"

"In a suburb near Lisbon. It's a Moslem neighborhood, and I bought it under an assumed name."

"So you've got ten thousand to get started."

He laughed lightly. "You know how far that will take us. I've already made plans for my sister to go to school. Both she and my younger brother, Ahmed, need a lot of work on their teeth. We need a car . . . "

"You've trapped yourself, Hafiz."

"Perhaps," he seemed to admit. "But I'm banking on my value to Garand, especially as a witness to the kidnapping. There's also the good chance that I can be of further use to him in dealing with Kasim."

He was rationalizing, but she knew it would do no good to tell him. "So what happens to me?"

"We'll be leaving here soon in order to cross into Lebanon before dawn. Our papers are still good, so you and I will continue to pose as man and wife if our papers are checked. Arrangements are being made for me to pick up a jeep with a radio transmitter after we cross into Lebanon. You'll go with me in the jeep. There'll be little time left by then, so it won't matter if you are seen, anyway. You'll be free to go at noon. The Christian sector is only a few kilometers away, and I'll drop you off within walking distance."

For some reason the relief Anne Hunt felt was not so profound as she had expected. Inwardly, she began thanking the Lord and praising His name. "I will continue to pray for you, Hafiz," she said then.

"You are most fortunate," he told her. "If it were not for my desire to get out, you know that you would be dead by now. So, I suggest you thank your God for that decision."

That he considered her fortunate reminded her of Alan. "Are you certain you know nothing about my husband?"

"I would not lie to you about that, especially now. Besides, he could very well be safe for all you know."

Anne supposed he could be right. She had no actual evidence or even a hint that Alan and Joshua had not completed their end of the operation without incident. She resigned herself that she would have to wait until after noon tomorrow to find out.

When the small compact sedan reached the street fronting the water, the driver stopped obediently at the intersection's stop sign. Jerome Mason looked out across what he could see of the darkened port of Beirut. It was going on eleven o'clock, the time of curfew, and there were only a few vehicles left on the streets now. Several seconds passed, and he looked to his left to see that his driver was carefully studying the rear view mirror.

"Someone on our tail?" Mason asked quietly, and he resisted the temptation to look back over his shoulder.

The driver, who looked young enough to be in high school, shook his head negatively as he shifted into low gear. He turned left, moving at a more moderate speed. The driver's precaution suggested they were getting close, and Mason noticed that most of the buildings away from the water were retail stores and restaurants with only a few showing any lights. The car turned left at the next corner, then left again down the narrow alley. About a third of the way into the block, they pulled in to park in a narrow, dirt-covered lot. Leaving the engine running, his driver spoke for the first time since they had left the American Embassy.

"You go through that door," he told Mason, jerking a thumb toward the building facing the lot.

Mason thanked him and got out with his jacket over his arm. The car backed out of the lot to move away down the alley. There was the heavy smell of the docks in the air, and it was getting chilly, causing Mason to pull into his lightweight sportcoat. He couldn't read the Arabic sign running along the top of the metal-faced building, the larger part of which was taken up by a wide swing-down door. Taking a deep breath, he walked across the sandy dirt to the smaller door pointed out by his driver. He tapped on the door twice.

David Sheldon let him in without comment, nodding just once before turning to lead him diagonally across the more open part of the small crowded warehouse. They passed by a panel truck with its rear doors open, and Mason could see enough of its lighted interior to identify at least one man working on some kind of equipment. The truck was a commercial vehicle, but, again, Mason could not read the Arabic characters painted on its side. Feeling disoriented and out of place, he followed Sheldon into a small and cluttered office, where he complied with Sheldon's gesture to sit down in a wooden chair next to a desk.

"Doesn't anyone in this country ever talk?" he asked drily.

As Sheldon sat down behind the desk he was smiling appreciatively. "Most of us have too much on our minds," he offered. "Besides, this city's like a powder keg. And, the rumors are starting that the Syrians might be pulling out any day."

So the blood-letting might start again, Mason thought as he watched Sheldon open a thin-line briefcase. "I'm beginning to think Joshua Bain is more right than wrong," he suggested, "when he claims there's more insanity than good sense in the world."

"Joshua is under the worst kind of pressure," Sheldon said.

Mason studied him closely. "You've got some news, haven't you?"

Sheldon arranged several papers in front of him before he answered, "Kasim has been reported in the Rafid sector. He was seen yesterday morning in a car, along with two other men. The identification is reliable, coming from a trustworthy informant."

"That has to be good news."

"My tendency is to view it as just the opposite. If Kasim can risk travelling in the open, then he probably has already disposed of his cargo and hostages."

Jerome Mason knew he had to agree with Sheldon's estimate.

"That's not all," Sheldon went on. "Maurice Garand has moved into an apartment on the east side, not far from here. The location was arranged by a Rashid Takla, a known flunky who would sell his services to any bidder with the cash. A few hours ago, they went out to eat, giving us the better part of two hours to bug and inspect the premises. Believe me, if you want to quote Joshua Bain, then you can say the situation stinks."

"So why not pick him up right now?"

Sheldon chuckled ironically. "It's simply too much of a risk. We could spook the radio transmission."

Jerome Mason noted to himself that they were all getting strung out. Operation Jordan was turning into a definite grind.

"What happened to your baby-sitter?" Sheldon asked.

"Your ultimatum worked. The Charge d'Affaires exercised his local authority in the best interests of the situation." Mason paused then, reviewing in his mind the classified Israeli note delivered to the Embassy, which stipulated that he could be permitted to join Sheldon's group so long as he was alone. "Your note suggested I'm an official observer. Do I represent the U.S. Government?"

"Yes, sir, you do," Sheldon told him, and he picked up one of the papers from the desk. "I have been instructed to inform you that earlier tonight the following official communique was delivered to your Tel Aviv Embassy. Briefly, it recognizes that three U.S. nationals are involved in the operation referred to as Jordan. By tomorrow morning, we will require a written statement from your State Department that we have U.S. permission to use whatever means we consider appropriate to secure the contraband plutonium and the release of the hostages."

"Why're you passing this across to me?"

"Because we want your personal endorsement."

"Why? It seems to me that you're going to do what you want to, anyway."

David Sheldon fingered his mustache thoughtfully. "We all know that's true. However, have you considered that there may be those in *our* government who argue that if we recover the plutonium that we keep it ourselves? Last week it was in the Caribbean, today it's right in our lap."

Mason grunted appreciatively. "But they must be in the minority, otherwise you wouldn't have issued the communique."

"That's true. But, with us, a minority can become a majority overnight."

"So what's your point?"

"We've added a kicker. If we're successful in recovering the plutonium, it will be immediately transferred to Ben-Gurion Airport, where it will be available for inspection. And, it must be understood that Israel be given due credit for its recovery."

Jerome Mason chuckled. "You don't want my personal endorsement; you want the communique leaked."

"Ah, Mister Director," Sheldon said affably, "your astuteness knows no bounds. I'm surprised you're not in politics."

Mason smiled back at him, thinking that David Sheldon was really the one who had missed the calling.

Chapter fourteen

The sleeping quarters for the IDF forward base was built like a bunker into the adjoining hillside. As Joshua Bain pushed through the heavy door, he estimated the adjacent concrete wall was at least two feet thick. The Israelis had obviously constructed the small barracks to withstand a rocket or artillery attack of the kind occasionally coming from the Lebanese side of the nearby border. He pulled up to wait for Dan Iser, who followed behind him. Both men were dressed in field combat gear.

"Where to now?" Joshua asked. He had slept for seven straight hours, soundly and without dreaming, and he was now anxious and ready to get started. The midmorning sun came down sharply, reflecting off the low wall of the barracks, and even with his dark glasses he was still squinting against the glare.

Dan Iser turned up his watch, before putting his left hand to his throat. "We're due for briefing at ten o'clock, about forty minutes from now. We can get something to eat first."

"Where's Shira?"

"She left before dawn. She's working one of the field triangulation posts, and it was necessary that she be in position before daylight."

"It seems we ought to be more forward," Joshua suggested. "If Sheldon has a reliable report on Kasim's location, the closer we are the better."

"We will probably move out about eleven-thirty," Dan explained. "If we tried to get closer now, our movement could alert Kasim, perhaps even cause him to move away. You see, these hills have both eyes and ears."

Joshua calmly accepted Dan's explanation, thinking that there was indeed a time for all things, but that waiting was one of the more difficult. He fell in stride beside Dan as they moved across the open compound. They had arrived by helicopter late last night from Ben-Gurion Airport, and the features of the small base had been dark and indistinguishable. Now, in the strong light, his military background enabled him to identify and appreciate the features of the small base. At least a dozen ready helicopters were spread randomly behind the protection of cement-lined revetments. Several armored personnel carriers were more evenly placed on an outer perimeter. He noticed two manned guard towers beyond the armored vehicles in an obstacle lane of barbed wire. He supposed the concertinas were laced with trip flares, behind an even broader perimeter of strategically placed land mines and listening devices. The camp was well defended against infiltrators. "Where exactly are we?" he asked.

"Do you remember Avivim?"

"Yeah," said Joshua soberly. Death in the afternoon, children on a bus, he seemed to remember. A cruel and senseless insanity.

"We're about ten kilometers away," Dan told him. "The border is just over that hill," and he pointed north across the compound. "This is primarily a patrol staging base."

Joshua followed his direction, looking both left and right

to appraise the countryside. The first wind was starting to move across the open ground, and he was reminded of the high desert of Rancho Canaan. He then realized the terrain was really only similar in profile. The rocks strewing the sandy ground were more white and weathered, as if they had been bleached under the millennia of sun and wind-driven sand. What plant life he could make out also seemed to be brutalized, and he caught himself thinking that the impression was ancient and skeletal, as if the crooked rocks and strains of exposed hardpan were the protruding remnants of what was once living. The land looked dead. "So this is the Holy Land," he heard himself commenting.

"You are not impressed," Dan observed.

They pulled up in front of another bunker. There was a small wooden sign over the metal door with Hebrew characters that Joshua couldn't read.

"Most new arrivals feel a sense of exultation," Dan went on. "It's like there's something here, in the air, pervading everything. History in this land seems to have a substance to it."

"I suspect it's all in your mind," Joshua suggested quietly. "I felt a little of it last night at the airport." Feeling awkward, he reached up self-consciously to pull on his left ear. "Perhaps in time I will come to appreciate it more."

He followed Dan into the bunker, which turned out to be the mess hall. It was comfortably cooler inside. The eating tables were almost all vacant, except for one at the far end of the room, where three men dressed in flight suits were seated drinking coffee.

One of them waved a greeting to Dan Iser.

Joshua was comfortable in the military atmosphere, and by the time they took their seats to eat he was feeling less out of place. Taking toast and coffee only, both men were quiet for several minutes.

Finished with his food, Dan Iser broke the silence first. "Those three over there," he said, gesturing toward the three pilots seated at the other end of the room, "will be flying the gunships for the strike."

Joshua removed his dark glasses to study the three pilots more closely. He saw now that they were younger than he had at first supposed. "They're just kids," he said quietly.

"They may be young, but they are well trained and quite able to do the job. The one on the right, the one who waved to me, is Haim Resnik. His father was my battalion commander in '67." Dan Iser was beaming as he went on. "His father is in fact the one who led me to the Lord."

"What about the son?" Joshua asked idly.

"I'm glad you asked, because Haim accepted the Lord last year."

Joshua nodded politely as he stared at the three pilots. "That's not a bad average. Like one out of three."

Dan Iser smiled broadly. "The average is more like one in ten thousand."

Joshua contemplated the remark. "That perhaps might be the lowest of any people in the world."

The expression on Dan's face turned more somber. "From what you told me at Port-au-Prince, I suspect you're more keenly aware of the average than you seem to pretend."

Joshua smiled thinly. "You may score one for the man with the rocks in his pockets."

"I suspect your good friend, Alan Hunt, may also be, shall we say, intrigued by the circumstance."

"A better word would be bugged."

"Ah, yes, but then it helps to understand why."

"A rabbi by the name of Feldman has been trying to get me to understand why for a long time now."

Dan Iser checked his watch, before returning his left hand to his throat. "You are a unique challenge to both of us, Joshua."

"You mean because I was raised a Gentile?"

"Oh, yes, indeed, and it's even more noteworthy that you use the term Gentile, because in so doing you admit to the separation which is integral to the situation. You see, a native-born Swede in Stockholm who accepts Christianity does not in any way become less a Swede. Would you agree to that?"

"Yes."

"Well, then, why is it that when a Jew in Tel Aviv becomes convinced that Christ is the Messiah, he is suddenly no longer considered a Jew by most of his fellow countrymen? Why is he openly called an outlaw, a renegade?"

"The answer to that is complex."

"It is made so by those who want it to be complex. Look at me, Joshua. Or, look at Haim. Do either of us strike you as being less a Jew than, say, David Sheldon or Shira Elazar? And, before you answer, decide also if it is so complex a thing to consider."

Joshua realized he was smiling as he answered, "From what I can gather, both David Sheldon and Shira look upon

Dan Iser as some kind of Israeli hero."

Dan looked aside. "You know what I mean."

Time turned back a year, and Joshua remembered Benjamin Caplan standing in an open hangar and the brief passage of anger across his friend's face. "I know what it's like to be called an assimilationist," he said evenly.

"Then you're right next to the key to the Jewish rejection. Our people are not nearly so much antagonistic to the fact of the Messiah as they are to the alleged loss of their cultural identity." He shook his head sadly. "The truth is that there are those who use the word assimilation not as a logical argument but as a bogeyman to frighten us into rejection."

Joshua thoughtfully sipped his coffee. It was beginning to dawn on him why Alan Hunt seemed to have had so much trouble in trying to reach him. "I understand the Holocaust connection now," he mused quietly. "The Nazis tried to destroy a whole people, an entire race. So that now, too, we are just as fearful of any kind of *religious* conversion because it can be viewed as an effort to reduce our numbers *racially*." He nodded vigorously. "But I don't understand why it is necessary to link the two together. Like the Swede in Stockholm, your personal convictions on religion ought not to affect you racially." He frowned then. "In fact, what you think has nothing to do with your genetics. And, to claim that it does actually suggests a form of racial superiority."

"A strange view for a Jew, wouldn't you say?" Dan offered. "However, there is a distinct difference between the Swede and me. In my case, I know I am much *more* a Jew in accepting my Messiah. Despite my critics, I am still very much the seed of Abraham. They can't take my birthright away from me. They may disown me, but our God hasn't. Also, since I'm so successfully able to remain here and demonstrate my Jewishness, I'm a special kind of problem to the orthodoxy. You see, I'm not really asking them to accept something, in their view, so much as I'm telling them to give something up. They've been conditioned. The myth of assimilation is the veil drawn across the minds of our people, so that they cannot see the truth. As it is said even until today, when Moses is read, the veil is upon their heart."

"So why keep pushing?"

Dan Iser stood up after checking his watch. "Because I am a Jew, and I love my people." He turned away toward the door.

Joshua got up to follow behind him. As if on cue, the three

pilots had also left their table, obviously heading for the same briefing.

Joshua stood aside while Dan Iser hugged his young friend, Haim Resnik. They separated and began to talk to each other in Hebrew. The affection between the two men was warm and apparent. Watching them, Joshua was conscious he could detect nothing different about the two men.

They were Jews.

The certainty of the fact was so obvious, he couldn't imagine anyone trying to deny it.

The reverse slope to the ridge line was gentle, and Hafiz had quietly nursed the jeep to within a few meters of the crest. With Anne Hunt following behind, he had walked the short distance to where he could start to see over the crest itself. Motioning for her to drop down, he crawled forward to where he could use the binoculars.

Anne pulled even with his shoulders to follow his line of sight. The ridge overlooked a gently sloping valley, and even without the glasses she could make out the low stone farm building on a small knoll. She estimated that their position was almost directly due north under the strong overhead sun on a line roughly two kilometers from the farmhouse. The wind was strong coming up the valley directly into their faces.

Hafiz handed her the glasses.

Anne studied the distant farmhouse more closely. It was a typical peasant farmer's home. The stone walls were gray and unpainted under the low, flat roof which had accumulated enough earth and sand over the years to support seasonal weed growth. There was a small fenced courtyard in front, where at least a burro and several goats would be stabled, but there were no animals to be seen. She guessed that the family working the barren farm had left for some reason. Aside from a lone sentry, the only sign of habitation was the several sleeping mats draped over the courtyard fence. "Are you sure he's there?" she asked quietly.

"Yes, he is. You can see the hood of the Fiat parked under the lean-to on the west side of the house. The sentry is one of Kasim's own personal bodyguards. Besides, this site is on the schedule. He was supposed to relocate here some time over the weekend."

She lowered the glasses, handing them to him awkwardly because of the handcuffs. Taking the glasses, he studied her briefly before reaching into his shirt pocket to pull out the key to the cuffs. "You might as well be comfortable," he told her, handing her the key.

She removed the cuffs. "So what happens now?"

"In about thirty minutes I will make a radio transmission. Supposedly, that is the end of my assignment. I have decided to take you into Beirut, where you can go directly to the American Embassy. It will be safer for you that way."

"I appreciate that," she told him sincerely. "Can I be of any help to you in Beirut?" She was rubbing her wrists, one at a time, while she waited for him to reply.

"What do you mean?" he finally asked.

"You should prepare yourself for a disappointment. I frankly don't believe they will give you the money."

"I am prepared to face it."

"Regardless of your pride, I'm still going to tell the American authorities that you helped me and that you're responsible for my being alive. And, my motive is the welfare of your family."

He chuckled as he leaned forward again to inspect the farmhouse.

"Why can't you send the radio message while we're on our way to Beirut?" she asked him then. She now found the waiting intolerable.

"We must wait here until noon. If we run into a Syrian patrol or check point, they'd confiscate the radio. Plus, we're on high ground here. And, for a far more important reason, I want to be as sure as I can that I haven't betrayed those who have always been my friends."

Anne realized they would have to wait. Hafiz was responding to both his conscience and curiosity, a combination too powerful for her to deal with. "I presume it's now safe for me to formally meet your family?" To her, the Barcas were only jumbled voices heard through a layer of dirty canvas.

He lowered the glasses, staying in place with his forward weight on his elbows. "When we finish here."

"Do they want to leave?"

"My younger sister, Maya, would rather stay. She imagines that she is in love with a soldier, a Jordanian sergeant who struts around the camp like a rooster."

"How old is she?"

"Eighteen, last month."

"You will have trouble there," she warned him thoughtfully. She picked up the empty handcuffs, turning them in her hand. "You may have to use these."

"Her mother and younger brother are both watching her."

So that meant there were at least three members of the Barca family in the van hidden in the small gorge at the base of the valley behind them. She dropped the handcuffs in the sandy dirt beside his elbow. "What happened to your father, Hafiz?"

"He died several years ago."

"In the fighting?"

"He died of boredom and humility, in his sleep," Hafiz explained after a moment, and he turned to rest on his left elbow, looking on past her impassively. "A few days before he died, he told me that he could feel the fat building up around his heart. It was a useless way to go, but I could tell he preferred that above the life he was forced to live. It was less a family tragedy than it was a kind of personal triumph for a kind and gentle old man who just couldn't take it anymore."

There was a closing tremor in his voice, and Anne Hunt looked away to stare at the shadowless terrain. She felt her own frustration in trying to deal with an injustice the cause of which was so shrouded in dispute that it seemed to defy discussion let alone explanation. But the absurdity of it was too apparent for her to let it pass without comment. "You may not be willing to accept it, but the fact is that your father was more—"

"Not now," he said sharply. "I must check the radio and get the antenna ready."

Anne took a deep breath, one of resignation and acceptance, watching then as he froglegged away from the crestline. She was beginning to realize that she was getting involved again. Her emerging feelings were strong enough to be identified. She turned away to pick up the binoculars, fingering the knurled focus ring absently while she reminded herself that it was nearly over and there was nothing she could do to alter the outcome.

She thanked the Lord again that she was being spared.

Closing her eyes, she prayed for the Barca family.

A warm breeze worked its way up the opposite slope to move across her face, and she repeated to herself again, *That which was dead lives, and that which lives . . . loves.*

The refrain had become a part of her.

At exactly ten minutes to twelve, Maurice Garand put his

left forefinger to his mouth, motioning for his accomplice, Rashid, to stop talking. The two men were in the apartment's small dining room adjacent to the kitchen. Garand was standing next to the service counter, his right hand on the rocker switch of a tape recorder on the counter. The anticipation turned in his stomach. He was smiling as he depressed the switch.

Rashid was also smiling as the machine started.

The recording was an edited part of the conversation between them on the night before at the restaurant where they had eaten dinner. Garand remained still long enough to be satisfied the volume level was proper. He took a note out of his shirt pocket to place it on the recorder, before he quietly led Rashid down the connecting hallway to one of the back bedrooms, where he carefully closed the door behind them. He had already cleared the room of its one bug, but he still motioned for Rashid to keep his voice down. Quickly then, they pulled the mattress off the double bed, lifting it next to the closet door. Garand steadied the mattress while Rashid slipped into the closet.

"Don't start it until the door's closed," Garand warned him quietly, referring to the small sabre saw Rashid had picked up from the floor. With the closet door closed, Garand secured the mattress with the box spring from the same bed. Finished, he tapped once on the nearby wall. He could hardly hear the saw when it started.

He checked his watch, aware of his nervousness now, to see that they were a full minute ahead of schedule. Taking a deep breath to help calm himself down, he next moved the room's lowboy dresser to a position directly in front of the closed hallway door. He had already mounted a small brass eyelet next to the jamb at the knob level. It took him less than two more minutes to set the booby trap of plastic explosive stored in the dresser. Finished, he stood up to briefly assess his handiwork. The trip line of nylon fishing line was a little too loose, and he carefully moved the dresser away to tighten the line. The explosive was meant to be a diversion only, enough to allow the final part of the plan to unfold with the maximum chance of success.

He checked his watch.

Operation Jordan was nearing its end.

He was sweating heavily, and as he pulled off his glasses to wipe them with a handkerchief, he reflected that today might find the score evened up for Colonel Calvin Price.

The tension in the panel truck was equal to the heat and humidity. Jerome Mason was in the passenger side of the front seat, where he was trying to do his part by watching the rear of the apartment building. The small truck was parked just far enough down the alley to allow him an unobstructed view. There were two other men on the surveillance team covering the front as well. David Sheldon was behind him in the truck, monitoring the listening devices in the apartment. The truck's shortwave receiver was also on, turned to the designated frequency of the expected noon message, and was manned by a waiting operator. The truck was also equipped with a separate transceiver with an open line to Tel Aviv, where the cryptographers were standing by their computers, in case the message came in code.

He heard Sheldon exclaim something, and he turned to look at the Major, who was shaking his head in obvious disgust. "Can you believe it!" Sheldon was saying heatedly. "Less than one minute to go, and they're talking about Rashid's love life." He grimaced even more angrily as he returned the microphone to his left ear.

As he turned back to watch the apartment building, Mason reached up with his left arm to again wipe the sweat from his face. The narrow alley was like a furnace. The heat waves boiled off the hood in front of him. What little wind there was did more harm than good as it pushed the dust in from the unpaved alley through the open window. He'd thought to close the window, but he knew they'd suffocate in minutes with the truck closed up. He anxiously checked his watch. Thirty seconds to go.

He looked over his shoulder again. "No change?" he asked.

Sheldon shook his head negatively.

"So what do you think?" Mason asked concernedly.

"I think we're being had," Sheldon said angrily, but he kept the headphone glued to his left ear.

At fifteen seconds, Jerome Mason realized that right up to the final second they had no choice but to wait and hope.

Hafiz Barca had removed the map from its canvas pouch. The topographical map was at a scale of 1:25,000 and he had at once located the ridge line, which was identified with its elevation number. He had been ordered to report Kasim's location in two different ways. The first, and simplest for him, was to designate the farmhouse by denoting its distance and azimuth angle from the nearest main and easily identifiable road junction. He had plotted the degree angle on the way in with a military compass and was familiar enough with the local terrain to accurately estimate the distance. The second method was to report the grid coordinates, using the map provided, which he was supposed to identify as UTMG dash seventy-two. He had checked both calculations twice.

He presumed that Garand was worried there could be a mistake in locating the site. He had already decided that with what he was going to report, Maurice Garand would have to be an absolute bumbling fool to miss finding the farmhouse, even in the dark.

At five seconds to twelve, he activated the shortwave transmitter. Almost casually then, he double checked the frequency setting.

He idly checked the antenna jack again.

At twelve o'clock, noon, he started sending.

David Sheldon took the message pad from the operator sitting next to him. In one glance he verified that the message seemed authentic. He held up the pad to show Jerome Mason, telling him, "It's in the clear, and it could be the real thing."

"What about the strike team?"

"Our comm' people have the message too. The chances are the strike team is already airborne."

He noticed that Mason was grinning.

Sheldon lifted his eyebrows in response, a questioning and unconvinced gesture, as he picked up the headset connecting him to the listening devices in the apartment. The conversation between the two men was still actually casual, even indifferent. There was no talk at all about receiving a radio message. Again frowning, he turned the volume up on the receiver. It caught his ear then; a tinkling sound that had bothered him before. The background noise was the sound of silverware, like that usually heard in a restaurant!

"It's got to be a recording," he hissed angrily.

Startled, Jerome Mason watched as Sheldon quickly snatched up his walkie-talkie to call the two men stationed in front of the apartment building.

"We hit the apartment now!" Sheldon snapped into the transceiver.

Chapter fifteen

The Huey transport helicopter was the last ship in the diamond formation, which had been airborne for about twenty minutes. Besides himself and Dan Iser, Joshua had counted fourteen uniformed commandos, all fully combat equipped, at the muster before they all boarded the aircraft. Three Cobra gunships, armed with tow missiles and 20mm cannon, made up the remainder of the strike formation.

The firepower of the small force was awesome.

For Joshua Bain, it was the rites of war all over again. The differences were small but significant. The efficiency and no-nonsense performance of the IDF personnel was not unlike that of his own Special Forces unit in Vietnam. But the equipment was more sophisticated and automatic, designed to reduce the human error factor, which also allowed the Israelis to destroy their Arab enemy, and vice versa, with a certain detachment.

In Vietnam, the transistor had started the phenomenon of men killing each other at a distance, though there was still the need in the jungle for the bayonet. Remote control there was in its experimental infancy.

Now, it was micro-chips and third-generation computers.

In another ten years, a patrol leader could wear white gloves.

They were on absolute minimum low-level approach, and the Huey topped a rise and dipped to slip down the ascending face of its falling away slope. Joshua swallowed against the balloon pushing against his lower esophagus. Captain Dan Iser was strapped in next to him in the aluminum dropseat attached to the bulkhead separating them from the engine compartment. The helicopter was in combat trim, and the exit doors on either side were open for quick exit, only partly covered with a restraining canvas mesh for flight safety.

The young intelligence officer who had briefed them said they had no idea what the target might be. They could be hitting a cave, a fortified bunker, or maybe even a tent. The way their luck had been running, Joshua figured they were flying straight into the teeth of a waiting Syrian division.

The intelligence officer stood out from the other commandos because he had a 35mm camera strapped to his chest. It occurred to Joshua that in the old days when the cavalryman bearing the unit's colors went down, there was another ready to pick them up. He now wondered if one of the other commandos had been assigned to pick up the camera if the intelligence officer went down.

Conscious of his pessimism, Joshua looked aside to see that Dan Iser had closed his eyes under the forward rim of his tightly fitting combat helmet. The metal whistle strung around Dan's neck was more than just a routine part of the equipment issued to a soldier of his rank; the whistle was his voice in the field. Dan's lips seemed to be moving, and Joshua looked away as he guessed the husband of Sharon Iser might be praying for his hostage wife.

Joshua self-consciously checked the automatic rifle between his legs.

He guessed they were down to less than three minutes.

He closed his eyes.

The sounds around him were also the same.

The engine less than an arm's length away was revved to near maximum RPM behind its armor plate and insulation and was giving off a more bass roar than the higher frequency of the wind tearing at the ship's hull and open doors.

Joshua Bain prayed for his friend, Alan Hunt.

The briefing officer had assured him that they would do everything they could to protect the hostages.

The front door to the apartment was unlocked, and David Sheldon entered first, lunging in to pull up in a crouch. The three other men in the team followed fanning out across the more open living room. Sheldon sprinted across the carpet to the small dining room. He stopped again to listen, hearing nothing. He gestured to the other three men to search the premises.

Where were Garand and Rashid? They'd not been seen leaving the apartment, yet it was illogical that they could still be hiding there.

Baffled, he moved to the kitchen counter to turn off the tape recorder, which was turning on an empty reel. He saw the handwritten note then, and scanned it quickly:

FROM THE DESK OF CALVIN PRICE, ESQ.
Operation Jordan is now concluded.
As a postscript, it is my opinion that the destruction of
my villa was the act of a petulant child. I expected more
from the State of Israel. So, I am therefore comforted
to suggest you inspect the Bonn securities you so tact-
lessly stole from the exchange team. Like the shekel,
their value is in doubt. Also, I hold Israel responsible
for the unwarranted death of Karen Laswell, and I expect by the time you finish reading this, that score, too,
may also be counted even.

The final sentence of the unsigned note had not yet fully
registered in Sheldon's mind when the explosion ripped
through the opposite end of the apartment.

In the alley, Jerome Mason first saw the blast effect as a
portion of the rear wall of the apartment building came out in
one ragged piece, blown across the short intervening yard into
the alley. The blast wave slammed into the truck, and he
ducked instinctively as the vehicle bounced once on its springs.
A spray of debris pelted the truck, and he looked up to see the
alley was filled with dust. Stunned for a moment, he tried to
assess the situation. He had no idea whom to contact or how.
Still confused, he sensed that he should try to help Sheldon
and his men, who, he presumed, had entered the apartment as
planned. He realized he had no weapon, but he pushed the
door open to climb out of the truck, anyway. By the time he
reached the rear of the apartment building, the dust was clearing enough for him to see down the rest of the alley.

The Mercedes Benz 450-SL backed out of the garage.
Rashid shifted expertly from reverse to low as Maurice
Garand glanced through the rear window. There was the outline of a man emerging from the dust still swirling behind the
apartment building, but Garand could not fix the man's features quickly enough to recognize him.

On impulse, he lifted his left hand in a kind of farewell
salute.

It was all over, and the gesture seemed appropriate.

Joshua knew they could not negotiate with Kasim.

He had reluctantly consented that the armed strike was the
only alternative available to them. To the Israelis, the quick

use of force offered a brutal balance of response to the enemy who in taking hostages had retreated to an especially despicable niche in the human order of things. The certainty of punishment, usually violent death, was both swift and absolute.

He came out of his thoughts to hear radio chatter coming over the intercom. The langauge was Hebrew, and he turned curiously to look at Dan Iser. They were apparently close enough to break radio silence.

Dan Iser pointed to his watch. It was too noisy for his voice transmitter and he slowly formed the words with his mouth.

"Thirty seconds," was the message.

Hafiz Barca picked up the sound of the approaching aircraft before they came into visual contact. The distant first sound was the typical *thump-thump* of the rotor blades on the approaching aircraft, which normally came before the noise of the engines. It was a sound he was familiar with, and he jumped to his feet, tipping his head against the intervening breeze.

"What's wrong?" Anne asked him.

"Helicopters," Hafiz snorted, and he used the binoculars to search the reverse slope to the lower ridge line to the south and west.

Anne Hunt was confused. The only hint she had of the developing situation was that Hafiz was apparently angry. "What does it mean?"

Hafiz said nothing, because he wasn't yet sure himself. Then, the first gunship popped over the ridge line. The ship's profile registered at once. He counted three more ships following in tight formation. "Jews!" he spat angrily. He dropped the glasses to start for the jeep. "They're coming in right down the azimuth line," he went on, the bitterness heavy in his voice.

Anne came to her feet to follow him. Now stunned, she watched helplessly as he climbed into the jeep.

"No, Hafiz," she pleaded with him, and she reached across the passenger seat to try to stop him from starting the engine. "You can't change it now. Don't you see, it's too late!"

He jerked his hand away, cocking his arm as if he might hit her.

She was biting on her lower lip, almost hard enough to break the skin.

Hafiz looked at her, and he let his breath go then with a rush. He reached under his seat to pull out a manila envelope, handing it to her. "There is money in here and the papers for my family. If I don't get back, then you must promise me you will take them to the address on the envelope."

She shook her head. "You must do it yourself." She was frantically thinking that she had to stall him as long as she could.

He tossed the envelope to the ground beside her. "It will be on your conscience if you don't," he told her evenly, and he reached down to crank the starter handle.

She stepped back as he slammed the four-wheel drive into low gear. The jeep lurched forward.

"You don't owe them!" she screamed after him, starting to follow as he pushed the vehicle over the ridge line. "They're still using you! Please, Hafiz! Please!" and she stopped then, her voice trailing off as he started down the opposite slope.

Anne Hunt turned away.

The lone sentry posted at the farmhouse was under the lean-to, dozing in the noon-day heat. The distant sound of the approaching jeep was not yet loud enough to disturb him, but he jerked awake as he thought he had heard a gunshot. The report had been flat and hollow, like that of a pistol, and he moved curiously to the edge of the courtyard. He saw the jeep at once, which was trailing a cloud of dust. It first occurred to him that the driver was either drunk or insane.

Hafiz fought the jeep to keep it under control. He had his revolver in his right hand, and he lifted it a second time to fire another warning shot.

The sentry stiffened. Drunk or not, there was something wrong with the driver. He hurried to the front door, whacking it with the butt end of his rifle while at the same time shouting a warning to the men inside.

The copilot in the lead gunship was tracking the jeep with his gyro glasses.

"What is it?" Lieutenant Haim Resnik yelled at him.

"Probably an outguard."

"Take him on manual with the two AP spares," Resnik told him. "We'll bracket the house with WP." He opened up his mike to issue the WP salvo order to the other two ships. He had already confirmed the farmhouse as their target. The first rockets were to be white phosphorus, for both smoke and concussion effect. If it were not for the hostages, the house would be destroyed by the more deadly AP rockets.

The copilot had already leaned forward to peer into his

scope, locking in on the jeep, which was moving only slightly away with a closing angle so ideal he could take it with minimum help from the computer. He thought for a fraction of a second that it was a little like target practice.

Joshua heard the two missiles buck away from the lead gunship.

Anne Hunt had finally turned, feeling inside that maybe there was at least the hope that Hafiz would make it. Like him, she was also familiar with the silhouettes of the rapidly approaching helicopters, and she looked back now because she was praying the attack would center on the house.

Hafiz realized he was screaming. He had fired another shot, and he was close enough now to see the figures tumbling out the front door of the small house.

He had succeeded in warning them!

He came off the accelerator, jerking the wheel to the left as the jeep started to slow. He was aware of the formation's closing angle, and he was trying to turn broadside.

The evasive maneuver came too late.

The lead rocket was actually a miss, passing harmlessly across the hood of the jeep. The second caught the jeep at its left rear wheel.

The blast and immediate eruption of smoke and dust obscured the jeep momentarily.

The copilot locked in on the house, itself a stationary and more temptingly simple target. He made the decision to target the courtyard.

Anne stood horrified. The momentum of the destroyed jeep carried its shattered parts on down the slope, splaying out in a fan of small dust trails which remained only briefly as the wind pushed up the slope. A single wheel continued on, bouncing lazily on down toward the house. Her mouth had been open, because she was involuntarily trying to say something, but she now closed it, feeling the dryness of her lips.

Several more pairs of rockets raced down the valley so swift and straight they seemed to be running on tightly stretched wires.

Like the jeep, the house simply disappeared under the explosions which were spaced so close together the effect was as if one huge bomb had gone off.

She flinched when the sound first reached her.

The larger helicopter angled in to disappear behind the thickening smoke, apparently landing close upwind. There were other more minor explosions then, mixed in with the chatter of many automatic weapons.

Unable to watch any longer, she turned away.

Joshua had tumbled out of the hovering transport right behind Dan Iser. The pilot of the large Huey had speeded up and trimmed his rotors to help push the WP smoke away from the target area. Held back by Dan, Joshua watched the assault unfold directly to their front. The commandos literally swarmed over the farmhouse, firing continuously as they advanced. Several concussion grenades went off in the house, and they both ducked.

Dan bolted forward then, heading for the courtyard side of what was left of the house. Following and ready with his own weapon, Joshua thought there could be a chance for the hostages. The strike had been lightning swift, taking only seconds. The gunfire had ceased.

The two men pulled up before the front door, which had been practically destroyed by automatic fire.

Joshua was holding his breath.

A uniformed Israeli stepped out the door. He started shaking his head as he looked down to the ground. The barrel of the Uzi in his left hand was still so hot it was smoking all the way to the receiver. The young commando spoke to Dan in Hebrew, the words low and quiet.

"There're no hostages," Dan translated with his left hand at his throat.

"Are you sure?" Joshua blurted incredulously.

The commando was still shaking his head as he went on briefly. Finished, he pushed by them, reaching out with his right hand to squeeze the arm of Captain Dan Iser.

Joshua felt his shoulders sagging. The disbelief was like a curtain drawn across his mind.

"One of them is still alive," Dan stated. There was the same metallic neutrality in the words, but Dan Iser's face verified the same disappointment and grief. Movement in the doorway caught his eye, and he looked back to see the intelligence officer who had briefed them. He had a dirty rag in his hand, trying to wipe what looked like blood from his left forearm. The 35mm camera strapped to his chest was open with its lens exposed.

"Is one of them alive?" Dan asked him.

"Not anymore," the officer told him in English. "But he lasted long enough to swear that Kasim hasn't been out of the country in months. He also knew nothing about any hostages, or a shipment of anything like plutonium."

Joshua was too stunned to speak.

"I tend to believe him," the Israeli officer went on. "He was a Muslim, and he knew he was dying."

"You're sure we got Kasim?" Dan questioned.

"There's no doubt," the officer assured him. "The wounded man also verified the identification. We shall not be bothered by the mad dog again." He turned up his watch. "We only have a couple minutes left, and I must get more photographs."

Watching him move back into the house, Joshua finally started to put a coherent thought together. "We must face it," he said bitterly. "They're both dead. They have to be now."

"Don't say that," Dan said quickly.

Joshua looked into his face to see an angry kind of determination.

"We will find them," Dan went on, "and when we do, they will be alive. Until then, we will keep our faith." His eyes narrowed down threateningly. "We will both keep the faith, won't we, Joshua Bain?"

"I just don't know, anymore," Joshua told him after a moment. "It seems so hopeless now," and he turned to look away, closing his eyes against the tangible feel of death hovering heavily in the air.

Jerome Mason waited patiently in the passenger seat of the panel truck while David Sheldon finished with the radio in the back. It had been about twenty minutes since the explosion, and the alley in front of them was jammed with emergency vehicles. One of Sheldon's men had been killed and another badly wounded by the blast, which was assumed to have been a booby trap to give Garand and his accomplice the time to slip away through the adjacent apartment. They apparently had cut their way through a closet wall.

While he had no way to verify it, Jerome Mason was convinced he had seen Garand making good his escape in a Mercedes Benz coupe. The Christian militia were searching for the car, but by the time the bulletin had gone out the 450-SL had probably been miles away.

He came out of his thoughts as Sheldon entered the driver's door to sit down heavily behind the wheel.

"How'd the strike go?" Mason asked him.

"Without a hitch. They got Kasim for sure."

"What about the hostages?"

He shook his head wearily. "There weren't any hostages. And, no plutonium either. In fact, one of Kasim's men made the dying statement that Kasim hadn't been out of the country for months."

"Oh, my God!" Mason exclaimed.

"I expect that's about the same thing Dan and Joshua said."

"We've been ripped off," Mason went on.

"And I went for that part of it without doubting it for a minute," Sheldon admitted. "For me, it started in the morgue in Kingston. When I saw the little finger missing from Hank Koman's hand. It was an emotional gimmick that stung me into believing. They even tripped up Alan Hunt, who tried so cleverly with his Bible fragment. We were all duped, so magnificently." He paused, shaking his head again. "I've run into some clever tricksters in my time, but Calvin Price has to be the grand wizard of them all." He reached into his shirt pocket to pull out a small folded piece of paper, which he handed to Mason. "Read this, then we can all sit down and cry together."

Mason unfolded the note left by Garand, read it slowly. "You mean the Bonn notes are counterfeit?"

"I haven't reported it yet, but when I do I'm sure we'll find out they are."

Mason assessed the development before he asked, "So what happened to the real notes?"

"They went up in the seaplane explosion. That's why Garand spent three days in the salvage operation at the dock in Port-au-Prince. He was looking for the money. I must've dropped the satchel charge right on top of the briefcase. I remember seeing a duffel bag right next to where it landed. The bag must've belonged to Karen Laswell." He leaned forward to hit the truck's starter. "I've got to get to Tel Aviv to report this. You can come along if you wish."

"With or without my CIA escort?"

"How would you like to jump around him?"

Mason chuckled under his breath. "I expect one more setback for the day won't hurt anything."

Sheldon punched the truck into reverse and began backing down the alley.

"It must be some consolation," Mason suggested, "that

Price at least lost the money in the seaplane explosion."

"A minor trade-off," Sheldon observed, "since he's probably already collected from the next buyer." At the street intersection, he turned away from the alley to start in the direction of the port area. He chuckled then, even more ironically. "The nerve of the man. He was planning to use our payment to finance the whole scheme, which would've given him a nice double profit."

"I'd say several million is a nice profit."

"And he'll probably recover it. Since he was the last holder of record, he has likely already filed a claim with the German government. It will take a time of waiting, but he'll be reimbursed eventually. You see now why he insisted on the German notes. If Israel tries to dispute the claim, who do you think will come out the winner?"

Jerome Mason didn't bother trying to answer the rhetorical question.

Chapter sixteen

It was turning dusk, and the traffic below in the narrow street was starting to thin as Joshua Bain stepped out onto the small balcony fronting the apartment belonging to Dan and Sharon Iser. The sixth-floor vantage point allowed him a fair view of the city of Jerusalem, but he was staring listlessly without seeing. He had moved to the balcony for no other reason than to give him something to do, to keep moving, to do anything except to sit and think, to remember, to try to make some sense out of the tangled happenings of the past week. He was vaguely aware then that Dan Iser was standing beside him. They had arrived at the apartment only a few minutes before, and were both still dressed in their camouflage fatigues.

"That's the King David Hotel," Dan told him, and he pointed to the large square building which in the late evening distance was turning orange under the declining sun. For Joshua, the appearance of the hotel only served to remind him that one more day was about finished. The air around them was heavy and stagnant. The chemical smell of cordite and phosphorus was still in his nose. The dried blood of the Arab terrorists he had helped to arrange in the courtyard of the farmhouse was still on his forearms and thighs.

"To your left," Dan was saying mechanically, "that higher ground is—"

"I'm sorry," Joshua interrupted, and he turned to start back into the apartment, "but I'm not in a tourist mood right now."

Dan followed him into the living room. "Why don't you take a shower and change clothes," he suggested. "You will feel better." He moved on past Joshua to the adjoining dining room and small kitchen. "I'll fix us something to eat. Shira is due here any minute. And, Sheldon should be calling us soon."

Watching him, Joshua could restrain himself no longer. "It's all over, Dan," he said disconsolately. "Sharon is gone, too, you know. So how can you be so calm . . . like maybe a magic phone call is going to clear it all up, or something," and his voice trailed off on an even more dejected note. "We have to face the facts, as much as I dread saying it . . . "

Another moment passed before Dan told him, "Don't be misled into thinking I am indifferent. It's just that I'm dealing with it in another way."

Joshua sighed heavily as he started to slowly pace the floor. "A couple of years ago," he started slowly, "I remember Alan responding in the same way. I could not understand it then, either. You both are amazingly similar. Can you believe that I once even accused him of not caring?"

Dan leaned forward to rest his left elbow on the kitchen service counter. "How many times have you heard the expression *Shalom*?"

Joshua felt a slight ironic smile cross his face. The Hebrew word had brought instantly to his mind the image of a bronze plaque on a brick pilaster in front of a house halfway around the world. *Shalom.* The brief mental association only served to further heighten his bitterness and frustration.

"It is that peace which you have mistakenly sought," Dan told him. "You are also in error when you assume Alan has found that peace. It is easy to see that you find *Shalom* to be an empty word. Its promise makes a mockery of the hope you perhaps thought it once held."

Joshua glanced at him, unaware that his bitterness was so evident.

"Oh, it's very obvious," Dan went on, showing his perception. "You see, I am particularly aware of your feelings, for they are the same as enjoyed by our people. If there ever has been a people crying for peace, Joshua, it has been the Jews. How we have sought it! We fight for it, and we die for it. Israel is a virtual monument to the quest. Yet, we as a people seem to be on an ever-widening angle of separation from peace." He seemed to pause thoughtfully. "You've seen it yourself on the streets of Israel. Thousands of us wearing T-shirts marked with the word peace, walking elbow to elbow with our soldiers carrying guns."

Joshua moved to the coffee table. He pointed down to Dan's open Bible. "If that be the case, why then is the word peace quoted in there so often?"

Dan's own face slowly began to turn into an expression of understanding. "I guess Alan and I tend to take certain things for granted," he seemed to admit. "Let me try to explain by starting with your point of view. Inside, perhaps like before, you are turned upside down because you are *trying* to deal with the *world*. You are seeking a peace which can never be realized. You are doomed to failure. So, you look at Alan and you cannot understand how it is that he seems to be at peace. Would you say that's generally correct?"

"That's about the size of it."

Dan moved around the corner of the counter to sit down on the couch beside the coffee table. "That's incredible," he finally offered. "For years I've been reading it and living it myself, and I never really realized the significance of the distinction." He lowered his left hand to begin to turn the pages of the Bible. He stopped to return his left hand to his throat. "Yes, here it is. *Peace I leave with you, my peace I give unto you: not as the world giveth, give I unto you. Let not your heart be troubled, neither let it be afraid.*" He looked at Joshua. "You see, Joshua, there is a distinction between what you've been trying to find and what Alan already has. You cannot understand it because it is a gift that only Alan can share. And, there is no way he can really explain it to you. Small wonder that you both have been frustrated."

Joshua shook his head wearily. "You're not much help, I'm afraid."

"I'm trying to be," Dan told him as he turned further in the Book. "Paul can help us both as he tells us that the peace of God, *which passeth all understanding*, shall keep your hearts and minds through Christ Jesus."

"So it's one of your mysteries, after all," Joshua offered critically.

Dan was smiling. "I don't understand electricity, but I still prefer it over kerosene."

Joshua lifted his eyebrows in reluctant appreciation.

The doorbell rang.

Joshua tensed involuntarily.

Dan stood up to move toward the front door. He paused with his right hand on the knob, looking at Joshua over his shoulder. "You explain to me what caused that bell to ring, and I'll enlighten you on what it means to have the peace of God in your heart. For my part, I would start by telling you that the love of the Messiah is what makes it happen. You push the button, and He makes the bell ring."

Shira Elazar stepped into the room.

Dan embraced her warmly.

Joshua nodded to her, noticing that she looked worn out and somber.

She moved to the couch to sit down.

"Any news?" Joshua asked anxiously.

"Not from our end," she answered. "You were debriefed on the operation?"

"Yes," said Dan.

"The only thing I can add," she said quietly, "is that one of the bodies has been identified as Hafiz Barca."

"Oh, no, no," Joshua groaned.

"It's not conclusive," Dan pointed out quickly. "Anne Hunt could still be a hostage."

Joshua did not answer, but as he turned away to stare out the sliding glass door fronting the balcony, he was thinking that the Barca report somehow or another did not surprise him. It was the final crushing blow. They were both gone now. He clamped his eyelids shut.

Dan had moved forward to put his hand on Joshua's shoulder. "You must eat something, get cleaned up."

Joshua turned to face him. "Not now." He reached up to rub his forehead. "I think I'll take a walk, get outside."

Shira pushed herself up. "I've got to get home. Can I take you someplace?"

"Yes, maybe you can."

Left alone, Dan Iser moved about the apartment lethargically. Everywhere were the things reminding him of Sharon, not so much in her own personal articles as in the way she arranged things, revealing her own personality. She had been alone in the apartment often, and she had fussed with it, organizing it carefully. He prayed for a while in the privacy of their bedroom. Afterwards, he moved into the bathroom, where he finally broke down and cried. His grief was not just for Sharon alone but also over the realization that he had not shared enough with her during the past few years. He had wanted to become a missionary in his early enthusiasm for the Lord, wondering from time to time if he might not have neglected the calling. But, he recently had come to understand that he was already a missionary in the fields which were in the most need, the land of his own beloved people. And, he had neglected his family.

He leaned over the bathroom sink to wash his face in cold water.

Back in the silence of the kitchen, he checked the wall clock to see that Joshua had been gone for nearly an hour. Realizing he was hungry, he was turning toward the nearby refrigerator when the phone rang.

The call was from David Sheldon.

"So you made it," Dan commented into the receiver.

"By a narrow margin. We lost one man, with another badly hurt."

So the casualties were continuing, Dan thought.

"Garand got away," Sheldon went on. "They picked up his accomplice about an hour ago. He delivered Garand to a private strip south of the port area. All he knows is that Garand took off on a southwest heading."

"Could be headed for Cairo," Dan suggested.

"Or Benghazi. Or he could've faked the heading and changed toward Cyprus."

Dan noticed the dejection in Sheldon's voice. "So can you talk about it on the phone?"

"It doesn't make that much difference now. The latest analysis suggests the Beirut ploy and the Kasim sacrifice was too sloppy to qualify as one of Price's better plans. What they're saying is that it could've been some kind of add-on thing, like a contingency."

"Meaning what?" Dan asked in the following silence.

"Price could've been in a time bind. So he threw us a bone to stall us. As weak as it is, it's the only hope we've got left."

There was a pause. "But I personally think it's all over."

"You sound terrible," Dan told him.

David Sheldon laughed bitterly. "This may turn out to be the embarrassment of the century for us. We just got confirmation that the payment money was fake. So we literally have nothing now. The cost to us in lives alone has been tragic enough, not counting the time and funds we've exhausted."

"So it's that bad," Dan noted.

"It's humiliating," Sheldon admitted. "Price's strategy worked so well that by now Jordan must be in the hands of the final buyer. Which means, of course, that we can scratch the hostages as well. I'm sorry, Dan, but there's no other way I can put it."

"I'll believe it when we find them."

"Suit yourself, but how's Joshua taking it?"

"Very badly. He's out now, trying to sort it out."

"If he's in that frame of mind, then you better get him inside."

Dan glanced at the wall clock again. "Where are you now?"

"At my place in Ramat Gan. Jerry Mason is here with me now. We'll be going out to eat, then back here to get some rest. For whatever help it might be, we're still on red alert, so we haven't officially given up yet. If Jordan is in Arab hands, then the disaster is going to escalate into a catastrophe. The whole mess is in the process of turning political right now."

Dan said good-bye and hung up.

After a thoughtful second, he picked up the receiver and dialed the private number for Shira Elazar.

Shira had dropped Joshua off at the Damascus Gate to the Old City, where he had started to follow the small posted signs directing him "To the Wall." Most of the small cellular shops crowding the narrow vaulted streets were closed now after dark, though it was still early enough for the area to be busy with those who lived there. It was cool and after the dinner hour and obviously a time for the older inhabitants to visit and relax. Joshua assumed that during the day the narrow streets of the Old City would be a scene of near bedlam, but the tourists had apparently left with the sun's passing. The mood of those on the streets was happy and open, which suggested the day's sales of everything from filigreed pendants to prayer rugs had been profitable.

He went unnoticed in his Israeli field uniform.

He supposed that some things never changed as he noticed an Arab beggar woman scratching in the trash left in front of the steel-enclosed vendor stalls. The Arab kids, too, fortified now with a meal, were back on the streets looking for a final hustle to finish off the day. His vague impression was that here the survival of a destitute Lazarus was less a staged thing for the benefit of the pilgrims than it was a reality.

He pulled up at the intersection of Via Dolorosa, the Way of the Cross.

The rough and uneven stones and steps wound irregularly down and away on the path represented as the one trod by Jesus Christ on His way to the cross. Joshua was finally beginning to feel the weight of history in the air around him. According to Shira, the chances were that the actual pathway walked by Jesus was fifty or sixty feet below the present Via Dolorosa, which was in reality the last of many which had been added in succeeding layers of construction during the past two thousand years. Still, it was an impressive experience, the closest one could get to the real thing.

Intervening rubble could not alter the original fact.

He moved on south, down Al Wad Road.

Joshua was still in a numbing kind of daze.

He thought again that Alan and Anne ought to be there with him, that it was wrong for him to be there without them. He woodenly turned left at the next sign, drawn along now by a sense of purpose or reason he could not break out and identify . His clumsiness was an extension of his own inner turmoil and lack of resolution. He was vaguely aware that the area was more quiet, with fewer people on the streets, and he supposed he was in or near the Jewish quarter.

He passed under an archway with an open steel gate.

The Wall was higher than he expected.

There were several low benches placed along the base of the Wall, and the plaza in front was now deserted except for a couple strolling slowly toward him. He stood still for a long time, staring blankly at the monument which was the most sacred relic that could ever be possessed by the Jews. It was called the Wailing Wall because it was here the Jews came to pray and cry out with tears over the destruction of the Temple and their exile and persecution. He could see in the chinks between the huge lower supporting stones the small rolled-up papers, the notes of prayers or names of loved ones.

He made a move to start forward.

"You're supposed to wear a cap."

The voice which was like a recording came to him from behind.

Joshua stopped short, turning to see Dan Iser standing next to the black iron gate. "How'd you find me?" Joshua asked, and he licked his dry lips.

Dan shrugged before he stepped forward. "It was just a guess. Shira told me she had dropped you at the Damascus Gate." He pulled up next to Joshua, facing the other way. "How did you find it?"

"Followed the signs," Joshua told him. "Which might be a disappointment to you. I suspect it might've been more appropriate if I had just stumbled in here by accident."

"It doesn't matter; the important thing is that you're here. If you like, we can get skull caps from one of the attendants."

Joshua took a deep breath as he self-consciously kicked once at the stone plaza. "It's like everything else here," he finally said slowly. "I don't understand what the people are saying. The smells are strange, the food different. The way many of them dress," and he shrugged his shoulders listlessly. "I might as well be a visitor from Mars."

"That's natural," Dan tried to assure him.

"No, it isn't!" Joshua exclaimed, and he looked up helplessly to the sky turning black. "Don't you understand? I came here looking for help, but I'm nothing more than a stranger in this place." His voice was bitter as he went on, "I stand here and look at this Wall, which means so much to so many, and all I see is a bunch of stones stacked one on top the other. It's an engineering marvel. It's sacred, and I try to respect that and all that it means." He held up his hands in a further helpless gesture. "So now I feel even worse. . . . Don't you understand?"

"More than you can imagine. Just before I left the apartment, I had to assess and measure myself also. I started to think about Sharon, to remember, especially how I had left her alone for these past few years. I went into the bathroom and I cried. Sometimes, Joshua, it comes down to this, so that you have nothing, absolutely nothing. You are naked. You are in the pit . . ."

"I would accept all that, right now, in exchange for Alan and—"

"Forget it," Dan interjected. "There's nothing you can

give, steal, or borrow to change things. With all our great skill and intellect, we consistently prove ourselves to be the most helpless of God's creatures. What makes you think you're any different?"

"So what's left for us, Daniel Iser?"

"Faith."

Joshua finally looked aside.

"Are you really in a worse position now," Dan went on, "than our father Abraham when he made ready the knife to sacrifice his beloved son Isaac? What do you think was running through his mind at that moment? Or, how about Moses standing by the awesome obstacle of the Red Sea, looking over his shoulder to see the dust cloud raised by the pursuing Egyptian chariots? And, do I need to mention Gideon, David, Samuel? I don't recall them rolling over and playing dead like you're doing right now. You both insult and waste their brave example."

Joshua had to move away. As he pulled up beside the steel gate, a young woman moved across his line of sight, and in the poor light he thought for a startled moment that it was Anne Hunt. As she passed closer by, he realized it was just a young girl who favored the wife of his best friend. He closed his eyes, swallowing against the brass-like taste creeping up his throat.

He knew he would never see them alive again.

It was all over.

Joshua wept.

After a moment, Dan Iser moved tentatively forward to stand beside him. He allowed a few more seconds to pass before he suggested, "The tears of a man ought not to be wasted on himself."

Joshua reached up to dry his face on his left forearm. He had to clear his throat to reply, "You just finished crying for your wife."

"Like you, I was really crying for myself, not her."

"Then your heart must be colder than I thought."

Dan didn't answer. Instead, he reached out with his left hand to take one of Joshua's. When Joshua pulled his hand back, he looked down to see a small stone in his palm. Closing his fingers around the stone, he looked up at Dan. There was in the man's eyes the look of concern and affection, a reflection of some inner substance, which he had seen before in the face of only one other person, Alan Hunt.

Joshua sensed the power of the substance.

"So what must I do?" he asked quietly.

"Accept Him, Joshua."

"All right, but I don't know what to do."

"Will you now surrender, give your life to the Messiah, Jesus Christ?"

Joshua contemplated the question briefly. "If that's what it takes, then yes, I do."

"Then say it," Dan insisted. "You must confess Him with your mouth, Joshua, and you must repent of your sins."

"I accept and believe in the Messiah, Jesus Christ," said Joshua evenly.

Dan Iser literally jumped off the pavement, clapping his hands at the same time. He leaned forward then to grab Joshua in a bear hug, threatening to break his ribs. Letting Joshua go, he reached up to his throat.

"Praise the Lord!" he exclaimed, causing Joshua to think he might blow his circuits.

"Now guess where we're going?" Dan went on as he grabbed Joshua and started pulling him through the gate.

"I can't imagine," Joshua answered.

"To the River Jordan, and you're going to get a bath with your clothes on. And, you must mark this date because it's your new birthday."

"Birthday?" Joshua questioned as he hurried to stay with the rapidly striding Dan Iser.

"Of course. You see, it happened not far from here—in fact, when Nicodemus came to question Jesus, who told him that except a man be born again of water and of the Spirit, he cannot enter into the kingdom of God."

"I'm not so sure I understand."

"Neither did Nicodemus, come to think of it. However, we will read about it when we get back to the apartment." He pulled up to stop abruptly. "So how do you feel now?"

Joshua frowned slightly. "Not really different, except that I'm hungry as a bear."

"You see, a blessing already."

Joshua could not help but smile.

Chapter seventeen

Anne Hunt was familiar enough with the city of Beirut to have crossed into the eastern sector without incident. It had been dark about an hour when she turned the white van onto Qadisha Street. Hafiz's sister, Maya, was in the passenger seat beside her, with the remaining two members of the Barca family behind them wedged in among their few personal belongings.

Anne had not yet told them that Hafiz Barca was gone.

The once younger brother, Ahmed, was now the eldest son.

She downshifted to second gear, slowing to check the house numbers.

"Will Hafiz be here?" Maya asked her. She spoke in her native Arabic, the only language the Barca family knew. But the Western influence was evident in both her manner and clothes. She was dressed in old worn jeans and a cotton blouse open at the neck, and, with her nearly black hair long down her back, she could've passed for a teenager out for a stroll on a Southern California street. Maya Barca was also an intelligent and pretty young girl with alert dark brown eyes, who of the three in the family seemed the most aware that there was something very wrong.

Anne Hunt told herself again that the time was not right to tell them about Hafiz. "I don't think he'll be here," she answered, and she changed the subject by giving the girl the house number.

Maya peered obediently out her window. "It must be in the next block," she said then.

Anne speeded up to cross the next intersection. She had no idea what she would do when they found the address. She was convinced that Hafiz had simply been used in some sort of intrigue, and that there was very little chance his family would collect any further payoff. Still, she did not know what else to do.

"We're almost there," Maya was saying quietly. Like her

brother and mother, the young girl was openly cool and suspicious toward Anne, who had to appreciate their position. Hafiz had apparently not told them anything, so that they, too, were confused and uncertain.

Anne again slowed the van.

"Soldiers!" Maya exclaimed under her breath.

Anne had spotted the two militiamen at the same time. She cruised on past the apartment building after double checking the number on the alcove. Even in the poor light she could see that the ground-floor unit on the right had sustained some kind of heavy damage.

She carefully speeded up.

"Was that the address?" Maya asked.

"Yes, it was."

Ahmed came forward to kneel down behind their seats. "Did you see Hafiz?" he asked curiously. Ahmed Barca was only twelve years old, but, like his sister, he was also alert and wise beyond his years, the product of the camp system he had grown up in.

"No, we didn't see Hafiz," his sister told him tartly.

Anne turned the next corner to curb the van at the first available parking place. She left the engine running while she tried to think. It had taken an especially twisted mentality to lead Hafiz Barca and his family to the address. If he were alive now, Hafiz would be on everyone's wanted list.

"What are we going to do?" Maya was asking her.

"I don't know."

"Hafiz would know," Ahmed pointed out.

Ignoring him, Anne pulled away from the curb. There was nothing more she could do. She circled the block to pull up in front of the apartment.

"You keep quiet," she told the two of them sternly. Before she opened the door, she turned to look at their mother, who was sitting quietly toward the rear of the van. "I'm going to talk to the soldiers," she told her quietly, trying to sound reassuring. She pushed her way out of the van. One of the militiamen met her at the sidewalk.

"You cannot park here," he told her at once. "This is a restricted area." He was about her age, with a rifle slung over his left shoulder. His companion stayed behind in the alcove, smoking a cigarette.

"My name is Anne Hunt," she told him in as authoritative a tone as she could muster, "and I am an American citizen. I have been held captive by PFLP terrorist elements for over a week, and I have just escaped."

The young soldier frowned. "Let me see your papers."

Anne took an impatient breath. "I do not have any papers. I was kidnapped in the United States and forced to come here."

"How did you get here without papers? I saw you pass here before, and you were driving the vehicle."

Anne Hunt debated whether to try to explain. Her travel papers in the van were false and in another name, and if she showed them to him it would only lead to further delay. "Will you please contact the American consulate. I have identified myself as an American citizen, and I need help."

"Wait here," he told her, and he walked to the alcove to start an animated conversation with his companion. They both moved to the sidewalk.

"I will take you to our CP," the first soldier told her.

"What about those people?" Anne asked him, gesturing toward the van.

"Who are they?" the second soldier asked her.

"Three Jordanian nationals, and I am responsible for them."

The first soldier was frowning again. "If you were kidnapped, as you claim, then why is it you have these people in your custody?"

Anne fought to control herself. She was exhausted in both mind and body. Tempted to lash out, she bit down on her lower lip as she reminded herself how it must look to them. "Please take us all to your CP. Place us under arrest if you wish. But, please, do something."

Louis Morganstern was a sabra Israeli who had lived in Cairo, Egypt, for nearly five years. He had initially arrived in Cairo on a French passport from Paris, France, where Israeli intelligence had planted the documents and evidence to support his inheritance from a sympathetic baronage family.

His cover name was Jacques Lamont.

His actual parents had immigrated from France to Palestine in 1929, so that he spoke fluent enough French to easily pass for a native. With the reputation of a Mediterranean playboy, his function had been to infiltrate the inner circle of the Egyptian military elite and their families. His periodic secret reports to Tel Aviv contained the less public details enabling Israeli intelligence to update the dossiers it maintained on virtually every Arab field grade military officer. He played tennis with the wives and daughters of generals, and was known for his lavish parties at his expensively furnished Cairo bachelor flat.

On Monday night, at a few minutes before 9:00, he had finished dinner and was preparing to consolidate his notes from the weekend's activity. He was in his study when the doorbell rang. Irritated with the interruption, he waited impatiently for his personal butler to answer the door. Hearing a commotion in the foyer, he got up to walk to the front door to investigate, where he found his butler in an argument with a man who looked as if he might have been a waterfront laborer.

"What's the problem?" Lamont demanded harshly.

His butler shook his head in obvious exasperation. "He insists on delivering a letter addressed to someone else."

Lamont took the letter himself, turning it to the porch light. It was addressed to Louis Morganstern! The shock passed through him instantly.

"You fool!" he exploded at the stranger standing on the porch. "You disturb this house this late at night!" he raged in an apparent fit of anger, and he turned to his butler, who had taken a step back, "Call the police at once," and he gestured angrily with his free hand. "Now, do you hear!"

His butler turned in response, heading for the telephone.

Jacques Lamont pulled the door closed behind him as he stepped out onto the porch. "Who gave you this?" he hissed, and he reached out to grab the arm of the startled messenger. He heard the sound of a car engine then, revving into gear, and he looked to the curb of the street to see a dark coupe pulling away down the street. He ran along the entryway, yelling at whoever it was to stop. At the curb, he pulled up to see it was useless. He turned in time to see the man who had delivered the envelope was also gone.

Back in the house, he caught his butler in time to tell the police that he had taken care of the problem. He had hidden the envelope in the fold of his robe, and, as he started for his study, he stopped short. His butler was at the front door, revealing his nervousness as he fumbled with the night chain.

"By the way," Lamont asked him casually. "What was the name on the envelope? I didn't get a good look at it."

The butler was frowning as he tried to think. "I'm sorry, sir, but I can't recall either. The fool was yelling at me to call the master of the house, and I was upset. I can only remember that it wasn't Jacques Lamont."

Lamont thanked him before turning into his study. At his desk, he could hear his heart pounding in the silence of the room as he unfolded the note. There was no salutation or signature to the hand-written message, which was in code.

The only hint to the message's content was the word, "Jordan," which appeared at the beginning and at the end. The cypher technique was as ancient as printing itself. There was an introductory group of four numbers which identified a specific edition of a published book. The body of the message was a long series of digits in sets, one set per letter, which listed the page in the book, the number of lines from the top of that page, ending with the number of letters in from the left margin. The code was absolutely unbreakable without knowing the source book.

It was of special interest to Jacques Lamont that the group of four numbers used to identify the source book was of the type used by Ha Mossad field operatives, including himself.

The master index, of course, was only on file at The Institution.

The message was therefore obviously intended for Tel Aviv.

Jacques Lamont was at once perplexed. The code name, Jordan, was in a manner of speaking on the entire network's hotsheet. He ordinarily would therefore make immediate contact to report the message. Yet, someone had used his real name, the knowledge of which had to be confined to no more than two or three people in The Institution itself.

Was his cover blown?

If so, he wouldn't have the time to pack his bags.

He calmly rejected the temptation to run.

The Jordan connection had to be the key.

It dawned on him then that whoever had prepared the message had deliberately used his real name as an emergency guarantee that he and he alone would receive and open it. That someone should risk using his real name also suggested that the message might be of far greater importance than he might imagine.

Tel Aviv would have the message in less than an hour.

On his way to his bedroom to change into street clothes, his mind continued to turn. His real name on the envelope had been printed in English. The messenger was a type to very likely be illiterate, certainly unable to read English. Had he been selected for that reason?

He figured that only the driver of the dark coupe could answer the question.

The command post for the Beirut military sector was in a garage behind a gas station destroyed by shellfire, which Anne Hunt presumed had come from Syrian artillery. The Christian militiamen, who had turned out to be Phalangists, had treated her and the Barca family rather indifferently, since it was the stated opinion of the duty officer that she did not look, act, or talk like an American. However, he had after some delay finally called the American Embassy. After hanging up the phone, his first order was to pull the two guards off the van, which had been parked near the front door. He then offered them all coffee and free run of the building if they liked.

Anne spent the next few minutes trying to find a way to tell the mother of Hafiz Barca that her son had been killed in an exercise so insane that she didn't know how to even begin explaining it. Instead, she found herself answering the questions of Maya and Ahmed about the country where she lived. Waiting impatiently now, her conversation was terse and forced, and she realized her nerves were dangerously close to the breaking point.

She shushed them into silence as an official-looking sedan pulled in to park directly behind the van. The two men who climbed out were escorted directly to the duty officer, who came himself to get Anne Hunt. Inside the garage, she was introduced to Walter Stimpson, the American Charge d'Affaires, and Curtis Hamilton, who also appeared to be an American. Excusing himself from the duty officer, Stimpson pulled her aside so that their conversation would be private.

"It is extraordinary that you are still alive," Stimpson told her first.

"Yes, I've been very fortunate."

He turned to the other man. "Mister Hamilton is with the CIA, and he has some questions he would like to ask you."

"Do we have to do it now?"

"It is important," Hamilton told her quickly.

"All right, but only after you tell me where I can reach my husband."

Hamilton looked down to the cement floor between them. "He is still missing, and we do not know where he is." He looked up then. "That's one of the questions we were hoping you could help us with."

Anne Hunt was struggling to control herself. "What do you mean when you say he is missing?"

"He was taken captive when the Jordan shipment was hijacked. Until today, we presumed that a man named Kasim had been responsible."

Anne caught her breath in her throat. "You mean he was with Kasim?"

"No, ma'am. That's what I'm trying to tell you. The Israelis killed Kasim today, but there was no trace of any hostages at the scene."

"Thank God," said Anne to herself.

"Isn't there anything you can tell us?" Hamilton asked her.

She could only shake her head slowly. "I'm sorry," she finally offered. "All I can tell you is that I was kidnapped by one Hafiz Barca, and I was alone with him for the entire time. I never met, saw, or heard from any other person he might have been associated with. He was killed today, as you may know. I also want to formally report that he spared my life against his orders."

There was a following pause, broken by Stimpson, who addressed himself to Hamilton, "Is that all for now?"

Hamilton looked discouraged. "Yes, I guess so."

"You mean you have no clues, or anything?" Anne asked.

"We have nothing, ma'am."

"What about Joshua Bain?"

"He's all right," Stimpson told her. "He's in Israel now, and we can get word to him, but it'll take some time to work through channels. Meanwhile, we've made arrangements for a hotel room. I can drop you off now. Perhaps we'll have more information tomorrow morning."

Anne sighed heavily. "You'll have to make room for three more people in your accommodations. They're outside in the van."

"I don't understand," Stimpson said.

"They're what's left of the Barca family. The mother, a young woman, and a boy of twelve."

Stimpson nodded that he understood. "The officer here can make arrangements for them to go to one of the camps south of the city."

"No, he won't," she told him flatly. "They are my responsibility, and if they go to a camp, then I go with them."

"That's impossible," Stimpson protested. "They are foreign citizens, and they may even be wanted on charges."

"So I've thought about that, too," she said. "And I'm acting legally on their behalf in requesting political asylum with the American Embassy."

Stimpson scoffed, "You can't be serious—"

Anne Hunt, her temper finally stretched to its limit, stalked quickly to the makeshift desk of the duty officer, who looked up at her with a startled expression on his face.

"Will you escort me and my party to the nearest refugee camp?"

Walter Stimpson was already by her side. "All right," he said quietly. "We'll take you all to the hotel. I'll check first thing in the morning to see what we can work out."

Anne Hunt closed her eyes.

Stupified by heavy sleep, David Sheldon groped for the phone receiver. He had to clear his throat twice before he could respond to the voice on the other end of the line. His head cleared and he noticed that the clock on the nightstand reported just past midnight.

Jerome Mason came awake at the same time. Seeing that Sheldon had pushed himself to sit up on the edge of his bed, Mason followed suit, putting his feet on the floor in the narrow space between the two single beds as Sheldon hung up the phone.

"You feel like a boat ride?" Sheldon asked him, and he started toward his closet.

Jerome Mason's first thought was that there was no way he could continue to keep up. He was still exhausted, and he could feel it in his bones. Still, he somehow managed to push himself to his feet, noticing that David Sheldon was already pulling on his trousers.

It was like a firehouse drill.

"Why a boat ride?" he asked.

"Don't know for sure, yet. But there're three gunboats already under way, and we're going to meet them at El Arish. All I could get over the phone was that we've got a lead on a ship, which we might have to intercept near Egyptian waters."

Listening closely, Mason had moved to the chair valet holding his clothes.

Sheldon was buttoning his shirt as he went on, "So we've got two phone calls to make before we leave. While I make us some coffee, you can help by calling your contacts in Washington." He paused to stare hard at Jerome Mason. "It's important, very important, that an American source contact the Egyptians at once, hopefully within the hour, to advise them that three Israeli warships are now moving toward their waters. But," and he emphasized the coordinating conjunction carefully, "we are pursuing a critical matter of internal security only."

Mason figured he understood, but he still commented, "You have diplomatic relations with Egypt now."

"Yes, thank God, and we're already working that channel. However, to hear it from your side will make it more palatable and believable. Remember, there may be American hostages involved."

Jerome Mason was awake and alert enough to understand the Israelis were not merely looking for help as much as they would like to have an endorsement this time. He was composing what he might say as he moved toward the telephone. He hesitated, his hand on the receiver. "You said you had two calls to make?"

"When you're finished, I'll get Dan Iser at his place. We can pick up him and Joshua at Kalandria on our way out."

Chapter eighteen

Nick Villon assumed his watch at 0400 hours. With a cup of black coffee in his hand, he stepped onto the weather deck to catch some fresh air before going below. The small Liberian freighter was a rust bucket, typical of the trading vessels working the open ports from Karachi to Marseille, and he was thankful his watch was scheduled during the cooler early morning hours. They had cleared Port Said, after leaving the canal, at a little after midnight. He guessed the ship was making about eight to ten knots, which meant they should be reaching their Benghazi destination within the day. The weather looked clear enough over the low running swells of the Mediterranean.

Maurice Garand was below, asleep in his cabin next to the Captain's.

The Jordan cargo was in the forward hold.

Standing at the rail, Nick allowed his thoughts to drift to Port-au-Prince. Garand had told him when he boarded at Ismailia that it was doubtful Colonel Price would rebuild the destroyed Haitian villa.

Nick Villon was thus not certain of his future.

He threw the rest of his coffee over the side before turning to go below. The two hostages were locked in a compartment aft, and as he slowly worked his way down the connecting ladder he realized that their time, too, was running out, though for a different reason and with a different ending.

Standing before the closed hatch, he idly checked the lock and chain securing the release lever. Satisfied, he moved on toward the galley to return his cup.

The sound of the chain scraping against the metal door had moved across Alan Hunt's mind. It took a moment for the noise to register, and he opened his eyes, listening. It was pitch black in the small compartment, and he guessed they were not far from the engine room. The rhythmic roll of the ship's engines had been steady for several hours, which suggested they finally had reached open water. Their Arab guards had continually refused to talk to them, so that their location was still a mystery. Until two days ago, when they had boarded the ship, they had guessed they were on the Red Sea. But they had been blindfolded during the time of their transfer aboard a smaller power boat.

It was Sharon's latest guess that they had negotiated the Suez Canal.

Sharon Iser's spirits had started to ebb again during the last twenty-four hours.

He couldn't blame her.

Neither of them could guess whether it was daylight or dark anymore.

If their guards didn't kill them soon, the small compartment would. The air was almost unbreathable. The stifling heat never seemed to let up. Their only toilet facility was an iron bucket.

He closed his eyes and started to pray again. The twenty-third Psalm, for what might have been the hundreth time. *The Lord is my shepherd; I shall not want . . .*

The clear image of Anne intruded into his mind, and he pushed it out.

Remembering had become a cruelty.

He maketh me to lie down in green pastures—

Joshua Bain stood spread-legged on the covered bridge of the starboard gunboat. He was also braced against the nearby bulkhead, literally hanging on for his life. The three ships were in a vee formation, avoiding each other's wake and enabling them to move at their maximum speed of fifty knots. According to David Sheldon's estimate, the three ships combined rocket firepower was enough to cripple a battleship.

Dan Iser was aft with the boarding party under his command. Joshua glanced over his left shoulder to see that the sun had broken the horizon. Tactically, he supposed having the sun behind their backs was an advantage, but even that seemed absurd as he considered the ship's sophisticated fire-control capability.

The Israelis weren't taking any chances this trip either.

Somewhere in front of them was a small freighter, whose location had been accurately fixed by an anonymous tip. The freighter's cargo, hopefully, was the Jordan shipment and two hostages. Jerome Mason had received the report that Anne Hunt was alive and well in Beirut, and Joshua again remembered her words to him concerning her husband: *Just bring Alan back home.*

Joshua closed his eyes.

Hopefully . . .

The ship's intercom crackled with an exchange from the lead ship, but Joshua couldn't follow the Hebrew communication.

A few seconds later, Dan Iser entered the bridge. "They've got a target on radar that fits the freighter's profile," Dan told him.

"What's the plan?"

"We board her at once."

Joshua felt the butterflies starting in his stomach. He looked forward then to see a dark black smoke trail against the slightly lighter horizon behind it.

"You better get aft and draw your weapon," Dan told him.

Joshua noticed that Dan already had his Uzi machine gun under his left arm. There were two concussion grenades hooked to the canvas straps coming down from his shoulders on either side of the black metal whistle looped around his neck.

Another more extended exchange came over the intercom.

Turning to go, Joshua stopped short as he noticed a concerned expression cross Dan's face. "Something wrong?" he asked at once.

"Don't know," Dan answered. "The radar also has aircraft on the screen. The Captain says their approach angle suggests they're Egyptian fighters."

Joshua felt the sinking sensation willowing down to his belly. They supposedly had the Egyptian thing cleared. The Israelis had held back their own aircraft because of the possible territorial complications. "What do you think?" he finally asked.

"We'll just have to wait and see."

The freighter's first officer escorted Maurice Garand to the bridge. Like the rest of the ship, the wheelhouse was rundown and cluttered. The crewman at the wheel was bare to the waist, and from the smell in the air Garand assumed they all hadn't had a bath in days. The ship's Captain was bald and fat, and when he spoke his voice was nasally and high pitched, as if he suffered from a serious sinus problem. Upon seeing Garand, he pulled his cap off to wipe the sweat away from the folds of his face.

"You said there would be no trouble," the Captain complained.

"What exactly is the problem?" Garand asked wearily. He suspected the fat old man was setting the stage to ask for more money.

"The problem is simple," the Captain assured him, and he pointed out the port side window. "There you see three gunboats." He pointed up, tipping his head as if he might be listening to something.

Garand heard it then, the closing sound of aircraft.

He frowned, before demanding, "Are we holding next to Egyptian waters?"

"Yes, we are," the Captain told him. "We are less than one kilometer away."

Garand moved thoughtfully to the port door. Pushing it open, he stared at the approaching gunboats. "Can you make out who they are?"

"Yes; they are Jews."

Garand stepped onto the deck, looking up. He counted eight jet aircraft, which were separating into two groups of four each. He stepped back into the cabin. "What about the aircraft?"

"The lookout says they're Egyptian." The Captain put his cap back on. "What are your orders? I hope you are aware that the gunboats could sink us in a matter of minutes."

Speaking rapidly in Arabic, Garand addressed the first officer. "Send a message to the gunboat commander, informing him that we have two hostages on board and that we are in Egyptian waters. Then, transmit a message to the flight leader of the aircraft, advising him that we are in a mayday condition and are seeking sanctuary." He turned to the Captain. "Alter course at once to enter Egyptian waters on the most direct line. Also increase speed to the maximum." It was his gamble that the Jews could not get an accurate enough fix to know for sure that the ship was not at the moment still in International waters.

David Sheldon and Jerome Mason were on the bridge of the lead gunboat. The formation had slowed almost to a stop with the arrival of the Egyptian military aircraft. Sheldon lowered his binoculars to address the Captain, "She's altering course and heading for Egyptian waters."

The Captain was tall and slender, his face angular and clean shaven under the bill of his cap. His reply to Sheldon's statement was to reach up thoughtfully to stroke his chin.

A crewman entered the bridge to hand the Captain a message on a clipboard. After reading it, the Captain told them in English, "The ship claims she has two hostages and that she's already in Egyptian waters. She's also asking the Egyptian flight leader for assistance."

David Sheldon swore under his breath.

The Captain looked at Sheldon, his eyes impassive. "What is your advice, sir?"

"Board her now. I say she's still in open water, and if we catch her soon enough, who's going to dispute it?"

The Captain pulled the wall mike to issue a terse order in Hebrew.

The boat lurched forward.

On the bridge of the starboard boat, Joshua Bain grabbed at the nearby bulkhead as the gunboat surged forward. He and Dan had come forward when the formation had slowed.

"We have a go now," Dan told him, and he motioned for

them to again return aft. They stopped as a radio transmission cleared the intercom.

"This is air patrol flight leader to commander of Israeli ship force. Come in please to acknowledge." There was a pause. "I say again, please acknowledge."

Joshua was holding his breath. The Egyptian flight leader sounded clear and crisp, his voice inflected with the confident British influence.

The Israeli gunboat commander acknowledged.

Joshua shook his head.

"He had to do it," Dan commented.

"Thank you, sir," said the flight leader. "You are advised to reduce power and stop pursuit of freighter. I repeat again, you are advised to reduce power and stop pursuit at once."

Joshua stood stunned.

David Sheldon hammered his fist against the nearby bulkhead.

The Captain addressed the mike in his left hand. "Negative, I say negative. Ship in question is believed to hold contraband material vital to our security. We are under orders to board her, and we intend to do so. We consider ourselves in a legal chase condition. Repeat, a legal chase condition."

"They're supposed to be standing clear!" Sheldon exclaimed angrily. "They said they wouldn't interfere!"

The flight leader answered in the same sober monotone, "If you continue pursuit, you will be boarding her in Egyptian waters, and your government will have to answer for what is an act of war. I repeat, you will be boarding her in Egyptian waters."

The Captain did not ask for advice before he issued the all-stop order into the wall intercom. He held up his hands in a gesture of helplessness.

Maurice Garand had been watching from the aft rail of the bridge deck. Seeing the gunboats slow to a stop, he lifted his right arm in a gesture of victory and jubilation. A few of the watching crewmen began to yell. Garand took off his cap to start waving it in an arc as he tried to thank the pilot who had managed to stop the Jews.

David Sheldon was so furious he could not speak. He had been watching Maurice Garand giving his victory dance, and he finally lowered the binoculars to stare unseeingly at the gray water between them and the escaping freighter.

"We still have a chance," Mason tried to reassure him.

"They should be impounded, and there are legal means—"

"You know better," Sheldon interjected bitterly. "Price will find the way to get the plutonium removed. And, if the hostages are in fact still alive, I can guarantee you their throats will be cut and their bodies thrown overboard within the hour."

Joshua Bain had not moved nor spoken since the stop order had been issued. He could only watch now as the Egyptian fighters maintained their protective umbrella. He was convinced that Alan and Sharon were on the ship.

They had been so close.

He realized he did not feel angry, but there was still within him a deepening sense of disappointment that he could not repress. He turned to see that Dan Iser was staring soberly at the escaping freighter.

"Does He always make it so difficult?" Joshua asked him slowly.

"It's not His work, Joshua. Or, if it is, then we have to believe that it's for a reason which in time may be revealed to us."

Joshua looked down to the gray paint of the deck.

"I swear to you from my own experience," Dan went on, "that you will later on get down on your knees and ask Him to forgive you for your present doubt and lack of faith. But, don't feel alone in your unbelief. We both should remember Peter, that blustering, bold fisherman, who managed to get more than his feet wet in the Sea of Galilee."

In the lead gunboat, David Sheldon had finally turned to look away.

Watching him stare at the gunboat's Captain, Jerome Mason could not imagine what might now be passing through the minds of the two men. He knew that in the government chambers of Tel Aviv and Jerusalem there were those who were at that moment waiting anxiously for the report these two men would shortly have to convey.

They had failed.

Feeling awkward to be watching them, he looked back to the window. He noticed then that the lead fighter from one of the two hovering groups had winged over and was starting down toward the freighter.

Joshua Bain, at the same moment, had also witnessed the aircraft starting to make its dive. A fighter pilot himself, it took only a second or two for him to realize the pilot was in a maneuver which could be a run on the freighter!

He stood transfixed, his mouth hanging open.

David Sheldon looked up in time to see the fighter's rockets break away, a full salvo which seemed to converge on the fantail of the freighter!

The explosion was savage enough to knock an astonished Maurice Garand to the deck of the bridge. The freighter's Captain, too, went down heavily, a look of total surprise on his fat face.

The sleek fighter shot up into a half loop and as it gained altitude it rolled over in a simple Immelmann, snapping over to the horizontal.

To Jerome Mason, the maneuver looked like a salute.

The intercom crackled with the voice of the flight leader. "Base, this is flight leader for patrol six, repeat for patrol six. We have observed intruder in our waters at approximate position eighty-two on coastal grid pattern. Intruding vessel appears now to be disabled, repeat, disabled. Strong currents this area will return her to International waters in about five minutes. However, there are several ships this area to assist her mayday condition. Am returning to base now. Over and out."

Joshua Bain was too dumbfounded to cheer.

David Sheldon also didn't know what to say as he lifted the binoculars to inspect the stricken freighter. The rockets had been expertly placed in the ship's fantail to disable her running gear. She was without a rudder or power.

Dan Iser was busily praising the Lord.

Jerome Mason watched curiously as David Sheldon turned to face the tall Captain.

"So maybe peace works," the Captain suggested solemnly.

"Yeah," Sheldon had to concede. "I wish I had that Egyptian pilot's name," he went on after a moment. "I'd send him a couple crates of oranges."

Jerome Mason couldn't help but chuckle.

The gunboats started forward.

Jerome Mason realized it wasn't over yet.

The freighter's Captain ordered his crew to the nearer starboard rail, where they stood in an even line with their hands clasped on their heads. The five Arabs working for Maurice Garand approached Nick Villon, who had moved forward on the weather deck. There was not yet any evidence of fire from the rocket damage, but he was worried the engine room might go up at any minute. The man who had so cleverly impersonated Kasim asked him for his advice.

"Surrender," Nick told him flatly.

"Garand says we should fight."

Nick shrugged. "So do what you want to do."

"You are giving up?"

"Of course I am."

The Algerian pondered the option for only a moment. "So we will join you."

The options for Maurice Garand were narrowing down. Once it became apparent they were going to be boarded by the Israelis, he had first hurried to his cabin, where he has hastily made sure there was nothing in his belongings which could incriminate him. The only evidence in the cabin was a single piece of scratch paper which contained the bare notes for the Benghazi exchange. He tore it up and flushed it down the toilet. Next he quickly tried to assess his position. He sensed the hostages were his last resort. With them under his control, he could at least negotiate. Needing explosives to carry out his plan, he headed for the quarters of the Algerian hijack team.

Using grappling hooks, the Israelis boarded the freighter from two sides simultaneously at amidships. The prisoners were rounded up by the starboard team led by David Sheldon. Nick Villon at once volunteered the location of the two hostages aft, and Sheldon passed the message to Joshua and Dan Iser, who had boarded with the opposite port team. He also warned them that Maurice Garand was still loose on the ship and unaccounted for. While the rest of the port team spread out to search the ship, Dan and Joshua quickly headed aft to locate the two hostages.

Garand had obtained the only explosives he could find, a canvas satchel partially filled with fragmentation hand grenades. He had hurried aft along the connecting companionway to the intersection leading to the compartment holding the hostages. Nervous and fumbling now, he had to stop to wipe the sweat from his glasses. He stepped up then to see that the doorway to the compartment was chained and locked! He cursed his bad luck, figuring either the Captain or Nick Villon had the key. He jumped as he heard the sound of feet scuffing on the nearby steel ladder leading topside. Garand dashed back the way he had come, turning behind the protection of the companionway corner.

Joshua led the way, with Dan covering, down the ladderway to the deck below. At the bottom of the ladder, he held up for a moment to let his eyes adjust. He had a firm grip with both hands on the Uzi machine gun as he stepped aside to allow Dan to join him.

As Dan settled on the deck, he reached up to put his whistle in his mouth.

Maurice Garand was holding his breath while he listened carefully to hear that at least one person, maybe two, had come down the ladder. He held a frag grenade in his right hand. He had already pulled the pin.

His contingencies were down to one.

Joshua gestured with his weapon toward the locked hatch.

Dan Iser started forward in a crouch.

Garand lobbed the grenade down the hallway.

The spring-actuated safety lever popped off.

The metallic *cling* was like an explosion in itself.

Dan's whistle shrieked a warning—

Joshua froze.

He saw the cast-iron grenade bounce once on the metal deck, at a point about even with the compartment door. Dan Iser also saw it coming at him, and his impulse was to kick out at it, knowing that Joshua was right behind him; but in that split second of decision-making, he realized that it might go off in front of the compartment door.

Joshua was still locked in place.

In the closed confines of the steel-walled companionway, the grenade would get them no matter which way they turned.

He started to spin away in a move to at least protect his head and face. As he turned, he saw that Dan had started to fold down to his left in an unaccountable dropping motion.

The grenade's burning fuse detonated its TNT charge at the same instant Dan Iser trapped it between his left hip and the deck.

Chapter nineteen

The small hospital room was on the fifth floor, facing

southeast across that part of Tel Aviv now turning a brilliant orange under the declining sun, and Joshua was reminded of Jerusalem on the evening before. It was the golden hour in the Holy Land. The recollection brought the image of Daniel Iser once more into his mind, and he had to swallow hard against the sorrow which was still so much a part of him.

Alan Hunt was on the bed behind him, there only for observation at the insistence of the Government officials who had met them upon their return from capturing the freighter. Alan's mood was understandably one of quiet satisfaction, since Anne Hunt was en route from Beirut and due to arrive within the hour.

The Armatrex plutonium was under heavy guard at Ben-Gurion Airport, there awaiting transport back to the United States.

Joshua had just been discharged from his own room, after being declared fit by a doctor who apparently was accustomed to treating such cases. His only physical ailment was a minor scratch on his right thigh from a grenade splinter. In his parting comment, the doctor had correctly diagnosed that Joshua Bain seemed to be hurting much more on the inside.

"So it's over," Alan said to him.

Joshua turned to face his friend. Alan looked gaunt and pallid, the result of his confinement, but he was otherwise in good physical shape. "It seems to be," Joshua agreed. "Mason and Sheldon will be here any minute. Maurice Garand and Nick Villon are apparently singing like canaries."

"What about the Colonel?"

Joshua could only shake his head. "The old man is still at large. The only consolation we've got is that he's counting losses instead of gain."

Alan studied him briefly, before asking him, "What about your balance sheet, Joshua?"

"The loss of Dan Iser can never be balanced." Joshua paused then to look down to the floor. "Incredibly enough, in the space of a few hours he not only gave me new life, he also saved it as well."

Alan waited deliberately before he observed, "While I never knew him, I'm sure Dan Iser would've been the first to point out that it is the Lord who gives and the Lord who takes away."

"Yes," Joshua consented. "But like I told you on the boat, it was Dan who led the way."

Alan Hunt closed his eyes, leaning his head contentedly into his pillow.

Jerome Mason pushed his way into the room. Like Joshua, he was still dressed in camouflage fatigues. He looked tired and worn, and his great mane of graying hair was disheveled even more than usual. As he fell into the chair next to Joshua, he groaned contentedly.

"Where's Sheldon?" Joshua asked him.

"He's with Shira Elazar. They're checking on Sharon Iser."

"How is she?"

"Still in shock. But I think she's conscious."

"So what's with Garand?" Joshua asked.

"Not a whole lot, beyond what we had figured," Mason told them. "The major squiggle which threw us the most, of course, was that the real Kasim was never involved. With Garand's background in Algiers, he was easily able to recruit the Arab hijack team. With Hafiz Barca's help, he obtained all the inside details he needed on Kasim's MO, description and personality. It was thus simple for him to come up with a look-alike to play the role. Hafiz Barca, by the way, had no connection with the operation beyond kidnapping Anne, and, finally, to pull the string on the real Kasim to throw us off."

"And got himself killed," Joshua noted.

"And it happened because of a fluke. The hijack team was delayed while en route," and he looked to Alan for confirmation.

"That's correct," Alan said. "We were held up at one point by a Bedouin tribal chief who refused to allow us to move on until he cleared it with someone on up the line. And I figured we were delayed about thirty-six hours."

"Which accounts for the Beirut ploy," Mason added. "Price and Garand had figured on a delay contingency, and they had to lead the Israelis in the opposite direction. If nothing else, Price had an appreciation for Israeli intelligence."

Joshua moved thoughtfully to the end of Alan's bed. "We still don't know all the facts about Karen Laswell."

"And we never will," Mason suggested. "She was totally underground and on her own. She was using the operation, of course, in some way. All we can guess is that the money was involved."

"What about the anonymous tip on the freighter?" Joshua asked then.

Mason reached up to rub the beard on his chin. "Sheldon's people are working on it now. The only hint I have is that there is a connection with the cypher technique used in coding the message. Sheldon did mention that they're supposed to acknowledge receipt of the message in the Jerusalem *Post* tomorrow. Whoever sent it obviously wants to make sure it was delivered."

"They'll probably never release the name even if they do work it out," Joshua mused.

"More than likely. My hunch is that it was someone who had a score to settle with Price, or maybe Garand."

Joshua returned to the window, where he saw that the golden color to the city had turned a dirty brown. He realized that Operation Jordan was finally winding down and was about ready to be entered into the books. The matter of Karen Laswell persisted in his mind, as it had done since the beginning. For him, the incidents in the seaplane were still an open book.

He was the last witness to the deaths of the two principals involved—Karen Laswell and Michael Brav.

Except for one David Sheldon.

He turned to ask, "Where's Sheldon?"

"He said he'd be in the waiting room," Mason told him, and he started to get up.

"You stay here," Joshua commanded.

He found Shira Elazar in the waiting room. As she stood up from her chair, Joshua noticed that she had on a skirt and blouse. As he took her extended hand, he felt his face turn into a smile. "You are much more a woman than I had guessed," he told her warmly.

She was also smiling as they both sat down. "It's not often that I get to dress like one," she admitted.

"It's very becoming, and you should do it more often."

She looked aside. "How's your friend?"

"Alan is just fine, aside from a slight case of nerves while he waits for Anne to get here."

"I can imagine."

"What about Sharon Iser? She was in a bad way on the boat."

"She is still in shock. Major Sheldon is talking to her doctor. It seems he wants to talk to her as soon as he can." She turned to look at him. "And what about you, Joshua? How have you survived it all?"

"I'm still in one piece."

"Mister Mason told us that you've become a Christian."

The remark was unexpected, and Joshua looked at her squarely while he turned it in his mind. There was nothing he could detect in her eyes. "I accepted the Messiah," he told her evenly.

She dropped her eyes.

"Does that surprise you?" he asked, curious at her concern.

She nodded yes. "In a way it does."

David Sheldon walked into the room before Joshua could respond. Shira stood up at once to ask him about Sharon Iser.

"Her condition is the same," Sheldon told her. "The doctor recommends we come back tomorrow morning." He checked his watch before asking Joshua, "Is Jerry Mason with Alan?"

Joshua told him yes as he stood up.

"We should get going," said Sheldon. "We're all very tired."

Joshua looked at Shira. "I have a couple details to clear up with the Major, so would you mind getting Mister Mason while we talk?"

With Shira gone, Joshua sat down again, gesturing for Sheldon to take the chair next to him. "Has Garand given you any new details on what happened to Karen Laswell?" Joshua asked him quickly.

"Nothing new, really. Why, what are you getting at?"

"Like I told you before, I've always had a strange feeling about what happened on the seaplane. I had been knocked out, so my mind was not as clear as it could have been. I'm pretty straight on most of it, except for the final exchange between you and her." He leaned forward then. "Try to remember exactly what happened."

Sheldon leaned his head back, closed his eyes. "There's not much to tell. I came to the doorway of the seaplane on the catwalk. I remember noticing that the door had been torn off. She came forward to meet me."

Joshua had also closed his eyes, and he tried to visualize the scene in his own mind.

"She whispered her name to me," Sheldon went on, "before she handed me the briefcase. I asked her if the money was all there. She said that it was. She then told me that you were forward in the cockpit and that I should forget about you.

Then, she insisted that she leave with us." He paused then.

"Then you shot her."

"Yes, and that was it. I set the timer on the satchel charge and pitched it into the cabin."

Joshua bit on his lower lip. "What about the briefcase?"

"What about it?"

"The chain for the cuff. Did you bother to check to see how it was cut?"

Sheldon delayed for a second, before answering, "The chain was intact. I know for sure, because when I got back to our boat, I snapped the cuff closed to make sure someone wouldn't accidentally put it on his wrist."

"You mean the cuff was unlocked and still on the chain when she handed the briefcase to you?"

"Absolutely, and I can guarantee it."

Now it was beginning to make sense to Joshua. He remembered, then, seeing Karen Laswell hand the briefcase to Sheldon in the doorway. *That was what had bothered him all along.* The only key to the cuff had been handed to him by the courier from Tel Aviv back at the lagoon. There was simply no way any one of them could have had a duplicate. Brav had taken the key from him later, and it had then gone out the doorway in his pocket. How then, had Karen Laswell removed the cuff from her wrist?

Joshua figured he knew what had to be the answer.

He stood up abruptly, feeling a new enthusiasm. "What about the anonymous tip?" he asked calmly. There might be more, and he decided to go after it all.

"We still don't know. Frankly, we normally wouldn't care. We receive such friendly tips all the time, usually from sympathetic supporters who don't want to be identified. However, in this instance, the message came to us through a contact which, shall we say, we're not able to discuss."

"You mean one of your residents?"

David Sheldon simply smiled at him. "The official release will say no more than there was an anonymous tip received by the Government."

"May I ask why you're so anxious to talk to Sharon Iser?"

"Routine debriefing."

Joshua sensed there was nothing more Sheldon would tell him. It didn't matter, because he already had enough. "One last thing. I understand from Jerry Mason that you're supposed to acknowledge receipt of the message in a newspaper."

"Yes, that's true."

"Give me a minute," Joshua said thoughtfully, and he turned to walk to the nearby nurse's station, where he borrowed a slip of paper and a pencil. A few seconds later he returned to hand Sheldon a folded note.

"Run this with the acknowledgement," Joshua told him.

Sheldon unfolded the note, reading it. "What's this supposed to do?"

"I don't know for sure," Joshua admitted truthfully, "but I need to get on a flight out of here tonight."

Frowning, Sheldon put the note in his shirt pocket. "They're arranging a ceremony for all of us tomorrow morning. The State of Israel wants to thank you publicly, all of you."

Joshua considered the comment. "Israel has rewarded me enough already in allowing me to have known Daniel Iser."

Sheldon nodded appreciatively. "All right. We can drop you off at the airport."

It was after ten o'clock when Joshua climbed out of the sedan at the curb of the passenger loading zone at Ben-Gurion Airport. Jerome Mason was in the front seat next to Sheldon, and he rolled his window down to take Joshua's hand.

"Why won't you tell us where you're going?" he asked, his voice tired and concerned, and he held onto Joshua's hand until he answered.

"I'll be all right," Joshua assured him.

Shira Elazar came across the rear seat to follow Joshua out of the car. Before she closed the door, she asked Sheldon to please wait for her.

A little surprised, Joshua took her arm as they moved away from the curb.

"I had to talk to you before you left," Shira said as they pulled up next to an empty baggage checkstand.

Joshua let his hand slip down her arm to take her hand, not knowing what to say.

"Will you be coming back?" she asked.

Joshua surveyed her face, thinking that she was uptight about something. "I would like to, especially if I can see you again."

She pulled her hand away, crossing her arms self-consciously across her chest. "That's what I wanted to talk to you about," and she paused, looking down to the pavement. "My heart wants me to say yes, but all the rest of me is in confusion.

You see, you should really know what it's been like for Sharon Iser during the past few years. And, you must remember that we were raised together, so I've been emotionally involved with her through it all."

It was beginning to dawn on Joshua. "You mean because of Dan's belief in the Messiah?"

"Yes, and it's not easy for me now, especially after what's happened."

"What are you trying to say, Shira?"

"Both our families are orthodox," she said quietly, pausing once again. "Didn't you notice that there was no one there at the hospital?"

Joshua shook his head, trying to clear it. "You mean her relatives—"

"That's right, Joshua. She was disowned when she decided to stay on with Dan after he was converted."

"Oh, wow," Joshua offered disbelievingly. "You mean after what Dan did today for this country—"

"Oh, that's not all. Sharon will have trouble finding a cemetery which will accept him for burial."

It took several more seconds for Joshua Bain to react and then sort out his feelings. He waited to be certain his mind was clear. "For some reason," he finally told her, "I can only feel a certain kind of sadness instead of anger right now. Maybe it's the legacy of Dan Iser himself." He paused once more. "In an ironic way, it's good that he's not alive now to sit alone in a hospital waiting room."

"You shouldn't judge us this way," she pleaded with him. "If it's a great wrong to you, then you've only seen the worst. You need more time—"

"I've had time enough," he interrupted, and he nodded his head approvingly. "You've actually done me a favor by telling me this, which was something not even Dan could do, probably because he was ashamed. You see, he was proud of his Jewishness. Oh, Lord, how proud he was . . . " His next breath was thoughtful and his words carefully composed. "In fact, he loved you all so much, I doubt he would ever have admitted he was the victim of the cruelest of intolerance. But, the truth shall be made known, in time, for all of us."

She started to speak, but he held up his hand to stop her, because he was already turning to walk away, telling her over his shoulder, "So go back to your family, Shira, and I wish you all the best of luck."

His parting comment was loud enough to reach the car. As

Jerome Mason rolled up his window, he presumed that Joshua had some deep concern for the family of Shira Elazar, for Joshua had just promised to remember them in his prayers, assuming he now shared the belief of his friend, Alan Hunt. . . .

That luck was the will of God.

Epilogue

On Wednesday morning, the following personal advertisement appeared in the classified section of the Jerusalem *Post*:

MESSAGE FOR JORDAN RECEIVED WITH OUR THANKS. SHIPMENT RECOVERED. ALSO OF INTEREST THAT BONN PAYMENT WAS ERSATZ.

The closing sentence concerning the Bonn payment had been appended at the request of Joshua Bain.

Routinely, the Wednesday edition of the paper was delivered via Nefertiti Airlines and distributed to Cairo newsstands by late that afternoon.

By late Thursday night, Joshua was fully awake and alert as he waited in the small abandoned building on the pier at the top of the lagoon. He had slept soundly for most of the day, after arriving from Kingston in the military helicopter arranged for by Inspector Bradford. The rain was now coming in across the lagoon in the same fine mist that had been falling on the fateful Monday evening. The wind, though, was less fitful, so that the sheltering crush of undergrowth and trees was more quiet.

The stage was appropriately set.

Joshua used his flashlight, shielding it inside his nylon windbreaker, to pour himself another cup of coffee. Carefully then, he covered the alcohol burner and put the small pot aside. With the wind down from seaward, he wasn't willing to risk the odor of brewing coffee in the still air.

That morning, he had called David Sheldon from Kingston. As he had hoped, Sharon Iser had come around enough to make a complete report, a part of which further verified that his hunch had been correct.

The black stainless steel briefcase was under the cot near his feet. He hadn't bothered to force the lock, because he knew the genuine Bonn notes were still inside.

He had been staring hard through the small window facing the far end of the pier, and he closed his eyes to rest them. He tried to think about Rancho Canaan, but the events of the past few days kept moving in and out of his mind. It would take a long time to assess Operation Jordan, to break it down to the logical sequence of what really had happened. For the moment, Joshua was content that it was nearly over.

He was aware that it had been the individual courage of a few who had enabled the rest of them to survive.

There was a young Egyptian pilot who had the guts to take a chance.

And one Hafiz Barca, who had been led to unusual bravery by the influence of a former sister-in-arms whose love and concern was more persuasive than either of them probably realized.

And forever inscribed in the heart of Joshua Bain, the epitaph of Daniel Iser: *Greater love hath no man than this, that a man lay down his life for his friends*. . . So that now in Abraham's hope to save the Promised Land, he had one less in his search for just the ten asked for by his God.

And, of course, Karen Laswell, whose performance to this point was still shrouded in mystery.

He opened his eyes, blinking to help clear his night vision. The small boat turned into the lagoon so slowly and quietly that he had to look twice to detect it. He reached under the cot to pick up the heavy metal briefcase. As he stood up, he debated whether to palm the Viper out of its holster. He expected only one person in the boat, and he decided that he probably wouldn't need a weapon. Carefully then, he moved out of the building to the pier.

The small launch tied up at the far end of the pier. Joshua waited in the shadows until he heard the soft splash of a body entering the water. He moved forward, and, as expected, he found the boat empty. At the end of the pier, he squatted down to wait again. The water next to the pier was about ten feet deep, and he could see the underwater light moving to and fro. The diver worked along the pier to a point well beyond where the seaplane had been tied up. The bubbles from the air supply broke the surface with an irregular gurgling sound under the softly falling mist. The light moved back to the boat.

Joshua took a deep breath as the diver broke the surface next to the boat.

Michael Brav removed his face mask.

"You looking for this?" Joshua asked him, and he held out the briefcase.

Brav moved his light across Joshua's face first before turning it on the metal case. He was breathing heavily from the exertion of the dive, and he had to catch his breath before answering hoarsely, "I was afraid you'd beat me to it." He pulled himself heavily into the boat.

Joshua watched while Brav pulled out of his air tanks. The lantern was on the control panel, and Joshua could see in the reflected light that Brav was moving clumsily and breathing hard. There was a heavy white cast on his left leg from his hip to below his knee. He was also wrapped heavily around his rib cage, the bandage white under the darker skirt of his leather neck brace. Out of his diving gear, Brav reached forward to turn out the lantern.

Joshua helped him to the pier. As the older man sat down beside him, Joshua noticed that the bandage around his rib cage was blotched under his left arm.

"Are you bleeding?" Joshua asked him.

Brav reached around with his right hand to inspect his side. "Feels that way," he commented. "I probably broke it open when I pulled over the side."

"I presume that's where Karen Laswell shot you."

Michael Brav answered with an ironic chuckle.

"So the cat made it one more time," Joshua heard himself saying. The man was really there, sitting next to him, but he almost felt it was necessary to reach out and touch him again just to make sure. The fact of Brav's survival was not really so outlandish. Joshua had already calculated that the man's fall from the aircraft in both speed and distance was actually less than that experienced by a man going off the Golden Gate bridge. Still, it had been a feat, one which he was admittedly curious about. "How in the world did you make it?"

"A combination of things, I suppose," Brav explained. "I was stone drunk, which helped because I had to be fairly relaxed." He pushed himself back away from the edge of the pier to ease the pressure on his left leg. "I must've hit the water feet first, because I tore up my legs. My left leg was almost wrenched off at the knee. The neck brace probably saved my life more than anything else."

Joshua realized the truth of the last statement. The heavy brace, which was laced tightly around Brav's upper chest and back, had no doubt protected his critical upper spine.

Brav reached up to finger the foam rubber ring around his neck. "I was knocked unconscious when I hit. Or, I just passed out. Anyway, the foam rubber kept my chin out of the water, like a life preserver."

So it wasn't so miraculous, after all, Joshua thought. "Who picked you up?"

"An elderly retired couple on a private cruiser headed for Santo Domingo. They patched me up, and I talked them into dropping me off at Jacmel. I found a doctor there who for the right price fixed me up and gave me the drugs I needed to keep on the move. I moved on to Port-au-Prince the next morning."

"You sent the Cairo message, didn't you?"

"I didn't realize it was that obvious."

"I don't know that it was so apparent. For me, until this morning, it was just a hunch."

"Why this morning?"

"Sharon Iser reported that you gave her a micro-transmitter to hide in one of the plutonium containers. Is that what you were talking about when you told me on the seaplane that you weren't a complete traitor?"

"So you remembered that," Brav commented laconically. "I gave the transmitter to Sharon Iser in Miami with instructions to plant it in one of the containers during the inspection phase at the villa. I originally planned that she would eventually tell Sheldon, if she were to survive a hijack attempt. However, as things progressed and I began to get a feel for what was coming down, I decided to leak the fact to headquarters after I got away with the money. But, once I went out the door of the seaplane, I figured it would be better if I just stayed dead." He reached out to run his hand over the wet surface of the metal briefcase. "How were you able to put this together?"

"The same way you did when you found out the Bonn notes taken by Sheldon were phoney. It took a little longer for me, because, like the rest of us, I presumed that the real money was blown up when Sheldon blew the seaplane."

"That bothered me, too," Brav admitted. "I started at Port-au-Prince myself, working out of there until Friday. I was aware of Sheldon's bravo orders to kill Karen and blow the plane, so I also presumed the real money had been destroyed. It was either that or you had it, since you were the only survivor. When I read the personal in the Jerusalem *Post*, I assumed that the real money had not been recovered. My first impulse was the Port-au-Prince seaplane dock, but I knew that Price's people had salvaged that site thoroughly." He held up his hands. "So, this had to be the only logical place left."

"Karen Laswell was with Interpol."

Michael Brav turned painfully at his waist to stare briefly at Joshua. Even in the poor light, Joshua could see the disbelief in his face.

"That explains some things," Brav said after a moment's thought. "I was suspicious that she would be so willing to throw over such a lush position as she had with Price. My estimate was that she would in the long run pull a whole lot more money out of him than she could realize from her cut from me. But, then, she stroked me. Don't you see, she was going to use the real money to lure Price into the open."

"That's what I figure," Joshua added. "But you fouled up her plan when you decided to go with the seaplane."

"I understand that, but how did she make the switch?"

"It's so simple, it's almost embarrassing. She already had the fake money in a duplicate case in her duffel bag when we landed at the lagoon. The whole thing had been obviously arranged by her and Price. The Tel Aviv courier gave her the real case, which she inspected and approved. She took it and put it in her duffel bag. I had stepped out to the dock to call Alan for help in transferring the containers. When I stepped back in, I saw that she didn't have the briefcase, and I ordered her to lock it on her wrist. She acted upset, but she reached into her bag and pulled it out. Of course, she picked up the duplicate, leaving the first case in the bag. Later, after you had knocked me out, she must've dropped the original case out the doorway into the water."

Brav grunted his understanding. "You're right. After I knocked you out, I left the plane to get Hank Koman on his way, and she took longer than I thought she should to start the engines. She had plenty of time to drop the case over the side."

"With you aboard," Joshua pointed out, "she knew she had to dump the real money then and there, because she didn't know what your plans were for both her and the plane. All she had to do was come back and pick it up herself later on."

"Which was also why she shot me," Brav mused.

Joshua eased himself up against the nearby piling. He took the next ten minutes to fill in Brav on what had happened after Port-au-Prince.

When he finished, Brav spoke approvingly, "So it all worked out after all. We even got Kasim to help even out the score."

"You're including Hank Koman and the alpha team, of course."

Michael Brav shifted again to stare at him. "I never knew for a fact that there was going to be a hijack."

"So why did you get on the seaplane?"

"I suspected there might be a hijack. Or, to put it another way, why should I get caught in a crossfire if there was one, no matter what the percentage. I presume you remember the engine trouble on the cabin cruiser just before the exchange?"

Joshua nodded his head. "I should've aborted the mission right then."

"Regardless, a part of my deal with Karen was that I would delay the transfer boat for thirty minutes. When I asked her why, she claimed she could use the delay to help her when she arrived back at Port-au-Prince."

"That was a scam. She arranged the delay to guarantee darkness for the hijack ambush. There's no advantage to searchlights in daylight."

"We're all aware of that now," Brav observed. "However, I was reviewing my options coming into the lagoon, and, the closer I got to that money the more I was convinced I should stay with it. As it turned out, I was right."

"What was your original plan to handle the money?"

"I was to get it from Sheldon on the *Bushnell*, after the operation, and then courier it back to Tel Aviv. Of course, I was simply going to disappear en route."

"I was disappointed that you had Karen Laswell killed."

"Then take it up with Maurice Garand. After Karen and I had our meeting to firm up our agreement, the little fox informed me that he had recorded our conversation, and, unless I cooperated he was going to turn it over to the Colonel. His fee for silence was the execution of Karen Laswell. She was apparently the kind of competition he couldn't otherwise handle."

"He ran a beautiful con on you. The Colonel already knew about your plans to steal the notes, which is why he had them counterfeited."

"A ton of hindsight is still worth less than an ounce of foresight. You were suspicious yourself, but you didn't follow up either."

"What do you mean?" Joshua asked defensively.

"The motel in Los Angeles when we met on Saturday. You made a point of wondering why Price had set Port-au-Prince as his base point instead of the villa. Now, it's obvious he did it to allow Sheldon a more open opportunity to steal the notes. Price set us all up, Joshua."

Joshua grunted appreciatively as he pushed himself away from the piling. "All I've got left is to ask how you found the freighter?"

"It was a bit tricky but not really difficult. When I got on my feet at Port-au-Prince, the only lead I could follow up on was Nick Villon. The Wednesday papers in town carried a report of the *Arosa* turning up beached on Morant Point. The trawler had been badly shot up, but the authorities claimed it was a narcotics thing. I knew better, of course, and I stuck with Villon like glue. With my limited resources, he was my only shot."

Joshua realized how close they had come to disaster. "Why didn't you just report the transmitter frequency? We could've blanketed the entire area, the approach routes."

"I was afraid to at first, because I was worried Tel Aviv would realize I was still alive. You have to remember that everyone thought I was dead, the perfect cover, and I didn't want to risk breaking it. However, if Villon hadn't booked himself on the flight to Cairo, I was prepared to report it. At any rate, after Villon arrived in Cairo, he went directly to Ismailia. The freighter didn't arrive until the following Monday night, and I couldn't get a positive fix on her until she cleared Port Said." He took a deep breath, wincing at an apparent pain in his left side.

"You need a doctor," Joshua told him.

"I'll see one in Kingston."

"You're aware that Tel Aviv is probably onto you, since Sharon has told them about the transmitter. And, I think you might've tipped yourself in the Cairo message itself."

"Couldn't help it. It was the only way I could make sure it reached the right people in time. You see, I knew it was going to be close."

Joshua noticed the final kind of note of resignation in his voice. "So what are you going to do?"

The mist was thickening into a light rain, and Joshua stood up after picking up the briefcase.

"That might depend on you," Brav offered.

Joshua thought over the comment. "I came here to get the money, nothing else."

"So you're going to turn it in."

"Of course. But there's the consolation of a ten percent finder's fee."

"Not bad pay for a night's work."

"It's going into a trust account. It seems Rancho Canaan is sponsoring the relocation of an Arab refugee family, and I can't think of a more appropriate way to finance it."

Michael Brav chuckled appreciatively, wincing then against the pain in his side.

"You still haven't said what you're going to do," Joshua reminded him.

"I don't know, now. I'm tired, beat down worse than I've ever been. To show you how bad a shape I'm really in, I haven't had a drink since I went out the door of that seaplane."

Joshua reached into the left front pocket of his trousers to pull out a small smooth stone, which he handed to Brav.

"What's this?" Brav asked, turning the stone in his hand.

"What would be your guess?"

Brav thought for a moment. "Well, if I had a slingshot, I suppose I could play David."

"That's remarkable," Joshua observed quietly. "You only missed it by a hundred pages or so." He reached down then to help Michael Brav to his feet. "Since you're in such bad shape," he went on, "then let me give you some help before you leave." He gestured toward the small building at the top of the pier. "I've got something in there I want you to read. We can put on some coffee and relax for a while."

Feeling a guiding hand on his shoulder, Brav stepped out to hobble along beside Joshua. He noticed that the rain had started to let up.

"What I have to show you," Joshua explained carefully, "was written by a man called John."

The two men moved slowly along the wooden pier, their gray forms blending into the night shade, and beyond them in the higher trees the night birds could be heard in their own chorus, a sound said by some to resemble a choir of angels celebrating some joyous event.

Selah!

Concluding note

The Canaan Trilogy is a response to an injunction made over 2,500 years ago:

> *Son of man, I have made thee a watchman unto the house of Israel; therefore hear the word at my mouth, and give them warning from me.*

So be it . . .